WHERE THE DEVIL
DON'T STAY

AMERICAN MUSIC SERIES

Jessica Hopper and Charles Hughes, Editors

Peter Blackstock and David Menconi, Founding Editors

ALSO IN THE SERIES

WHERE THE DEVIL DON'T STAY

DON'T STAY

TRAVELING THE SOUTH WITH THE DRIVE-BY TRUCKERS

STEPHEN DEUSNER

UNIVERSITY OF TEXAS PRESS ❧ AUSTIN

Requests for permission to reproduce material
from this work should be sent to:
Permissions
University of Texas Press
P.O. Box 7819
Austin, TX 78713-7819
utpress.utexas.edu/rp-form

♾ The paper used in this book meets the minimum requirements of
ANSI/NISO Z39.48-1992 (R1997) (Permanence of Paper).

Library of Congress Cataloging-in-Publication Data

Names: Deusner, Stephen, author.
Title: Where the devil don't stay : traveling the South with the
Drive-By Truckers / Stephen Deusner.
Other titles: American music series (Austin, Tex.)
Description: First edition. | Austin : University of Texas Press, 2021. |
Series: American music series | Includes bibliographical references and index.
Identifiers:
LCCN 2021005210
ISBN 978-1-4773-1804-1 (cloth)
ISBN 978-1-4773-2392-2 (library ebook)
ISBN 978-1-4773-2393-9 (ebook)
Subjects: LCSH: Drive-By Truckers (Musical group) | Rock musicians—
Southern States. | Rock music—Southern States—History and criticism. |
Southern States—Civilization.
Classification: LCC ML421.D72 D48 2021 | DDC 782.42166092/2—dc23

LC record available at https://lccn.loc.gov/2021005210

doi:10.7560/318041

Contents

▼

WHERE THE DEVIL THE DON'T STAY

Introduction

▼

It is August 2016. The present is bleak and the next few months are only dimly promising when Patterson Hood takes the stage for an intimate acoustic solo set at Saturn in Birmingham, Alabama. The club is decorated with old computer motherboards and spaceships and assorted space-age bric-a-brac—the futuristic technology of an era long past—but Patterson sits alone onstage in a metal folding chair, the kind you might see at a church potluck, facing the crowd of 150, maybe 200 fans, armed with his guitar and his ragged voice and a seemingly inexhaustible catalog of story-songs about what his band, the Drive-By Truckers, like to call "the Dirty South."

Tonight is not a rock show but one of the many solo gigs Patterson plays every year, when he pares his songs back to their barest elements and lets his characters move around a bit. He plays "Heathens," a song about the rural poor from 2003's *Decoration Day*, then launches into "My Sweet Annette" from that same album, a song about leaving a woman at the altar (based very loosely on a real event in the Hood family). Even stripped down to just vocals and guitar, shed of the two- and sometimes three-guitar attack that defines the Truckers' sound, his songs are imaginative and engaging, southern storytelling at its finest, with Patterson giving voice to characters who typically don't have a say in popular music: roustabouts and criminals, misfits and ne'er-do-wells, the rural poor and the small-town working class. These aren't the pickup-driving cowboys and homecoming queen beauties who populate mainstream country music, but *rednecks*, each drawn with such care and imaginative precision that they feel life-size rather than mythic or romantic. The crowd at Saturn knows every word.

It is an important moment for Patterson, the calm before the storm: the Truckers are not quite two months away from releasing their eleventh album, *American Band*, which will turn out to be one of the best rock records of that year as well as the most explicit political statement of their two-decade career. It chronicles American life late in the age of Obama, addressing racial tension, white culpability, gun control, identity politics, national and regional history, fake news, real news, and most of all the way politicians have cynically spun these issues first into public grievances and then into votes and often into violence. The Truckers had tackled these topics before, but never so directly and not without the filter of characters and stories. These new songs are the most straightforward of their career, the most outraged, but they are tempered by humor and empathy and passion.

It is a bold departure, in more ways than one: the year before, Patterson had moved out of the South—the region of the country with which the Truckers had long been associated—and up to the Pacific Northwest. Mike Cooley, his friend and co–front man, remained in suburban Birmingham. And instead of an illustrated cover by unofficial Trucker Wes Freed, whose stylized folk-art renderings have adorned almost every one of the band's albums, they have chosen a black-and-white photo of an American flag blowing languidly in the wind. It is anything but blithely patriotic.

Very consciously the band is expanding its scope and subject matter, refocusing its gaze to take in not just the South—which they had portrayed on numerous studio and live albums as a place of great ugliness and great beauty—but all of America. *American Band* is a pivotal moment for the Truckers, one that will make them more relevant and more popular than ever even as it threatens to alienate a considerable portion of their core fanbase. Just the year before, Patterson had signaled this new direction with an editorial in the *New York Times*, which fervently argued against the Confederate flag as a worthy symbol and expressed the need to devise new icons of a more progressive South. "Why would we want to fly a symbol that has been used by the K.K.K. and terrorists like Dylann Roof," Patterson wrote, referring to the young white man who killed nine members of the Emanuel African Methodist Episcopal Church in Charleston, South Carolina, in a violent attempt to incite a race war. "Why would a people steeped in the teachings of Jesus Christ and the Bible want to rally around a flag that so many associate with hatred and violence? Why fly a flag that stands for the very things we as Southerners have worked so hard to move beyond?"

Toward the end of the set at Saturn, Patterson introduces a new song, one that he has played only a handful of times. The crowd is already standing and remains on its feet as he launches into "What It Means," soon to appear on *American Band*. Few in the audience have heard the song before, but each listener leans in, rapt and so quiet it's disconcerting, as he addresses the heartbreakingly insoluble contradictions of race in America. Patterson begins with a plaintive guitar theme, subdued and spare; he mostly plays electric rhythm guitar in the Truckers, occasionally taking solos but generally responsible for gargantuan southern-rock riffing. When he plays "What It Means," he makes sure the guitar does not intrude on or distract from the lyrics.

The tune opens with an image all too familiar to anyone keeping up with the news: "He was running down the street when they shot him in his tracks." We know instinctively the victim is Black before Patterson even mentions it, before he brings up Trayvon Martin in the second verse. We know the song is about Eric Garner, Michael Brown Jr., Philando Castile, Freddie Gray, and too many other Black lives lost. "If you say it wasn't racial when they shot him in his tracks, well, I guess that means that you ain't black," Patterson sings, underscoring his own whiteness as well as the whiteness of his audience. "That means that you ain't black." That line—and especially Patterson's repetition of it—is complicated: it's less about assuming unearned knowledge of the Black experience and more about challenging white listeners to listen, to empathize, to acknowledge the racial motives behind such crimes.

"What It Means" moves on from the shooting of Black Americans by white cops to consider the fallout from such incidents: the exoneration of George Zimmerman for the murder of Martin, the quelling of any public debate on gun violence by the NRA, the unconscionable resistance to the idea that Black lives matter, the mere assumption that there is more than one side to this issue. "They'll spin it for the anchors on the television screen, so we can shrug and let it happen without asking what it means."

Here in Birmingham, Alabama—home to civil rights heroes; the site of some of the most dignified demonstrations and the most cravenly violent responses; a city nicknamed Bombingham for all the white terrorism aimed at Black men, women, and children; ground zero for racial conflict in America throughout the mid-twentieth century and a hotbed of racial instability ever since—"What It Means" hushes the crowd. Patterson sings his throat raw, shredding those syllables until they are bloody and pulped, drawing out that title phrase: "What it MEEEEEEEEANS." That long vowel is fingernails on a chalkboard, an exasperated cry, an anguished screech: the sound of despair devouring all hope for a better world and better selves. Singing those words visibly wounds Patterson, and he appears somehow smaller, his back bent, not proud or patriotic but exhausted and empty. He has left part of himself in the song and has emerged not victorious but ravaged and shaken.

There is a beat of pure silence as the last note fades, and in that moment we all seem to wonder what to do, how to react to something so tremendous and so horrific. What do you do when rock and roll shows you something so grave? All we have at our disposal is the usual concert behavior: clapping hands and shouting, whistling, stomping feet.

Patterson takes a moment to recover and then proceeds with the show. But my mind lingers in that moment. It feels as if I have glimpsed an ugly future. It is not an epiphany, more like the first gnash of a gnawing doubt that will culminate three months later when Hillary Clinton, who had run her campaign as though she couldn't understand why anyone would vote for her opponent, wins the popular vote but loses the electoral college, initiating years of political and social chaos, base opportunism, and barely checked corruption. There had been a dream of progress, but like a prophet, Patterson tells us that the dream will wither without our outrage, our anger, and our actions. Are we so naive to think the worst couldn't happen, when the worst already happens on the streets of America every day? "And it happened where you're sitting, wherever that might be," the song goes. "And it happened last weekend, and it will happen again next week." And sure enough, it has happened far too many times in America since he wrote those words.

At Saturn, "What It Means" sounds like one of the most important songs a white American man could sing—a composition that might enter into a national conversation, a sympathizing response to Kendrick Lamar's "Alright" and Beyoncé's "Formation." It doesn't speak truth to power, but grim realism to naive optimism or, worse, pious ignorance. "What It Means" is a mirror held up to the nation to show us how twisted things have become. Months before the election, "What It Means" sounds like a eulogy for a country that had lost its way.

That's an awful lot for one song to hold. After introducing it into his setlist for a short solo tour, Patterson was asked by a fan if he was going to play it in St. Louis, which is near Ferguson, Missouri, where Michael Brown was shot and killed by white police officers and where the ensuing protests brought increased national attention to the issue. As he told me some years later, "I felt like I had to. If I don't play it there, then I don't have the right to play it ever again." The response was encouraging: a standing ovation in the middle of his show. A few weeks later, he played it in Selma, Alabama, site of the famous civil rights march across Edmund Pettus Bridge, where, in March 1965, peaceful demonstrators were attacked by police and bigots, an event so violent it has become known as Bloody Sunday. A few people made a show of walking out the door, but overall the audience was, Patterson later said, "extremely supportive."

Perhaps "What It Means" was the song that so many people needed at that time—a song that didn't pretend to give answers, that didn't attack any one group specifically, but simply asked questions about what these atrocities say about America in the twenty-first century. Looking back on the song, he told me, "When I wrote it, I didn't even know if it would ever be something the band would want to do. I was just trying to get everything down. It was eating at me. It thought it'd be relevant for maybe the next ten minutes, which was obviously wishful thinking. That didn't happen at all."

A few weeks later, *American Band* revealed a full band pondering these issues rather than a lone singer. The studio version of "What It Means" has a loping pace, less desperate and more pensive, as though the band is just walking down a crowded street. There's nothing violent about its verses, but that calm assessment can rattle the listener, especially toward the end of the song, when the vocals fall away. There are handclaps and a churchly organ solo from Jay Gonzalez, a gospel chord progression from bassist Matt Patton that reaches higher and higher. It could be any church in America; it might be Emanuel African Methodist in South Carolina, or it might be Sixteenth Street Baptist in Birmingham. But the Truckers are no closer to figuring out what it means.

Hailed for its topical and immediate songwriting, *American Band* didn't represent a pivot toward the political for the Truckers. They had been confronting issues of race and class, regionalism and nationalism, what it means to be southern and what it means to be American for more than two decades. "Our whole approach to it—the way we've always written about political things—is to write about a personal thing, where one of us is playing a character, somebody we know or somebody we made up, and put them in a situation to tell their story," Patterson told me. (All interviews in this book, unless otherwise noted, are from interviews I conducted with the band over several years.) "One of the problems we have as people in this country is this lack of empathy toward other people's points of view and life situations—what puts them in the position they're in and what makes them have the beliefs they do. That's always been a part of what we do. *American Band* on the surface might be a little more direct than records in the past, but it's what we've always done."

Was it possible to feel pride in the South? Could anyone find some sense of identity or fulfillment in a place so closely associated with prejudice, hate, and violence? Or was there only shame and penance? "The duality of the southern thing" is a line from a song on the band's breakout double album from 2001, *Southern Rock Opera*, and it's by far the most quoted lyric in their sprawling catalog. Actually, it might be the most quoted line about the South in the twenty-first century. That phrase puts words to my own vague struggles about where I come from: disgrace and pride, forgetting and remembering, change and stasis. Here was a band saying that the best choice—the only real choice—was all of them.

On *American Band* the Truckers enlarged that duality to apply to the country as a whole. *The duality of the American thing*: the shame and pride of being American. The album continued a trajectory they began when Patterson and Cooley first began playing together in the 1980s, first as

Adam's House Cat and later as the Drive-By Truckers.[1] They explored various aspects of what is largely known as southern rock: not just the boogie riffs of Wet Willie or the masculine drama of Lynyrd Skynyrd or the expansive improvisations of the Allman Brothers but also the southern soul that was refined in their own neck of the woods, the sound of Muscle Shoals. Almost every band member hails from North Alabama, and Patterson's father, David Hood, was a member of the Swampers, a famed group of backing musicians who played with everyone from the Staple Singers to Arthur Alexander, Paul Simon, Aretha Franklin, and Etta James.

In 1998, not long after the band had formed and self-released its debut, *Gangstabilly*, Patterson and Cooley started writing some hard-knuckle southern tales set in small communities well off major highways, what the novelist Harper Lee referred to as "tired old towns." The lyrics are populated with the kinds of folks who rarely appeared in depictions of the South except as backwards antagonists driven by racism, stupidity, boredom, or enough religious certitude to frame an innocent black man in *To Kill a Mockingbird* or to stalk small children in *Night of the Hunter*. Rather than render them as strawmen in the culture wars, the Truckers portrayed these characters as complex, sometimes but not always sympathetic, occasionally contradictory, and always compelling. They embraced it as their own identity but rebelled against the stereotype perpetuated in so much popular culture: "We do have some redneck in us," Patterson told the *Guardian* in 2020. "We don't necessarily let anyone tell us what to do."

Spread across several of their early albums, the Heathen Songs (as they would come to be known) now form the core of the band's catalog and the bedrock of their reputation. They arose from a period of intense creativity and productivity in the late 1990s and early 2000s, during which the Truckers would tour behind one album while recording the

---

[1] The Truckers are a band with many nicknames and no tattoos. Patterson Hood is often called Sasquatch, but I'm going to refer to him simply as Patterson rather than use his last name, because it just sounds right. Cooley is just Cooley. He's often called Stroker Ace, but he is never, ever called Mike. He's like Cher or Madonna; all he needs is the one name.

next and writing the one after that. It was a heavy workload, but the result is a string of records that feel thoroughly interconnected and consistent as they conjure a world that's large yet specific, familiar yet exotic, real and imagined. This is their Dirty South.

It's important to note that they didn't coin that term. When they used the phrase as the title of their 2004 album, they borrowed it from some of their southern contemporaries: namely, Atlanta rap artists like Goodie Mob, Outkast, and others who adopted that moniker in the 1990s to distinguish their strain of southern hip-hop from New York and LA varieties. These artists made music that was rebelliously weird, that acknowledged their southern roots in all their complexities and contradictions, that ultimately unmoored hip-hop from its coastal poles. The Truckers are all hip-hop fans and have been influenced by the genre's emphasis on vérité storytelling as well as its regional milieu, and they recognize that this form of music is often cited as violent when white genres of music are not. As Patterson explains, "No one cares that Johnny Cash sang, 'I shot a man in Reno just to watch him die' because he's a white country boy, but everybody was pissed at Public Enemy and N.W.A. We thought we could address this in the context of our type of music. *The Dirty South* [album] was named as an homage to the Atlanta rap scene. We thought we would tell the other side of the story as our statement about that musical form of racism."

It's a noble idea that perhaps some years later shows how even most well-intentioned white engagements with Black culture can slide into something akin to appropriation (although, for the record, the band largely abandoned the term after the record's release). And yet, keeping in mind Patterson's phrase "the other side of the story," the Dirty South is a useful designation, rooting out a racial duality in the southern thing. Theirs is a *white* Dirty South, a place in time where we see new portrayals of southern white men in film, literature, and music in which they're positioned as rebels in a winking nod to the Lost Cause: that romantic notion about the Civil War that the South fought to ensure states' rights rather than to perpetuate the brutal institution of slavery.

It's a place where mass-market notions of southernness are passed down through pop culture venues like *The Dukes of Hazzard* or *Smokey and the Bandit*. It's a battlefield in a cold war against the strides made by Black Americans, with statues lionizing Southern generals, Confederate heroes, and Klan wizards as the weapons. If you're looking for the beginning of this Dirty South, you might look to 1961, when Arthur Alexander put Muscle Shoals on the map with his R&B/country hybrid song "You Better Move On." Or you might look to 1963, when white bigots bombed the Sixteenth Street Baptist Church in Birmingham and killed four Black girls. Or perhaps 1964, when President Lyndon Johnson signed the Civil Rights Act into law and Buford Hayse Pusser became sheriff of McNairy County, Tennessee.

Whenever it starts, this Dirty South is the culmination of several trends affecting rural and urban areas around America but especially in this region. The twentieth century had already seen vast migrations from the countryside into the city: the Okies traveling west to California, Black southerners moving north for factory jobs. But that rural exodus was continual. Small towns have long been places to leave, big cities places to arrive. That meant that rural areas lagged far behind the rest of the country economically. A special commission launched by President Johnson found that one-third of Americans in rural areas lived below the poverty line and that those communities were ill equipped to provide access to jobs, education, and health care. That trend only gradually improved into the 1980s, when the idea of two Souths emerged, defined not by race (although that's always part of it) but by economics. There was the South that led the way and the South that got left behind. Emphasizing education, leadership, and industry on a purely local level, this perception was popularized primarily by two politicians: Arkansas governor Bill Clinton and Tennessee congressman Al Gore.

As they devised ways to portray these distinctive Souths, the Truckers' storytelling and world-building ambitions culminated on *Southern Rock Opera*, their 2001 double album that tells the story of the three great Alabama icons: Paul "Bear" Bryant, football coach of the University of Alabama Crimson Tide; George Wallace, the governor who first thwarted and then supported civil rights; and Ronnie Van Zant, lead singer of Lynyrd Skynyrd. But the backdrop is their own origin story: growing up in the South, going to concerts, starting their own bands. *Decoration Day* in 2003 and *The Dirty South* in 2004 further established the Truckers as some of the most important voices coming out of the South.

The Truckers and their mission would persevere through almost constant upheaval. Born as a band with no set lineup, they initially consisted of whoever could show up for a gig, settling into a formidable quartet only several years later. After guitarist Rob Malone left the band in 2001, Jason Isbell went out on the road with them and introduced himself as an observant and inventive songwriter, a favorite among their growing legion of fans. He left in 2007, followed by bassist Shonna Tucker and pedal steel player John Neff in 2011. Only recently has the lineup settled into a solid quintet, with Patterson, Cooley, and longtime drummer Brad Morgan joined by Athens, Georgia–based keyboard player Jay Gonzalez and Mississippian Matt Patton on bass.

"The secret to a happy ending," Patterson sings on "World of Hurt," "is knowing when to roll the credits." They were contemplating that very idea not too long ago, wondering whether they might have overstayed their welcome. Just when the band thought they might settle into something like cult status, with their audience shrinking to diehards or at least leveling off, *American Band* renewed interest in the Truckers as sober voices from the South. "I'm doing more press for this record than any record we've ever done," Patterson told me at the time. "That's exciting, because the last couple of records, I felt like people considered us this old band that didn't know when to break up. We hadn't embarrassed ourselves yet, but it felt like each record was getting less attention than the one before. So it felt good to have a record that everybody wants to write about and fight about."

With all the comings and goings over the last twenty-five years, the Drive-By Truckers are really defined by core members Patterson and Cooley. They're the chief songwriters, the main singers, and the only two members who've been in the band since its first rehearsal/recording session back in June 1996. By that point they had already been playing together for a decade and had weathered a few highs (in both senses of the word) and many lows. They have an unusual chemistry, polar opposites who somehow seem to fit together neatly. Patterson is an extrovert who is active on social media, posts often on the Truckers' Facebook page, and does almost all the press for their albums. He's a born songwriter who started penning lyrics when he was just eight years old and wrote full concept albums as a teenager. Where some folks have an internal monologue, I suspect Patterson has an internal rock show.

Cooley is literally none of that. He doesn't talk a whole lot, preferring to choose his words very carefully; as he sings on "Marry Me," "Just 'cause I don't run my mouth don't mean I got nothin' to say." He has never logged on to any form of social media and generally hates doing press, yet he can explain clearly and eloquently, in that deep voice and North Alabama accent, how the band's songs and ideas all fit together. He's a deft guitar player who blends punk and classic rock and country and bluegrass, but he admits that he's not a natural songwriter. He didn't come to the pursuit until he was in his thirties, and he's nowhere near as prolific as Patterson.

Theirs is a curious partnership between lifelong friends whose creative minds overlap in unexpected ways. They write separately, Patterson usually finishing a song in one quick burst and Cooley painstakingly assembling one over months, sometimes years. Yet their songs more often than not complement each other and address the same topics: their frayed marriages, for example, or the suicide of an old bandmate. When they met to trade songs for *American Band*, they were surprised that they had both become so explicitly political. Neither of the songwriters believes much in hoodoo or spiritual connections, but there is something between them that can't be explained or severed very easily. "I can't imagine what sort of gutpunch it would take for Patterson and Cooley not to do this together," says David Barbe, who has been producing Truckers records for twenty years. "Maybe a nuclear bomb going off or something."

Furthermore, Patterson and Cooley share a mad devotion to the rock show, where those ideas about the South, about America, about resistance and healthy rebellion play out in unexpected ways. As sturdy as their albums are, the stage may be their natural setting and the place where they leave their deepest mark. It's where they can rewrite their old songs every night, where they can interrogate their ideas about the Dirty South and about America more generally. And there are some kick-ass guitar solos.

It is a long tradition within the Truckers—dating back to their earliest days in Athens, Georgia, when they had only a loose lineup that changed seemingly every night—to forgo setlists in favor of just winging it. A few minutes before they take the stage, they'll figure out which song they're starting with, but after that song is done, even the band members don't know where they're going. There are, of course, some rules: Patterson and Cooley usually trade off songs so that neither of them dominates the proceedings. There are some songs that make good openers, like Patterson's "Putting People on the Moon" or Cooley's "Ramon Casiano," which set a scene or a tone early in the show that the band can sustain or twist as it proceeds. Similarly, other songs work best in the middle of a show, deep into the second act, just as there are a handful of tunes that are best played late in the evening, songs like "Angels and Fuselage" or the boisterous eulogy of the Jim Carroll Band's "People Who Died." They've played thousands of concerts but haven't repeated a setlist. Each show is its very own sacrosanct thing.

Fuck with the rock show at your own risk. They will stop a song cold to dog-cuss someone waving a rebel flag or creeping on a woman near the stage. At a HeAthens Homecoming show in Athens in 2017—one of their annual three-night stands at the 40 Watt that have become a tradition for the band and the community that has gathered around them—Patterson stopped "What It Means" to have a guy ejected. He held a quick trial because he "believe[d] in the justice system." Then he heard testimony from witnesses: "He was being an asshole," one fan shouted. And for the crime of interrupting Patterson's song, the convicted asshole was escorted out of the 40 Watt. As further punishment, Patterson tried to guess the guy's favorite Truckers song just so they could play it after he was gone. When the band released that live show through Bandcamp in 2020, that false start and mock trial got its own track and title. It's called "The Incident," which makes this guy's infraction and the crowd's response to it canon.

The rock show can be a political rally, a town hall meeting, a front-porch hang, a community potluck (usually without casseroles, though), even a discussion salon, and while it's a cliché to compare a concert to a religious experience, the rock show can be a church service, too. There is something of the preacher in Patterson, something like sacramental wine in the bottle of Jack they pass around onstage. These are songs about damnation and redemption, and the band plays them like true believers who really do want to save your soul. Most of their performances culminate in a simple yet powerful affirmation of life's immense value, Patterson shedding his guitar, sweating profusely, lugging the microphone stand around the stage, pleading on his knees, giving everything. Their best performances—and most of their not-best, too—have something of a moral to them, a challenge to their fans to be better, to do better: You're not alone in your pain, because everybody is going through something. And because everybody is going through something, don't make it worse for them. Don't be racist. Don't be sexist. Don't be assholes. Be heathens. "Love each other, motherfuckers," to quote Patterson quoting Patti Smith.

In the following pages, I attempt to tell the band's story, albeit in a roundabout way. It's not a chronology but a travelogue of sorts, a road trip through the southern wilds to visit the places the Truckers have been writing and singing about for more than twenty-five years now. More ambitiously, this book speaks to the power of music—the Truckers' albums in particular and southern music in general—to do more than simply reflect a larger culture. Rather, music can frame and shape that culture, prompting us to question certain assumptions we make about ourselves and other people, whether we're listening on headphones in our rooms or with other people at a bar in downtown Birmingham.

In crucial ways the Truckers have provided a rip-roaring soundtrack for a very personal reckoning with my own southern roots. I was born in one of the places they sing about: McNairy County, Tennessee, home to Sheriff Buford Pusser of *Walking Tall* fame and setting for three Truckers songs. I grew up there, got baptized at the First Baptist Church of Selmer, and played in the McNairy Central High School marching band. When I left, I took a bit of the place with me.

I first heard the Drive-By Truckers in 2003, when I bought a copy of *Decoration Day* at a record store in Newark, Delaware. I had heard of the band, but like many I had immediately dismissed them based on the name alone; in fact, I'm still a little embarrassed to say *Drive-By Truckers* aloud, especially to civilians who might not have heard of them. And they know it's bad. They understand that it's held them back, although it might actually make their success all the more impressive: they did all *this* despite having *that* name. As Patterson says, "There are probably a lot of people who will never listen to us because our name's so stupid but who might actually like us if they heard us. But I don't know what to do about that at this point except just keep doing what we do."

When I first heard the band, I had recently moved away from my home in Tennessee for the first time and was still reeling from the recent death of my father. Burdened by loss and grief, somewhat adrift in life, I was looking for something to make me feel a bit more at home in the world. If you had asked me what exactly I was looking for, I wouldn't have been able to tell you, at least not with any specificity. And that was why I was so stunned to find this record.

It wasn't an immediate thing, certainly. My world didn't explode the first time I heard *Decoration Day*, but my curiosity was piqued. It wasn't country music, although it had country elements, especially the heartsick "My Sweet Annette." It was southern rock, but not the kind I was expecting: no Confederate flag-waving, bro-hugging, "Free Bird"–yelling, beer-hoisting anthems with long guitar solos, a life soundtrack for every guy who ever wanted to beat me up in high school. It was a little bit of that, of course, although certainly not the flag-waving part.

These were wordy songs full of concrete images, proper nouns, references to a Ford Mustang Mach 1 and a heaping serving of nana pudding. It took a few listens to take it all in, the boogie guitar riffs and rock-solid drumming, the trade-offs between the three songwriters and vocalists: Patterson, with the higher voice, a pronounced Mid-South accent, and a dense lyrical style; Isbell, gruffer of voice and so specific in his details that I wouldn't have believed he was only twenty-three years old; and Cooley, a bit looser and wilder, author of story-songs that had to have been based on guys I knew from back home, ready with a turn of phrase that is literary but with none of the pretensions the word *literary* might imply.

With each listen I got to know these guys better and better, and they gradually constructed a wide and amazingly detailed world that I recognized as the one I had left behind. Driving through the Brandywine Valley every morning and evening, a commute that allowed me to listen to exactly one full-length album, I was taken back to my home in Selmer, to the curvy country roads I had raced along in my first car, windows rolled down and stereo cranked up. As a teenager I longed to escape my small rural town, to drive those back roads right out of the county and into another world, but at that moment, as an adult living in Delaware, listening to *Decoration Day* every day for months, all I wanted to do was go home again.

It would be wrong to say that *Decoration Day* cured my homesickness. What it did was make my homesickness more acute. It filled in my sense of self at a time when I felt emptiest. It convinced me that I was a southerner, a Tennessean, a small-town guy, an exile in the First State. And that renewed identity changed the way I saw my new surroundings and eventually the way I saw the whole world.

All this was despite the fact that I was never the guy who would end up in a Drive-By Truckers song. I was never the guy with the muscle car and no prospects beyond high school; I was never the guy who knocked up his girlfriend; I was never poor. I had fired a shotgun only in high school recess class, where gun safety was a crucial part of the curriculum. I was, in fact, a reasonably book-smart, generally well adjusted, shy-around-girls, middle-class white kid who never developed much of a southern accent. But I recognized something in the Drive-By Truckers' songs. I knew the characters and the setting from my own life. I had lived in this world, even if I had left it behind. More crucially, I heard something in the Truckers' music that sounded like a similarly complicated relationship to the South.

The South, I knew by then, is not especially defensible. It is renowned for its art: the blues and rock and roll; the sublimely patterned quilts of Gee's Bend, Alabama; Faulkner and Carson McCullers and Eudora Welty; Ernest J. Gaines and Zora Neale Hurston; Hank Williams and R.E.M. and Howard Finster; Carroll Cloar; Big Star, Louis Armstrong, and Johnny Cash. In every other way, however—politically, socially, racially, economically—the South is fundamentally compromised. "Their music makes you feel okay to be bitter about the place," says Isbell, who was a Trucker from 2001 to 2007. "It makes a lot of people think, *Okay, I've had issues with the place where I grew up and how I was treated and made to feel like an outsider, and these guys make me feel okay about that.* They're pissed about it, too."

I had seen it all up close. Growing up in Tennessee and Alabama, I heard ugly jokes about Black folks told by people I loved and otherwise admired, like it was nothing—just a casual kind of racism. I witnessed what we called salt-and-pepper fights in the halls of my high school, violence sparked by a stray word spoken by a white kid—*always a white kid*—who might be trying on a particular prejudice the way he might learn to drive his daddy's pickup. In college I had heated conversations with friends from northern or western states who dismissed the very idea of the South, despite having chosen to attend a southern college. As a college student in Memphis, I delved into the history of Sun and Stax Records, an acolyte's lessons in racial collaboration, and found some beauty in hits by Sam and Dave, Otis Redding, and Booker T. and the MGs.

Until I heard the Drive-By Truckers, however, I had heard the South described only in terms of its trajectory: the bad of its history, the promise of its present moment, the rosiness of its future. I had experienced the geographical South, the cultural South, the South as philosophical concept and national scapegoat. And I had studied in college the New South, which I understood to be a tricky term that originated in the years just after the Civil War, when regional pride engendered a widespread optimism that the war-ravaged region could shed its agrarian poverty and embrace an industrial prosperity modeled on the North. The term was resurrected during the civil rights era of the 1950s and 1960s, less as a description of the place and more as a hopeful goal: they marched toward a New South.

There are, in fact, many different Souths: what the Indigenous scholar Jodi A. Byrd poetically described in 2014 as "shadow souths, phantom souths, fugitive souths, and occasionally the imperial norths against which proper Souths, in all their cross-culturalities, come to reveal themselves." This is important to note, especially when the South is commonly portrayed as politically and culturally monolithic. It's a sea of red states on electoral maps, where public servants embrace rank conspiracy theories, where the rebel flag still flies. But that seems to be changing: the massive mobilization of Black voters turned Georgia blue in 2020, a feat that once seemed impossible but perhaps heralds a new political reality in the Peach State.

The South is an ever-shifting terrain, as is the Dirty South that the Truckers conjure in their songs. Its defining virtues were passed down not via oral tradition or even lived experience. Rather, we learned our southernness through pop culture: the television show *The Dukes of Hazzard* most of all, but also the *Walking Tall* films, southern rock bands like Lynyrd Skynyrd, and country singers who sang slickly produced songs about rustic life. When so many white southern writers seemed so caught up in the racial certainties of the past, the Truckers by necessity were confronting the South head on—not as it was in years past but as it is in the present. I listen to these songs years later and they still sound relevant. They still sound like they're happening *now* rather than *then*. Patterson, Cooley, and Isbell sound like they're singing about a South where old prejudices haven't yet been swept under the rug, a South that can't congratulate itself for getting on the right side of things, a South still dirty from the muck of history. Sadly, the way things are going, it'll be a long time before it comes clean.

Because I first heard the band when I was far away from my southern home, because they evoked the specifics of that region so vividly, and because they undertook their mission with such dogged determination, the idea of place has always been inseparable from the Drive-By Truckers. It determines how I hear them, how I think about them, and how I recommend them to readers and friends. I'm not alone. In fact, in order to fully understand their music, it helps to consider it in geographic and cultural terms, each song depicting another acre of their Dirty South. In that regard a chronological account of the band's formation and development would be not only redundant (the 2010 documentary *The Secret to a Happy Ending* does a good job covering their first fifteen years) but also extremely limiting. Their story hits on the events common to so many rock bands, tracing a familiar arc from teenage flirtations with music through early lineups to landmark albums. To date, they haven't burned out or faded away; they remain a viable and relevant act, and likely will for years to come. What they've built is perhaps more important than how they went about building it.

I write about places here because that's what the Truckers write about. Their songs are decidedly set in deep corners of the South, with a keen understanding of what those particular locales mean to the characters and what they mean to the listeners. It's about geography, of course, but also geology: the fact that Birmingham was founded in one of the few valleys where all the ingredients for steel occur naturally, the fact that the Shoals sits at a bend in the Tennessee River where the current slows for a few miles, as though reluctant to leave it behind. The Truckers understand that our notion of place is informed by its history, by its politics, by economic forces outside pushing in and inside pushing out, by the music made there and the food cooked there. They understand that place defines its people just as people define their place, which means hometowns and old haunts can sit cockeyed in our psyches, exerting a strange pull on us—like the woman in Cooley's song "Pulaski." She leaves her Tennessee town for the Pacific breezes and TV promises of California but finds herself tugged homeward. It ends tragically, as though they're rewriting the old Bobby George and Vern Stovall classic "Long Black Limousine."

So let's take a road trip using their songs and albums as a map. Let's ramble through the Dirty South, sit in its diners and attend its churches, listen as preachers extol the love of God then leave the pulpit to do unspeakable things. Let's shop at the strip malls and drive the long, mean highways. We'll start in the Shoals, one of the unlikeliest music capitals in America, a place that hosted historic sessions by Aretha Franklin and Wilson Pickett and the Rolling Stones. Patterson and Cooley grew up here, formed their first band here, and kept it going for six long years despite local apathy.

Memphis may seem like a curious detour, considering the duo lived there for only a few months before leaving in defeat. But that city is important not least for its impact on how they thought, wrote, and sang about race in their Dirty South. And there's a legendary shock rocker and a chance exchange they overheard at a local greasy spoon, both of which inspired a foundational Truckers tune that hints at the band's mission. It's a long drive from the Bluff City down to Athens, Georgia, where the Drive-By Truckers played their first notes together. A small college town renowned for its thriving music scene, Athens showed them that a band could be anything they wanted or needed it to be.

We'll dip down to Auburn, Alabama, as we trace the Truckers' route to a uniform warehouse in downtown Birmingham, where they finally managed to record *Southern Rock Opera*. We'll head over to the soggy bottomland of southern Mississippi to a place with no real name where Lynyrd Skynyrd's plane crashed. And then it's back up to the Shoals, a completely different place by now with a very different view of its own musical legacy. Many more years away from its heyday, the music scene found new opportunities for young musicians, including Jason Isbell and Shonna Tucker, two band members who helped goose the Truckers in new directions.

We'll take Highway 72—subject of one of Cooley's finest songs—east out of town, then head north to Richmond and catch up with Wes Freed, the artist who developed a unique visual style for the band, setting them even further apart from their peers and becoming something like an auxiliary member himself. We'll go back to Tennessee, to my old haunts in McNairy County, where the Truckers have set several of their songs and where many of the myths and truths of the Dirty South intersect in the figure of Sheriff Buford Pusser. From there we'll go . . . who knows.

These are places real and imagined, sites of mythmaking and myth-shattering, defined by a strange southern calculus of water and mineral, music and food, racial violence and racial collaboration, economic boom and bust. They're constantly in flux, constantly changing and putting their own histories into brand-new contexts. The Truckers can't speak to every aspect of these places, nor do they try. Their Dirty South is largely populated with white characters, as is their audience, but they do not simply ignore the larger, multiracial South. Rather, they refer to it constantly, persistently, reminding you that it is there, this larger world.

It's a bumpy ride for sure. There are so many moments when the band might have crashed into an oak tree or driven off an embankment. Although they found success in their thirties—at an age when most rock-and-roll hopefuls would have long ago given up—they still made bad decisions, nursed grudges against each other, harbored serious doubts about their mission, lashed out, drank too much, and maybe took a few too many drugs. Somehow they hung on, keeping the tour van between the ditches. "Oh, we were in the ditches!" Patterson corrects me. "But we just kept going anyway. I can't account for what kept us going, other than just plain old stubbornness."

Writing this book and taking this road trip, I have cried over the fate of Bryan Harvey and his family, murdered in Richmond and eulogized by Patterson in "Two Daughters and a Beautiful Wife." I have watched with no small disgust as white parents posed their children for photos, all dressed in their Sunday best, at Stone Mountain outside of Atlanta, moving the camera to afford the best view of the Confederate heroes in the background. I have visited abandoned moonshine stills far from any road in McNairy County. I have gotten lost driving in downtown Birmingham listening to Patterson theorize that *A Blessing and a Curse* is the Truckers' worst album. I have made friends with Cooley's dog Bowie. I have sat with Matt Patton at Crestwood Coffee in Birmingham. I have geeked out over power pop with Jay Gonzalez. I have walked the railroad tracks in Athens to visit the kudzu-clotted ravine that appears on the cover of R.E.M.'s *Murmur*. I have thought long and hard about my own history as a white southerner, and that reckoning produced this book. It doesn't stop with these pages. It's something I'll be doing until my last breath.

Until then, let there be rock.

The Shoals

▼

There are catfish as big as cars in Wilson Reservoir, near Florence, Alabama. At least that's what locals say. Some people won't venture into the water to swim or to fish, fearful that they might meet up with a gargantuan bottom feeder: whiskers as long as saplings, teeth like shovelheads, mouth like a bathtub. You might get gulped up whole. You might not even see that fish if it was right behind you, its maw opening around you. And you might not see that old cabin that was covered up when the dam water flooded the hollers. Or that gun used in an unsolved murder from '82. Or that set of shin bones projecting from a concrete block.

This is one of those places where reality blurs into legend. That gargantuan catfish is one of those tall tales you wish were true, even though you know it can't be, like the Boggy Creek monster over in Arkansas or the Bell Witch up in Tennessee. In fact, the largest catfish ever caught in the Yellowhammer State was only about 120 pounds, and it was hooked down near Tuscaloosa. But that old gun and those human remains, they might actually be down there. There have been bodies disposed of at the dam, and more than a few were still kicking when they made the plunge.

"There's folklore about people being thrown over the spillway, especially in the Redneck Mafia era that we sing about on *The Dirty South*," says Patterson Hood. "I don't know if that's true or not, but it's a great story. And those songs are based on some truth. Some of it is very true, and some of it is local tall tales, stories that have been passed down."

The Drive-By Truckers have been exploring this divide between the truth and the yarn almost since their first notes. Patterson and Mike Cooley, not to mention Jason Isbell, Shonna Tucker, and Rob Malone, grew up in the shadow of Wilson Dam, in this odd coalition of municipalities—Florence, Muscle Shoals, Sheffield, and Tuscumbia—that have bled together into what is sometimes called the Quad Cities and sometimes called the Shoals. It's a place of many places: a metropolitan area that sprawls across two counties, that has absorbed numerous municipalities, that has spawned very particular cultures separated by just a mile or so. They were all defined by the dam, which not only brought labor and industry to the area but delivered light and electricity into the darkest corners of North Alabama. It's a century old, built to supply electricity to nearby nitrate plants. Nitrate was intended as a new ingredient for gunpowder during World War I, which would have made the Shoals region crucial to the war effort had the war not ended before construction even began in 1918.

It was a massive undertaking by the US Army Corps of Engineers and dangerous work for the laborers they hired. There were rumors of workers who perished on the clock, their bodies unceremoniously blended with the concrete of the dam itself, their bones supporting the spillways. It prodded the local economy as entrepreneurs opened movie theaters, general stores, churches, and hotels to accommodate this new working class. But mostly it was vice that profited: drugs, liquor, gambling, and prostitution.

The Truckers have depicted the dam and its history—their region's history—in human scale, showing how it might benefit many people while erasing others. "Thank God for the TVA," Isbell sings on his song simply titled "TVA." This was one of his first songs as a Trucker, and they were playing it during some of his earliest shows with the band in 2001. Those live performances were wild and wooly, anthemic and epic, although when they got around to recording it for *Decoration Day*, the song had become a more languid, mostly acoustic tune. The original studio take is a slow soul number that sounds easygoing at times, bittersweet at others, desperate by its final notes. It's spare, with Isbell's rough-edged voice and some guitar fanning the melody and an organ riff churning the humid southern air. It was scratched from that record and finally saw the light of day four years later on a rarities collection called

The Fine Print. Even after Isbell left the Truckers in 2007, he kept it in his setlist and recorded a searing version for 2012's *Live from Alabama.*

"TVA" is a quiet testimonial, as Isbell's narrator—who may or may not be Isbell himself—relates three generations' experiences with the dam and the landscape it created. He and his father bond while fishing in the reservoir, the old man regaling him with stories of "Camaros and J. W. Dant"—the former a muscle car and the latter a cheap and therefore popular brand of whiskey, both understood to be used together too often. In the next verse he recalls sitting out on the locks with his girlfriend, making out and "watching the raccoons and terrapins dance on the rocks," which suggests he's moved on to something stronger than liquor.

The song climaxes with his great-grandfather, a farmer whose land is drying up and whose ten children are starving; they are saved when government men show up and recruit him to work on this new project. There's some pride here: "He helped build the dam, gave power to most of the South," Isbell sings, "so I thank God for the TVA." Every time he sings that grateful refrain, he sounds nothing but sincere. There's no sarcasm; there's nothing beneath the lyrics except perhaps a generational guilt for lounging and tripping on the blood and sweat of his forebears.

During Isbell's early shows with the Truckers—when Patterson would introduce him as the "nearly famous Jason Isbell!"—they would follow up "TVA" with "Uncle Frank," a much less celebratory, much more sober account of the construction of Wilson Dam. Bound together in Truckers lore, these two songs comment on each other, two sides of the same double eagle. Even musically they complement each other, both with a pace as steady as a river's current, one leisurely and the other a bit more frantic. The title character isn't Cooley's actual uncle, although he says he did base the character on stories he heard growing up. "I remember visiting my granddad when I was a kid," says Cooley, "and he would get to talking about stuff. One time he definitely got my attention. He was telling me about a guy he knew from that era who wound up killing himself. The guy had been forced off his land, and he ended up living in a housing project. It had something to do with the TVA project."

Uncle Frank is one of many Alabamans who were displaced by Wilson Dam, whose land was seized, whose homes were flooded, whose independent way of life was obliterated. This version might be a fictional character in a story-song, but his circumstances were real. "What's under the river, there were people living down there," says Cooley. "This guy would cut and sell timber off his land. He had to be a conservationist back then, because if you cut it all down without replanting, you got nothing to sell the next year. So he would cut what was mature, sell it, live off it."

In the song, the government agencies building the dam fill Uncle Frank with promises of jobs, electricity, and shiny cars. "I added the part about the auto industry, but Ford was looking at Muscle Shoals around that time," explains Cooley. In fact, in 1921 Henry Ford attempted to lease the dam for ninety-nine years, offering a paltry $5 million and intending to build what Ford called the Detroit of the South. More than a decade later, when he visited the region with President Roosevelt, their party wanted a touring car fit for both the leader of the free world and the richest man in America. The only person who owned such an automobile was the local madam—or at least that's the story they tell around the Shoals. "Who else," says Cooley, "was making that kind of buck? Pussy's a natural resource everywhere."

It wasn't a southerner who thwarted Ford's ambitions, but a Republican senator from Nebraska named George Norris. He opposed the automaker's plans for a decade, until Franklin Roosevelt was elected president and created the TVA in 1933, which *still* oversees the development of natural resources in the region. Locals still like to play what if. "Think about the Black migration north," says Cooley. "Detroit and Chicago were where all the Black folks leaving Mississippi and Alabama were going. But they would have come to the Shoals otherwise. It would have changed the landscape up there and down here. What would race relations have been like in the South if that had happened?"

But it didn't happen. Ford never purchased Wilson Dam, the region never developed into an industrial center to rival northern cities, none of those jobs came to town, and Uncle Frank and the very real people like him were left homeless, jobless, and unemployable: the detritus of progress. Wilson Dam became just another means for the rich to get richer. As Cooley sings on "Uncle Frank," "the price of all that power kept on going straight uphill. The banks around the holler sold for lakefront property where doctors, lawyers, and musicians teach their kids to waterski." That is a tongue-in-cheek dig at his friend and bandmate:

Patterson's dad, David Hood, was a musician, and he raised two kids right on the banks of the river.

In the song's final verse—one of the finest, most startling moments in the Truckers' catalog—Cooley recounts Uncle Frank's fate over a winding guitar lick that sounds like the grinding of industrial gears:

> Uncle Frank couldn't read or write,
> so there's no note or letter found when he died.
> Just a rope around his neck
> and a kitchen table turned on its side.

"TVA" left the band's setlists when Isbell left the band in 2007, but they still play "Uncle Frank" regularly and still have to dispel certain misperceptions the song invites. "I've always felt like 'Uncle Frank' might have given people the wrong idea about us," says Cooley. "It's critical of the government, and it comes from a real place. There are always casualties in progress. There are always unintended consequences. You can't deny that, but a lot of people got the idea that I was coming from a right-wing libertarian point of view, which is not who I am. You're going to throw stuff out there and people are going to cherry-pick parts of it that fit their own ideologies, maybe make you more one of them than you really are. No, buddy. I'm not part of that club."

Even without Ford, Wilson Dam changed North Alabama profoundly, bringing electricity out to remote hollers where there wasn't even running water, let alone working lights. And it brought power to Florence and Tuscumbia and Sheffield, even to Muscle Shoals, which was then mostly cornfields. Wilson Dam produced the power that ran the reel-to-reels that captured "You Better Move On," a song written and sung by a local bellhop named Arthur Alexander and recorded in 1961 at a makeshift studio above a drug store by another man named Rick Hall. Wilson Dam powered radio stations and home radios around the South, many of which broadcast "You Better Move On" to fans who didn't even know where it was recorded, or really even care. And those same radios broadcast a cover of the song by the Rolling Stones, who less than a decade later would camp out in the Shoals to record one of their best and most popular albums.

Like Detroit, the city Ford intended it to rival, the Shoals became a music town in the 1960s. By then it had already produced two men who exerted a profound influence on twentieth-century popular music. W. C. Handy was born in Florence in 1873 but moved to Memphis to work as a bandleader. There he wrote and notated scores of blues songs, not inventing the genre but documenting and innovating it. Sam Phillips, another Florence native who migrated to the Bluff City, would record scores of blues musicians at Sun Studio before producing early sessions by Elvis, Jerry Lee Lewis, Carl Perkins, and Johnny Cash. Not everyone left town to make their mark. Many stayed local, including Hall, a white man who opened FAME Studios—short for Florence, Alabama, Music Enterprises. His first crew of white session players—including bassist Norbert Putnam, keyboardist David Briggs, and drummer Jerry Carrigan—soon hightailed it up to Music Row, where they became part of a coterie of local musicians known as the Nashville Cats and played on records by George Jones, Tammy Wynette, Elvis Presley, Bob Dylan, and Neil Young, to name just a few. Hall replaced them with another group of locals that included David Hood on bass, Jimmy Johnson on guitar, Barry Beckett on keyboards, and the great Roger Hawkins on drums. Together they came to be known as the Swampers, presumably for making any groove sound humid, tight, *swampy*. These white players were often mistaken for Black, which earned them a certain renown when they backed visiting Black artists like Wilson Pickett and Aretha Franklin, whose Shoals recordings helped revolutionize R&B music in the mid-1960s.

The Shoals was the place where the Staple Singers cut "I'll Take You There," "If You're Ready (Come Go with Me)," and other anthems of the post–civil rights era. It's where Arthur Conley and Otis Redding created "Sweet Soul Music" to serve as a kind of mission statement for the genre that they were helping to redefine both commercially and artistically. "Do you like good music, that sweet soul music?" Conley sings on a song that celebrates Sam and Dave, Wilson Pickett, Lou Rawls, and Otis Redding himself (who produced the song). "Just as long as it's swingin'. Oh yeah, oh yeah!"

It's also where tween titans the Osmonds recorded some of their biggest hits in the early 1970s, with Donny standing on a Coca-Cola crate to sing into the microphone. It's where Paul Simon and Bobbie Gentry and

Bob Seger and the Rolling Stones and Clarence Carter and Cher booked sessions. And it's arguably where the notion of southern rock was born, when a session player named Duane Allman shredded eloquently at the end of Wilson Pickett's 1968 cover of the Beatles' "Hey Jude." Just a few years later, a rock band from Gainesville, Florida, with a confusing name cut their first sessions, although those Lynyrd Skynyrd recordings weren't released until their singer, Ronnie Van Zant, was dead. Even after that flurry of activity died down in the late 1970s, even after the Ford plant closed down in 1982, even when the local economy tanked, the Shoals remained an unlikely music publishing mecca, mostly in the country genre.

And here is a very different blurring of legend and reality. The Shoals scene around FAME, and later Muscle Shoals Sound Studio, has been celebrated as something of a racial utopia in the middle of the South, an example of Black folks and white folks creating great music together, while down the road in Birmingham and Selma, civil rights marchers were met with violent opposition from law enforcement. This is the crux of Patterson's "Ronnie and Neil" on *Southern Rock Opera*, which frames these strange contradictions within the story of Neil Young and Ronnie Van Zant. In the 1970s the two men had a friendly war of words that played out in Young's "Southern Man" and Skynyrd's "Sweet Home Alabama." Addressing the intense racism and poisonous notions of masculinity that defined the South in the popular imagination, the former is an overbearing song, steeped in lurid, backwater imagery and the kinds of stereotypes you might encounter in exploitation films like *2000 Maniacs* or *Mandingo*. If you're a living, breathing soul reading these words, then you've certainly heard Skynyrd's response on classic rock radio, in movies or commercials, or *somewhere* out in the world. With its catchy boogie-rock riffs, "Sweet Home Alabama" is a tricky, contradictory song about a state the band never called home, praising the Swampers ("they've been known to pick a song or two") and possibly booing Governor George Wallace. But it also points to Watergate to suggest that political corruption is not exclusive to any one region of the country but widespread, and Van Zant flips the bird to Young and his fuzzy portrait of the South: "Well, I heard Mr. Young sing about her," Van Zant sings, not snarling but certainly defiant. "Well, I heard ol' Neil put her down. Well, I hope Neil Young will remember: a southern man don't need him around anyhow."

Those lines always struck me as lacking sting, more concerned with maintaining a rhyme scheme than with expressing a sentiment. But as I listened to it after hearing *Southern Rock Opera*, it sounded sneaky more than snarky, essentially taking Young to task for generalizing about the South, for not realizing that there is as much nuance among southerners—even among white southern men—as there is among any other regional population, that there are men (like Patterson and Cooley, for example) who are fighting to be on the right side of history. This is the very thing that Skynyrd were fighting and years later the Truckers would keep fighting: this idea that the South is one thing or the other, that it generates racism while the rest of the country does not, that everyone down here is ignorant of these problems.

Around the time the Birmingham public safety commissioner and civil rights villain Eugene "Bull" Connor turned the hoses on peaceful Black demonstrators in downtown Birmingham, two hours up the road there was some sweet soul music being made in multiracial recording sessions: something beautiful to combat the ugliness. The musical activity in the Shoals stands in stark contrast to the violence in Birmingham, maybe not brighter than the darkness but something like a small step forward as Patterson sings about all the artists who came to town— Wilson and Aretha and Skynyrd—before they were famous. "They met some real fine people," he declares in the first verse, "not no racist pieces of shit." That experience informed, among other songs, "Sweet Home Alabama," not just its defensiveness about place but also the nuance of it, the contradictions that have defined Skynyrd's biggest hit for so many years. The Truckers acknowledge that thorniness, emphasizing the unlikely bond that formed between Young (who loved "Sweet Home Alabama" and wrote "Powderfinger" specifically for Skynyrd) and Van Zant (who often performed wearing a Neil Young T-shirt, although the rumor that he was buried in it is false).

Instead of racial conflict, there was in the Shoals something like a first step toward racial cooperation. This is true only up to a certain extent, as recent histories by Charles Hughes and other scholars have made clear: many of the artists who came down to the Shoals were Black, but the infrastructure at these studios was almost exclusively white. Most of the money went into white pockets. That shouldn't diminish the talents or contributions of the Swampers, not when Roger Hawkins's drumming on

Wilson Pickett's "Land of 1000 Dances" remains one of the most electrifying beats in rock history, not when you can hear Mavis Staples cajoling David Hood on the Staple Singers' ebullient "I'll Take You There," not when Spooner Oldham's beautiful organ intro to Aretha Franklin's "I Never Loved a Man (The Way I Love You)" rolls out a red carpet for the Queen of Soul. Rather, so volatile and violent was the turmoil that engulfed so much of the South that even meager racial progress appeared profound, even utopian.

Which raises a few questions: Why here? Why did this happen in the Shoals? Why not some other place along the Tennessee River? Why not some other place in the South? Why not Selmer? Why not Birmingham? Nothing about this place seems likely, nothing obvious. There are other places like it, many of them better located and more easily accessible. In fact, the Shoals is slightly removed from the world. You can drive in, but you'll drive for a while even after you take the exit off I-65. There's a small airport in nearby Huntsville, but very few commercial flights land there. Almost none offer direct flights from anywhere. The Shoals existed in a bubble, cut off from the rest of the world. "To get here," says David Hood, "you have to want to get here."

Rick Hall had a pretty obvious explanation. Once, before he passed in 2018, I had an opportunity to ask him why the Shoals had become a musical powerhouse when other cities did not. His answer was short, direct, and exclamatory: "It was me!" It's hard to argue with him. A poor kid who grew up in the Black Hills of Franklin County, Alabama, right on the Mississippi border, he could remember when his family first got electricity. To seek his fortune away from the family farm, he moved south to Florence, where he played in country bands and set up a makeshift recording studio in the space above a drugstore downtown. He was driven, and it's said that his work ethic alienated his business partners. So he moved FAME out near the dam, then out to its current location in Muscle Shoals. He cut deals with Jerry Wexler at Atlantic in New York and Jim Stewart at Stax in Memphis, and they sent many of their artists down his way.

A savvy businessman who steered FAME through several decades of changing music industry trends, Hall was also an inventive record producer. He manned the boards for Arthur Alexander's "You Better

Move On," not to mention Jimmy Hughes's magisterial "Slip Away," the Osmonds' infectious "One Bad Apple," and Bobbie Gentry's lush empowerment-via-prostitution anthem "Fancy" (which remains one of country music's finest story-songs). He maybe didn't dream it all up, because who in their right mind would have dreamed up such a story? But Hall made it happen. "There was all this talent to pull from," says Cooley, "and Rick Hall was the one who knew what to do with it. He started the businesses and he hired all those guys. He provided the jobs."

Initially he provided those full-time jobs to white players, although after the Swampers left FAME in 1969, he did hire more Black musicians, including members of the legendary FAME Gang, a new and larger studio band that released *Solid Gold in Muscle Shoals* in 1969. These were working-class musicians who would have worked at one of the local factories or the Reynolds aluminum plant if they couldn't book recording sessions. "And they knew it," says Cooley. "It provided a lot of incentive for them to not just be talented but to be really good. They knew that if Rick Hall didn't keep calling them back for those sessions, they were going to be putting in applications for that shitty-ass job in a 150-degree blast furnace. You're gonna play your damn ass off for him!"

Perhaps Hall succeeded because he stayed put. At neither the height of his success in the 1960s nor its nadir in the 1980s did he leave town; he never picked up and moved to Nashville or New York or Los Angeles. He could be tough on his employees, ornery by most accounts, so much so that the Swampers eventually set out on their own, defecting from FAME to open Muscle Shoals Sound Studio in an abandoned coffin factory out on Jackson Highway. (A quirk of place-names in the Shoals: FAME may stand for Florence, Alabama, Music Enterprises, but it's located in Muscle Shoals. Muscle Shoals Sound Studio, however, has never been located in the town that gave it a name. Both of its locations—the coffin factory and the larger facility down by the river—are actually in Sheffield.) Hall emerged as the central figure in the Shoals music scene, with a personality bigger than the place and a will bigger than the obstacles the place posed for him. And he lived long enough to see the city revived, to see music tourism become another major industry.

Among his many obstacles was the fact that the Shoals was mostly dry, which meant that selling alcohol was prohibited. There were few clubs around town that offered live music, so working musicians, including the

Swampers, had to drive up to the Tennessee state line, which was littered with bars that hired bands for the night. Or they had to trek south to Birmingham, or over to Huntsville. Every other place offered better gigs and therefore better pay than the Shoals. But those FAME sessions and later the Muscle Shoals Sound Studio sessions were enough to keep a lot of musicians out of the local factories and, in some cases, the local jails. It also meant that locals weren't always aware of the pop music being made in their own backyards, which in this case might have been an advantage rather than a disadvantage: they might have gawked at the freaks and longhairs in the Stones and Skynyrd, but they weren't getting angry over white musicians and Black musicians working the same recording sessions.

Says Cooley, "It was Black and white musicians working together at the height of the segregated South, and they talked about feeling the hate whenever they would go anywhere and eat together. If it had been more public, it might have been controversial around town, but the fact that nobody knew what was going on and nobody was paying attention to it, it could be this thing that just kinda happened."

Patterson was born into the Shoals music scene. His father took him to FAME and Muscle Shoals Sound Studio when he was just a kid; he even took him on the road from time to time. When Patterson was around ten years old, he made his first visit to New York City, when his father was producing Maggie and Terre Roche's 1975 album *Seductive Reasoning.* "One night they ended up knocking off work early and my dad and mom and Maggie and Terre took me to Greenwich Village," Patterson told the podcast *Fidelity High* in 2017. "So I have this real vivid memory of me at ten years old walking hand in hand with Maggie and Terre Roche as they're pointing out all these places in Greenwich Village and in Chinatown, and we rode the subway for the first time. It really literally kind of blew my mind, because I was a misfit kid at home and didn't really feel like I fit in at school. I think even a lot of my songwriting was a result of being a lonely, weird, misfit kid."

John Michael Cooley, on the other hand, knew nothing of that world. Word hadn't reached that far out into rural Colbert County, not far from where Sam Phillips was born. So he didn't realize that those songs he heard on the radio were made just across the river in Florence. "I wasn't aware of what all was being recorded there," he says. "I was really young, and 'When a Man Loves a Woman' was already an oldie by the time I was paying attention. But most people weren't aware of what was happening, and most of them didn't give a shit about Cher or flower children or that scruffy-looking Willie Nelson."

Back to the question Why here? Why the Shoals and not some other town in the South? Bono has a theory: maybe it's something in the water. In the 2013 documentary *Muscle Shoals*, locally referred to as "that movie" or "the film," the U2 front man pontificates, "It always seems to come out of the river. It's like the songs come out of the mud." Directed by Greg "Freddy" Camalier, that movie opens with a lengthy meditation on the Tennessee River, which hits a sharp turn at the Shoals and slows its current for a few miles. The idea is that there is magic in that water, accumulating like silt along the banks and worshiped by Indigenous people long before whites colonized the region—an attractive and romantic idea that always struck me as bogus. After all, that same water flows for hundreds of miles before it reaches northern Alabama, and it flows for hundreds of miles after it leaves northern Alabama. There are many other twists and turns along its length, not to mention many other dams: Chickamauga Dam near Chattanooga; Kentucky Dam up near Paducah; Pickwick Landing Dam, just a stone's throw from McNairy County. To credit so much amazing art to some sort of supernatural effect ignores the efforts and ingenuity of so many singers, instrumentalists, songwriters, producers, and engineers.

But Patterson says, "Yeah, it's totally the river." His sister Lilla says the same. The Hood siblings dispute some of the documentary's claims but accept that there's some kernel of truth to its assertions of waterborne magic. "We all knew about the Trail of Tears coming through here, because you learned all about it in history class," says Lilla, who lives in Birmingham and does design layout for the Truckers' albums. "We never called it the 'Singing River.' But when I saw that movie, I thought it might be true. The river does sing to you. There's something about it that is very special, and maybe that has something to do with the creativity in the Shoals area. When I drive up to Florence, I drive across that bridge and I feel like I'm home. My dad didn't leave because of that river, and I see that now. As I've gotten older, I see it more."

The Tennessee River draws people to it, to its magic and its industry, but it can divide as well as unite Alabamans. "I'm from Florence," says Lilla, "and I meet people all the time who say, 'I have a friend in Muscle Shoals. Do you know them?' No. I never know their friends. You didn't cross the river. You stayed on your own bank. You never knew the people on the other side of the river. They were *those people across the river.*" In other words, you let your bank of the river define you, at least against the people on the other side.

"It's like East Germany and West Germany," says Patterson. "I played in a band in high school with some guys from the other side of the river, and that was weird. I would introduce them to my Florence friends, and they'd say, 'You can't bring them here. They're river rats!'"

The river isn't a gigantic racial metaphor like they have down in Birmingham, where Red Mountain used to separate the Black inner city from the white suburbs. It's a metaphor for something different, separating the poor from the rich—or at least the people who perceive themselves to be rich from the people they perceive to be poor. The north side of the Tennessee River—especially Florence—is generally considered to be more urban and perhaps therefore richer, while the south side is more rural and perhaps therefore poorer. But wealth radiates outward from the water: the banks of the Tennessee are home to the biggest houses in the Shoals, and the further you get from the river, the poorer the people you meet.

These two future Truckers were separated by only a few miles, but their worlds were very different. Patterson was a city kid, while Cooley says he "went to a pretty backwards county school [from] kindergarten through fifth grade." Switching to the city school system was an eye-opening experience for the kid. "These schools were only a few miles away from one another, but there's a stigma. The city kids looked down on the county kids, and the county kids looked down on the city kids. But the city kids . . . they're rednecks, too! Big time. They lived in a subdivision—that's about the only difference. But in that small degree of separation geographically, people look at each other differently. They have a different set of values, even though the schools are only three miles apart."

One thing these two Southern boys did have in common was the presence in their lives of strong women—in particular, Patterson's grandmother Lilla Ruth "Sissy" Patterson and Cooley's grandmother Glady

Sizemore. "We both grew up being raised largely by and being very close to our maternal grandmothers," says Cooley. "Both of my parents worked all the time, so I would get dropped off at my grandparents' house. They were a farm family, so they were home. Same with Patterson. Our maternal grandmothers had a lot to do with shaping us. They were people we looked up to. They were figures of strength and integrity, and they both came from generations where women weren't exactly given their due. Both of them knew that, too."

Cooley wrote about his grandmother on "Space City," on the 2006 album *A Blessing and a Curse*. Specifically, he wrote about her death, which left him adrift, wandering around town wishing he were "about as half as tough" as he pretended. The music is acoustic, lonely, rooting his grief in his hometown and in the NASA complex in nearby Huntsville: "Space City's one hour up the road from me, one hour away from as close to the moon as anybody down here is ever gonna be." As quiet as Cooley may be in real life, in song he can be eloquent and vulnerable: "Somewhere behind that big white light is where my heart is gone, and somewhere she's wondering what's taking me so long." It's a song about fighting his feelings, trying to man up, putting on a brave face for the world, wondering if that's even a good thing to do: in the face of death, those ideas of masculinity mean nothing.

"The idea that women might deserve a little more respect was something I started getting hip to at a young age," says Cooley.

I was being dragged to these fundamentalist churches. All religions are cultish, but Church of Christ is a lot more cultish. They make Baptists look reasonable. It's a very patriarchal culture. In fact, if I had to get down to the one thing that made me question religion and the whole fundamentalist Christian church [it] was that women were to be seen and not heard. *Keep your mouth shut* was the message that they preached. It gives men who might be prone to be violent license to be violent. And I saw women accept that as normal and okay. You have to be strong to do that. It's strength in the appearance of weakness. Men can't do that. I'm not strong enough to keep my head down.

Cooley's songwriting is marked by a poignant empathy toward female characters, especially those at loose ends. "Panties in Your Purse," his first Truckers song, describes a woman who stops him at a show to relate her life's story, one that hits the usual country marks: cheating, divorce, public humiliation. She emerges not as a punchline but rather as a deeply sympathetic character who retains a kind of smartass humanity despite her troubles. Even more affecting is "Birthday Boy," which Cooley sings in the voice of a stripper who calls herself Trixie. He records her inner and outer monologue, mixing her practiced come-ons to patrons with some of the harsher aspects of her job ("flat on her back under a mean old man, just thinking happy thoughts and breathing deep"). Odd as it may be, he connects these songs to the influence of his grandmother. "She instilled a lot of goodness in me, and I saw this woman who was very, very strong but would never get credit for it. That really had an impact on me, the way women are treated."

For Patterson, playing music wasn't about following in his father's footsteps. He wanted to front a band, go on the road, rock stadiums, get groupies, be a star. His career started early, when he wrote his first song at eight years old. "When I started writing as a kid," he says, "I wrote whole albums. I didn't even know how to play yet, but I could write a whole concept album. It was fun. And it was the '70s." Because he gravitated toward writing and away from sports, he was bullied in grade school, but a growth spurt in high school and a bit of teenage rebellion made his high school years much easier. He played trombone in the school orchestra, but he practiced guitar more often and with more determination. As he grew up and learned about his hometown's history and his family's place in it, Patterson's mission became more about expanding and continuing the Shoals' legacy: he wanted to represent the region to the world. Perhaps that's naive, but it's also noble, especially since he never wavered in the face of what turned out to be local indifference, a string of hard setbacks, and some truly bad luck. Ultimately, Patterson would have to leave town in order to put it on the map.

He has written about his upbringing often, mining it for material on many of the Truckers' albums. "Let There Be Rock" on *Southern Rock Opera* opens with him dropping acid at a Blue Öyster Cult concert. He sings, "I thought those lasers were a spider chasing me." Later, he drinks a fifth of vodka and nearly drowns in a toilet before his friend's sister pulls him out. Opening the album's second disc, the song feels like a very specific form of personal mythmaking, presenting the details of an ordinary '70s adolescence as something extraordinary.

By the time he started playing in neighborhood bands with friends from his high school, Patterson had been a songwriter for half his life. He wrote scraps of lyrics in notebooks; some of those words would eventually make their way into Truckers songs many years later. Those ambitions, however, did little to endear him to other teen musicians and certainly not to audiences. Few of his friends were willing yet to learn his songs, or any new songs, for that matter. For many young men, fulfilling their rock-and-roll dreams extends no further than covering their favorite songs and aping the famous moves of their heroes. New songs offer far fewer chances for showboating; you have to make your own moves, which can be intimidating or, worse, might seem invalid. For Patterson creating new songs was not just part of the process but the entirety of it.

While the Truckers may be famous for their liberal reformulation of southern rock and for their endless variations on classic rock riffage, Patterson was way more into punk and new wave growing up: the Clash, the Replacements, and most of all R.E.M., the band from Athens, Georgia, who taught him (and me and so many others) that southernness could express itself in different ways. It didn't have to be rednecks and rebel flags, but something more obscure, something in the turn of a phrase or the crackle of a guitar riff or the push of a drumbeat or a pervasive air of mystery.

After graduating high school, Patterson stayed in Florence and enrolled at the University of North Alabama with tuition money from his grandmother Sissy. "I don't think I went to class the last two months I was enrolled," he admits. "I was a fuckup. I realized I was spending all this money to go to school, and I wasn't getting anything out of it. It's a good school, but it was such a part of my hometown that it felt like I was in thirteenth grade of high school, then fourteenth. That was the attitude I had then, and I really needed to get out of my hometown. I couldn't appreciate it. But it made my grandma cry."

His father agrees. "I wanted him to finish school because I didn't finish school myself," says David Hood. "I wanted him to finish school and get a degree in something like pharmacy, get a regular job. But he has a real mission, which is a good one, to keep the South alive, to keep some of its traditions alive but also to dispel some of the bad things, if possible."

Disappointing his folks still weighs on Patterson, as does his thwarted education. He wasn't a good or committed student, but that doesn't reflect his high intelligence or his curiosity. It merely reflects his restlessness. Perhaps there was a feeling that he wanted his life to get going, that he was ready to shoulder the mantle of rock stardom. That would take quite a while, though. In fact, it would take so long that he would actually be old enough to appreciate it properly and would have the perspective to make what modest celebrity came his way mean something.

Remarkably, UNA recognized as much and gave him an honorary degree in 2015, which involved wearing a gown, donning a mortarboard, and addressing the graduating class. "Being asked to do a commencement speech for a school I basically flunked out of was beautiful," he says now. Speaking to those students, he described their new degrees as, at the very least, something they could fall back on: "When people asked me what I planned to fall back on," he told them, "I'd say, 'A knife.'" It's not just a dramatically fatalistic line, but a reference to a Maggie and Terre Roche song his dad had produced: "There ought to be something to fall back on," the sisters sing, "like a knife or a career."

Like Patterson, Cooley wasn't the greatest student, but he was drawn to music, even if he didn't have many ways to hear it. There was no cable television that far out, and his parents didn't own very many records. But he listened to the radio constantly. "We had a few radio stations at the time," he says. "If you go back and look at what was playing on the radio around that time, that's what I was hearing. There was some Kiss here and there, even Ted Nugent. I didn't know any better then. When I was in my early teens, I got Lynyrd Skynyrd's first live record and wore it out. I loved it."

While Patterson was exposed to a wide range of artists, Cooley's musical tastes were more circumscribed. "If I'd heard *Raw Power* when I was twelve, I would not be the same person I am today. I didn't hear it until I was an adult, and it came closer to making me feel twelve again than any other album ever has. But it never has the power to hit you again, no matter what you do to make it sound better, no matter how much equipment you buy. It's never going to sound as good to you as it did when you were going through puberty."

He bought a guitar and took lessons, learning the basics from local instructors who specialized in bluegrass rather than rock. Among them was a fiddler originally from Virginia named Al Lester, who gave lessons in his backyard studio when he wasn't doing sessions around town, and Cooley had no way of knowing at the time that his teacher had played on Boz Scaggs's 1969 self-titled debut or on Willie Nelson's 1974 album *Phases and Stages* (both recorded at Muscle Shoals Sound Studio). "I was learning to play old bluegrass stuff, which is actually really cool—way cooler than I thought it was at the time. I didn't learn or absorb nearly enough of it. I was learning what I was being taught just for the sake of learning how to play, but I wasn't really into the whole hillbilly thing. I was rejecting that. I wanted to be a little too cool for it."

Those divergent interests—the bluegrass lessons, the classic rock he loved, the devil-may-care teenage angst—combined into a playing style that a lifetime later still doesn't let technical precision get in the way of punk immediacy: Cooley plays sharp boogie rhythms on electric guitar and picks intricate patterns on acoustic, all with a sense of abandon and urgency, as though capturing the messy moment is more important than getting each note exactly right. He has become perhaps the least fussy guitar hero imaginable.

By the time they met in the mid-1980s, young men just moving away from home and enjoying their first adult freedoms, both Patterson (then twenty-one) and Cooley (just nineteen) were already adept musicians and—somewhat less common among their peers—keen observers of the world around them, in particular the region of Alabama they called home. With that came a belief that the Shoals was every bit as legitimate a setting and subject as Southern California or New York City or any other place was. It was here they found the raw material for the music they would make together and for their vision of the South that they would construct over the next thirty years, whether it was the treatment of women in church or the economic disparities on either side of the river or all the tall tales they heard growing up.

Patterson in particular is fond of fictionalizing local tragedies and conflicts, often blurring the lines between legend and fact until something remains that is not true but somehow truer than true. That's the case with "The Great Car Dealer War," an outtake from *The Dirty South* that was included on *The Fine Print*. "When I was in high school, all the car dealers in town burned down in about a one-year period," says

Patterson. "Every few weeks there would be another one that burned down, and one in particular burned down twice. They rebuilt it bigger and fancier, and it burned down again. So they rebuilt it again. Right after it reopened, the proprietor, the guy whose dealership it was, was shot and killed right there in the dealership. That was the end of that. No more dealerships burned down after that. The official reason for the shooting was that somebody was disgruntled with a seventy-five dollar repair bill, but nobody really believed that."

There's something so mundane about a car dealership that makes such violence all the more fascinating and lurid, and Patterson sings from the point of view of the fictional arsonist setting those fires, a redneck who sees himself as a foot soldier in a larger feud and therefore less culpable than the businessmen giving the orders. There's an intriguing self-regard to this arsonist, who might be Charlie, the protagonist in Patterson's short story "Whipperwill and Back" from the 2016 collection *The Highway Kind: Tales of Fast Cars, Desperate Drivers, and Dark Roads*. In that case it's an inside job, because that character is a daredevil in the Tuscumbia Volunteer Fire Department. A pyromaniac who sets the fires he later fights is a bit like the preachers Patterson often writes about, the men of the cloth who practice the sins they warn against from the pulpit. He's written not one but two barely fictionalized songs about Elizabeth Dorlene Sennett, who in March 1988 was found beaten and stabbed at her home in Colbert County. She had obviously fought hard against her attacker but died on the operating table. When her husband, the Rev. Charles Sennett of the Sheffield Church of Christ, was named as the prime suspect, he shot himself outside their son's home. A few weeks later, police arrested the three men the preacher had hired to make him a widower.

"Home," says Patterson, "was more violent than the big cities in a lot of cases."

Before they were bandmates, Patterson and Cooley were roommates in Florence, living with two other people on Howell Street in a basement apartment that had no house on top of it. They had shit jobs, and most of their money went toward rent. But they still jammed together on their ratty couch, and from those sessions was born their first band, Adam's House Cat, which took its name from one of Patterson's new songs.

It's a southernism, a colloquial term: *I wouldn't know him from Adam's house cat.* The band outlasted the apartment. "We were not meant to be roommates," says Patterson. "It was Jack and Walter. It didn't last long, because Cooley's girlfriend graduated and he went and moved in with her. But he still paid rent and maintained the premise that he lived with us because she had a very old-school, religious family. The live-in boyfriend thing wasn't going to fly with them. She lived in fear of her mother dropping by without calling, and catching him in her bed."

They needed a rhythm section, so they put up notices on the bulletin board of Counts Brothers Music Store in Muscle Shoals. The first responders cycled in and out of the band quickly. A bass player named John Cahoon, son of the mayor of Florence, quit after being shot by the drummer; "It just grazed the skin," Patterson recalls, but how do you trust a drummer after that? They would go through several other players before Cahoon rejoined a few years later. Their next drummer, Charles M. "Chuck" Tremblay, was more than ten years their senior and had to commute down from Huntsville, but even before their first rehearsal ended, he knew they were something special. "I could tell real quick that this is what I wanted to do," he says. "I told them, 'I don't care what we've got to do to keep it going, but we're gonna do it.' I was there 100 percent."

Tremblay, who served as a casual mentor to his younger bandmates, had been playing since he was a kid in California, banging on his pots and pans until his mom got him a drumkit. After relocating down South as a teenager—"I was used to seeing buildings and everything, and then all of a sudden I'm seeing farmland everywhere!"—he studied jazz at Hinds Community College in Raymond, Mississippi. He tells me, "The best advice my instructor gave me...he says, 'Chuck, no matter what you're playing—a slow piece, a fast piece, a midtempo piece, whatever—if you can't make the beat cook, then you're no good to anybody.'"

Playing out in clubs around Jackson, rough joints with bullet holes in the walls and chicken wire strung up between audience and performer, Tremblay developed an open-handed technique that mixed the solid timekeeping of southern soul drummers with the flashier elements of white '70s blues rock, which served him well when he went on the road with a band from Baton Rouge called Murphy Howze. Playing boogie rock in the Skynyrd vein, they were road warriors, touring the country nonstop but never making it as far as recording anything. "That's where I was happiest, just sitting up there on that drum riser," Tremblay says.

His experience impressed Patterson, his maturity anchored the band, and his playing kept the guitarists nimble and inventive. Plus, he relished the opportunity to perform originals rather than work up the same classic rock covers that everybody in the Shoals was doing. They rehearsed constantly, hours per day and well into the evenings, running through the same songs over and over. For a while they rehearsed at the insurance office of bassist John Cahoon's father, which was located right next to the jailhouse. Says Tremblay, "We'd take a break and go outside, and the guys in the jail were shouting, 'Hey man! Do y'all know this song?' The prisoners were shouting requests!"

Soon, Adam's House Cat relocated their practice space out to the Norwood Park neighborhood of Florence, where Patterson's grandmother offered them the use of her basement. As Patterson tells it, she never once complained about the noise. David Hood wanted his son to get a real job outside the volatile music industry, which had seen its ups and downs in the Shoals, and the mid '80s were a particularly grim down. But the rest of the family encouraged the kid. His great uncle George A. Johnson gave him money for a PA, and Patterson paid him back years later by writing "The Sands of Iwo Jima" based on his memories of watching black-and-white war movies together—including the 1949 John Wayne and John Agar flick that gave the song its title.

That PA enabled Adam's House Cat to start playing around and eventually outside of town. They drove down to the Nick in Birmingham, up to the Tip Top in Huntsville, out to the Antenna Club in Memphis, and over to Jackson, Mississippi, where on a hot night one club owner took a chainsaw to the walls in order to air-condition the venue. But they never strayed far from home, playing no more than a few hours' drive away, which severely limited their options and exposure. For all the great music that has been made in the Shoals, it wasn't a town with much in the way of a live scene. That's partly due to the fact that the local industry is based around studios instead of clubs, partly due to the economic straits the region was weathering after the closing of the Ford plant in 1982, and partly due to the heavy Church of Christ presence that kept the surrounding counties very dry. There were few places in town for Adam's House Cat to play, much less to play enough to hone their chops and build up much of a following.

Worse, any place that booked bands preferred cover bands, because Top 40 and classic rock, even old-school country and R&B, brought more people in than slightly punk originals. What little scene for live music existed in the Shoals was not amenable to bands that wrote their own material. Patterson was developing into an idiosyncratic songwriter with a keen eye for local color and southern lore, and a few of his most popular Truckers songs were written during the early House Cat days, including "Lookout Mountain" and "Tornadoes." Originally titled "It Sounded Like a Train," "Tornadoes" describes the carnage left in the wake of some F4s that hit the Shoals the night Adam's House Cat played a homecoming show in Florence; the Truckers rerecorded the song for *The Dirty South*. Tremblay says that kind of deeply idiosyncratic songwriting "was exactly what [he] was looking for: original music that was well written. A lot of the cats that came into the group just wanted to play something that would make them money. We were making a little money here and there, but it was a very commercial thing people were used to. A lot of people who came to see us were like, *Um, okay, whatever*. But we played our asses off wherever we went, and we were constantly working on new material."

So they ended up practicing even more often than they played shows, tightening their dynamic for no one but themselves. They would go six hours at a time, sometimes five or six times a week, until they got their set into rip-roaring shape, until they could play off each other instinctively. "We'd start up at four or five o'clock in the evening and play till midnight," Tremblay says. "Once we got started, we didn't want to quit. We wanted to keep on going, keep on going, keep on going, because we had that momentum all the time. We were always practicing."

They also used the time to work out new songs.

If I wasn't working my daytime job, I was talking to Pat, or the three of us would all be practicing in his grandmother's basement. I'm surprised she put up with it. There were a lot of good songs that came out of those rehearsals, like "Child Abuse." Cool Daddy [Cooley] started off with that riff, and I jumped into it, and we played the whole thing through. Pat was upstairs with his grandma, and he came flying down the steps. "Oh, man, I love this song!" He picked up his notebook and started writing "Child Abuse." That's how fast it would come sometimes.

A friend of friends of the band, Jenn Bryant became a devoted fan when she first saw Adam's House Cat play. She will figure prominently into the Truckers' story, a crucial component of their early success and longevity, but initially she was just happy they weren't another cover band. "I was impressed that they played almost exclusively original material," she says. "A few other bands had some originals but more covers. Adam's House Cat was the best, but they also tended to piss people off because Patterson didn't pull any punches lyrically. They put more punk rock into their music than almost anyone else, and they were a refreshing change from the jammy pop rock that dominated the area."

Despite grounding their songs in the local, Adam's House Cat was, in other ways, a band from another place. They didn't fit into what counted as a Shoals scene, and most professional songwriters in the area frowned on Patterson's fondness for southern gothic imagery, for gory details, for deaths both gruesome and ironic. They had a handful of fans, mostly their friends and other struggling musicians, and were quickly growing frustrated.

One of the catchiest, most pop-oriented numbers in their growing repertoire was written as a middle finger to a promoter who refused to book Adam's House Cat. There was far too much death, he said. Not enough love and sex. So Patterson penned "Smiling at Girls," a short and highly accessible song with a hyperactive bassline courtesy of Cooley, a lo-fi guitar riff not unlike what the Replacements or Soul Asylum were doing at the time, and lyrics about death and flirting, or maybe flirting with death. Possibly the death of flirting. "Notify my next of kin, caught me doing it again," Patterson shouts gleefully. His sin: "Smiling at girls, smiling at girls."

What started as a bitch session turned into one of their most popular songs and the closest they got to a hit, at least with their fans. So, in 1988 when *Musician* magazine held its Best Unsigned Band Contest, Adam's House Cat sent in "Smiling at Girls" and didn't expect much to come of it. There were, after all, 1,962 other acts across America and Australia crossing their fingers that the judges—Elvis Costello, Mark Knopfler, T Bone Burnett, and Mitchell Froom—would pick their song. Among the prizes was a bundle of recording equipment, including a state-of-the-art Otari eight-channel recorder, but the big reward for the top ten was a spot on a Warner Brothers sampler CD and, surely, a record deal.

Adam's House Cat had never received any outside feedback on their music, or much feedback at all that wasn't outright hostile. So they weren't sure what to expect, balancing a grim realism with indestructible rock dreams. "I thought we might make it to a certain level," says Tremblay, "but I also thought, *They'll probably hate us.* Then we got to the next level. *Okay, that's probably as far as we'll make it.* But then the next thing I know, we're in the top twenty. *Are you serious, man?*"

When the results were announced in August 1988, Adam's House Cat didn't win. That distinction went to a singer named Lonesome Val, who impressed the judges with a country song called "Front Porch" that sounds a little like k.d. lang or Lone Justice. The runners-up weren't ranked, but they were listed in alphabetical order, so Adam's House Cat could pretend they placed higher than Exude from Anaheim and Idle Hands from Massachusetts. They were the only band from the South to make the top ten, and they were only one of two bands from what you might call a flyover state (the other being the Subdudes, then based in Fort Collins, Colorado).

Here, finally, was the opportunity they had been working toward for so long. Here was a chance to show the world that the Shoals could still produce exciting, original music. Here was a way that Adam's House Cat could put their town back on the map. Especially when that Warner Brothers sampler CD was released in fall 1988, it looked like all the work they'd put into the band was about to pay off. But it didn't. "They didn't know what to do with us," says Tremblay. "It was the '80s, and they were all looking for something that would have these nice little guys with these big haircuts. They were looking for Poison. We were *not* a Poison kind of band. We were totally different, and they didn't want to take a chance on us."

The few labels that did express some interest didn't express *enough* interest, at least not enough to make it worth the band's while. "We didn't like the contracts, because it was taking too much from us and cutting into our profits," says Tremblay. "David Hood helped us a lot with that stuff, which we really needed. We really needed somebody to be a good manager for us. But we didn't have that. Things probably would've gone a lot different if we'd had a real, honest-to-god manager who could have negotiated for us. Usually, a band is their own worst manager. You're into it too much. You're too emotional about it. You lose your sense of what you're trying to accomplish."

Their excitement quickly dulled, and Adam's House Cat found themselves exactly where they had started out: without a label, without much of a fanbase, without the money necessary to tour beyond the South. About all they had between them were Patterson's songs, which were growing increasingly bitter and openly hostile toward their audience and especially toward their hometown. They had put in the work, played some blazing shows, dreamed big dreams, and had less than nothing to show for it all. "I put part of the blame for that on the absolute zero support we had at home," says Patterson. "We were hated there. And I felt like we were misunderstood—all the things that young punks think about their hometowns. Typical. In retrospect I can say we did everything in our power to be misunderstood."

"We just couldn't catch a break," says Tremblay. "We were working hard. We were doing everything you're supposed to do, but it just wasn't the right time."

Onstage, that frustration became more and more volatile with every show, often lending a fire to their performances but doing little to win over new converts. Their bad behavior got them banned for life from two local festivals, the W. C. Handy Festival and the Helen Keller Festival, a punishment that carried over to the Drive-By Truckers for many years. "When we had a chance to headline the Handy Festival many years later," says Patterson, "the committee was like, 'Hell, no! They might piss on our children. They might take the lord's name in vain.'" It took them twenty years, but in 2011 the Truckers not only played but sold out the festival.

Even as it was confounding the band professionally, that tension between Patterson and the Shoals inspired some of his best songs and the first hints of what he would do with the Truckers. Named after the popular tourist attraction on the Tennessee-Georgia line, "Lookout Mountain" is both a suicide note and an antisuicide anthem, as Patterson games out the aftermath of his own death: "Who will end up with my records? Who will end up with my tapes?" he asks, not quite rhetorically. "Who's gonna mow the cemetery lawn when all of my family's gone?" It's a curious idea, too, given that he's not singing about jumping from the Wilson Dam. Instead, he'd drive the three hours to Chattanooga and off himself in front of all those vacationing families. It's almost like he would need some degree of anonymity to summon that kind of courage, which is something he didn't have among friends and especially family in the Shoals.

Patterson wrote "Lookout Mountain" in about the time it takes to play the song, on a night when everything was weighing heavily on him: a failing band, a hometown that ignored him, and family members he knew wouldn't be around forever. On top of everything else, he was also a newly married man, although the relationship was irreparably frayed before they even walked down the aisle. He was burdened by a sense of deep dread that he couldn't shake, but he saw "Lookout Mountain" as at least a step forward. He was on to something. He had something to offer as a songwriter. By facing those fears head on, by owning up to this desire for self-annihilation, he found his voice.

"We were really just disheartened," says Patterson. "Everybody hated the band. We knew we were good. At that point in time, we had been practicing several nights a week for six years. We were red-hot tight and I was writing crazy prolifically. We just kept working and working. We could go in anywhere, plug in, and just throw it down. Yet nobody liked it because it wasn't cool. Everybody wanted something that sounded like Red Hot Chili Peppers or Jane's Addiction. We didn't sound like any of that shit, mainly because we didn't like any of that shit."

So, they doubled down. Two dismal years after their big *Musician* magazine victory, still without the support of a label or management, they booked time at Muscle Shoals Sound Studio to record what they considered to be their proper debut album. They already had a collection of lo-fi recordings, which they dubbed to cassette and called *Trains of Thought*. The band created homemade covers and sold their makeshift album at shows or gave them to anybody who expressed any interest in what they were doing. But this would be more professional, more effective. It would give them something to send to record labels, potential managers, and even booking agents. Having been burned before, they were wary of thinking much beyond that.

When Adam's House Cat arrived on November 25, 1990, they set up in the studio upstairs, where the high ceilings would produce a bigger, more dramatic sound. They invited their friends to stop by, made it something like a party, and cut fifteen songs in one day, tracking all the instruments live. "We didn't do a whole lot of overdubs," says Tremblay. "Pretty much when I laid a track down, we did the whole song right then and there. We only had the one day to do everything. We went in at eight that morning and we got out of there at two the next morning. Once it got pretty late in the evening, I told the guys, 'I'm starting to hear things that aren't there. I've done got ear fatigue.'"

Several months later, right when President George H. W. Bush was launching Operation Desert Storm, Patterson went back to Muscle Shoals Sound to record vocal takes. It took them several more months to mix and master the thing; because they could pay only piecemeal, producer Steve Melton, a veteran of the local recording industry, would master the record over several sessions. In the meantime, the band tried to hang on long enough to see the record's release. Bassist John Cahoon quit before it was finished, reluctant to sign on as a permanent member of a failing band. His replacement, Chris Quillen, known for his long golden hair and shredding abilities, was a close friend and one of the most talented musicians in the Shoals. He knew it, too. "He would tell you he was the best guitar player in town, flat out," says Patterson. "'Who's the best guitar player in town? Oh, other than me?' He was the cockiest motherfucker I ever met." ("Motherfucker" is one of Patterson's favorite terms of endearment.) Quillen's dexterous playing meshed well with Tremblay's imperturbable drumming. But he had other bands vying for his attention, including two promising groups called Stained Mecca and Fiddleworms, and everybody understood that he was there only temporarily.

These two players would figure prominently into Truckers lore, although neither of them was ever a member of that band. Cahoon took his own life in 1999, inspiring two songs on *Decoration Day*: Cooley's "When the Pin Hits the Shell" and Patterson's "Do It Yourself." Both songs express anger that he would do that to himself and his family ("It's a sorry thing to do to your sweet sister") but still maintain compassion and understanding. Patterson had, after all, been in similarly dark places. Amazingly, neither knew the other was writing about Cahoon until the Truckers started recording. "I loved John, but he was very troubled,"

Patterson recalls. "He was a fun guy to hang out with, but he had a dark side that would come out, usually late at night. It was like someone flipped a switch. The last time I hung out with him is something I still have nightmares about. It was several years later when he killed himself, and it really beat me up that I didn't know what to do for him."

Quillen was actually supposed to be a Trucker. When Patterson was putting the band together, he called up his old bandmate and invited him to the sessions. However, just days before his trip to join them, Quillen was killed in a one-car accident that still puzzles his friends. For one thing, he was notoriously scared of cars and didn't know how to drive. "The fact that he died in a car wreck was weird enough," says Patterson, "but the fact that he was driving freaked us all out, because we didn't know he could drive. *What the fuck's he doing driving a car?* And he wasn't even wearing a seatbelt that night. No one will ever know what happened."

On a night after Quillen's death but before his funeral, Patterson, Cooley, Rob Malone, and their friend Jenn Bryant all had the same dream. "I could feel and smell and hear him as if I were awake," says Bryant, "so much so that I almost convinced myself that his death was the nightmare and this dream was reality. He noticed that I was crying and leaned back to look me in the face, chuckling. 'You worry too much,' he said. 'Don't cry. Everything will be okay.' I woke up sobbing, feeling the dream steal him right out of my arms."

"It was like a conversation with Chris," Patterson recalls. "He visited us. We were all asking the things you ask: 'What the fuck? How did this happen? Why are you dead? Are you coming back?' He had this flashlight, and at the end of the dream he turned it on and shined it down a path. That's as literal as it could be. That was the path. I'm not religious. I don't believe in God. I don't think I do. I don't believe in ghosts. But that happened. And I saw it. Word for word the things he told us were the same."

Both Quillen and Cahoon were there for the *Town Burned Down* sessions in 1990, but Adam's House Cat were all but broken up. There wasn't really a band to shop the recording around to labels, much less promote and tour it. So it sat in the Muscle Shoals Sound archives, forgotten by everyone but the band members themselves. In the decades since, it has made the circuit as a bootleg traded among Truckers fans, sounding rough and even lower-fi than they ever meant it to be. After the Truckers established themselves as one of the best rock-and-roll bands of the twenty-first century, there was talk of finally giving the damned thing an official release, but nobody could locate the masters. Patterson and Cooley both thought the tapes had been destroyed. Muscle Shoals Sound had been bought out by a label consortium out of Jackson, Mississippi, called Malaco, which specialized in gospel and some southern soul. They moved the studio's archive of masters to their storage facility, which was destroyed by a tornado in 2011.

The *Town Burned Down* masters eventually did turn up, completely by accident, and they were mostly in good shape. The band had used some technology that was state of the art at the time but that sounded positively historical in the 2010s. Patterson called up Cooley and Tremblay, and the band reunited long enough to master the album, re-record Patterson's vocals, and play a few shows to promote the 2018 reissue. It sounds like a long-lost Truckers album, full of early versions of songs most fans already knew by heart, like "Runaway Train" and "Lookout Mountain." But there's something still compelling about that bootleg, which in its rawness retains a sense of intense desperation and recklessness. They sound like a band throwing themselves violently into every note, Patterson unleashing his frustrations about this place that they still called home, that they had promoted along with themselves, that they felt had thoroughly rejected them.

If the crucial question surrounding the Shoals is Why here? then the crucial question surrounding Adam's House Cat is Why stay here? Why didn't they just abandon the Shoals for a bigger city with a better music scene? His discontent with his hometown became Patterson's primary subject with Adam's House Cat, informing the vitriol of "6 O'Clock Train" and "Buttholeville," both of which appear on *Town Burned Down*. The latter, which they set to a coiled and scuzzy ZZ Top riff, reveals someone at loose ends, someone who finally understands that his fate is no longer bound to his hometown. "One day I'm gonna get out of Buttholeville," Patterson sings over a runaway-train guitar riff. "Gonna reach right in, gonna grab the till." He dreams up a life that trades the Shoals for the beach, where he drinks scotch and feasts on lobster and promises himself, "I'm never going back to Buttholeville."

It's perhaps the most direct and all-encompassing song he ever wrote about the Shoals, which explains why he continues to play it with the Truckers. Patterson needed that song: he needed the motivation to move forward instead of backward. He needed that reminder of why he was still pursuing that dream, even when he reached an age when most people would have given up. Of course he would leave the Shoals, and of course he would return. The big surprise was that he would return something like a hero. "The big mystery is why I stayed there for thirty years when every song I wrote for Adam's House Cat was steeped in trying to get out of there. But I never left. I just couldn't. I didn't want to leave my grandmother and my great uncle, who were a big part of raising me. I knew they were older, and I knew my time with them was limited. When I finally did leave, it was literally the most painful thing I'd done in my life."

Memphis, Tennessee

▼

Summer Avenue, a long and occasionally disreputable thoroughfare that cuts through several miles of Memphis, Tennessee, was once bracketed by nude women. The street begins in Midtown, where North Parkway meets East Parkway and becomes Summer; at this intersection in 1940 a Sicilian immigrant and businessman named Michael Cianciolo built what he called the Luciann Theater, named after his daughters Lucy and Ann. By the 1960s it had become a bowling alley and then it was converted into a dance club. Its most illicit incarnation, however, was the Paris Adult Theater: videos and toys in the lobby, films in the theater, booths off to the side, and in the back a parking lot for patrons worried their cars might be recognized by passing traffic. For nearly fifty years it was a seedy local landmark, finally closing its doors in late 2017.

Some ten miles down Summer, right where it intersects I-240, once stood two enormous neon strippers, three stories tall, as colorful a local monument as you could imagine, waving at passersby and advertising a topless joint that went by several names, including Dancing Dolls. In between these two landmarks are scores of anonymous strip malls, crowded dive bars, dusty antique stores, churches, drive-throughs, holes in the wall, garages, and used car lots, and at least one historic sight: the enormous neon sign that once advertised the local record chain Pop Tunes, which was painted over in 2007.

Almost right in the middle of Summer Avenue sat one of the city's greasiest spoons, a diner called Ferguson's, which attracted a diverse clientele: nearly every stratum of Memphian, from Midtown hipsters and cash-strapped students of nearby Rhodes College to suburbanites straying out of Germantown and churchgoers sporting their Sunday best. For a few short months in 1991, Ferguson's counted among its loyal clientele Patterson Hood and Mike Cooley, who typically placed their orders while hung over. They didn't have much money for booze, but booze was a necessity for survival in this town and during this phase of their lives. They had even less money for Sunday breakfast, but again it was necessary. They scrounged whatever change they could find in the sofa for hot coffee and all the refills they could want.

Ferguson's is the setting for one of the first and most pivotal Truckers songs, a reminder from one friend to another of what they do and why they do it together. Set at this most democratic of local institutions, the story involves strong coffee, *Gilligan's Island*, and thrown feces. But to understand the significance of this bit of Trucker lore, you have to understand what brought Patterson and Cooley to Memphis, and what they found once they arrived.

Many musicians have left the Shoals and found success in the Bluff City. W. C. Handy made the trek in 1909, after which he achieved notoriety for pioneering a new and specifically Black strain of popular music commonly called blues. A little more than thirty years later, an entrepreneur named Sam Phillips left his home in Florence, Alabama, to work at WREC, a radio station that broadcast from the famous Peabody Hotel downtown. But he's better known for opening Sun Studio just off Union Avenue and helping to translate blues into rock and roll in 1950. In fact, generations of musicians moved to Memphis to make it: Elvis from Tupelo, Mississippi; Johnny Cash from Dyess, Arkansas; Jerry Lee Lewis from Farraday, Louisiana. Country-come-to-town every one of them, Patterson and Cooley included.

The city always held a specific fascination for Patterson, mostly because it seemed so seedy and dangerous and therefore so exotic: "People would be like, 'Why do you want to go to Memphis? It's a cesspool. A hellhole. They'll shoot you. You'll be mugged and raped. You'll be *pillaged!*' Nobody goes to Memphis. Everybody leaves Memphis. *Well, we're going to Memphis and we're going to bring it back!* Adam's House Cat was going to be the band that put Memphis back on the map."

His excitement, while perhaps naive, was not misplaced. Memphis was one of the markets where Adam's House Cat actually attracted something resembling a fanbase—not a big one, but a loyal one. And they had a few fans with industry connections who believed that Memphis could be a viable launchpad for up-and-coming bands. "We had it going on as far as being a place where new, emerging artists could develop and get signed to major labels," says John Hornyak, who was one of those early fans. He co-owned a home studio in Midtown and regularly championed regional acts like the Gunbunnies and Adam's House Cat to major labels, producers, A&R men—whoever's ear he could bend. Today, he works as the senior executive director for the Memphis chapter of the Recording Academy. "There were great studios here and great producers and great engineers to work with. I thought it was one of the best places to be in America at that point if you were doing original rock and roll." Memphis was producing some notable acts, but few graduated to national prominence.

Hornyak saw considerable potential in Adam's House Cat and considerable talent in Patterson especially. "His songs were so well written and so well formed. He was obviously a student of songwriting, and what he did was so different from everybody else. And he was so prolific, which I thought was very important. It just seemed like he had the potential to do something special, and I thought they could be successful. What I remember most from that time, though, was that no one got it. The band never even got close to that next step."

"John took us under his wing and tried to manage us, maybe get us in the door somewhere," Cooley recalls. "He was still trying to work with us at that point." Says Patterson, "He had been trying to help us. He loved our band and thought we were great. He thought that somebody somewhere would love our band, too." Not long after they had finished recording *Town Burned Down* in November 1990, Adam's House Cat played an annual Memphis producers showcase called Crossroads, held on Beale Street and designed to promote local acts. Hornyak talked them up to a few people and got them a sizable audience. "We got up there and played this really rip-roaring set to maybe 100 to 150 people, 200 tops," says Patterson. "And we were met with indifference. Nobody gave a fuck."

Adding insult to injury, that same year the showcase was dominated by a band of teenagers called DDT. The *T* in DDT was Paul Taylor on bass, and the two Ds were Luther and Cody Dickinson, sons of legendary Memphian Jim Dickinson, who played piano on the Rolling Stones' "Wild Horses" and produced albums by Big Star, Ry Cooder, the Replacements, and many others. Listing the many accomplishments that made Dickinson important would demand an entire book, but I'll point to two: he helped Chilton deconstruct local rhythm and blues and rock and roll on a series of solo albums in the 1970s, and in 1979 he staged a concert at the Orpheum Theater called Beale Street Saturday Night, whose proceeds helped restore the iconic venue.

The Dickinson boys were only teenagers when the band played Crossroads, selling out a small bar called Lafayette's. "It was this little side bar," says Patterson, "and it was packed to the gills for this band of skinny kids playing an amazing set. I remember at the end of their set Luther threw his guitar down and it just kept feeding back. They walked off and went back to the dressing room, and that guitar is still squalling and the place is going nuts. Then these girls come up—these teenage girls—and they pick up their gear and carry it off the stage. I thought they were going to be huge."

It was soul crushing. "The next day I wrote 'Pollyanna,'" says Patterson. "It's all there in that song, even though it's all there *cryptically*. Every line of that song has something to do with all that without actually telling the story." Perhaps he was too close to that story at the time, because "Pollyanna" would go unrecorded for several years, finally showing up in the mid-1990s on a cassette Patterson sold at his pre-Truckers solo shows in Athens; he'd record it properly in 2009 for his second solo album, *Murdering Oscar (And Other Love Songs)*. Over a low-down boogie-rock riff, he sings about a woman who "had a warmth about her that could not melt an ice cube." I always assumed he had written it about his first marriage, especially as it describes a scene that confuses fucking and fighting: "The bed got sticky, the floor got sticky. The kitchen table went crashing down." But that unfaithful woman—the one Patterson finally gets unstuck from—could be rock and roll. It could be his band. It could be the audience that he imagined he might find one day. "Pollyanna doesn't live here," he pleads on the chorus, referring to the 1960 Hayley Mills flick about a young girl whose unwavering optimism redeems a dry, bitter town. Patterson rarely writes in such coded terms; more often his subjects are stated outright, with plenty of rich subtext ("the dirt underneath," to co-opt one of his own lyrics), so even when the song finally saw the light of day, it still sounded a little unsettled, as though it refused to make up its own mind what it was about.

By 2009, any rivalry between Patterson and the Dickinson boys was ancient history. DDT combusted when Taylor left to join another local act called Big Ass Truck; Luther and Cody formed the North Mississippi Allstars to showcase the legendary talent around their hill country home. In the late 2000s the Truckers and the Allstars even recorded some sessions together, with Jim Dickinson manning the boards from a barber chair he'd installed in the control room. It was a bright spot during a dark time for Patterson; tensions in the Truckers were high, ultimately leading to Jason Isbell's exit from the band. "I was really questioning whether or not I still had a band, if anyone was ever going to like my band," he says, echoing his concerns about Adam's House Cat. "It was a pretty dark moment, and then we spent several days at Zebra Ranch [the Dickinsons' compound in North Mississippi] and recorded that stuff. It was a beautiful and amazing experience, and Jim Dickinson was really encouraging to me. He made me realize it would all be okay. We had about half an album done with their dad and my dad. We were touring and they were touring, and then Jim got sick and died. Boom. For years nobody wanted to go back there and finish it. We were all heartbroken. He was a hero of mine."

In 1991, neither Patterson nor Cooley knew that nobody got Adam's House Cat, nobody cared, nobody would give them a record deal, nobody would make them rock stars. They might have had an inkling, but they still moved to Memphis with at least a little optimism, thinking they could use their small fanbase and their industry connections to finally make that next step. Patterson got a job at a booking agency with a cramped office in the old projection booth at the New Daisy Theatre, a historic venue on Beale Street. He was excited about the job, feeling like he was getting a foot in the music industry. "My boss knew I was a relentless hard worker who was crazy enough to do it for next to nothing. *Well, fuck, I found my calling! This is what I'm gonna do with my life.* When you're young, you're full of beans. You think you can do anything."

The only thing keeping Patterson in the Shoals was family, in particular his maternal grandmother and his great uncle George A. (whom he memorialized on "The Sands of Iwo Jima"). Otherwise, it was no sacrifice to leave home. The Shoals had rejected his band, so it wasn't like he was alienating local listeners. And his personal life was in turmoil. The relocation strained his already rocky marriage, although he admits that he might have leaned into that aspect of the move. Unhappily married, he wanted a divorce and needed some sort of ultimatum. "If there was one thing my wife hated more than me, it was Memphis. When I told her about the job, she said, 'Well, you picked the one place on Earth you knew I wouldn't go. So be it.'" He left with not much more than his record collection, then his most prized possession. "I didn't lose any of them in the divorce, which was a relief because that's all I had—a record collection and a stereo and the clothes on my back."

Cooley was a lot more receptive to the idea of picking up stakes and moving to Memphis. "He literally danced a jig around his couch," says Patterson, "like that scene in *The Three Little Pigs*. 'Who's Afraid of the Big Bad Wolf?' He was dancing around the room."

So, in September 1991, they packed up their meager possessions and headed northwest. The pair found a place in Midtown, not far from Rhodes College. It was small, but cheap: $200 a month. "It was this little, dumpy garage apartment barely big enough for one person, but both of us were trying to live in this thing," says Cooley. "We were not meant to be roommates." Cooley worked at a men's clothing store, while Patterson commuted downtown to his booking job on Beale.

To make extra money, they lugged gear at the New Daisy, helping touring bands set up for shows. "We'd work load-in crew," says Cooley. "We loaded in Dread Zeppelin, which was one of the easiest jobs I've ever had because they had almost no gear at all. Blues Traveler came and they had just become the biggest thing. They had a fuckin' semi and their crew were assholes. It was a long, miserable day. And you got paid the same no matter how easy it was or how hard it was, so it was well below minimum wage for Blues Traveler." Another band who played the New Daisy was Nirvana, in the weeks just before *Nevermind* changed rock and roll forever. "I didn't work that show," says Cooley, "but I heard there was hardly anybody there. They were fucked up and pissed off."

"I worked crew for Nirvana," says Patterson. "They played to 128 people right before 'Smells Like Teen Spirit' got added to MTV. And they were not good. But they played the 40 Watt in Athens and it's a legendary show."

All the while, Cooley and Patterson plotted the rebirth of their own rock-and-roll band. Chuck Tremblay had stayed behind in Alabama, working at a restaurant and meeting his bandmates for the occasional show. "When they moved, me and Pat kind of lost touch with each other. It was hard bouncing back and forth between Florence and Memphis, and it was hard to keep up with them," Tremblay explains. They were also on the hunt for a new bass player. John Cahoon had abruptly quit the band, briefly replaced by Chris Quillen, guitarist for the promising Shoals group Stained Mecca and one of the sharpest musicians to come out of the region in ages. He wasn't considered a permanent replacement, just a friend doing them a favor. The pool of musicians in North Alabama was small, but Memphis seemed to offer more options. "We thought we'd find one there," says Patterson. "There are a lot of great musicians there, so it felt like we had a chance to start over."

Any optimism they had packed for the move was lost almost as soon as they arrived in Memphis. They arrived on Tuesday, September 10, 1991. Patterson remembers that date because three days later, on Friday the thirteenth, his car was stolen. He drove a Honda CR-X, a tiny two-door hatchback sports car that was flashy but not especially useful for a touring band. Says Cooley, "He leaves to go somewhere one morning, and comes walking back in the apartment and says, 'Are you fucking with me?' This is a legitimate question, because I did fuck with him. Still do sometimes. 'You didn't move my car? No? Oh god.'"

The thieves had gone in through the sunroof. "I don't think it was ever right even after he got it fixed. Memphis always had a lot of organized crime, some of it highly organized and some of it barely organized. These folks were stealing specific cars and stripping the parts off that they needed, and you would always find the carcasses in the same place. I kept thinking the cops were in on it."

The police officer who filed the report was unconcerned and predicted—correctly, it turned out—that the car would turn up a few days later, stripped completely. "He said they'd probably find it stripped down by the river, and that's exactly what happened," says Patterson. "They found the carcass of it downtown, and I ended up having to get it rebuilt and put back together. I was driving the Adam's House Cat truck while it was being fixed, this old '65 pickup with a camper shell on the back. I drove it down to pick up my car, and the plan was that Cooley was going to give me a ride back the next morning to pick up the truck. So I just left it parked outside the wrecker yard for one night."

You know where this is going.

"When I got back the next day, the truck had been stripped."

Memphis, ultimately, represented more of a retreat than an advance. In reality, Adam's House Cat was floundering, playing the same clubs on the same circuit to some of the same general disdain or outright hostility. They had recorded an album, but it had been sitting in the vaults at Muscle Shoals Sound Studio for nearly a year, with no labels—local or national, indie or major—willing to take a chance on the band. To put it more direly, just as certain domesticated animals wander off into the woods to die, Adam's House Cat went to Memphis to breathe its last breath. They chose an appropriate destination, a city defined by death. In the 1870s the yellow fever epidemic had greatly reduced the population, claiming 70 percent of the white population but only 7 percent of the Black population. That more or less evened out the racial makeup and defined Memphis as a city where racial tensions would continue to bubble under the surface of its barely polite facade.

But the Memphis music scene in particular has been defined by death, at least since Martin Luther King Jr.'s assassination exposed some of the friction underlying its famously integrated sessions. Elvis died at Graceland and is buried there. Al Jackson Jr., one of the finest drummers of the rock and soul era, a lynchpin at Stax and Hi Records, was murdered in his own home in 1975, the killer never apprehended. Chris Bell, upon leaving Big Star and hesitantly trying to launch a solo career, wrapped his MG around a telephone pole on Madison Avenue. More recently, Jeff Buckley drowned in the Wolf River. Jay Reatard overdosed in his bedroom. The birthplace of rock and roll is also a place of its death.

Maybe Patterson and Cooley knew this. During the sessions for *Town Burned Down*, Adam's House Cat recorded not one but two songs about the King, both of which purport that Elvis never died, that he still lives in Memphis and commits mischief as well as miracles. "Elvis Presley Stole My Car" is a fairly witty but throwaway rocker that is neither as catchy nor as funny as Mojo Nixon's "Elvis Is Everywhere." But "Picture of Elvis Cured My Cancer" is better and shows how Patterson can take something as silly as a tabloid headline and find the humanity in it; it's an early indication of the complicated approach the Truckers would take to Southern culture, even its punchlines. The story is fairly straight-forward, capably summed up in the title, but he and the band emphasize the narrator's mortal dread, as though he's tried everything from che-motherapy to the 1967 cheeseball Elvis flick *Clambake*. The song may traffic in cornpone humor, but there's an edge of desperation in the way Patterson sings that chorus and the band elaborates on a tense guitar riff.

These two songs have gone in and out of favor within the Truckers canon. When they played an Adam's House Cat reunion set in 2006 for Nuçi's Space in Athens, they included both of these odes to Presleyana. However, when they remastered and finally released *Town Burned Down* in 2018, both songs were curiously omitted from the track list. "At the time there was a new tabloid every other day with an Elvis sighting, so those songs are directly ripped from specific headlines," says Cooley. "But now a lot of people would be like, 'What are they even talking about? Why would Elvis do that?' Those are fun songs, but it's a bet-ter record without them." Perhaps that's true, but there is something usefully disreputable about Elvis, a symbol of white encroachment into Black culture, who dies over and over again as he goes in and out of favor with each new generation of listeners.

Patterson and Cooley settled into life in Memphis...or tried. "It was miserable," says Cooley. "We were piss broke. Had no idea what we were gonna do. I think the idea was to get the band up there, but that was never realistic. It was never going to happen. Things weren't so good at the time. The city wasn't in a good place. Everybody in music was packing up and moving to Nashville. Also, there was a godawful heatwave. They were having to close schools because they didn't have air-conditioning. It seemed like the city had everything going on that could possibly make you miserable."

Those hardships—almost comical in retrospect, as many tragedies become—in some way defined the Truckers and helped to shape the songwriters' views on Blackness, their own whiteness, and class. Patter-son and Cooley had arrived at a pivotal moment in Memphis history, a big year for local politics. The city was in the middle of a very tense mayoral race between incumbent Dick Hackett and insurgent Dr. Wil-lie Herenton that remains one of the most racially charged city elections in US history as well as one of the closest. The tension was not neces-sarily between the candidates, who did not hold a public debate and were rarely in the same room at the same time during their campaigns. Rather, it was the voting populace who aligned themselves along very stark lines: white Memphis supporting the white candidate, Hackett, and Black Memphis supporting the Black candidate, Herenton. There was almost no deviation, no overlap. Hostility simmered in a city split neatly in half, the white suburbs pitted against the Black inner city: two very distinct Memphises vying for control. "There was just a lot of intense racial tension at the time," says Cooley. "Probably it was still left over from the riots in the '60s. Twenty or thirty years later, you could still feel it. You could definitely feel the hate in the air. It was bubbling under the surface."

Working down on Beale, Patterson saw that conflict up close. That street had been one of the most famous thoroughfares in America. Beginning in the late 1800s and peaking in the 1920s, it was a center for Black fashion, Black music, Black business, and Black vice: gambling, prostitution, hooch. And it was also a site of racial violence, where whites would occasionally lead mobs looting Black-owned casinos. During the 1968 garbage workers' strike, riots broke out downtown, and the next day National Guard tanks rumbled down Beale. The street sat in ruins for decades, many of its blockhouses razed and businesses shuttered, yet it remained central in the city's imagination. During the 1980s—as part of a larger Reagan-era movement to "clean up" cities by bringing in businesses for whites while disenfranchising people of color—it was resuscitated as a tourist attraction, with white-owned bars and clubs generally serving white tourists. There was concern that white money might radically alter this hub of Black culture. In 1986, city councilwoman Minerva Johnican clarified these issues to the *Tri-State Defender*: "The total goal or direction of Beale Street is the real issue. Blues and jazz made Beale Street internationally known. The Black community is not at all happy with what Beale Street has become, from the Elvis statue placed at the head of the street to the country and western music filling the air. . . . Most of the entertainment has been changed from Black to White."

Earlier in 1986, Carl Perkins had opened a new club called Blue Suede Shoes, modeled on the juke joints and roadhouses that he and other rockabilly stars used to play in the '50s. The venue had hosted one band that used a Confederate flag as a backdrop facing a window onto the street, and the club had left the decoration up long after the show. The sight of such a flagrant symbol of slavery and enduring racism on Beale Street sparked outrage from the city's Black populace. "I think the hanging of a confederate flag in any establishment serves as a symbol that Blacks are not wanted or welcome," Johnican continued. Echoing her concerns in the *Defender* article was Shelby County commissioner Vasco Smith: "Everything that is repulsive to me about the South and the relations between blacks and whites is represented by that flag." Originally Blue Suede Shoes management dismissed the concerns as blown out of proportion, but it eventually relented and removed the flag. That didn't stop two local white men from wrapping themselves up in a Confederate flag of their own and parading down Beale Street in protest.

When Herenton won the tense 1991 election by a tiny margin—fewer than 150 votes—Hackett's supporters threatened to contest the results and demand a recount, eventually discovering that several hundred votes had been cast by people who were dead. The city braced for chaos, for riots, for racial violence. "The community just went berserk," Patterson remembers. "We were out in front of the New Daisy hammering up boards in front of the windows because everybody thought Memphis was going to riot again. If that happened, everybody figured it would start on Beale. So we were . . . expecting the worst."

But the riots never happened in 1991. Hackett conceded the race, and the election of W. W. Herenton as city mayor was certified. He was not Memphis's first Black mayor; that was J. O. Patterson Jr., who had been appointed interim mayor in 1982. Instead, Herenton was the city's first *elected* Black mayor, and he proved both hugely popular and persistently controversial, holding office for nearly twenty years. He resigned in July 2009, then seemed to regret it immediately; he even tried to enter the special election his vacancy had triggered. He attempted to run for mayor again in 2019, even suing the city for allegedly blocking his name on the ballot.

But the tensions churned up by the election lingered in Memphis throughout the 1990s, and Patterson noticed it. "I grew up in Alabama, but I was naive about the level of racism I saw there. Muscle Shoals was so much different from Memphis or Birmingham as far as all of that goes. You definitely saw some racism and you heard about the racism, but it wasn't this big, ugly, festering, boiling sore. It was easy to pretend it wasn't as bad as it really was. It was easy to be naive about it. When we were living in Memphis, it broke my heart. It made me so depressed and unhappy."

Here may be the beginning of Patterson truly figuring out his position as a white man confronting the lived reality of racial tension. He says he was naive about racism in Alabama, but our truest beliefs aren't always challenged in our hometowns. Instead, they must be tested elsewhere, in a place that puts everything in sharp relief. It's impossible to be naive about race in Memphis. Through their experiences with the mayoral election and the deep-seated anxieties it aggravated in the city, Patterson and Cooley began to recognize these cues, possibly without even knowing it. Their time in Memphis was crucial to their development as a socially conscious rock-and-roll band. It's the source of their formulation of the duality of the southern thing, that mix of pride and shame that informs their—my, our—feelings about our home.

Race has rarely been the focal point of their songwriting. Arguably, the subject they feel most connected to or more comfortable with is class, specifically the desperation and resilience of the downwardly mobile. But awareness of race and racism is there in "What It Means" and "The Day John Henry Died" and "Ronnie and Neil." It's there in "The Southern Thing" when Patterson sings, "Hate's the only thing my truck would want to drag!" It's an awkward but righteous reference to the horrific 1998 killing of James Byrd Jr., who was abducted in Jasper, Texas, by three white supremacists, who dragged him behind their truck for three miles and then dismembered his body.

The Truckers don't ignore the South's history of racial inequality and violence in their songs, but they've learned to be observers, to ask questions and let others provide the answers. They work by implication, understanding that to be southern is to address the issue of race on some level. It's at the heart of every conversation you have about the South, whether you're talking about music or politics or cooking or literature. Race is the inescapable topic, *the dirt underneath*.

Patterson was depressed when he moved to Memphis, and the city did little to alleviate his depression. In fact, it only deepened it. The divorce, the stripped vehicles, the threat of riots, and the sad fate of his rock-and-roll band all accumulated until the weight threatened to break him. "It was a horrific time, and I was suicidal. I remember more days than I can count when I woke up thinking, *Is this the day? Is this it?* And then I would think, *I want some soul food. That'll make me feel better.* I'd always find something to talk me out of it, but I never stopped thinking about it."

Cooley wasn't faring much better. "I had been in a band that wasn't well respected, but it was respected enough. We had a great time. There were lots of girls, and I was single. All of a sudden the spigot turns off. Where'd everybody go? We weren't done partying. We didn't want to grow up yet. The last half of our twenties were a letdown. My thirties were better, and my forties were a lot of fun. That's when the Truckers were doing great."

One method Patterson considered for offing himself was Cooley's .22 caliber pistol. Instead of turning it on himself, he wrote a song about it, immortalizing the firearm in "Nine Bullets," which would end up as the B-side on the Truckers' debut seven-inch single in 1996. "My room-mate's gun got nine bullets in it, nine bullets in my roommate's gun," Patterson sings over a scrawled guitar riff. "Gonna find a use for every last one." One's for "the love who chose to betray me" and another's for the man she betrayed him with. There's one for his boss, another for the lady at the laundromat stealing his socks, three for his immediate family (because he knows they'll be disappointed in him), one for himself, and one for his roommate (because "after all it's my roommate's gun"). Despite the subject matter, the mood is light-hearted, and I've watched crowds sing loudly and lustily along with that chorus during more than one live show. The Truckers even punctuate it with a riff on "Shave and a Haircut...Two Bits," as though the whole violent scheme has been a joke. Or maybe it's life that's a joke.

"Nine Bullets" is funny but not. Patterson's tonal shifts reveal a self-deprecating sense of humor (missing socks, really?), even as he confronts something as horrific as murder and suicide. But the song plays poorly today in the era of mass shootings, when too many men take too many guns on too many sprees. For a sense of how much both the times and the Truckers have changed, compare that early tune with one of their most recent, "Guns of Umpqua," from their 2016 release *American Band*. It opens with a strummed guitar riff similar to that of "The Living Bubba" except slowed down, melancholic, even serene. Patterson paints a bucolic picture, heavy with the tactile details that immerse you in the scene: "I see birds soaring through the clouds outside my window, smell the fresh paint of a comfort shade on this new fall day."

Then he obliterates the idyll: "Hear the sound of shots and screams out in the hallway." Very carefully he reveals the final thoughts of a teacher trying to protect his students from a school shooter, barricading the door with a chair and praying for survival. Based on a real incident at the Umpqua Community College in Roseburg, Oregon—ten killed, seven injured—it's the inverse of "Nine Bullets," told from the perspective of a victim rather than a perpetrator and emphasizing the beauty of life rather than its hopelessness. It's a crushing song, both simple and complex, the work of an imaginative and intuitive storyteller, one who is able to look beyond himself to practice empathy and compassion. "I was at home with my family when the news [of the shooting] broke and I walked around all day in a daze of questioning and sadness," Patterson writes in the liner notes for *American Band*. "I wrote 'Guns of Umpqua' on a flight back to Atlanta a few days later. It's fictionalization but there's far too much truth within it."

Cooley is philosophical about their time in Memphis and wonders if the darkness they saw was a product of their age. "I didn't realize it at the time, but I think your twenties—in particular, your mid- to late twenties—can be an especially dark period. The magic age is twenty-seven. That's the age that kills so many people, and we were both approaching that. I turned twenty-five in Memphis. You start reexamining everything you've ever believed, everything you were ever taught to believe, holding it up to the light of reason and love and hate, and you start processing it all. It can drive you crazy. Some people can't see past that age."

What kept Cooley and Patterson from turning that gun on themselves or on each other? There was soul food. There were favorite albums and favorite songs. "I was listening to Big Star's *Third*," says Patterson. That's not anybody's idea of an uplifting album. Neither is Neil Young's *Tonight's the Night*, another record he associated with this time. He balanced them out with the Plastic Ono Band and John Prine. "I listened to *The Missing Years* a lot. That's probably why I didn't kill myself."

Patterson has moved far past that bleak period in his life, but he makes sure those dark days are never too far away. They're crucial to his songwriting, allowing him to empathize with characters as they navigate their way to rock bottom, as they make foolish choices out of desperation, as they contemplate their own deaths. It all feeds the rock show: when he's shouting at the top of his lungs, "It's motherfucking GREAT to be alive!" or when he's eulogizing his fallen friends, wondering about the afterlife, or bitching about politicians, he's drawing on all those dark moments to make the bright moments almost blinding. And with that comes an awareness that his band might do for someone else what Big Star and Yoko Ono and John Prine did for him.

One of the defining aspects of Memphis is its rivalry with Nashville, the state capital a few hours up I-40. Memphis considers its music gritty, authentic, urban, and raw compared to the slick, polished, professional *product* that rolls off the Music Row assembly line. To give you a sense of the one-sidedness of the rivalry, few people in Nashville are even aware of it. Nashville has never really known a time when it was not a music town. Ever since WSM started broadcasting the Grand Ole Opry in the 1920s, Nashville has always been closely identified with country music, and it has managed to adapt to industry changes and audience tastes with remarkable flexibility. Many Memphians will suggest that this is due to the fact that Nashville manufactures glossy radio hits; it's a factory town, whereas Memphis is a soul town. Nashville's problems with racial tension are notable, but it is generally considered a white town that makes white music.

So it makes a perverse kind of sense that although Adam's House Cat went to Memphis to die, the band actually breathed its last breath in Nashville. They played up there every once in a while; Nashville audiences were okay—not the best but reasonably responsive. After one set Patterson and Cooley were sitting in the parking lot and sharing a box of Kentucky Fried Chicken, a meager meal that cost much of the show's paycheck. As they were eating, perhaps dreaming of a future when Adam's House Cat was touring the country in a bus, a homeless woman approached them and asked for a leg. "You could tell she had been on the streets for a while," says Cooley. "She's looking hard at our KFC, so we give her the rest of this chicken. As she's standing there eating, she's talking about, 'Oh yeah, I used to write songs for Ronnie Milsap.' She names a few others. We look at each other, thinking, *She might be telling the truth. It sounds like a crazy person making stuff up, but she might be telling the truth. Is this our future?* Welcome to the cold hard facts."

Suddenly, the greasy chicken didn't taste so good. Suddenly, that tour bus seemed like science fiction. There was no official breakup, no air-clearing fight, no unceremonious fax, no onstage brawl, no drama. It was as if the energy it took to keep Adam's House Cat alive just dissipated and the band simply ceased to be. "We didn't really break up," says drummer Chuck Tremblay. "There was no memo to each other that said we quit or the band was over. There wasn't any falling out between us. It was more a falling out with other people, because people just lost interest in us all of a sudden. Everybody just disappeared. It just happened, and we just wandered off like a bunch of little animals."

They weren't even upset, not specifically, no more than they already had been about the fate of the band. Eventually they would all realize how poorly timed it all was, how their fortunes might have changed if they could have just struggled on for a few more weeks. "Not only is our band breaking up and not only do we not know what the hell we're doing," says Cooley, "but within a few days everything about rock-and-roll music and the way it was processed and consumed had changed. Everything was different, and we didn't know what to do with any of it. Maybe if we'd been able to get on the road . . . or if we'd even known how to go about getting on the road, we might have been able to fit in with that new wave, but who knows? I think we were that band that had been around a little too long."

Says Patterson, "A week after we broke up, Nirvana's 'Smells Like Teen Spirit' came out, and the entire music scene completely changed. Bands that were doing what we had been doing were finding homes. We probably could have found a home, because we didn't really sound that different from what became a really big thing that year. Our big song was even called 'Runaway Train,' just like the Soul Asylum hit."

That's not sour grapes. Adam's House Cat weren't that far removed from the bands that broke big in the early '90s, during the wave of alt-rock that rippled out from the grunge explosion. In fact, when Adam's House Cat's sole album, *Town Burned Down*, was finally released in September 2018, critics compared the band to groups like Dinosaur Jr., Hüsker Dü, the Replacements, and even early Soul Asylum. "We weren't that different from Pearl Jam, really," says Patterson. "They took elements of arena rock and southern rock and mixed that with elements of post-punk rock. That was that sound. But we were actually from the South. We came from closer to the source of it all. You can count the Skynyrd licks on *Vs*. It's astronomical."

Could Adam's House Cat have found a home in this dramatically altered landscape? Could they have represented a southern outpost in the grunge explosion? Or would it have only intensified their frustration? It's impossible to say, but, says Patterson, "it made [their] utter failure and breakup that much harder to take." Cooley is more philosophical when he reminisces about the moment in "Self Destructive Zones" from the Truckers' 2008 album *Brighter Than Creation's Dark*. "The pawnshops were packed like a backstage party, hanging full of pointy, ugly, cheap guitars," he sings. "Deaf, fat, or rich, nobody's left to bitch about the goings on in self-destructive zones." Personal angst had replaced rock star hedonism, but the impulse to play music in front of an audience was the same.

They lingered in Memphis for a few months more, drank a lot and endured their hangovers at Ferguson's, and finally left town around Christmas. All in all, their Memphis sojourn lasted only four months, and it was a disaster from start to finish. "I didn't want to go back home and be defeated," says Cooley. "I was going to keep getting my ass kicked and be miserable somewhere else before I was going to let that happen. And I did!" The duo retreated further south to Auburn, Alabama, where Patterson shacked up with his sister's college roommate and Cooley managed a Subway. "Lousiest job ever, but it paid me what felt like real money for the first time," Cooley says. "I'd been broke for years, almost homeless sometimes and probably should have been. I was working fifty-plus hours a week in this awful fast-food environment—corporate nonsense. But even there it was nice just to not be broke all the damn time."

He and Patterson started and abandoned a few acts, most notably an acoustic duo called Virgil Kane and a *something-or-'nother* called Horsepussy. Eventually, Patterson returned to the Shoals, sheepish and ashamed. "I was 29, living at my mom's house, still wanting to blow my brains out. I'd turn on MTV and there was fucking 'Runaway Train.' Did I want to kill myself? Or did I want to kill Soul Asylum? Or did I want to kill them and then myself?" Years later Patterson became close friends with Soul Asylum's bass player, Karl Mueller, who turned out to be a huge Truckers fan. "He and his wife, Mary Beth, would take me out to dinner whenever we came to town. Wonderful people." Mueller died of throat cancer in 2005. "Before he got sick, I told him the story of 'Runaway Train' and he laughed his ass off."

Cooley fared much better down in Auburn. While working at a local Subway, he met a nursing student named Ansley. They fell in love, and he followed her to a residency in Durham, North Carolina, and finally to Birmingham. During that time he started writing songs. In Adam's House Cat, Cooley played lead guitar, sang backup occasionally, but left the songwriting and vocals to Patterson. Upon leaving Memphis, however, he thought more and more about how to express himself.

> I started writing songs the way everybody starts writing songs—by taking personal experiences. It started out as a therapeutic thing because I was in such a dark, sad place. I was trying to get stuff out of my system, and it felt pretty good. I was going back to childhood memories and trying to paint pictures with words. That's how it's always been for me. Play the image. Create the scene and go from there. When I liked a song or any kind of writing, that was what I was looking for. That's what I liked about it. I can see that kitchen and the people around the table. Or I can imagine what it smells like in that bar.

Patterson remembers his friend playing a song called "One of These Days," about the often contentious relationship between fathers and sons, which even includes a dig at the Bluff City: "I remember him saying that Chicago was a hell right here on earth," Cooley sings, "and twenty-five years later I was saying the same thing about Memphis." Says Patterson, "Cooley turned out to be a real-deal songwriter. He was already as good as I'll ever be, and he was just getting started. He'd written maybe ten songs by the time he wrote 'One of These Days,' and I'd written thousands of horrifically bad songs before I wrote something like 'The Living Bubba.' Fuck that guy!"

Most of his earliest compositions are lost and forgotten, possibly but very doubtfully preserved in a notebook somewhere. But they served their very important purpose: they were the stepping stones for him to become a songwriter, one as distinctive as Patterson, albeit far less prolific. Cooley's earliest recorded songs have the arc of southern short stories—a little bit Barry Hannah, a little bit Flannery O'Connor. His first recorded tune was "Panties in Your Purse," which appeared on the Truckers' 1998 debut, *Gangstabilly*. With a gangly acoustic shuffle and Cooley drawling his words, it's a country song as a small one-act play, a bit of tough and tenderhearted dialogue between a musician and a woman who lays her life story on him. It involves a walk of shame, a bad divorce, and a night out at a club as a precious escape from the shambles her life has become.

"I was in a cover band in Tuscaloosa," Cooley recalls, "and we took a break one night and this one girl came up and started talking to us, like they do in these places. That was what she was telling me and that was who she was: already middle aged in her thirties. I took that and ran with it." His details are cinematic—"Saw you standing in the hallway, red plastic cup and one of them big long cigarettes"—but what really makes the song, what really startles you as a listener, is how vividly and especially how compassionately he portrays this female character. She is desperate but intelligent; she acknowledges her mistakes but remains determined to get *something* out of life. She doesn't quite fit the mold of women found in pop songs. "You asked me if I could play you some Dylan," he sings. "I said, 'Dylan who?' and you told me to kiss your ass." Every time he sings that song, Cooley lets her get the last word.

But that song and the band that would record it were a long way off. Cooley says, "1991 to '96 is really not that long, just a few years, but man, it felt like an eternity just wandering in the wilderness."

Let's go back to Memphis now. Back to Summer Avenue. Back to Ferguson's.

Neither Patterson nor Cooley remember the date—it was sometime in November 1991, probably right before Thanksgiving—but they both remember the day, despite it being a fairly typical Sunday. Groggy, dehydrated, piss broke, and pondering bad choices and worse luck, they took a booth next to an older couple who couldn't have been any more different from them: well-dressed, sober, obviously fresh from praising God and likely on their way back to their well-appointed home in Germantown. Patterson recalls that they sounded like Thurston Howell III and Lovey from *Gilligan's Island,* a high-society accent so extreme, it could have been a parody of moneyed uptightness. They were reading the *Memphis Flyer,* the local alt-weekly, rather than the Sunday edition of the *Commercial Appeal,* which might have been for them a kind of slumming. Thurston was reading aloud to Lovey an article recounting a recent show—if you could call it that—by someone or some*thing* called G. G. Allin. "Honey, if I ever pay ten dollars to have somebody shit on me, I hope you have my head examined."

Despite their hangovers, Cooley and Patterson nearly fell out of their booth laughing. "We're both sitting there listening to him describe this show to his wife," says Patterson. "We're sitting there with a mouthful of mac and cheese trying not to spit it all over the table. I was turning blue. We could hardly eat, we were laughing so hard."

They knew who G. G. Allin was, and they knew that Thurston and Lovey did not know who G. G. Allin was. The son of a New England apocalypse preacher who made his wife and kids dig their own graves just so they would be handy in a worst-case scenario, the man originally named—no shit—Jesus Christ Allin developed a reputation in the 1980s as the most extreme performer in the already extreme genre of punk. Before the internet, before YouTube and viral videos, before memes and TikTok, before Two Girls One Cup, Allin was a word-of-mouth sensation for his chaotic, visceral live shows. Most punks did little more than gob on the crowd and get gobbed on in return, but Allin took it to the level of boneheaded performance art, different from works by Pyotr Pavlensky or Vito Acconci only in setting and intention: backed by a rudimentary punk band dubbed the Murder Junkies, he performed in clubs instead of art galleries, with no greater purpose than churning out shock and spectacle. *Hustler* magazine called him "punk rock's answer to Gallagher," referring to the comedian best known for smashing watermelons.

Allin didn't have fans so much as he had morbidly curious ticket buyers. Attending a show bestowed upon punks not insignificant bragging rights, hardcore bona fides. In that regard, it's tempting to romanticize him as punk's unchecked id, as the logical conclusion to a musical form that prized anarchy, lawlessness, and confrontation. There are several homegrown documentaries that try, fairly unsuccessfully, to paint him as a deeply misunderstood artist while excusing his racism, misogyny, and homophobia. Allin served time for sexually assaulting a woman onstage, and he attacked many others during his shows. He died in June 1993 of a heroin overdose.

Just two years before his death, he played the Antenna Club, his only Memphis performance. It was, briefly, as legendary among locals as the Sex Pistols' concert in January 1978. This was the show that Thurston was reading about, and it began and ended as a typical G. G. Allin gig. He was in some state of naked before the first song was finished. He hammered the microphone into his forehead until blood trailed down his face. He chugged beers and threw the bottles into the audience. Having downed a handful of Ex-Lax pills before the show, he defecated profusely on the stage, smeared himself with excrement, then threw great handfuls into the audience. At some point he may have sodomized himself with the mic. Had the show continued, he might have masturbated onstage, as he occasionally did. Instead, he chased the audience out of the club and across Madison Avenue. When the shit-sprayed punks returned, he chased them out again and again until, reportedly, a woman drew a knife on him and ran him off. End of show.

Neither Patterson nor Cooley attended that show, but they heard all about it from Thurston. Over time it became an inside joke between them, and then it became a song. "I wrote 'The Night G.G. Allin Came to Town' as a birthday present for Cooley during our breakup," says Patterson. After Memphis and Auburn, after the demise of Adam's House Cat, after countless deflated rock-and-roll dreams, the tension between the two old friends bubbled up to the surface. "Basically ten years' worth of stuff that we had been fighting about came to a head over probably nothing. That was the lowest point in my life. So I wrote 'G.G. Allin' as a birthday present to him, because I knew it would make him laugh. Every line of that song is just spot on a moment in time from our lives when we were so down and out and laughing hysterically."

"It wasn't quite as bad as a falling out," says Cooley. "Just late-twenties bullshit. Involves pride. We just needed to go our separate ways for a little while and figure some shit out. And we did."

One of the first pieces Patterson wrote for the Drive-By Truckers, "The Night G.G. Allin Came to Town" is a country song, totally unlike the music Allin was known for (to the extent that his music was ever known). It begins with a loping bass line and what sounds like a series of rim shots from the drummer, as Patterson offers a bleary prologue: "We were bored, there was nothing going on. Might as well stay home, drink until we pass out again, drink some more when the morning comes." This was more or less their life in Memphis. As Patterson describes the scene at Ferguson's, complete with Thurston reading from the *Flyer*, John Neff's pedal steel supplies a weird sense of majesty, and the Truckers make the most of the contrast between the stately pace of the song and its subject matter. In fact, the whole thing bears a perverse resemblance to Johnny Cash's 1987 single "The Night Hank Williams Came to Town," substituting scatological wordplay for hazy nostalgia.

Patterson has some fun with the lyrics, indulging some gross-out humor (Allin was "gone before the shit came down") and even time-stamping the song ("Antenna Club 1991!"). It's a story within a story within a story-song, sharp and surprisingly sophisticated. As fine as some of those Adam's House Cat songs are, there's nothing on *Town Burned Down* that hints at the clever conceit of "The Night G.G. Allin Came to Town," nor at its unique tone. It's hilarious, yet the song is shot through with a potent melancholy, with something like resignation for the fate of Adam's House Cat. "Memphis was sinking into the Mississippi," Patterson sings. "We were doing our best just to ride 'er down."

Released as the final track on the Truckers' second album, *Pizza Deliverance* (and dedicated to "Adam's House Cat 1985–1991"), the song commemorates their brief, miserable sojourn to Memphis and perhaps marks the moment when Patterson realized his band was going nowhere. That G. G. Allin had fans to befoul perhaps struck the hardworking, long-suffering bandmates as deeply unfair; perhaps they didn't want to sully themselves so thoroughly just to get an audience. Buried deep in "G.G. Allin," then, is an idea about how to be a rock band: Don't let the spectacle distract from the music. Always have a good song to back you up. Don't throw shit at people who pay good money to see you play those good songs. Don't beat yourself up till you bleed. Don't beat up other people either.

More than ten years later, Cooley would write something like a spiritual sequel to "The Night G.G. Allin Came to Town," chronicling a very different bit of Memphis lore. "Carl Perkins' Cadillac," from the Truckers' 2004 album *The Dirty South*, is about Carl Perkins and Sun Studio. Nothing so pedestrian as a keep-it-real anthem, it's about being in the music business for the right reasons, about knowing what the right rewards are. The story goes like this: In the mid-1950s, as his stable of local talent was gaining in popularity, the Sun Records owner and producer Sam Phillips decided to spur some friendly competition between his artists. The first one to get a gold record would win a Cadillac. For a bunch of boys from the sticks who knew only poverty, a Caddy was more than just transportation; it projected wealth and success and *control*. It told everyone who saw you speeding by that you had come to Memphis and you had *made* it. Everybody figured Elvis would be driving that prize convertible, but in fact it was Carl Perkins who got to gold first with "Blue Suede Shoes." Of course, Phillips took it out of Perkins's royalties.

With its breezy melody and jangly Byrdsesque guitar riff, "Carl Perkins' Cadillac" was inspired by one of Cooley's first concerts, when his father took him to see Perkins play in Tuscumbia. The show inspired Cooley to be a rock musician, to be a performer, but there is no personal history here, only rock history and, more crucially, rock mythology: Elvis grousing about losing that Cadillac, Johnny Cash already high on the pills that would nearly kill him, Jerry Lee showing enough respect for Phillips that he called him—and only him—"Sir." And then there's Carl Perkins, the only one to absorb the lesson in the story: "Carl drove his brand-new Cadillac to Nashville and he went downtown," Cooley sings. "This time they promised him a Grammy. He turned his Cadillac around." It's an empty promise, not least because what the hell are you gonna do with a "little gold-plated paper weight"?

Along with "G.G. Allin," "Carl Perkins' Cadillac" reckons with the business of music, with personal standards and lines drawn, about what you do and why you do it. "Memphis," Cooley says, "was obviously a necessary part of getting to where we ended up."

Memphis kicked them around, but they still loved the city. They loved the music and the food and the weird vibe of the place, and they still had heroes there besides. Or at least heroes still associated with the city. When Booker T. Jones, organist at Stax and front man of Booker T. and the MGs, wanted to make a new solo album in the late 2000s, he knew he wanted lots of loud rock guitars, and he knew he wanted the Truckers on it. Booker knew Patterson's dad, and Patterson knew the MGs first and foremost from samples in his favorite rap songs growing up, so he was ecstatic to hole up together down in Athens. The sessions at Chase Park Transduction went haltingly at first—so poorly, in fact, that the band feared they would be fired. But Booker realized that they were a band used to playing to lyrics and vocals. They were lost without that element, so he went to great pains to describe each song to them: the memories and feelings they evoked for him. "Then they gave themselves musically over to me," Booker writes in his memoir, *Time Is Tight*. "My melodies and my guitar parts came to life in their heads and their hands, and we became a musical family." *Potato Hole*, as he called the album, is more about rock and roll than the R&B he'd long been associated with, concluding with a churchly cover of Cooley's "Space City," where Booker doesn't need lyrics to convey the overwhelming sense of loss. His Hammond B3 is as expressive as any voice.

Almost twenty-seven years to the day after Patterson and Cooley left Memphis in defeat, their band returned once again to record a new album. Their summons came via Matt Ross-Spang, the producer and engineer who had worked on *American Band* in Nashville, had gigged at Sun Studio and produced Margo Price's first solo record, and was by 2018 running the historic Sam Phillips Recording Studio on Madison Avenue. They had come full circle, in a sense. What would happen when the band returned at a professional high point, after they had expanded the scope of their songwriting and gotten some of the best sales and reviews of their career?

At first it looked like the same old city they had known in 1991. Flying in from a one-off show in Richmond in September 2018, they landed at an airport that was mostly empty, many of its gates closed off and its baggage claim deserted. Memphis had lost its Northwest hub when Delta bought the airline in 2008, and that cut air traffic in and out of the city by two-thirds. The city had spent the last decade trying to strategically shrink the facility, and Patterson recalled that it looked like a scene from one of George Romero's zombie movies. And yet, despite being the only customers in a lot full of cars, it took them hours to get a rental van.

En route to their Airbnb—a local mansion that had been redesigned to cater to visiting musicians—they drove past a crime scene: a presumably dead body in the parking lot of a convenience store, surrounded by officers who looked like they were interested in anything but the corpse at their feet. The light turned green and they kept going. "Already we're thinking, *Are we in the thick of it already?*" recalls Patterson. "We don't even start rolling tape until tomorrow, and we're already in the thick of Memphis." They turned it into a joke: any time somebody had to wait for food or got caught up in some nonsense, they got "Memphised."

But that joke didn't last long with them, because that initially dismal impression of the city didn't last. They went out to restaurants that weren't around when they lived there (not that they would have had the money to spend). Beale was still a tourist attraction, but there was also the Rock 'n' Soul Museum, the Stax Museum of American Soul Music, the W. C. Handy House Museum, the Blues Hall of Fame, the Earnest Withers Collection—all relatively new institutions suggesting the city had finally learned to embrace its musical heritage rather than erase it. The band stopped by Crosstown Concourse, the massive vertical village built in the old Sears building on North Watkins. It had been a sleeping giant for the last thirty years, a symbol of a once thriving city left to decay, but it had been transformed into the city's arts hub: a facility with restaurants, theaters, music venues, apartments, art galleries, studios, schools, and even a health clinic serving the neighborhood.

When Patterson says that Memphis is like a character in the songs they recorded at Sam Phillips, it is this version of Memphis he is referring to, scrappy and strange and thriving, just like the band itself. "We knew going into the sessions that the whole Memphis thing was going to be a part of the recording experience," Patterson says. "The hope was that it was going to be a positive thing. And it was. We were reveling in those kinds of details rather than having those details beat the shit out of us."

Cooley is a little less sentimental about the city than his old friend is. "I'd love to dig around in my ass and come up with some bullshit that cast Memphis in a really poetic light, but that's not who I am," he says, laughing.

The Unraveling, released in January 2020—just months before the COVID-19 pandemic hit the United States, thwarting their touring plans—is as politically fraught as *American Band*. It had to be. After years under one of the most corrupt presidential administrations of their lifetime, they knew they couldn't back down from the subject matter they had explored previously. Much of the material they recorded at Sam Phillips was upbeat and steeped in their love of Memphis music, so much so that they at one point thought about releasing a sprawling double or even triple album that might be called *Memphis Hollywood Disco*—a tribute to their Airbnb. The more they tinkered with the sequencing, however, the more a very different album began to emerge. "You know what? I don't think they heard me the first time," says Cooley. *"I don't think you assholes are pissed off enough.* I don't want these people to think we're walking away."

Some of these songs are even more outraged than those on *American Band*, especially Patterson's "Babies in Cages," with its swampy groove and rust-industrial drumbeat soundtracking the horrors at the United States' southern border. (The song features Cody Dickinson on electric washboard.) But the album is a true sequel in that it extends and expands those ideas, with both Cooley and Patterson not merely writing about the horrors they see but dreaming up grand punishments for their perpetrators: Cooley's "Grievance Merchants" imagines a very special hell for anyone who might stoke or profit from the suffering of others: "An eternity for every tear they mock," he demands. On "Thoughts and Prayers" Patterson not only criticizes politicians for rendering that title phrase meaningless in the wake of more mass shootings but imagines a day when we can hold them responsible: "They'll throw the bums all out and drain the swamp for real, perp walk them down the Capitol steps and show them how it feels." That sounds like they might have hope, and perhaps that hope is rooted in the setting, in a city that had once seemed dead but has found new life.

Athens, Georgia

▼

Near the corner of Clayton and Jackson—spitting distance from the University of Georgia campus—the High Hat was a townie drinking establishment nestled among the frat bars and greasy pizza joints in what passed for a sketchy neighborhood in Athens. Most nights during the late 1990s, but especially on weekends, the street would fill up with rowdy, intoxicated bros, a throng sometimes resembling a riot flowing out of open doors, blocking cars, and clogging traffic. It was only half a mile from the west side of downtown, where the Caledonia Lounge and the 40 Watt anchored an artsier district that was quieter, less crowded, less rowdy, and less Greek, but some nights the High Hat could feel like it was in a different place altogether.

Home to legendary bands like the B-52's, Pylon, R.E.M., Widespread Panic, and Neutral Milk Hotel, among many, many, *many* others, Athens has always enjoyed a diverse music scene, never defined exclusively by one particular sound or style but united in a like-minded approach to music-making that values freedom and invention. Psych-pop bands rub elbows with hardcore punks jostling for stage time with country-rock outfits sharing equipment with jangly guitar groups sharing members with noodly jam bands hackeysacking with reggae artists. Blues, however, has not historically been among the most popular local styles, partly because that first wave of house party bands sprang up almost in opposition to the blustery, blues-rock machismo of the 1970s. At the time of the High Hat's opening in 1994, you could have counted the number of local blues acts on one hand and still had plenty of digits left over to strum a guitar.

Opening a blues club might have seemed like folly, but a very Athens sort of folly. The scene is built on a philosophy of accommodation: if you make something you truly care about, it's likely someone else will show up to see it, even if it's just your friends. Perhaps that made it seem like a sustainable enterprise, location be damned. The High Hat struggled, often dead even on show nights. Gradually, the owners—Drew Alston and Tony Eubanks—expanded the club's purview to include a wider array of popular styles that might actually entice people to brave the bros and pay the meager cover charge. They started getting smaller touring acts, bands too new or too obscure or too esoteric to fill the 40 Watt. By nobody's plan, the High Hat became something like a hub for what in the mid-1990s was becoming known as alt-country, insurgent country, or—if you prefer puns—y'alltternative. This focus put the High Hat slightly ahead of the curve: while groups like the Jayhawks and the Bottle Rockets were already defining the movement, the genre's bible—a magazine titled *No Depression* in a nod both to Uncle Tupelo's 1990 debut and to the Carter Family's signature song—wouldn't hang out its shingle until 1995.

When Patterson moved to Athens, Georgia, on April 1, 1994, he was still licking his wounds from that disastrous stopover in Memphis and a few years in the wilderness: Auburn for a little while, then back to the Shoals, neither place doing much to curb his suicidal thoughts. Actually, he had intended to land in Atlanta, where there was a burgeoning scene of musicians mixing country and punk in the Cabbagetown neighborhood, known among themselves as the Redneck Underground: bands included the Vidalias, Jennie B. and the Speedbillies, Slim Chance and the Convicts, the Blacktop Rockets, and the Diggers. When he visited a friend in Athens, however, he got immediately drunk on the spirit of this college town and its weird history. A music boomtown as improbable as the Shoals, Athens was home to R.E.M., a band he had counted among his favorites ever since he hand-sold copies of *Murmur* at the Record Bar back in Florence. Besides, the rent was cheaper and the environment a lot less Memphis and a lot more Shoals. After moving into a place on Ruth Street, not far from the Oconee, which he was dismayed to discover was a mere creek compared to the Tennessee River, he found a job at a restaurant (his first of many gigs in food services), and he set about embedding himself in the local scene. He wrote songs, played a few gigs at a burrito place called Frijolero's, and even recorded a lo-fi album on a boombox in his apartment, calling it *Murdering Oscar (And Other Love Songs)*, and giving the cassette away to new friends.

Patterson's first solo show at the High Hat went well enough that Alston invited him to play again. "I was so stupid and ignorant about how things worked in clubland—it's not like Adam's House Cat ever got that many club gigs—that I called him on a Saturday night to follow up about booking. He was like, 'I don't have time to talk right now. The sound guy didn't show up, and I'm in the weeds trying to soundcheck a band.'" Patterson sensed an opportunity. "I told him I was a sound guy, which was totally a lie. I sorta knew how to do the basics of it, because we'd had a PA in our practice space. But I'd never done sound for a band." So he bluffed. How hard could it be?

Plenty hard, it turns out, because the building wasn't really designed to serve as a club. Let's say you survived the murder of bros on the sidewalks, paid the cover charge and had your hand stamped, and maybe recognized the local musician Kevin Sweeney or Nick Bielli working the door. You then walked down a long tunnel into the venue proper. A bar ran the length of one wall, crammed with drinkers. In the opposite corner was a cramped, diagonal stage that barely fit the full bands playing that night. For a while the original sign from Tyrone's OC hung over the stage, a nod to Athens' glory days in the late 1970s and early '80s and to the club that hosted early shows by Pylon and R.E.M. and Love Tractor. Next to the stage, a staircase led up to a tiny mezzanine holding four or five tables and a door leading to the manager's office. A thick cloud of cigarette and pot smoke pushed at the ceiling. It was an odd space, logistically and acoustically, made all the more awkward by the placement of the soundboard up in a crow's nest, separate from the mezzanine and accessible only by a rickety ladder.

"It was a nightmare because it sounded totally different up there than it did on the floor," says Patterson. "I had just enough sense to learn pretty quickly that I had to set the levels, then climb down the ladder and listen on the floor. Then I'd go back up and tweak it. I was up and down that ladder all night, and I got really skinny."

He was as shocked as anybody else that his first night running sound at the High Hat wasn't a complete disaster. In fact, he was hired for full-time work that night, despite Eubanks's initial suspicions about the stranger in the crow's nest. It was Tony who invited Patterson to work a regular Tuesday night gig by a local pickup group called the Hot Burritos, whose Gram Parsons–derived band name hinted at the style of music they played. Tuesday nights were given over to a cosmic, toke-happy strain of country music performed by a quartet of acoustic strummers including William Tonks and future Trucker Barry Sell. They would play their own set first, then come back for a second set fronted by a guest artist—usually locals, but sometimes someone from Atlanta or beyond. Vic Chesnutt did a Hot Burrito night. So did Kelly Hogan, Anne Richmond Boston from the Swimming Pool Q's, Greg Reece from Redneck Greece Deluxe, Ben Reynolds from the Chickasaw Mud Puppies, Andy Pike from the Continentals, Mike Mills from R.E.M., and Gregory Dean Smalley, who you'll read more about later. "It was a who's who of the southeastern Americana set," says Patterson, "and we all became buds."

From his perch high in the crow's nest, he watched a lot of bands put their own twists and spins on acoustic country music, sometimes respectfully and often irreverently. For someone raised on punk and new wave, who counted R.E.M. as a favorite, who lied to his parents and drove to a Springsteen concert in Mississippi, who harbored dreams of being part of the next Replacements or at least the next Soul Asylum, this was an awakening, an apprenticeship in twang, as Patterson saw this genre that he had spent much of his life dismissing and disdaining reinterpreted by people like himself. Maybe they had never stepped inside a honky-tonk or tasted moonshine or spent a weekend in county jail, but they could still deliver a convincing version of "Mama Tried" or "$1000 Wedding." A new sensibility crept into Patterson's songs to match an aw-shucks humor in his lyrics, and he began to experiment with characters other than himself and stories other than his own. Country helped him become a third-person songwriter, which would carry over to the Truckers.

Things were loose at the High Hat, casual even for a rock club, which attracted a very specific clientele. "There was a lot of drinking," says Nick Bielli, a member of local bands Hayride and Japancakes, "and a lot of, 'Hey, why don't you hop up onstage and play "Cat Scratch Fever" with us?' Everyone who worked there played, so we would always play there. It was like having a treehouse with a bar in it. You'd think that it's only three blocks away from the campus, but it was like another planet because no one wanted to go down there." Some nights there were more employees than patrons. "You'd book these incredible shows and it was like pulling teeth to get a hundred people to show up. Forty people came to see Daniel Johnston. Nobody wanted to walk those three blocks to the High Hat."

Most nights Patterson brought his guitar with him, in case there was a slot that needed to be filled or there was a band that didn't show. He could jump onstage at a moment's notice and deliver a semiprofessional set of original songs, and he took every opportunity that came his way. That put him in front of an array of concertgoers and introduced him to a small network of musicians in the region. In fact, nearly everyone who figures prominently in this chapter met Patterson at the High Hat or at the very least knew him as "that sound guy." And he became a concierge for touring bands. Many nights he would invite the headliner to crash with him at the haunted house he shared with his new wife out on Jefferson Road. "I would often take bands home with me. My second wife was a killer cook, so in the morning she would cook them breakfast before they left. We called it the Redneck Ramada. Lots of bands slept on the floor of the Redneck Ramada, and lots of bands left toward the next day full of some really good cooking."

Occasionally David Barbe would stop by to set up his mobile recording equipment or to play with his band Buzz Hungry. He was something of a local hero, having worked on Uncle Tupelo's third album, *March 16–20, 1992* (an early alt-country landmark), and played bass with former Hüsker Dü front man Bob Mould in the short-lived alt-rock power trio Sugar. But Barbe was done with touring, having decided to stay in Athens, focus on his family, and open up his own studio. His long friendship with Patterson began in that crow's nest overlooking the High Hat stage. "It's a tiny place that barely held one person, let alone the two of us who were just hanging out," says Barbe. "I was recording bands and he's running sound, and that was the foundation of our friendship, just me and him hanging out in that little sound booth." Barbe would produce all but three of the Truckers' studio albums, at one point even steering the band away from the brink of self-destruction.

This was Patterson's life in Athens: climbing up and down that ladder, checking levels on the floor and near the ceiling, playing last-minute gigs, hanging out with whoever came to town, smoking weed, drinking whiskey. They would close up the High Hat, walk over to the Manhattan with Bielli or Kevin Sweeney or John Neff from the local country group the Star Room Boys or his old friend Earl Hicks from back home or whoever was around, and then drink until the crowds dispersed. They'd head home at four or five in the morning, sleep all day, and get up and do it all over again. Somewhere in between, Patterson would write songs, wordy compositions about his rock heroes, about broken branches of his family tree, about his first and current wives, about this corner of the country he called home. He played in a few bands, including a rock outfit called, regrettably, the Lot Lizards. And he started to dream up a new band, one with no fixed lineup and no rehearsals, one that could swing from hard-crunching southern rock to jangly acoustic alt-country, one that would specialize in barely keeping it between the ditches: raw, powerful, gloriously sloppy. He wanted something that was unhinged and wild and unpredictable even to those onstage, but also he wanted something with the flexibility of the Hot Burritos, something that could accommodate more personalities and songwriters than just himself. Before he gave his notice at the High Hat and graduated to the 40 Watt sound booth, the Truckers would be up and running, testing this concept with some harebrained schemes, some shit-eating grins, and a lot of seat-of-their-overalls touring. "It was a magical spot," Patterson says. "That was the job that really changed my life, because it put me right where I needed to be at the exact moment that I needed to be there to do what I needed to do."

Around the time all of that was happening, the city organized the inaugural AthFest, a three-day event intended to answer South by Southwest over in Austin. It never did rival that crowded music industry expo, but it has come close. Today it features hundreds of bands, locals and nonlocals alike, playing at venues all over town, and the Truckers have played it multiple times. Back then, it was just sixty or so local acts playing on the courthouse steps. Nearly every player was shocked to receive a bill from the city charging the musicians a workplace tax. Suddenly the new event looked like an especially pernicious con, a means of collecting info on local bands in order to levy charges that few could afford to pay. Most of them simply ignored the bill, but Nick Bielli remembers Patterson sticking his letter on a nail in the wall of the sound booth, like Martin Luther affixing his ninety-five theses to the cathedral door. Then the Drive-By Trucker wrote in big, bold letters nearly legible from the stage: EMERGENCY TOILET PAPER.

Patterson wrote many of his best songs while living in Athens, but he wrote very few songs *about* Athens. Still, he lived there at a time when the local scene, which is always active, was especially bustling and especially diverse, and when the internet was changing how bands toured, how they made music and what kind of music they made, and how they interacted with their fans. Through a combination of luck, desperation, and gumption, the Truckers found themselves right on the cusp of so many different trends, and this college town helped put them there.

Athens, Georgia, was something like hallowed ground for a music nerd like Patterson. He could drive around town and see the house on Milledge Avenue where the B-52's played their first show back in 1977. He might walk by the building where Pylon drummer Curtis Crowe opened a small club that took its name from its sole source of light—a bare 40 Watt bulb hanging from the ceiling. He could visit Dudley Park, where the train trestle that appeared on the back cover of R.E.M.'s 1983 debut album, *Murmur*, still stands, preserved as a local landmark. Or he could walk the train tracks to see the kudzu-clogged ravine from that album's front cover—one of those pilgrimages nearly every fan makes at some point. For a time he lived in an apartment near Weaver D's Delicious Fine Foods, a cinder-block building on East Broad painted bright green, famous among R.E.M. fans for providing the title of their 1992 album, *Automatic for the People*. Much later Patterson might drive by the house where Neutral Milk Hotel lived when they recorded *In the Aeroplane over the Sea* or down Sunset Drive past the house owned by Ross Shapiro, mastermind behind the Glands, one of Patterson's favorite local bands.

What he couldn't have known at the time—what he might have only dreamed of when he first moved there, when he started running sound at the High Hat, when he put together his first Athens band, the Lot Lizards—was that he was participating in that history, extending it, expanding it, and establishing his own local landmarks around town.

Athens was very different from Auburn and worlds removed from the Shoals, where Patterson had fought and ultimately failed to make a place for himself and for his music. In the late 1970s, right when the Shoals scene was sputtering, Athens's was just kicking to life. Driven not by one man or by proximity to some magical river, it was fed by young college students leaving their cloistered small towns or sprawling suburbs and finding new tribes that allowed them more opportunity for self-expression. It was the province not just of good ol' boys but of queer kids, art nerds, misfits: a very different breed of dreamer. Originality was prized; cover bands were sneered at. It was "a new kind of small-town bohemia," asserts Grace Elizabeth Hale, who lived in Athens and played in several local bands in the 1980s and 1990s, in her indispensable 2020 book *Cool Town: How Athens, Georgia, Launched Alternative Music and Changed American Culture*. "Life should be about making art for and with friends, combining creativity and pleasure and personal relationships, and living within and sharing a culture that you made yourselves. Money and fame were not necessary. They might even be lethal, killing the experience of creative pleasure."

Ever in the shadow of Atlanta, which got all the big touring acts, Athens was a place where you could make your own fun slightly out of the public eye. And that fun could take any shape you might want. The B-52's started among friends who might spend an evening walking around town in full drag, flipping off the rednecks who shouted insults from passing pickup trucks. Pylon started among students at the art school, who dubbed their sound "feasible rock" and wryly preached caution and moderation. Oh-OK initially consisted of two women, a keyboard player and a bass player, who wore outlandish outfits and rarely played a song that lasted more than two minutes. In a state known for its R&B and southern rock—Macon, home to both the Allman Brothers Band and James Brown, was just a two-hour drive down 129— Athens represented a very different, but no less southern, music scene, one not nearly as enthralled with prevalent ideas of southern masculinity. This was about as far from *The Dukes of Hazzard* as you could get without leaving the Peach State.

One band in particular convinced Patterson he could make a place for himself in a southern bohemia like Athens. "I thought if R.E.M. could do it there, I could do it there. I didn't know enough about Athens then to know the difference between there and Florence. Athens had venues and an infrastructure to support a scene. They had college students who were into the idea of people doing something different because of the huge arts school there. They had an instant audience to build from."

The acts that defined the Athens scene were not native to venues like the High Hat or to studios like FAME or Muscle Shoals Sound. Local music—the coiled spring of Pylon's grooves, the sharp jangle of R.E.M.'s guitars, the ebulliently subversive kitsch of the B-52's, the barbed whimsy of Oh-OK, the two-man attack of the Method Actors—was forged primarily at house parties, where bands would set up in a corner and play for their friends. It was dance music, party music. Made out of something like necessity, it flourished in these makeshift spaces, like the house of studio art professor Bob Croker or the quasi-abandoned St. Mary's Episcopal Church on Oconee Street, where members of R.E.M. lived and played their first show together on April 5, 1980.

Because Athens is a college town, music is an endlessly renewable resource, with a new wave of hopefuls arriving with each new class of freshmen at UGA. Many students stay in Athens even after they graduate, if they even bother to graduate at all. There are always bands forming and breaking up and reforming. In the '80s and well into the '90s, the city saw the rise of groups like Dreams So Real, Kilkenny Cats, the Bar-B-Q Killers, Widespread Panic, Vigilantes of Love, Five-Eight, and Jucifer. Add to that musicians who moved to Athens not for school but for the scene itself, people like the members of the Possibilities (Bainbridge, Georgia, right near the Florida line) and almost all of the Truckers themselves: Patterson, of course, came from the Shoals, but longtime drummer Brad Morgan hailed from Greenville, South Carolina, where he'd played in punk bands. Jay Gonzalez was from New York State. Rob Malone and Earl Hicks followed Patterson from Florence to Athens.

But relocating from elsewhere can be a tricky proposition in Athens, where musicians can be suspicious of outsiders. "People who moved to Athens to play music were almost without exception derided and ridiculed," says Dave Schools, who moved to town in 1983, co-founded Widespread Panic a few years later, and met Patterson when his band played the New Daisy in Memphis. "There was this protective bubble around the townie musicians and the art-school kids, the people who really make the culture of Athens into something so special. So you can't move here with the intent of being a local. You have to be natural-ized. You have to roll burritos and maybe take some classes and live in a punk rock house or a hippie commune. You have to start a couple of weird bands. And then you're one of us." Schools says he didn't encourage Patterson to relocate to Athens, because it might have been too hard for him to find a niche. "If anything, I probably told him it's a really cool town, but don't bring your band here." Patterson paid him no heed.

In the mid-1990s, when Patterson was trying to pierce that bubble, Athens was just on the cusp of another wave of bands that would have nearly nothing in common with the Drive-By Truckers yet would represent a similar DIY ethos. Actually, the Elephant 6 collective began about 1,500 miles west of Athens, out in Boulder, where a small group of friends attending the University of Colorado were nursing an all-consuming obsession with '60s pop. They not only formed their own bands—including the Apples in Stereo, Synthetic Flying Machine (later known as the Olivia Tremor Control), the Sunshine Fix, and Neutral Milk Hotel—but also devised something like a community of like-minded artists, all putting their own personal twists on pop psychedelia, mixing it with drone and noise and a new kind of narcotic fantasy. They called this coterie of groups, this band of bands, the Elephant 6 Recording Company, after nothing in particular.

Eventually, the bands came down from the mountains and resettled in Athens, where Elephant 6 bucked the odds and managed to insinuate itself into the scene and expand to include a dizzying array of artists, some local (Elf Power, Of Montreal) but some from elsewhere (San Francisco's Beulah, Denver's Dressy Bessy). Together, they remade the familiar tropes of '60s pop into something newly weird and unpredictable, a palette for experimentation, and the late 1990s saw perhaps the greatest uptick in musical activity and influence in Athens in more than a decade, thanks to adventurous records like the Apples in Stereo's *Fun Trick Noisemaker* (1995), the Olivia Tremor Control's *Music from the Unrealized Film Script: Dusk at Cubist Castle* (1996), Neutral Milk Hotel's *In the Aeroplane Over the Sea* (1998), Elf Power's *A Dream in Sound* (1999), and Of Montreal's *The Gay Parade* (1999).

While they developed in parallel, there was very little musical overlap between the Elephant 6 bands and the Drive-By Truckers (although Kevin Sweeney, a doorman and sound guy at the High Hat, did split his time between the Truckers and the Sunshine Fix, which also included Bill Doss from the Olivia Tremor Control. But that may be the exception that proves the rule. (Sweeney also played in the Glands, an Athens band that should be mentioned as often as possible.) What they did have in common, aside from geography and a determined creative independence, was a certain informality about what they called a band. Membership might change from one show to the next, or from one album to the next, but it usually centered around one guiding creative force: Jeff Mangum in Neutral Milk Hotel, for example, or Robert Schneider in the Apples in Stereo, or Patterson in the Truckers. In fact, most Athens musicians played in multiple bands, some in as many as four or five. It wasn't about hedging their bets professionally. Rather, it was about goofing around with friends, trying out new ideas, playing different styles of music. *Incestuous* is an overused word for such a scene; *promiscuous* might be more applicable. Some bands might be a one-night stand, others a long-term relationship. So Athens is the rare place where there are more bands than musicians, however statistically impossible that might sound. A band might exist for only one show or one night, or it might persist for decades, long after its members have started families and careers. The Truckers were conceived as the former but grew into the latter, to almost everyone's surprise.

Patterson arrived in Athens at a crucial moment in the city's history. In 1991, the city and county governments had unified into one entity that would oversee all of Clarke County. That made the mayoral race in 1994 crucial, and it marked the ascendancy of a Democratic city council member named Gwen O'Looney, who represented several historic districts in Athens, was supported by donations by several local musicians (including members of R.E.M.), and made preservation a cornerstone of her campaign. That issue helped ingratiate her to the local misfit constituency. Despite shepherding the city toward unification, O'Looney had two contenders in the Democratic primary, voting for which was held on July 19, 1994. She would face a runoff before becoming the first Athens–Clarke County mayor.

Just five days before, Patterson had attended an O'Looney fundraiser at the 40 Watt, headlined by Kevn Kinney from Drivin' N Cryin' and local singer-songwriter Vic Chesnutt. Patterson knew Kinney, but not

Chesnutt; that's why he was there. He'd been hearing that name over and over and over since he arrived in town. Chesnutt was, by most estimations, the greatest songwriter in town, with three albums to his name (two produced by Michael Stipe, even) and a very avid fanbase that was just beginning to creep beyond local. So Patterson's curiosity was piqued, and he planted himself at the lip of the stage.

Chesnutt and what he dubbed his "scared little skiffle band" had just finished recording his fourth—and, arguably, best—album, *Is the Actor Happy?*, and were performing an entire set of new songs. The performance took the top of Patterson's head off, and Chesnutt immediately became one of his songwriting heroes. That show served as an introduction to an artist who embodied two important aspects of the Athens music scene. First, Chesnutt was completely DIY. After moving to town in 1985 and briefly playing in a band called the La-Di-Da's, he established himself locally with a weekly residency at the 40 Watt, where his shows occasionally were loopy and weird and distracted and more than occasionally brilliant. He'd signed to a tiny indie label (Texas Hotel, now defunct) and, despite a celebrity like Stipe manning the boards for his first and second albums, seemed to harbor neither ambition nor inclination toward rousing a larger audience. The work itself was too important.

Second, Chesnutt had a *sound*—one born of tragedy and ingenuity and orneriness and guile. When he was a teenager in Zebulon, Georgia, a small town about two hours southwest of Athens, a car accident left him paralyzed from the waist down, with limited mobility in his hands. He taught himself guitar again by gluing picks to a glove, turning what might have been limitations into a spare and evocative style that played freeze tag with the meter. He combined that with a reedy voice that split words in unusual places and bent notes into odd shapes, and used it all to perform songs that savored regional turns of phrase, hinted at local details, took playful digs at his friends, and found deep meaning in the ceremonies of childhood: building rabbit traps in the backyard, waving a sparkler on the Fourth of July, watching *Speed Racer* after school. It was an aesthetic that didn't lend itself to fame and fortune, although he did release a straggler of an album on a major label and establish a career as a cult hero.

Patterson, nearing thirty, was actually eight months older, but Chesnutt had already found his voice, had already discovered what was unique about himself as a songwriter and performer, and was already crafting a singular body of work. Patterson was still impressionable: he had an idea of what he wanted to do but hadn't quite figured out how to do it, much less how to sustain it as something resembling a career. "As a writer, I definitely felt a kinship between what I felt like I was trying to do and what Vic did. I was in awe. His stuff's so funny yet so dark and twisted and beautiful. So many things at the same time. I loved how bathed in his southernness he was willing to be in his writing. It was very freeing to me."

That show at the 40 Watt in 1994 stuck with Patterson, but it was another show fifteen years later that still haunts him. In early November 2009, Chesnutt played a show at the 40 Watt during the tour for his album *At the Cut*, with Guy Picciotto from DC punk stalwarts Fugazi among others backing him. But the Truckers were headed out on the road the next day, and Patterson didn't want to start that tour with a late night. So he passed. He went to bed early, hit the road fresh. It was Chesnutt's final Athens show: he died on Christmas Day from an overdose of muscle relaxants. He was forty-five years old, roughly the same age as Patterson.

Since then, he's written at least two eulogies for his hero, one of which—"Sitting in the Sunshine (Thinking about Rain)"—he has never released officially. The other was, fittingly for Athens, a collaboration: "Come Back Little Star" was based on a stream-of-conscious poem by Kelly Hogan, a Redneck Underground veteran. She passed it along to Patterson, who with her blessing edited it down and set it to music. They cut it as a duet for his 2012 solo album, *Heat Lightning Rumbles in the Distance*. Anchored in a tender piano theme, it's a solemn song, drawing more from Shoals soul music than Chesnutt's peculiar folk. "We both had these dreams too long to let them slip through your hands," Patterson sings, trying to make sense of the loss before Hogan joins him on a pleading chorus: "Baby, don't go . . . take me with you." It's a song that reaches out but can only touch absence.

Patterson himself had more than one side hustle going. He worked day jobs at various restaurants, including the Athens Country Club and a place called Pasta Works. "Patterson was my prep cook, and I was a line cook," says Brandon Haynie, an old friend from the Shoals and his roommate in Athens, about the latter. "I remember him writing 'Dead Drunk and Naked' while he was cooking pasta. No guitar, no nothing. He just thought of it and wrote the lyrics down on the back of a pasta box." In addition to solo gigs at the High Hat, Patterson had started the Lot Lizards with a pair of brothers from southern Georgia, guitarist Kevin Lane and drummer Matt Lane. Taking their name from the slang for truck-stop prostitutes, they revived some of Patterson's old Shoals tunes, including "Lookout Mountain," along with a few he had written in the meantime, including "Nine Bullets." They played a handful of shows in Athens and Atlanta and recorded some songs for a cassette they sold at shows, but it wasn't a band that was meant to last. "It was well known that this was just a thing to do for a little while," says Matt Lane. Patterson wasn't particularly bothered by that band's unceremonious demise, especially since that limited shelf life was built into the concept he had for a new band. This group would have no dedicated lineup but would consist of whoever could make the next gig. Some nights it might be a loud, unwieldy septet, some it might be six guitarists and no drummer, or some just Patterson and his guitar. There would be absolutely no rehearsals. They would just make it up as they went along. In fact, at the very beginning there weren't even any live shows planned.

On June 1, 1996, Patterson invited a handful of friends to record a batch of songs at the High Hat with recording equipment on loan from a local band called Hayride. Cooley drove in from Birmingham, joining Barry Sell from the Hot Burritos on guitar, John Neff from the Star Room Boys on pedal steel, Adam Howell from Patterson's short-lived band Horsepussy on bass, and Matt Lane on drums. Together they ran through a handful of Patterson's songs, working up impromptu arrangements and setting them to tape before they sounded *too* rehearsed. Patterson had written "Nine Bullets" back in Auburn, but the others were newer and, for the most part, fairly twangy. "Margo and Harold" sounds like a George Saunders short story set to music, about a couple in their fifties still acting like they're indestructible twentysomethings. "Zoloft," a hokey ramble about the joys of mood medication, is the only one that has aged poorly.

Almost all of these initial songs remain live staples of Truckers shows, but the standout among them is "Bulldozers and Dirt," which makes a perfect introduction to what Patterson wanted this band to do, even if he couldn't quite articulate it just yet. A deeply uncomfortable song, it opens a cappella, with Patterson intoning that first syllable and holding the note just a beat longer than you expect, longer than the meter warrants, before getting to the rest of the phrase. It's like an overture: "Bulllllllldozers and dirt, bulldozers and dirt, what's your mama got hidden up her shirt?" Against the sharp clip of Cooley's mandolin and the sloshed stagger of Neff's pedal steel, Patterson relates what might be described as a redneck meet-cute: the narrator breaks into a woman's trailer and tries to steal her color TV. She holds him at gunpoint until the cops arrive, then bails him out the next day. They shack up. That was eleven years ago, when her daughter was only three years old; now the girl is a teenager and the object of the narrator's wayward attraction.

Undertones of incest certainly align with a cartoonish view of the rural South, according to which people marry their own cousins and the branches of family trees grow right back into the trunk. "Bulldozers and Dirt" plays up some of these hick stereotypes—there's a pickup on blocks in the front yard of their mobile home—but Patterson treats the characters with gravity and humanity. What makes the narrator so relatable and so much deeper than caricature is how he tries to resist that temptation by driving his bulldozer around in the backyard: "Them red clay piles are heaven on earth. I get my rocks off, bulldozers and dirt." The song ends unresolved, as though this errant lust was a permanent, perhaps even existential condition. He lives with that compulsion to wreck his marriage and his life, constantly distracting himself with heavy machinery.

That first session proved more fruitful than Patterson could have imagined. "I bought a bunch of beer. I bought a bunch of pizzas, we all had fun, so at the end of the day I said, 'Hey, do y'all wanna play a show together?'" They were officially a band, so they did what bands do. They played some shows and released some songs. The mid-1990s was the heyday of the CD format, and technology was such that even a brand-new group could manufacture a small run of discs and run some covers off at Kinko's. But Patterson had other ideas. A lifelong vinyl nerd who'd hauled his beloved record collection around the South, he wanted to release a 45 with "Bulldozers and Dirt" on one side and "Nine Bullets" on the other. It was a scheme born partly out of a kind of ornery contrarianism, partly out of a need to distinguish the band from every other upstart in town, and mostly from a desire to situate the band in relation to its influences: old country and classic rock LPs that were littering dollar bins at Wuxtry and Big Shot Records.

So they pressed up a small batch of records, commissioned artwork from their friend Jim Stacy, and printed up some sleeves. They ignored the fact that the PO Box number on the sleeve didn't match the PO Box number printed on the record label and started selling them at shows. You could argue that the Truckers predicted the vinyl resurgence of the 2010s—actually, you could argue that they predicted a lot more than that, which we'll get to presently—although they lacked the funds to press another vinyl run until the early 2000s. For the moment, the single was a curio on the merch table. It didn't garner much in the way of reviews or press, but they still considered it a success. "It gave us a merchandise item," says Cooley. "It gave us something to sell. It was novel enough and good enough to attract some attention and get people talking."

At first, nobody really expected the Truckers to go anywhere. It was just fun—a very particular kind of Athens fun. Both Patterson and Cooley had had their rock-and-roll dreams annihilated by the failure of Adam's House Cat, and while they couldn't have known it at the time, that failure helped to ensure the Truckers' success. It lowered their expectations. It kept them from overinvesting and therefore from overthinking. It allowed them to keep the sound raw and beautifully messy. And this might actually be the most Athens thing about the Truckers. Groups don't have to be formalized; they don't have to have decided membership; they can exist in whatever state best suits the musicians. "It was a fun ride playing those shows," says Cooley. "It could be a train wreck, but it could then go into this beautiful, moving, cathartic moment. Then veer back into the ditch. That's why people started coming to the shows. They wanted to see what would happen next. And we were having so much fun up there, and I think they wanted to have fun with us. Then those people started to bring more people. Next thing you know, we're selling out the Star Bar in Atlanta."

Cooley was making the drive from Birmingham, but when his wife got a nursing residency in North Carolina, he followed her to Durham and started painting apartments. "It was a pretty cool job for me because I can't stand people. So it wasn't a service industry. It wasn't restaurants. None of that bullshit. You'd just go into this empty apartment, knock it out. You're in there by yourself. And when you're done, you're done. It's not an hourly thing. You got paid for the job you did." It also allowed him ample time off for gigging with the Truckers and eventually touring. "Our shows were much later back then, and there were a lot of times when I would work my day job, come home, throw my shit in the truck, haul ass to Athens. I'd drive around looking for a parking place, get my shit out, plug in, and start playing."

Like Patterson, Cooley was impressed by Athens and intrigued by its history. He loved the scene and, as much as he could, enjoyed the camaraderie of his bandmates. But he knew he was never going to move to Athens. For one thing, jobs in his wife's field were scarce, and they both knew she could make more money in a bigger city like Birmingham or Durham. Plus, Cooley didn't want to spoil a good thing. "I thought maybe I ought to just keep it a nice place to visit. Let's not ruin this fuck buddy by actually going on a date."

"Be careful what you name your band," says Cooley, acknowledging that the Drive-By Truckers may not be that great a moniker. "How many bands are out there with these stupid names they give themselves just to go out and play a few songs, and then people start showing up. Oops. If we had known people were going to show up, we would have thought a little longer about it."

He's not wrong. Pretty much everyone agrees that Drive-By Truckers isn't a great band name. It's a little embarrassing in fact, maybe even something they had to overcome rather than something that helped them along the way. But that name is a relic of a particular time and speaks to something essential in the band's DNA. The first half—Drive-By—is a racially loaded term describing the assassination of enemies from a passing car. It was popular in gangsta rap, the gritty, violent, and nebulously defined strain of hip-hop pioneered by West Coast groups like N.W.A. in the late 1980s and early 1990s. The music was derided for its explicit depictions of murder, drug dealing, and prostitution, and it was praised for offering an unflinching depiction of life in American cities. Ice Cube included a skit called "The Drive-By" on his 1990 album AmeriKKKa's Most Wanted, presented as a hybrid radio sketch/news report, complete with ersatz Tom Brokaw concluding, "Outside the South Central area, few cared about the violence because it didn't affect them."

Patterson loved it all. He took notes on hip-hop's intricate storytelling techniques: how rappers could summon a whole world with just a few words, how they let the action play out in ways that weren't always obvious or expected. In particular, he loved the Dirty South scene just emerging over in Atlanta, which included Outkast and Goodie Mob. With their Georgia drawls informing the cadence of their flows, these acts helped to define a specifically southern strain of hip-hop with its own sound and perspective.

But drive-bys were also a useful tool to justify extreme policing tactics and exaggerate myths about Black-on-Black violence. "At the core of this violence," writes David Wilson in his 2005 study *Inventing Black-on-Black Violence: Discourse, Space, and Representation*, "was blackness rather than poverty, economics of class. . . . Race was the template applied to understand this violence. In media hyperbole, here was proof that inner city blacks had become dangerously distanced from civility."

The drive-by reference in the new band's name might have been ironic at first, underscoring the unlikelihood of combining hardcore rap with hardcore country. By aligning themselves with that scene, however, the Truckers were laying out their mission: to tell gritty stories of crime and violence in the rural South, with as much verve and verisimilitude as the Black artists they wanted to consider peers. So many years later, the Truckers' glib reference to hip-hop music and culture threatens to obscure or make light of Black accomplishments and tragedies, which is only heightened by the kitsch elements of country music. Patterson admitted as much in 2020, addressing the subject in an article for NPR titled "Now, about the Bad Name I Gave My Band." Writing that they've grown as individuals and as a band since their first recording sessions, but also admitting that the context of '90s alt-country and their own good intentions won't let them off the hook, Patterson writes: "Our name was a drunken joke that was never intended to be in rotation and reckoned with two-and-a-half decades later, and I sincerely apologize for its stupidity and any negative stereotypes it has propagated." He doesn't go so far as to say they're going to drop the *Drive-By*, but he does say they're open to suggestions.

As for the *Truckers* half of their band name, country music was something Patterson and Cooley had grown up with in the South, even if they had never counted themselves fans of the genre. "I came from a rural background—the actual culture that country is," says Cooley. "I rejected it. I wanted no part of it. I wanted to be cooler than that." But age and experience gave both Cooley and Patterson a better perspective on the music, especially at a time when their peers were reassessing country music. "A lot of hipsters at that time who were normally pretty snobby were starting to appreciate Merle Haggard, at least until they heard 'Fightin' Side of Me,' says Cooley. "And whether I like it or not, it's a part of who I am. So I can do it authentically. It became part of who we were and how we presented ourselves to the world. We eventually made our way back to rock and roll, but we started out by reexamining that music—in my case, my old man's music that I had rejected."

There was among '90s alt-country acts a tendency to condescend to the material or to present it as something kitschy, like a semi-ironic *Hee Haw* sketch. The Truckers flirted with cornpone novelty in songs like "Demonic Possession" and "The Tough Sell" and even "Wife Beater," which along with the band name led some listeners to dismiss them altogether. Patterson fielded questions along those lines early in their career. In a 1999 feature with the *Savannah Morning News* titled "Nothing Kitschy," Patterson is quoted defending the band against such accusations: "People tend to hear the name and see the artwork and say, 'Oh, they must be like Southern Culture on the Skids,'" referring to the long-running North Carolina band that wallowed in white-trash stereotypes and sang songs like "Carve That Possum" and "My House Has Wheels." "I love Southern Culture on the Skids, but I don't think we sound anything like them," Patterson continued.

But they generally avoided this pitfall by interrogating many of those redneck stereotypes, by generously emphasizing the humanity of their characters. "Some of our songs might come off as novelty on the surface, and they can be a little funny," says Cooley. "Then you realize, *Nah man, this is really dark and sad.* And it's *about* something. It ain't *Hee Haw* ... although I do love *Hee Haw*."

One song that critic Kandia Crazy Horse, who covered the band early in their career, singles out as "passionately human" is "18 Wheels of Love." "Their music focused on the people not descended from the planter class—their own families and folk from their communities in Alabama. The Truckers were a breath of fresh air because they came out self-consciously delving into the mythology of the New South and their accents were indelible. Their songs provided a strong intellectual perspective on the 'Southern Thang' equivalent to a college course's textbook."

Patterson wrote "18 Wheels of Love" at a time when touring alt-country bands like Son Volt and the Bottle Rockets were identifying some of their own road experiences in trucker anthems by Del Reeves and Red Sovine, and the song begins with a chorus that sounds ironic: "Mama ran off with a trucker! Mama ran off with a trucker! Peterbilt! Peterbilt!" It's got CB lingo and sweet potato pies, the kind of details that might lead to something like a punchline for other acts, but it never turns into a joke. Rather, it has an unrelenting sweetness as Patterson celebrates the genuine affection between a woman and her truck-driving man. The song is actually a true story, written in celebration of the second marriage of Patterson's mother. When the Truckers play it live, that story takes on even greater depths and that chorus sounds earnestly celebratory: the version on the Truckers' 2000 live album, *Alabama Ass Whuppin'*, begins with Patterson telling the story of his mother suffering through a tough divorce, finding work at a trucking agency, and eloping with a three-hundred-pound driver named Chester. On their 2009 release, *Live in Austin, TX*, he adds a new chapter detailing Chester's battle with cancer. The song is disarmingly sincere.

"I wouldn't say I thought they were a joke band," says onetime member Kevin Sweeney, "but there was a humorous side to it. 'Nine Bullets' seemed jokey to me. There was a novelty to some of Patterson's songs, but then he wrote 'The Living Bubba' about Gregory Dean Smalley. When I heard that, it was on a totally different level. I think that's the one that made a lot of people take them seriously."

Still a live staple and one of Patterson's finest, most moving compositions, "The Living Bubba" actually predates the Truckers. Its first performance—but not its first recording—was by the Lot Lizards, near the end of their run. Like so many of Patterson's songs, it tells a true story, in this case of Gregory Dean Smalley, an Atlanta musician who fronted several bands, including the Diggers and the Bubbamatics, and sat in with many more. He was also the force behind Bubbapalooza, a small festival that originally spotlit bands from the Redneck Underground before expanding to include national acts. Patterson met him, of course, at the High Hat, where Smalley played several times and even did a set with the Hot Burritos.

Smalley's tremendously busy schedule—several shows a week around North Georgia—was all the more impressive considering he was dying of AIDS. At first it wasn't noticeable, but he grew weaker from the medication, often unable to stand, sometimes slumped in a chair onstage. But he still managed to sing and play guitar, as though summoning strength from that part of his brain that lived for the rock show. In 1995, he asked the Lot Lizards to play the Star Bar in Atlanta. "When I called him to thank him for inviting us, his wife answered and said he was in the hospital and wasn't coming home. I wrote 'The Living Bubba' that afternoon. I hung up the phone, walked my dog, and when I got back, I sat down and wrote that song."

That sense of urgency carries over into the music. Patterson sings from Smalley's point of view, as though he's explaining himself to an audience: "I'm sick at my stomach from the AZT," he sings, referring to the controversial treatment known for its incredibly harsh side effects. "Broken my bank 'cause that shit ain't free. But I'm here to stay at least another week or two." Then he caps it off with what may be Smalley's motivating philosophy, which means it's also Patterson's motivating philosophy: "I can't die now 'cause I got another show to do." The song builds and subsides unpredictably, with no verse-chorus-verse structures and lyrics that seem to trail off. The song puts the listener right there in the moment with Smalley, which is another way of saying it keeps him alive. Patterson says he wept when they debuted the song at Bubbapalooza, with Smalley's widow and mother in the audience.

And who wouldn't weep? Right when the band is running up to the song's cathartic climax, right when they're hitting those big power chords, Patterson punctuates the song by simply saying the man's name, a small but incredibly poignant moment in any Truckers show. "The Living Bubba" makes clear that Smalley is Patterson's ultimate rock idol. He has written songs about icons like Ronnie Van Zant and Neil Young and Jimmy Page, but there's something definitive and incredible in this story of a musician who lived solely to play, who defied death in order "to bend that note in two." Smalley didn't do it for the fame he knew wasn't coming to him, not that he would have been around to enjoy it even if it had arrived. It wasn't for the money, because a club gig won't pay for your meds. It was for no other reason than playing that rock show. It might not have been pretty, but it's everything Patterson wants to embody as a rock star.

"The Living Bubba" appears on the Truckers' 1998 debut, *Gangstabilly*, arguably their most country-sounding record to date. Patterson funded the recording sessions himself with sweat and toil. David Barbe was building his studio, called Chase Park Transduction, and Patterson hung drywall in exchange for studio time. "We were a great drywall hanging team," says Barbe, "because Patterson is a great big, tall guy who can hold a piece of drywall up against the studs. I'm not so big, but relatively quick and agile and can zip up and down a ladder with a screw gun. We were dissecting the history of some bands and listening to records while we're working."

Even after spending a few months out on the road playing shows and selling CDs, the Truckers didn't have the cash for more studio sessions, so they recorded their second album, *Pizza Deliverance*, out at the Redneck Ramada in 1999. They borrowed equipment, snaked wires in and out of rooms, duct-taped microphones to broomsticks, stretched pantyhose across microphones. "The setup was pretty barbaric," says Patterson. "It was a real wing-and-a-prayer operation. That album is truly a field recording."

If it hadn't been for the generosity of an old friend, *Pizza Deliverance* would never have been finished. The Truckers were, to use Cooley's phrase, piss broke. Money was always tight, as it was for any band at this level. They were touring heavily, but if one of their trips broke even, they considered it an astounding success. They had no business plan, nor any plan to come up with a business plan. Even recording at Patterson's house, they didn't have the funds to mix and master the songs, much less press them on CDs.

Enter Dave Schools. He was the bass player for Widespread Panic, who were, aside from R.E.M., the biggest band in town. Mixing psychedelic southern rock with blues and jazz, lengthy improvisations with focused songwriting, they had held a free CD release party in Athens around the time the Truckers were making *Pizza Deliverance*. Estimates vary, but anywhere from eighty thousand to one hundred thousand fans from all over the world descended upon Athens for the show. "Panic was doing really well, and we were on tour a lot, and things were blowing up on a national level for us," Schools recalls. "For the first time in my life, I found myself owning a home and having a car that worked and paying my bills on time and even having a little extra." In true Athens fashion, he wanted to make sure other local bands could benefit from his success.

Schools had met Patterson back in Memphis, and they reconnected in the Shoals when Panic recorded their third album, *Everyday*, at Muscle Shoals Sound Studio. When Patterson moved to Athens, Schools was one of the few people he knew there. Schools was a frequent patron at the High Hat as well; Widespread Panic were far too big for such a small venue, but Schools would play the High Hat occasionally with Brute, his pickup group featuring his Panic bandmates and Vic Chesnutt. (Check out their two albums, *Nine High a Pallet* and *Co-Balt*, both terrific, underrated Athens records.) "Watching Vic backed up by Widespread Panic covering Olivia Newton-John's 'Have You Never Been Mellow' was absolutely one of the most punk rock things I have ever seen in my life," says Patterson. "Vic was singing with such power and emotion that I swear he was levitating out of his chair."

When Schools learned of the Truckers' financial woes, he drove out to Patterson's house on Jefferson Road and quizzed him on the status of the album and the band. "They were in this difficult spot—one of the first humps to success," says Schools. "You need to tour to satisfy the demand, but at the same time your gear is taking a beating, your van is taking a beating, and the money just doesn't match up yet. I've seen that hump take out a lot of promising bands." So he wrote them a check for several thousand dollars—an unexpected act of generosity that not only saved the album but allowed them to upgrade their touring van. "It wasn't a big deal. 'Just get out there and get over the hump. Pay me back when you can.'"

Patterson and Cooley both have come to see this act of generosity as a pivotal moment for the Truckers, a moment when they managed to make it to that next level. "Dave Schools saved our ass in '99," Patterson says. "We told him we didn't know when we could pay him back. We didn't have any money. 'Well, just pay it forward. Someday you'll have money to help someone else out.'" Schools might have served in a mentor role for the band had he not been so busy with Widespread Panic, who in the late 1990s were one of the top touring draws in the United States. Occasionally, when they weren't on the road, they would see each other around town, usually at the Grit, and spend a few minutes catching up.

The Truckers did eventually reimburse him for that check, and Schools immediately donated it to Nuçi's Space, an organization providing mental health services to local musicians. They continue to abide by that ethos, as though the idea of paying it forward was more valuable than the check itself. The Truckers make a point to pick most of their own opening acts, giving a boost to Athens artists like singer-songwriters Thayer Sarrano and Don Chambers. And their annual HeAthens Homecoming shows are as much about showcasing lesser-known acts and supporting Athens nonprofits like Nuçi's Space and Camp Amped as they are about spotlighting the Truckers.

A few shows had turned into a few years, and the Truckers had far surpassed Patterson's original concept for the band as a rotating group of friends showing up whenever they could. They had become a touring band, and with the funds from Schools, that model looked sustainable for the short term. This was something Adam's House Cat had never done, maybe couldn't do. Patterson hadn't known that he would need to leave the Shoals to make it, nor did he know then how to arrange a tour for his band. Even in Athens, he wasn't sure how it was done but had learned enough to wing it. Besides, their inexperience planning a tour did little to dampen their enthusiasm. The deprivations of life on the road had a certain punk romance: long drives in their cramped touring van, trading out driving duties, arguing about whose turn it was to pick the music, sleeping in pretzel positions among the gear. And when they arrived at their destination, they didn't mind loading in too much, and they even savored the rock shows in towns they never really got to see beyond the club and the back alley. They would go home with whoever might be willing to host an unshowered band for the night and stay up too late when those people wanted to talk or drink or party.

Along the way, they would hold hours-long conversations about music and movies and the legends they had heard growing up in the South, which fueled a burst of songwriting that would define their next several albums. As they traveled, as they stopped at different cities and saw new places, they realized just how different the South was from how the rest of the country perceived it. "Growing up in Alabama at that time was very different from anything I'd seen portrayed in the southern novels that I'd been made to read in high school," says Rob Malone. "Since we all came from basically the same place, we all cut our teeth on the same stories and myths. Like Buford Pusser—I don't even remember the first time I heard about him. It's like we always knew about that stuff. Those stories were always around, and they became ingrained in us. But there was a lot of truth in them as well."

One jaunt sticks out to Cooley, who remembers how they booked a December run in Michigan and Pennsylvania, not expecting the weather to suck or people to be sick. "The first night we were in Columbus, Ohio, working our way up north, the band that was hosting us, they were local and had kids, and one of their kids had come home with the flu. They were all puking in garbage cans in the dressing room. It ran through us, but somehow I escaped it." A few nights later, when the band was in Lansing, the snow started falling, and it didn't stop. These southern boys in Michigan were exhilarated by the sight of something they very rarely saw in Georgia, but that excitement dissipated into something like dread. "We had to go from Lansing to Buffalo, which is a long-ass way away," says Cooley. "We could have taken the shortcut across Canada, but we didn't know what the hell we were doing. So we went down around Lake Erie through Cleveland and up through Erie, Pennsylvania, during a blizzard. Somehow we made it home and were like, *I wanna do that again!* That's not what a sane person does. A sane person does not get thrown off that animal and then want to get back on. But we couldn't wait. We got better at it."

One thing that distinguished the Truckers from so many other bands they crossed paths with was their age: Patterson and Cooley were seven to ten years older than most of their peers, the Truckers a new act fronted by guys who were well past the age when guys were forming bands and going on seat-of-their-pants tours. But that only gave them perspective. It made them more determined not just to play a kickass rock show night after night but to get to that next town, to appreciate the hardship and savor the experience. And to not let their modest success go to their heads. "It probably kept me alive," says Cooley. "If I'd been one of those people who had any success when I was twenty-three, I would have made a much bigger ass of myself than Kanye West. I would have been really destructive. I'd probably be dead or at least missing a lot of years off the other end of the line. Not being in my twenties when I was being interviewed by *Rolling Stone* was really in my best interest. It was a godsend."

One of the most crucial Truckers at this point wasn't even a member of the band. Jenn Bryant was an old friend of theirs from back in the Shoals; a diehard Adam's House Cat fan, she was devastated by their breakup but heartened by the formation of the Drive-By Truckers, by which time she had moved to Athens, too. She was close enough to the band to get a shoutout in their hard-touring anthem "Hell No, I Ain't Happy," from *Decoration Day*: "Check my mail if you would please, Jenn," Patterson sings over a crunching guitar riff. "Collect my things till I'm in town again."

Bryant's day job involved doing desktop publishing for a local start-up that specialized in a very primitive form of online banking, which means she learned website design and development before most people had Wi-Fi. In her spare time she loaned out this new expertise to her favorite bands, creating sites for groups like Hayride, Slobberbone, and the Truckers. She kept the tour page updated and helped manage the Yahoo forum. "There were hardly any band websites out there, so we really were one of the first," she says. "I knew if a music fan would just go see them live, they would be hooked. And I was right. Their following grew rapidly online and in real life, because they just tore it up on the road and people could always find out when they were coming."

The practice of listing tour dates on your website—hell, even the very notion of having a website for your band—is so commonplace now that it's easy to forget just how revolutionary it was in 1997. "The internet was just starting to become something," says Cooley. "It was about where TV was in 1950. It wasn't in every home yet, but it was coming. It gave us a way to call ourselves a band and start booking shows. And people started showing up. It started coalescing the fanbase." Along with Brandon Haynie, who co-managed the band's very active Yahoo forum, Bryant and the Truckers were showing how an enterprising new band might use the internet to define itself, to book and promote tours, and to connect a far-flung community of fans. It also allowed them to reach what has become one of their biggest markets: southern expats. With their very detailed and idiosyncratic depictions of the South, the

Truckers became a band for people in other places, presenting a vision of home to southerners like me who were in exile from the place they considered home. And those people showed up at gigs, bought merch, and cheered the band on.

"Because of that, when we toured, we would go to a town we'd never been to and we would have people show up," says Cooley. "It wouldn't be a packed house, but there would be a dozen or so people who were there to see us and thought we were doing something special. That made us think we could turn it into a living, or at the very least have some of the experiences we grew up wanting to have before we said, 'Okay, enough of this foolishness. Let's be adults now.'"

Very quickly the Truckers surpassed any success that Adam's House Cat ever experienced. "Cooley and I had been playing together fourteen years by the time we put out *Pizza Deliverance*," says Patterson. "We'd watched Adam's House Cat die, and that damn near killed us. And everything we did after that was a dismal failure. So when the Truckers started up, we knew something was different. People seemed to like us."

"The difference between Adam's House Cat and the Drive-By Truckers," says Cooley, "was that with Adam's House Cat, we just tried so hard. It was so important. By the time the Truckers started up, I didn't give a fuck. I've always described Adam's House Cat as the guy at the party who's going home alone because he's trying too hard. The Drive-By Truckers are definitely getting laid, because they don't give a fuck. That's what the audience was relating to. There were no rehearsals. Sometimes the shows would fall apart. And we didn't give a damn. And then it could become really beautiful."

Starting a band in Athens is relatively easy. Much, much more difficult is keeping that band together, and the modest success they were enjoying didn't mean everything was going smoothly. Even just a few years into their existence, the Drive-By Truckers were hitting potholes, existing in what Patterson calls a "high level of dysfunction." Some of it was the usual wear and tear on any band, but "them's highway miles," as the song goes (the song being "The Tough Sell," from *Gangstabilly*). Even as they pared down to a sharp quartet—Patterson and Cooley, joined by Rob Malone on bass and Brad Morgan on drums—they struggled to balance the work and fun of the band with day jobs and families. All the band members were by then married except for Brad Morgan, who lived with his longtime girlfriend. Being in a band complicated those relationships, and those relationships in turn complicated the band. They brought the baggage from one into the other, until one day in 2000 things came to a head. Cooley recalls, "There was this one day when everybody's wife or significant other—except mine—called them up to say they were breaking up, their shit was out at the curb. Pretty much all of them in the same day. I think they all got together and went out drinking. They got to talking and one-upping each other and pushing each other's buttons, and they went home all pissed off and half-drunk. Then they lowered the boom."

They commemorated these fraying relationships on their 2003 release *Decoration Day*, in songs that sound all the more heartbreaking for being so self-effacing, so measured, so evenhanded. Writing about breakups can be tricky, as they're usually one-sided depictions of a relationship with a partner who might not have a public voice or a sympathetic audience. Patterson and Cooley manage to avoid that imbalance largely because they're less concerned with laying blame and more determined to face up to the tragedy of it. "(Something's Got to) Give Pretty Soon" is Patterson's autopsy of his failed second marriage, set to a fast tempo just shy of desperate and featuring one of his most urgent choruses. There's no bitterness, no recrimination, not even any self-loathing—just the realization that his ex needs more than he can give her. "It breaks my heart to see that it ain't meant to be," he sings, "but it ain't me." Perhaps on paper that sounds like he's shrugging his shoulders, but his delivery makes it sound like a deeply felt apology.

Even darker is Cooley's "Sounds Better in the Song," a mostly acoustic account of being outgrown by the woman you love. He makes explicit the effect the band has had on his marriage ("I might as well have slipped the ring on her finger from the window of a van as it drove away"), and rather than address the song to his wife, Cooley makes it sound like he wrote it to sing in front of everybody but her ("Lord knows I can't change / Sounds better in the song than it does with hell to pay"). And yet, Cooley's was the only relationship to survive that Armageddon. He met his wife, Ansley, when he and Patterson lived in Auburn, and they married just before the Truckers formed. "There's no special mojo," he insists. "I got lucky."

And then Patterson committed a dumbass mistake. "I did an unspeakable violation of the band's relationship and started sleeping with the person who was at the time our manager. I'm not someone who tends to have a lot of regrets, and there aren't a lot of things I'd say I'd do differently. Even the bigger mistakes I've made in my life I tend to be pretty philosophical about. But that's the exception. I fucked up pretty bad."

This seems like a cardinal rule in rock bands: don't fuck your manager. It's almost as obvious as Don't fuck your bandmate or your bandmate's partner. It wasn't a power play, Patterson insists, but the rash actions of a man still reeling from a second broken marriage and a band that he still couldn't quite believe was successful. "She'd been in and around the business for a while, and we weren't in any position to attract anyone who was equipped to really manage a band," says Cooley. "It would be a while before we picked up management that was capable of doing anything. Actually, we ended up going through a lot of managers before we finally got to where we are now. But it almost torpedoed the band."

"We certainly didn't think he was doing it to gain more power or some weird shit like that," Malone recalls. "He wasn't doing it to screw anything up. He was just having a good time. Cooley was the first one to put his foot down. He was smart, so he knew it was going to end up horrible. He knew it was going to fuck everything up." So they staged an intervention, calling a band meeting at Malone's basement apartment over by the hospital, and they confronted Patterson about his indiscretions. It did not go particularly well, but it didn't break up the band either. They hobbled along, barely speaking, holding in their resentment, and usually taking it out on a song.

Patterson and the manager broke it off, which effectively meant she was fired. And he apologized. The damage had been done, though.

As the Drive-By Truckers toured farther and farther from home, their coughing tour van rode in the shadow of more and more 18-wheelers crowding the highways to deliver to big box stores all over the country. Did they realize how much the Walmartification of America threatened to ruin their beloved Athens? In the early 2010s, an Atlanta-based development company announced plans to build a mixed-use shopping center near downtown Athens. It was essentially a high-end strip mall that would be anchored by a Walmart Supercenter, taking up nearly nine acres abutting the green space around the Oconee River. Locals were incensed, Patterson among them. He feared that the development would be too big for the small town, drawing money away from locally owned businesses and essentially squeezing out the weirdness that made Athens *Athens*.

Their fears weren't unfounded, either, because that is what Walmart has historically done in similar communities. According to studies dating back to 1988, by offering discounts greater than what mom-and-pop shops can match, the chain harms and often kills independent businesses that may have been operating there for generations. It's a consequence so widespread that it's become known as the Walmart Effect. And that's not restricted to their host towns either; the stores often pull business away from neighboring towns and counties, especially in rural areas and small towns. That can wipe out a town's identity, not only dampening its economy, but turning Main Street into a row of empty storefronts. Athens already had two Walmart Supercenters on its outskirts, along with a Walmart Neighborhood Market. Could it sustain or even survive another, closer to its center?

A more interesting question might be, Did it actually need a Walmart? That's a bit murkier. As Will Doig points out in an essay on Salon.com, "The truth is, the downtown desperately needs more practical retail. Right now, there's not even a grocery store, and there are more places to buy vintage skirts than paper towels." Criticism of the project became more about the type of shopping facility that would house the Walmart: a massive, multi-tenant complex that would essentially double the retail space in downtown and would likely damage greenspace around the Oconee River.

Fearing Athens might lose its essential Athens-ness, Patterson wrote a song about it: an ambling country-folk song called "After It's Gone" that imagines his town bled of its eccentricities. He wanders its streets as if in a nightmare, surveying blocks gone to seed and empty storefronts and apartment buildings that were hastily constructed and falling apart. It's a horrifying fate for his beloved hometown, but "After It's Gone" is the rare protest song that is defined by sadness rather than outrage. It's a song about barely keeping the wolves at the door; it's a song that knows they'll get in some day. "I'd rather be wrong than to have it all be gone," goes the chorus. "If it all disappears, there's no reason to stay here."

The song didn't end up on a Truckers album or even on the solo album he released in 2012. Instead, it became its own standalone seven-inch single, credited to Patterson Hood and the Downtown 13. It is something like a cross-generational all-star project, a local version of USA for Africa, featuring Lera Lynn, John Bell and Todd Nance from Widespread Panic, Mike Mills from R.E.M., and members of the Hernies, Hope for Agoldensummer, and Futurebirds. They recorded it during soundcheck at the 40 Watt, with Chase Park Transduction donating studio time to mix and master the song. The Truckers sold the record through their website, with proceeds benefiting an upstart organization called Protect Downtown Athens. Patterson had figured out a way to turn an Athens issue into something with national implications: "If all politics are local," he sings, "then I guess it starts here."

Eventually, those development plans were scuttled. But that doesn't mean there aren't more plans being drawn up right at this very moment. There is always the fear that the beloved barbecue joint or rock venue or record store or landmark might be razed to make room for something that can make somebody else a little more money. The town has changed dramatically over the years, with new condos for students and retirees and new boutique hotels for football fans. Like so many other artist enclaves and college towns (like Oxford, Mississippi, or even my own adopted hometown of Bloomington, Indiana), Athens is in danger of being overdeveloped, with rising rents and a higher cost of living squeezing out the musicians and painters and weirdos and misfits who have defined the city to so many outsiders.

"After It's Gone" aligns with other local conservation efforts in a city defined by its dual identities as an arts community and a college town. While its music history is unparalleled, Athens still attracts more Dawgs fans every year than rock fans. That lends a certain urgency to the efforts to protect local landmarks, including what is known as the Murmur Trestle in Dudley Park and St. Mary's Episcopal Church on Oconee Street. That structure was mostly destroyed in 1990, and now only the steeple remains.

As a result, the Athens scene is always taking its own pulse, always gauging its own health. Some folks will tell you it was better in '79 or '83 or '87 or '94 or last year, grumbling over this or that venue going out of business, this or that sound going out of style. But others see it less as peaks and valleys and more as a continuum. The city continues to support hundreds of bands, not to mention more studios, producers, engineers, labels, venues, and publicists than almost any other city its size in the country. In fact, arts in Athens, music in particular, seem to flourish under pressure, when players have something to push against. "There's always something good happening in Athens," says Dave Schools. "In fact, the more you try to send it down the drain, the more there's going to be. There's no way to stop it."

Certainly the Athens that Patterson moved to in 1994 barely resembles the Athens he moved away from in 2015. The High Hat closed in 1999, and the Truckers were one of three bands playing the final show. Tasty World down the street shuttered in 2010. Frijolero's is long gone. Schoolkids Records (where the Glands' Ross Shapiro held court) closed. Caledonia Lounge closed during the COVID-19 pandemic. Even Patterson's old house, a hundred-year-old structure on North Broad Street, is gone, razed by a developer after Patterson and his family left town.

But it's not all bad. The Grit is still there, as are Weaver D's, the Manhattan, and the 40 Watt. Wuxtry is still there, and another great record store called Low Yo-Yo Stuff opened near the 40 Watt. New West Records, which signed the Truckers in 2002, still has offices in Athens and is a completely different beast than the one that inspired Patterson's song "Assholes" on *Go-Go Boots*. The Georgia Theater was nearly destroyed by a fire in 2009, but it was refurbished, remodeled, and reopened in 2012.

It is February 2018, and it's cold in Athens. Not icy—this is Georgia, after all—but cold enough to make the crowd at the 40 Watt pack in a little tighter against the stage. Lilly Hiatt has just played an opening set on the third night of the HeAthens Homecoming, and now the crowd is getting rowdy and impatient. I'm standing about halfway between the stage and the door, pressed up against complete strangers, including a woman who introduces her mother as though I'm an old friend she's told her all about. They've driven down from Virginia to spend the weekend here in Athens, although they could get tickets only to tonight's show. The mother, who has a grandmotherly smile, hasn't heard a note of the Truckers' music but has faith in her daughter's good taste. Another guy next to me is here with friends from Alabama, all of them packed into one motel room out on the interstate. The crowd shifts, and within a few minutes these two groups have been pushed far away from me.

This is Homecoming: a weekend where Truckers fans from all over the world—seriously, they arrive from Japan and South Africa and other far-flung locales—descend on Athens and form one big community where nobody is a stranger. Every shop or restaurant has at least one person wearing a DBT concert shirt or drinking a beer out of a DBT coozie. Outside the 40 Watt, a man in an Adam's House Cat T-shirt is treated like a celebrity.

There is a bit of confusion from the crowd when the Truckers finally take the stage: an initial burst of applause followed by gasps and laughter. Every one of the Truckers is sporting a big pink pussy hat, recently made famous at the Women's March in Washington, DC. It's a strange sight but certainly not ironic, despite Cooley ending an especially frayed-nerve performance of "Women without Whiskey" by crooning, "...and a pussy hat on my head" like he's George Jones. On this third and final night of their fourteenth annual Homecoming, they're punchy, maybe a little fried after a long weekend, but that only feeds the rock show. Over the next three hours they play more than thirty songs, including a cover of Alice Cooper's "I'm Eighteen" and snippets of Prince's "Sign o' the Times" and Tom Petty's "Southern Accents." They repeat only one or two songs from previous nights, a testament to the sheer size of their repertoire.

This is a tradition that dates back to the mid-2000s, when the Truckers scheduled a run of 40 Watt shows to cap off one of their longest tours, behind *A Blessing and a Curse*. It was successful enough that they booked another set of shows the next year, and it has grown bigger and bigger ever since, turning into something like a music festival and fundraiser for Nuçi's Space and Camp Amped. Even after Patterson and his family moved all the way out to Portland, Oregon, and left only two Truckers remaining in Athens—Jay Gonzalez and Brad Morgan—the band still considers this town their home. They store their equipment here, keep their headquarters here, and most of their road crew still live in the area. There's way too much Athens in their DNA. They couldn't hold Homecoming anywhere else.

This annual tradition is not something the band set about inaugurating so many years ago, mostly because they wouldn't have thought it'd work. Instead, Homecoming is something that grew organically around them, motivated by fans' desire to see their favorite band in this particular town, in this particular club, on this hallowed ground. It is, in many ways, the culmination of the online community that Jenn Bryant and Brandon Haynie helped to build in the late 1990s, with many of the same people in the audience, some of them even sporting T-shirts from early tours and exchanging notes on shows by previous lineups of the band. And the activity spills out of the 40 Watt and into the town itself, where fans crowd bars and book Airbnbs and dig through crates at record stores.

"Most people who come to Homecoming in Athens aren't actually from Athens," Cooley clarifies. "They come from all over. Other countries. Everybody who's from Athens is backstage. We've never given an official award for who's traveled the farthest to get there, but that's always something everybody's trying to figure out. One year an old roommate of mine from back in Florence flew in from South Africa. He probably won that year. But it's all hard for me to fathom. I wouldn't go across town to stand in a room that crowded and watch me onstage. But that's me. I was never a good audience member. I like having my own space up on stage."

As with birthdays and holidays, HeAthens Homecoming is also a means of marking time, especially for the two main Truckers, who found success at an age when others might have put aside their rock dreams for full-time jobs and civilian lives. Every year brings some new milestone to commemorate, not all of them happy. In 2010 it was the death of Vic Chesnutt. In 2013 it was the passing of their longtime merch guy Craig Lieske, who suffered a heart attack and died one night during Homecoming. In 2018 it's Tom Petty, whose "Rebels" the band had covered on *The Fine Print* and whom Patterson eulogized for the online magazine *The Bitter Southerner*.

That gives Homecoming a poignancy missing from many such fan gatherings, and it's perhaps why the shows always end on such a cathartic note. At least one night per year, they wrap things up with "Grand Canyon," Patterson's song about Lieske's sudden passing. "Angels and Fuselage" is another favorite show closer. But on this Saturday night in 2018, it's a medley starting with "Hell No, I Ain't Happy," an angry touring song from *Decoration Day* that becomes an anthem of resistance even before Patterson starts spelling out "R-E-S-I-S-T" and Cooley starts asking if there are any farmers in the audience tonight. "You know bullshit when you smell it!" They've created a space that is unique to them, right at the confluence of southern rock and punk and R&B and every album they've ever loved.

Somewhere along the way, the song veers into a red-dirt psych jam version of Prince's "Sign o' the Times," then takes its sweet time getting back into "Hell No, I Ain't Happy." Patterson commands David Barbe to join them onstage, but before he can even strap on a guitar, they've launched into Jim Carroll's "People Who Died," which the Truckers have been covering for more than twenty years. Soaked in sweat, Patterson sheds his guitar, falls on his knees, rolls onto his back—"people who DIED! DIED!"—holds the microphone into the audience for people to shout along, chants the lyrics—"DIED! DIED!"—all while the band batter their instruments. It becomes a punk show, then a tent revival, then a wake, then something else entirely. It's a mass eulogy for Chesnutt and Craig Lieske and every other friend who died. "These people who made us feel invincible, they DIED!" Patterson preaches, his voice going hoarse. "Prince fucking died! David Bowie fucking died! Motherfucking Tom Petty fucking died!" Then he adds, "And I miss 'em!" There's really no life-affirming message here, nothing more than a fevered realization that death comes to everybody. Yet they make it sound defiant and majestic and real and sloppy—like that gloriously messy band he dreamed up twenty-four years ago.

Then, as the din dies down and the band starts to leave the stage, Patterson sends us out into the chilly night with a hearty "See you next year, fuckers!"

Birmingham, Alabama

▼

Vulcan is the god of the forge and the fire, craftsman of weapons for the Roman gods, but in Birmingham he is also the god of indignities. Eons after his mother, Juno, was so disgusted with her ugly newborn that she threw him out of heaven, Vulcan was chosen to represent the largest city in Alabama—specifically its booming iron and steel industry—at the 1904 World's Fair in St. Louis. An Italian immigrant named Giuseppe Moretti designed the statue, which stands fifty-six feet tall and shows the disgraced god hard at work: he stands nearly naked at the forge, wearing only an apron and sandals, a hammer resting in his left hand and his right holding up an arrow, which he eyeballs to ensure it is straight and true. Despite the fact that his bearded head is awkwardly out of proportion with his body, Vulcan made such an impression at the World's Fair that the New York–based Moretti became a celebrity down South.

After his original function had been fulfilled, nobody knew what to do with poor Vulcan. He lay disassembled for several years, enormous head removed from his body, but was eventually erected at the Alabama State Fairgrounds. Reportedly, workmen attached his limbs backwards before realizing their mistake. He became something like a billboard, his newly forged arrow replaced first with a giant Heinz pickle and later with a bottle of Coca-Cola. At one point he was stitched into an enormous pair of blue jeans to cover his exposed legs and ass.

It wasn't until the late 1930s, as Birmingham was recovering from the Great Depression and its foundries were glowing bright and hot again, that Vulcan was finally moved to the city as part of Roosevelt's WPA program, which local businessmen vehemently opposed. He was reassembled on the crest of Red Mountain, so named for the vivid rust-crimson hue of its hematite ore, and placed atop a large pedestal that gave him an unimpeded view of the city. Very quickly he became Alabama's most famous landmark, an odd civic presence but a distinctive and eventually beloved addition to the skyline. A decade later, Vulcan was drafted into service as a gigantic traffic cop, trading his arrow for a lamp that local historian Diane McWhorter has likened to "a radioactive popsicle." The thing changed color based on the conditions of local highways: red if there had been a traffic fatality that day, green if no one had died on the roads.

There he stood for fifty more years, his two-inch-thick cast-iron skin rusting in the elements and his apron clinging tight to his classically defined body. Because he faced north toward the city, the suburb of Homewood was granted a clear view of his bare backside, the joke being that there were two moons over the city. When a regrettable new lighting setup inadvertently spotlit the god's goods in the early 1980s, a local radio DJ penned a short ditty called "Moon over Homewood" and released it as a hokey country single credited to Chick Churn and the Chillydippers. "Moon over Homewood, we don't think it's fair," they sing in rough harmony, "that we have to look at his big derriere."

In his silent and stoic response to such indignities, Vulcan became sympathetic, a benevolent god halfway back to heaven high up on that hill. But what he saw before him more often resembled hell. Red Mountain, his home, serves as a massive racial divide in Birmingham: in the decades since white flight sent many well-off families scrambling out into the suburbs mostly to the south, the mountain has separated them from the working-class whites and nearly all the Black residents still inhabiting the inner city and its northern fringes. That made downtown off-limits in the minds of many generations of white Alabamans, unless you worked in an office or had a commute that took you over the mountain. The city emptied out after the workday was done. I remember my father telling me that they rolled up the sidewalks in Birmingham at night, and I always wanted to see that.

Vulcan has largely escaped any association with the racial violence the city became known for, despite that violence being bound up in the industry he represented. Birmingham prospered as an industrial capital largely because it sat in one of the few places in the world where all three main ingredients needed to make steel—iron ore, coal, and lime—were right there in the ground. The ore was mined in the surrounding hills and shipped to foundries in the city, including Sloss Furnaces, the most famous and last standing. Along with that ore came thousands of laborers from the countryside to the city, bringing with them some of their old rural prejudices. But those underlying resentments were stoked by mining companies to pit white and Black laborers against each other. It was a strategic offense that prevented workers from organizing and unionizing.

That's probably not what Mike Cooley had in mind when he wrote "Where the Devil Don't Stay," one of the Truckers' heaviest songs, about a moonshiner in Alabama back in the '30s. But that's what comes to my mind whenever I hear him sing about a time "before blacks and whites went and chose up sides and gave a little bit of both their way." The songwriter is fascinated by these divides—not just Black and white, but rural and urban. "That's one of the things I learned when I started traveling. No matter where you go, urban is urban and rural is rural. Why are the values so different depending on how much concrete is laying around? It's like two different planets. That's really where the politics divide all the way around. It's just as true in the Bible Belt as it is on the liberal West Coast."

As the civil rights movement chipped away at the Jim Crow laws that had made Black Americans something akin to second- and third-class citizens, Birmingham grew incredibly violent, eventually earning the grim nickname Bombingham. White terrorists loved their dynamite because it was as anonymous as it was destructive. A more apt word might be *cowardly*. One of their favorite targets was a neighborhood that came to be known as Dynamite Hill, built on land that had once been a dump but had been transformed into a latticework of streets lined with nice brick homes owned by Black families. That a Black man might own such a fine home incensed poor whites, to the point where explosions became weekly occurrences. It should go without saying that almost none of these crimes were ever solved or prosecuted. On Christmas Day, 1956, sixteen sticks of dynamite took off the wall of a house belonging to the

Reverend Fred Shuttlesworth, who just happened to be sleeping a few feet away from the bomb. Somehow, he survived with minor injuries and a steadier resolve to fight. He was already a civil rights leader, but four more failed assassination attempts turned him into a folk hero.

Vulcan saw every explosion, watched countless Klan rallies in the city's halls and streets. He watched the peaceful demonstrations that were organized at the Sixteenth Street Baptist Church and launched at Kelly Ingram Park just across the street. Vulcan watched as bigots burned the buses that drove freedom riders into town, then beat the freedom riders, then assaulted onlookers and passersby. Vulcan watched when Black children and teenagers skipped school to march in their parents' place, believing they would face less danger, and Vulcan watched when Eugene "Bull" Connor, a local despot and the city's commissioner of public safety, ordered white police officers and firemen to sic the dogs and turn the firehoses on those Black children. Vulcan watched when Martin Luther King Jr. arrived to bring more national attention to the local crisis, and Vulcan could not turn away that Sunday morning in September 1963 when a bomb went off in the basement of the Sixteenth Street Baptist Church and killed four Black girls: Addie Mae Collins (age fourteen), Cynthia Wesley (fourteen), Carole Robertson (fourteen), and Carol Denise McNair (eleven).

Vulcan was still watching when a white bigot named Robert Chambliss—known to friends as Dynamite Bob—was convicted for their murder in 1977. However, by the time his accomplices were tried in the early 2000s, Vulcan had been removed and disassembled, shipped away to clear seventy years of the city's grime and rust. Doug Jones was the district attorney who brought the bombers to trial and convicted them, yet fifteen years later the Democrat still had to fight to win a congressional seat against a Trump Republican accused of child molestation. The Truckers played benefit shows for Jones in 2018 and again in 2020, when he lost to a former college football coach exhibiting very little knowledge of or interest in state or federal governance.

For a small-town kid like me, whose family made several trips to Birmingham to visit grandparents, aunts, uncles, and cousins, seeing Vulcan from the window of our minivan always seemed magical. Dramatically framed by mountains—or what passes in the South for mountains—downtown appeared so big, so exotic, touched with a kind of glamour that was missing where I grew up. As my father maneuvered the tangle of overpasses that would take us over the mountain and to my Uncle Maloy's flower shop in Mountain Brook or to my Grandmother Love's house in Homewood, I kept a keen eye out to see what color Vulcan's torch was that day, which I would announce to my parents and brothers. I had no idea what all that sad god had seen from all the way up there. Later, when I learned to drive and could be trusted to make the trip by myself—stereo always blaring, speed limit dutifully ignored—I told myself that I wouldn't be the one to turn Vulcan's torch red that day. He was a reminder that death was always nearby.

Birmingham wasn't really magical to Patterson. He'd driven through it enough times on his way to and from gigs, back to the Shoals or off to Athens or down to Auburn or occasionally even over to Tuscaloosa. Long before he joined the Truckers, Patterson had passed through the city so often that he'd almost stopped noticing Vulcan up there on the mountain, or really any other local landmark. Back in his Adam's House Cat days, he, Cooley, Chuck Tremblay, and whoever was playing bass would drive the two hours south to play the Nick countless times. For a while they had a weekly gig at the small venue, which had been a B'ham's Finest Qwik Mart until it was converted into a rock club. Originally called the Wooden Nickel, it was shortened to the Nick in 1981 and was eventually dubbed "Birmingham's dirty little secret" by none other than Bono. It's one of those places that has accrued random bric-a-brac over the years: a giant American flag rescued from a car dealership, several generations' worth of black-and-white promotional photos from bands both legendary and obscure, and the like.

The Nick is one of the few small venues to survive so long in Birmingham, not because it adapted to the times but more because it doesn't bother to adapt. Located in the shadow of the Red Mountain Expressway in a neighborhood that doesn't look like it would tolerate a loud rock club, "it's not one of those places that has updated into some slicked-up version of itself," says Cooley. "It's still got exactly the same things now as when we played there. Smells exactly the same. When they drop the atomic bomb, the Nick will still be standing. In fact, if you're in there, you'll probably be just fine."

It is, in other words, the platonic ideal of a rock club, although

Patterson doesn't have especially fond memories of his former band's unofficial residency in the late 1980s: "It was always on a Monday night, and nobody would be there," he says. "And it would always rain." Cooley's memories aren't any rosier. "We opened for a few bands on weekends, but most of the time we'd drive down there, play on a weeknight, make ten bucks for gas to get back home. Of course, at the Nick, even if there are people there, they're all regulars and they're not charging them cover to get in. You might get your one-hundred-dollar guarantee, but they would charge you for your beer tab. Nobody's getting free beer."

One night in July 1989 they played to a particularly unenthused audience that hardly bothered to acknowledge them, which made for a long and lousy show. Only after they left the stage did the members of Adam's House Cat learn that there had been a murder the night before. A man had been shot trying to recover his friend's stolen purse, and he had staggered into the Nick's parking lot and died. As of this writing, the case remains unsolved. "We didn't even know about it until after the show," says Patterson. "We just thought the vibe was really weird that night. Then I found out about the murder and I wrote a song about it." It was a low-down bluesy number with a midtempo chug, but Patterson was never quite happy with it. So he stowed it away for more than a decade. It would come in handy while they were recording their breakout album.

And yet, their run of shows at the Nick tightened them up as a band and put them in front of occasionally hostile audiences that had to be won over. It was their trial by fire. And even though the Truckers outgrew the Nick, they still consider it something like home base, or at least a beloved old haunt. They recorded most of the album *Alabama Ass Whuppin'* in 1999 underneath all those glossy photos. More recently, following shows at larger venues around town, some of the Truckers will still repair to the Nick to play more music or just hang out with old friends. In November 2018, after a three-night stand at Saturn that coincided with the midterm elections, multi-instrumentalist Jay Gonzalez did a short set of covers and originals at the Nick, and Patterson joined him for a rousing version of Todd Rundgren's "Hello It's Me" ("one of my all-time favorite songs," says Patterson).

Similarly, even after Adam's House Cat broke up and they all moved away from the Shoals, Birmingham remained central to the Truckers, primarily because it sits right in the middle of all of those places. You can get from the Shoals to Athens by other routes, but the quickest and easiest way is to drive south for two hours and take a left when you see Vulcan. Birmingham is on the way to everywhere in Alabama. Plus, Patterson was dating a girl from Auburn, so they would meet up in Birmingham and shack up for a weekend. One night they broke into Vulcan Park for a tryst under the god's torch. Patterson recalls, "At the time, Vulcan was falling apart. They eventually had to take the torch down, because parts of it were falling off. It was in bad shape back then."

Not even a month after he'd moved to Athens in 1994, his old friend Earl Hicks from back home moved in with him, and the two rented a U-Haul to carry their stuff to their new apartment. Driving a route similar to the one in *Smokey and the Bandit*, they shot the shit, trying to entertain each other in a truck without a tape deck and a speed governor that wouldn't let them exceed fifty-five miles per hour. They talked enough that the conversation turned to Lynyrd Skynyrd, the notorious southern rock band that didn't survive the 1970s. They devised an idea to write a screenplay about the band, a somewhat fictionalized treatment that would draw from fact and from fabrication equally, that would pay as much heed to the legends surrounding them as to the actual truth of their lives and careers. After all, more people knew the lore than knew what they were actually about. "I had all these Skynyrd stories because of growing up the way I did," says Patterson. "I knew the inside shit on the band and the funny shit, but I didn't want to write a book about them because then you'd have to deal with Skynyrd, and they seemed like terrible people at the time. They were all fighting with each other and suing each other." A screenplay somehow felt like the more feasible option.

By the time they hit Birmingham, they were on a roll. Either Earl or Patterson pointed out Vulcan high on the mountaintop, and they devised a movie poster for their screenplay, one showing the Roman god with a Flying V guitar strapped across its shoulder. That instrument transformed the statue: what was a beacon for local drivers became instead Pete Townshend mid-windmill, poised for a colossal power chord that would shake the city and reverberate outward. Instead of iron and steel, it was heavy metal.

That's exactly the kind of harebrained scheme that comes from long road trips with insufficient soundtracks, and it does seem like one of those things people go on about and promise to see through to completion and then quickly forget all about. But Patterson and Hicks recognized something meaningful and maybe even important in this idea. Back in Athens with the U-Haul unloaded, Patterson wrote an outline for it and proceeded to talk about it for the next seven years. "Every floor we slept on involved us telling some poor soul at his apartment this crazy thing we were working on," says Patterson. "We'd see what people responded to. We'd watch their eyes glaze over, like they're thinking, *What the fuck are these crazy rednecks talking about?* We talked about it all the time, and that was part of our way of willing it into existence. If we talked about it, we had to deliver it, or else we talked a bunch of shit. And I really hate shit-talkers who don't back it up."

The idea grew more feral the more they daydreamed, blue-skied, and bullshitted, and eventually it mutated from a screenplay to a standalone concept album. "We weren't even going to call it a Drive-By Trucker record," says Patterson. "It was going to be its own thing. It was like a side project." But the kernel of the idea remained intact: a retelling of the Skynyrd story as southern mythology, mixing in their own personal reminiscences of growing up in the South and aspiring to rock stardom. And they came up with a title for the project: *Betamax Guillotine*. It was based on the legend that Ronnie Van Zant had been decapitated by a videocassette player that had been installed incorrectly in the plane that crashed. Fortunately, they abandoned it for the catchier and much more straightforward *Southern Rock Opera*, because that's what they had been calling it all along—the rock opera, the southern rock opera. (And most of the band members, including Isbell, still add the definitive article to the title.)

All along they knew it was ridiculous—not stupid, not pretentious, but wildly, even comically ambitious and so preposterous in the scope of its storytelling, songwriting, sequencing, package design, and funding that it becomes in its own way glorious.

To do it right, however, they understood that they had to grow into the kind of band that could deliver on that extravagance, whose chops matched the concept, whose resources matched their dreams. It seemed to take forever—during which they toured far and wide, played hundreds of rock shows, worked grueling day jobs, recorded two studio albums (one of them nowhere near a studio) and one barnstorming live album—and eventually it led them back to Birmingham. The city emerged as a crucial part of the story they were telling: the site of so much racial violence that it became a villain, a grim emblem of everything that was wrong with the South.

One night very early in the writing process, Patterson found himself alone at home in the haunted house he shared with his wife in Athens. She was working the late shift, and he was sitting around smoking a little dope and thinking about the rock opera. He and Cooley had already written several key songs for the double album, but he knew something was missing, something crucial that would tie everything together and give the thing a bit more gravity. He got to thinking about George Wallace, the opportunistic Alabama governor who essentially ruled the state from the early 1960s until the late 1980s. Wallace had run for president in the 1970s, survived an assassination attempt that left him without the use of his legs, and symbolized a very backward idea of the South at a time when the region was supposed to be redefining itself. Patterson hated seeing that old footage whenever he turned on the TV: Wallace bloviating about segregation now, segregation tomorrow, segregation forever and facing down the National Guard in a theatrical attempt to thwart the integration of the University of Alabama.

So he decided to write a song about Wallace arriving in hell, where he knew the old bastard would end up. He might have left office with a weirdly progressive record and one of the most integrated state governments in the country, but he got there by appealing to the worst in white Alabamans. So Wallace burns for eternity for his political opportunism that still mars the South today. "I wrote the song from the devil's point of view, and it went super quick—maybe twenty minutes—and I thought, *Man, this is part of the rock opera.*" Simply titled "Wallace," it's a gleeful comeuppance as Old Scratch gets out the fine china and prepares to welcome his new guest with all the southern hospitality a devil can muster. "If it's true that he wasn't a racist and he just did all them things for the votes," goes one particularly damning verse, "I guess Hell's just the place for kiss-ass politicians who pander to assholes." In other words, Wallace isn't lonely down there.

"My head was spinning in that direction, so I immediately wrote 'Let There Be Rock,'" Patterson says. It's hard to imagine a song more different from "Wallace": Patterson's second song of the night is an unabashed rock-saved-my-life anthem, a volley of lighter-raising riffs and shout-along choruses, a survey of ticket stubs for Ozzy, Molly Hatchet,

Blue Öyster Cult, and AC/DC but not, of course, Skynyrd shows. "I had the end of the first act with 'Wallace' and the beginning of the second act with 'Let There Be Rock,' so [I thought] I should just go ahead and write an ending. So I wrote 'Angels and Fuselage.' It probably didn't take three hours to write all three." That may sound like a boast, especially considering that he knew exactly where they would fall on the album, but he'd been writing concept albums since he was a teenager. "I knew how to create a narrative and when to veer off of it, all that stuff. Writing those songs put me back in touch with part of my youth, which was a theme of the record."

The Truckers took their first stab at making *Southern Rock Opera* in Dave Schools's basement studio in Athens, where the Widespread bassist and Truckers benefactor manned the boards for the sessions. Because Rob Malone had switched over to guitar, the band was short a bass player, so Schools sat in as one half of the rhythm section. Like many in the Truckers' circle, he was bemused by the idea of a rock opera recounting the Skynyrd story, although he admits he took it a bit too literally. "I was trying to get Patterson to listen to things like *Jesus Christ Superstar*," says Schools, suggesting a direction the Truckers most definitely did not take. "I was telling him about all this Broadway stuff where there's a specific template woven throughout all of the songs, certain characters that reappear, and there's always an overture. I thought it would be really different and cool to incorporate some of that stuff. But Patterson wisely changed his game plan and decided to put out that live album and establish themselves as a kickass live band. I don't think my idea would have landed with the same raw impact."

Schools was entering what he refers to as a "fog," so his disappointment over the direction of *Southern Rock Opera* didn't last very long. And the band emerged with a collection of rough demos rather than a completed album. "We didn't consider any of that to be working on the album per se as much as it was just getting a rough sketch to see where we were," says Patterson. "A lot of it wasn't even written. We weren't there yet. We were trying hard, though. I had to relearn how to play and to sing in order to play and to sing those songs. We were still a work in progress."

In March 2000 the band was still at each other's throats, but they managed to get their shit together and drive west to Auburn, where their old friend John "Pudd" Sharp lived. A native of Decatur, Alabama, just fifty miles east of the Shoals, he had until recently played in a band called the Quadrajets, who specialized in loud, raucous rock and roll with just enough twang to qualify as alt-country. Patterson had run sound for them back at the High Hat, and the two bands had played a handful of shows together, each upping the ante for the other. "The Truckers are a fun, partying kind of band, and the Quadrajets were, too," says Pudd. "We tickled that gene in each other." More than that, though, he appreciated their songwriting, how they reflected a corner of the South that he recognized as his own: "All of the people in their songs are people you already know from somewhere. The band channeled all this stuff that rubs against your own experience somehow, and they figured out how to put it and be funny and smart and eloquent."

When the Truckers asked Pudd to record some songs for the weird album they had mentioned, he jumped at the opportunity. The Quadrajets had disbanded, and Pudd says, "I wasn't ready to hang up my spurs just yet. I offered them my house in Auburn. I was living in a huge farmhouse from the 1840s or '50s. It had high-ceiling rooms, so it sounded good. I had a roommate, but I could run her off for a while. It was low cost, low impact, and everybody stayed at the house." He even agreed to play bass for them, learning the songs from the tapes from Schools's basement. Earle Hicks came along to engineer the sessions.

They had come a long way with the album, and when they set up at Pudd's place on Bragg Avenue—which he claims was inhabited by ghosts, which makes two haunted houses in this story—they all believed they were at long last recording the rock opera for real this time. They had added some important songs, filled in some glaring holes, and sequenced everything in a way that made sense. Just the week before, Patterson had written "Ronnie and Neil," which not only explored the supposed rivalry between Skynyrd front man Ronnie Van Zant and "rock star from Canada" Neil Young but also introduced the Shoals as the racial antithesis of Birmingham. "Church blows up in Birmingham," Patterson sings, referring to the Sixteenth Street Baptist Church bombing in 1963. "Four little black girls killed, for no goddamn good reason." He's a poet with expletives and finds catharsis in vulgarity, but that "goddamn" may be his most impactful lyric to date—a word that underscores the ungodliness of the violence, how it runs counter to the Christian faith of so many southerners. By comparison, the Shoals is a model of racial cooperation where Black and white musicians create sweet soul music together. "Ronnie and Neil" was sequenced early on the first side for maximum impact.

Yet the longer they stayed in Auburn, the more they realized—with no small amount of frustration—that they still weren't quite there. The recordings, according to Pudd, didn't sound terribly different from the final version of the album; it was more like they hadn't quite pushed the concept far enough or ironed out their own differences. They didn't leave their squabbles and resentments back in Athens, but packed them as carefully as they did their gear. "We were still fighting and bickering and still being assholes to each other," says Patterson. "At Pudd's house Cooley threw an entire glass of whiskey at me, and it smashed on the wall right next to my head. Whiskey went everywhere, including on one of the recorders. Earl was pissed. It was an ugly two weekends."

For his part, Pudd did his best to stay out of it. Working all day at the local Home Depot and recording this band of rowdies all night, he strategically played the role of peacemaker, which along with his bass chops may explain why they asked him to officially join the Truckers. It was a tempting offer, as he was still jonesing to play a good rock show. But his girlfriend had been accepted into a graduate program in Lafayette, Louisiana, and he felt he needed to follow her. "To be honest, it was the way things were going with those guys," he says. "Everyone was having their relationships fall apart. I understood what they were going through. I remember being on tour, all the calling cards, the phone conversations in the middle of the night. But things seemed especially rough for them. I thought, *You know what? I'm just going to get a job.*" (Pudd married his girlfriend and still lives in Lafayette, where he works at the Archive of Cajun and Creole Folklore, a division of the Center for Louisiana Studies.)

Patterson calls him a soulmate member of the band. "He was the sanest, most got-his-shit-together, badass motherfucker ever. Still is. I think we understood that he was making the right decision, because we knew we were all batshit crazy. I can't even begin to describe the level of dysfunction in our band at that time. But Pudd was the antithesis of all that. I remember thinking, *I don't blame you, dude. Wish I had someone worth moving away for.*"

The Truckers still weren't ready six months later, when they set up a makeshift studio at a uniform factory in downtown Birmingham, but damnit, they were as ready as they were ever gonna get. The situation was becoming more discouraging by the day, and the band felt like it was a do-or-die moment: if they couldn't make this album they had been talking about for years, then they couldn't survive as a band—they should all probably sell their guitars and find real jobs. Cooley's in-laws owned the warehouse and gave the band the run of the top floor for two weeks, the one condition being that they could record only at night. This wasn't an abandoned urban space; not only was the building still in use, but it was actually pretty busy during the day. "We'd go in at six in the evening," Patterson recalls, "and we'd be there until six in the morning. It was creepy as shit down there." Downtown Birmingham can empty out at night, which made the Truckers feel like they had the city to themselves.

Just a block or so away from the warehouse was the headquarters of the *Birmingham Post-Herald*, which thirty years before had been the old stomping grounds of their friend Dick Cooper, who'd taken on the role of mentor, tour manager, producer, and sounding board for the band. The Decatur native had worked there as a reporter while in college, then bounced around the country from one paper to another before landing in the Shoals as a photojournalist. He fell in love with the music scene after attending a session at FAME, which inspired him to leave his profession. In the late 1970s he managed the tours for the local duo LeBlanc and Carr, which featured songwriter Lenny LeBlanc and session guitarist Pete Carr. They were enjoying a hit with the soft-country love song "Falling" and opened for Lynyrd Skynyrd on that band's final tour. In fact, Cooper even came close to boarding Skynyrd's doomed Convair turbo prop in Greenville, South Carolina, which would have put him on board when it crashed near Gillsburg, Mississippi. A decade later he worked as the tour manager for Skynyrd's guitarist, Gary Rossington, who was doing solo sets opening for his own band's reunion tour.

"Dick had a ground-floor, front-row seat at all of these different events that happened surrounding the record we were making," says Patterson. "He made sure we got our facts straight on *Southern Rock Opera*. I didn't want to say anything about George Wallace and have it come back to bite me on the ass for being wrong. He was the only outsider who was there for the whole recording. Dick was there the entire two weeks."

It was a hot two weeks. Birmingham in the summer of 2000 was suffering through a withering heat wave, which seemed to melt the asphalt underfoot and made the air feel like warm water against the skin. By summer's end, Lake Purdy, one of the city's main reservoirs, had dried up almost completely. And temperatures stayed high well into September, at times exceeding one hundred degrees. That the Truckers were recording at night didn't help matters very much; the heat and humidity clung to the city even after the sun went down. The warehouse trapped it all, creating a hell that seemed just as brutal as the one Patterson writes about in "Wallace." "We couldn't even turn on a fan, because you could hear it in the microphones," says Patterson. "So we would close the windows, turn the fans off, and record until we were all drenched in sweat and couldn't take it anymore. Then we'd open the windows up again, turn the fans back on, air it out for a little while, and drink for a while. Then we'd close 'em and do it all again. We'd do that all night, every night."

For reasons both logistical and aesthetic, the band did mostly first takes. "Make it rough and leave it loose" was the mantra, as Rob Malone recalls. "It's kind of the Neil Young approach. Rough and ready. Just play it. The feel is the main thing. I don't know if nobody had the patience or they just didn't want it to be too perfect. You gotta admit, the whole perfection thing does take the soul out of a lot of stuff."

Like Skynyrd, the Truckers tend to thrive on a certain type of adversity, so in a way they were right at home. It was miserable, but it steeled their nerve and buttressed their collective mission to make a kickass rock-and-roll record. Even their own resentments toward each other seemed to wilt in the heat, at least for a little while. So it didn't matter too much that they were still working things out as they were recording or that Patterson was still writing songs. It helped that Earl Hicks had officially joined the band as the bass player after Rob Malone had switched to guitar. For years Hicks had occupied a strange place both in the band and not, joining them onstage every now and then but mostly working behind the scenes to record and produce *Pizza Deliverance* and *Alabama Ass Whuppin'*. Now he was doing double duty, which seemed to suit him just fine.

The nagging sense that something was missing carried over from their first two sessions, but this time Patterson had a better idea how to proceed. For one thing, he says, "there needed to be a song that illustrates how no two Southerners agree on what the *Southern thing* actually is. That was the idea, and I knew it needed to be a rocker and it needed to have a really bitchin' guitar riff. So we took one of those breaks where we opened the windows and turned the fans on, and I smoked a doobie and wrote 'The Southern Thing.'" That song became the lynchpin of the album and far and away its most quoted song: the source of "the duality of the Southern thing" that is still routinely included in reviews, profiles, academic papers, and books about the South. Drawing from his own views about his homeland as well as his family's history—including an ancestor who took up arms against the Union after northern troops occupied his farm—he wrote the song in not much more time than it takes to play it.

But there was something else bothering him. The city where they were finally recording the album, the city where they finally felt like they had become the band that *could* record the album, had assumed the role of the villain on what they were now calling *Southern Rock Opera*. And in some important ways, Birmingham did represent something dark and evil about the South, especially on "Ronnie and Neil," which implicates every southerner in the violence that once defined the city: "A whole lot of good people dragged through the blood and glass, blood stains on their good names, and all of us take the blame." We all bear the burden and guilt of that violence.

Was there a need to complicate that story, to show the city in the present as well as in the past? Patterson thought so. "You know, I'm bad-mouthing Birmingham at every turn. The city had become the villain in the story, but Birmingham was actually pretty cool in 2000, and there needed to be a song about that." Rather than write another song whole cloth, he remembered the one he wrote for Adam's House Cat about a murder at the Nick. It was more than ten years old, but it could quickly be updated to show this side of Birmingham, to emphasize the duality of the city with its ugly past but promising future. The bombings had stopped, the lunch counters opened up, and city and county institutions were no longer being used as bludgeons against the city's Black residents, as they had been during Bull Connor's era. There was still prejudice and resentment, still an imbalance of money and power and opportunity between the races, but Birmingham had managed to shed its identity as the most violently segregated city in America—or so it appeared to Patterson.

Recorded almost immediately after he wrote it, "Birmingham" opens tentatively, with a four-note false start and a stuttering drumbeat. Arriving midway through the first disc, it sounds like a throat clearing, as though announcing a break between acts. Once the song gets going, however, it doesn't sound much like a celebration of the city's revitalization, especially with Patterson singing about economic despair in the first verse and fictionalizing the Nick murder in the second. But the final verse subtly shifts toward a city that he wants to believe is overcoming its own worst impulses: "Vulcan Park has seen its share of troubled times, but the city won't admit defeat," he sings. "Magic City's magic getting stronger, Dynamite Hill ain't on fire any longer." But the Truckers include no big guitar solo and do not build to a cathartic climax, like they do on other songs. Birmingham hasn't earned its lighters and fist pumps just yet.

"Birmingham" isn't merely a toast to the town, but a song that gestures to an artist the Truckers have long admired and an album they refer to as the "original southern rock opera." Randy Newman and his 1974 story-album *Good Old Boys* exert an even greater influence on Patterson and Cooley than Skynyrd does, providing proof for them that all the dualities they had seen in the South could be confronted and expressed and maybe even partially unknotted in rock songs. Newman conceived and wrote *Good Old Boys* as a stage production and then reassembled it as a suite of ragtime and jazz songs. It opens in Vulcan Park, as a deeply bigoted steelworker named Johnny Cutler surveys the city sprawling at the foot of Red Mountain. Grumbling over the indignities he and other white racists face in a South that seems to be changing faster than he can process, Johnny contemplates where he belongs in this place but also where Black men and women belong. Mostly in cages, he concludes. Not just here in Birmingham, either: "He's free to be put in a cage in Hough in Cleveland . . . and he's free to be put in a cage in East St. Louis . . . and he's free to be put in a cage in Roxbury in Boston." Those are all historically Black neighborhoods, the implication being that America naturally segregates its Black citizens into their own neighborhoods, far away from the whites.

Rather than abandon such a foul character, Newman follows Johnny through several more songs, and he becomes a useful tool for deflating the popular image of the southern man in the early 1970s as virile, wily, street- but not booksmart, and completely unaffected by feminism or civil rights: the white man in his precivilized state. The joke is that Johnny grows more pitiful with each song, a man adrift and unfulfilled who understands only vaguely that the world has less and less use for him. On the song "Birmingham" he declares that this is "the greatest city in Alabam'" and that "you can travel 'cross this entire land, but there ain't no place like Birmingham." Presumably what endears the city to the character is how it has long separated Black folks from white, how it has absorbed that racism into its culture, and how that gives Cutler a group of people against whom he can define himself and to whom he can feel superior. That gives a touch of menace to the final verse about his "big black dog" named Dan, "the meanest dog in Alabam'." When Cutler says, "Sic 'em, Dan," even the dimmest listener doesn't have to think too hard about who Dan is about to sink his teeth into.

By contrast, the Truckers' depiction of Birmingham is much more hopeful and welcoming. "No man should ever have to feel he don't belong in Birmingham," Patterson sings toward the end, drawing out the syllables in the city's name. It sounds like a direct refutation of so much ugly history, tying the city's fortunes to its spirit of inclusion and equality rather than to its legacy of violence and white supremacy. But it's that *should* that sticks in your gullet, because it's Patterson suggesting that Birmingham isn't there yet. The city has come far, but it still has far to go.

While the Truckers were recording *Southern Rock Opera* in that hot warehouse downtown, Vulcan was not at his post. The Roman giant had been removed from his perch in 1999, largely for safety reasons, and he lay dismantled while the city raised funds to rehabilitate him. He was in bad shape, his skin pocked with rust and cracks. At one point in his life, someone had the brilliant idea to fill the hollow statue with concrete, believing it would stabilize and strengthen the structure. But concrete expands, and Vulcan was in danger of being torn apart from the inside out. The idea was to repair the poor thing and upgrade Vulcan Park into one of the city's nicest attractions—definitely not a place for late-night hookups.

He suffered additional indignities, though. When Birmingham applied for $3 million in federal funds to repair him, Arizona Senator John McCain used him as a symbol of errant government spending and misplaced fiscal priorities. "While the federal surplus is rapidly dwindling, why should federal dollars pay for a facelift of a Roman god in Alabama?" he lectured his fellow congressmen on the Senate floor. "I ask my colleagues to extinguish this Roman god of fire and strike a victory for taxpayers—and Metis, the goddess of prudence—by throttling down our insatiable appetite for pork-barrel spending." His bill blocking funding for Vulcan and similar projects, pagan and otherwise, was soundly defeated, although the US government kicked in only a third of the requested funds.

The fortunes of Birmingham often follow the fate of Vulcan, which made the early years of the twenty-first century a pivotal moment for both. Despite the fact that two of the city's biggest companies—McWane Inc. and HealthSouth—were both facing serious corruption charges, downtown was starting to get busier as new generations of Alabamans made their way over the mountain and small-business entrepreneurs converted old buildings for new uses. Breweries like Good People and Avondale Brewing set up shop alongside new venues like the Bottle Tree and (much later) Saturn. Pepper Place, housed in the old Dr Pepper plant down on Second Avenue, began hosting a weekend farmer's market that draws people from all over the city, and the old Pizitz department store was transformed into a giant food court specializing in world cuisine. And the old sites of civil rights marches and meetings were given historic designations: Kelly Ingram Park is full of sculptures and memorials to the movement, including one by local artist Ronald McDowell depicting a police dog lunging at a Black man. The Civil Rights Heritage Trail allows visitors to follow in the footsteps of demonstrators and children, without the firehoses.

Of course, *revitalization* is often used as a softer synonym for gentrification. Some of these leaps forward have emptied out neighborhoods that have traditionally been working class or Black, pushing those residents farther out to the fringes and further disrupting any sense of community they might otherwise enjoy. In this regard Birmingham is no different from so many similar-size cities throughout the country that have seen their urban areas flourish with an influx of new businesses. But in other ways Birmingham has embraced its history and is attempting to turn itself into a site of Black triumph: a battleground where those who fought so hard for civil rights finally emerged victorious.

"This is not the Alabama I grew up in," Birmingham native and *Daily*

Show writer Roy Wood Jr. wrote for the *New York Times* after a visit in 2018. "On the surface a lot of things are the same. There is for sure still discrimination. But Alabama has been the site of so many losses that it's a place where you count the victories, no matter how small. Because they often point to something larger."

The Truckers had finally become the band that could do justice to *Southern Rock Opera*, but they still had a few songs to get down, a few parts left to track, and a few cracks to smooth over. For one thing, they still needed a Cassie Gaines, who had been one of Skynyrd's backup singers known collectively as the Honkettes. Years before, Patterson had called up his friend Kelly Hogan, a veteran of Atlanta's Redneck Underground whom he'd met running sound at the High Hat, and pitched the rock opera to her, specifically asking if she'd be willing to sing the part of Skynyrd's main Honkette. Gaines was a crucial part of Lynyrd Skynyrd, a character of almost Shakespearean complexity, having gained enough power in the band to recruit her brother Steve Gaines as a full-time guitar player. Both siblings died in the plane crash.

"Patterson called me up one day and said they were writing this crazy rock opera and wanted me to sing her part," Hogan recalled. "I said cool; then I hung up and thought, *That'll never happen. He's really stoned today.*" So she was a little surprised when he called her up again just a few years later and said they were ready for her closeup. Still with no real funds for a proper studio, they set her up in the back bedroom of Cooley's apartment, and set up the control room down the hall in the kitchen. "I went in and I remember there were PBRs everywhere, tall boys or even king cans! I imagined I was in a tube top with roach clip earrings while I was singing, and at one point I was thinking of Ronnie Van Zant and I went, 'Whooo!'"—you know how he'll throw one of those in every now and again. I didn't think they'd ever use it, but as soon as I did it, I could hear them all in the kitchen going wild."

Especially after two weeks at the warehouse, these piecemeal recording sessions were bringing the rock opera to life and easing some of the tensions within the band. But those old grudges continued to curdle just under the surface, and when they finally packed up and left that warehouse in Birmingham, all the old complaints came flooding back in. Patterson, now divorced from his second wife, doubled down and moved in with their manager, growing defensive about the relationship. When arguments among the band members got louder and more hostile, just shy of violent but on the way there, he decided to call it quits. He wrote his thoughts down on paper, penning an eight-page breakup letter addressed to his bandmates, not on the computer (he didn't even own one yet) but handwritten in a notebook, like a suicide note. He worked as diligently on that missive as he did on a Truckers song, taking several days to get everything just right. Mixing *Southern Rock Opera* was already stressful enough, given the disorganization of the tapes. "They were all in crazy order," he recalls. "After recording in Birmingham, we'd done some overdubs at Cooley's house. There were some technical glitches, and there was a whole tape of songs that the kickdrum had been erased from accidentally." David Barbe had his work cut out for him organizing and mixing the tracks, while Patterson's depression deepened under the mess that the album had become.

One night at Chase Park Transduction, Barbe's studio back in Athens, after all the other band members had gone home to mend fences with wives and girlfriends, and likely to curse his name, Patterson holed up in a dark corner to scribble away at his epic breakup letter. Barbe saw him, asked what he was doing, and proceeded to join Dave Schools in the very small club of people who have saved the Truckers from veering head-on into the ditch. "I ended up spilling my guts to him, and of course he's so fucking cool and levelheaded about it."

"What I recall," Barbe says, "is that as fucked up as their personal situation seemed at the time, I thought they were on the precipice of something really good happening to the band. Patterson was in his mid-thirties, supporting his rock-and-roll lifestyle by working a bunch of crappy jobs. He's about five years past the point when most people just give up. But he was still at it."

After considering the matter, Barbe offered Patterson a deal. "I told him he had some good points, but 'I tell you what, why don't you take that letter, fold it up, put it in a safe place, and let's finish the record. After it comes out, if you still feel this same way, you can give them the letter then. But let's focus on the job at hand.'" Patterson did as he was told and resolved himself to seeing the rock opera through its final stages.

"Years later," he says, "I found that letter and was mortified. So I burned it."

It wouldn't be the last time the Truckers would barely avoid disaster—in fact, even darker times were ahead—but for the moment the band simply went on, gradually healing and saying more words to each other each day (or, at the very least, fewer expletives). Brad Morgan was forced to re-record his kickdrum part for several songs, and let's take a minute to appreciate the tedium of that job: just playing the kickdrum where the kickdrum needs to go, with no other drums or instruments. But Morgan has always been the band's secret weapon, not only a rock-solid time-keeper but a dependable peacekeeper as well. "I've learned to listen and I've learned to read the room," he says. "Okay, somebody's annoying Cooley and he's about to explode. I can see that shit coming a mile away, so let's get that person away from him. I'm usually the most laid-back person, but I can take care of business if I need to."

Even at their most ragged, the rock opera served as the anchor that kept the band united by a common enemy: all the record companies that couldn't be bothered to release the damn thing. They had shopped it around to various labels—some small and regional, others larger and longer shots—but had no luck convincing any of them that this strange double album could find an audience and recoup any kind of money. But the Truckers were all steadfast in their belief that it needed to be different. It needed to be absurd, with lengthy liner notes and gnarly artwork by their Richmond friend Wes Freed. They envisioned a triple-gatefold cardboard slipcase like a miniature version of the double albums of the '70s. Vinyl seemed like a foolish daydream, but they were adamant that it at least had to be two CDs (no matter that it would all fit on one). Says Cooley, "It was like, *If we don't do it this way, if we just put all those songs on a CD with a standard booklet in a plastic piece-of-shit jewel case, then we're just going to be another of the thousands of indie bands that put something out that maybe gets a few good reviews and nobody else gives a damn about.* And we were fucking *right!* It's one of the only things I've ever been right about in my life."

So convinced were they, the Truckers ultimately decided that they would have to do it themselves. Only they understood what the project needed, so why put it in someone else's hands? Rather than search for a single benefactor, the band decided to divvy it up. Perhaps their greatest asset at the time was the far-flung community of fans brought together by their website and busy Yahoo forum, so they hatched a plan as outlandish as the album itself: they would sell shares of the rock opera as though it were a company, allowing their fans to invest in the product before it was released. What has since become a common practice was almost unheard of at the turn of the century. The Truckers Kickstarted ten years before Kickstarter took its first pledge.

And it was successful. The Truckers raised more than $20,000 from about a dozen donors, more than enough to press the CDs, print the elaborate packaging, hire a publicist, and even make a down payment on a new touring van. What they didn't do was redefine how independent music is funded, marketed, and distributed. "What we should have done is invent Kickstarter," says Patterson. "We should have patented that part of it and then made a billion dollars. Then all this rock-and-roll shit would be my side hustle. I'd fly to gigs in a Lear jet. But we didn't have that much vision yet."

Birmingham was my second home growing up, but I actually knew very little of the city. We lived in Selmer, Tennessee, but we would make the four-hour drive down to see my mother's family several times a year. For all the time I spent there, I rarely went downtown. Instead, we were headed to the suburbs: Homewood, Mountain Brook, Vestavia, Hoover.

It was Grandmother Love's home in Homewood, right off of Lakeshore Drive, that truly piqued my sense of wonder. A massive brick house set atop a steep drive, it was like no other place I'd ever been. My grandmother was a regal woman with a schoolteacher's demeanor, able to turn anything into a lesson, whether it was the proper way to hold a fork and knife or the right way to make a bed. Most nights I slept next to her in her big four-poster bed, and she told me stories about Brer Rabbit and Brer Bear and Brer Fox, tales about the briar patch and the tar baby, and I would laugh as she did a different voice for each character. She would exaggerate her own deep southern accent, dropping consonants and running words together in a different way for each animal. I thought she was making it all up on the spot just for me. Only later did I realize that these were Uncle Remus stories, told from the perspective of a wise old slave who sacrificed his newfound freedom to remain on the old plantation. He was the creation of a white journalist named Joel Chandler Harris, who based Remus on the old slaves he knew back in his hometown of Eatonton, Georgia. While somewhat progressive by the standards of his era, Harris's legacy is complicated by the paternalistic view he took toward newly freed slaves, helping to secure education and suffrage for them while making a fortune from a character who is happy to remain on the plantation and loyal to his white master. I didn't know this back then. I didn't know that Grandmother Love had heard these stories when she was growing up or that she had passed them along to her own children. I didn't understand the subtle ways they reasserted the subordinacy of Black folks and the supremacy of whites—and I'm still trying to grasp that today. I just thought they were funny.

I've thought long and hard about what to do with these particular memories and how to feel about hurtful stories told with so much warmth and affection for the listener. It's a dilemma I hear the Truckers working through, especially on *Southern Rock Opera* and especially on songs like "The Southern Thing" and "Birmingham." It's that duality, that contradiction that I think every southerner has a story about—or they ought to. Often I wonder how Grandmother Love might have responded to the idea that these stories were hurtful, because even then I understood that I was supposed to identify with these caricatures of Black folks. They delivered the lessons, and lessons were the most important thing to my grandmother: Outsmart your opponent. Brains count more than fists. Always say "ma'am" and "sir." Those memories remain vivid to me so many years later, all the more precious for being some of the few ones I have of her. She died of lung cancer when I was eight years old.

Around the time I learned about the highly complicated legacy of Joel Chandler Harris, I also learned about the history of Birmingham and realized that I knew actually very little about the city. I'd heard the ghost stories about Sloss Furnaces, which sat like the rusted skeleton of a dinosaur downtown. I'd heard my mother talk about participating in evacuation drills, where schoolchildren were piled in the cars of volunteers and driven thirty miles out of town—a rehearsal for the day when our Cold War enemies were expected to bomb Birmingham's steel plants. I'd heard stories about a safer, rosier past when you could go downtown, but rarely about why you didn't anymore. I'd been told that the suburbs had no inkling of what was happening downtown in '56 and '63. It dawned on me that the Black experience of Birmingham was very different from the white experience of the city, from my experience of it. In retrospect, after the installment of numerous statues, plaques, heritage walks, and museums, this seems obvious, but at the time it seemed profound.

It meant that this place couldn't exist on some mythological plane, the way we think of Faulkner's Yoknapatawpha County or T. R. Pearson's Neely, North Carolina, or Margaret Mitchell's Tara. Even the fiction written about this place—Anthony Grooms's *Bombingham*, for example, or Sena Jeter Naslund's *Four Spirits*—is grounded in, even suffocated by, real events. Everything is too public, too well documented now, so that we can't get lost in Birmingham anymore, at least not the way we can lose ourselves in the back hollers and deep woods of the rural South. These and other voices disrupt the privilege of nostalgia, obliviousness, and forgetting.

It's the same for the Truckers. Birmingham and "Birmingham" keep the rock opera's wilder flights of fancy grounded in the real world—a real *white* world. They rarely sing in the voice of Black characters or speak to that experience of the South, but not out of any lack of empathy or any dismissal of values other than their own. Rather, they understand that they lack the expertise to inhabit the voice of Black characters or speak to that experience because they have not lived close enough to it. What the Truckers do instead is constantly remind you that this other South exists, whether it's by adopting a "dumb" band name or singing about the Sixteenth Street Baptist Church bombing or just locking into a swampy Shoals groove.

The Truckers don't write about white redemption in the South either, which allows them to avoid the faceplants of songs like Brad Paisley and LL Cool J's "Accidental Racist" and movies like *Green Book*. Their white fans can't get *too* comfortable in these songs or in the reminiscences they might provoke, which means the music implicitly challenges them—*us*—to be better white citizens, to question our own privileges and to think beyond ourselves. That idea has grown more explicit as the band has moved away from the South as its primary subject and widened its scope to America writ large, when they're hanging Black Lives Matter signs onstage and singing about Trayvon Martin and Ramón Casiano. They're trying to hold us and themselves accountable.

Not everyone is up for such a challenge. Especially in response to the Truckers' more explicitly political songs of the 2010s, some fans made a show of breaking up with the band. There were staged mass walkouts

at a few shows, but hey, they still bought tickets. Posts on online forums and social media routinely disparage Patterson in particular, and
a telling sign of the sharpness of his critique is the way it offends the
sensibilities of those hoping for another Kid Rock. According to the
Atlanta-based zine *Stomp and Stammer*, which already had an unhealthy
reputation for confusing cultural criticism with alt-right provocation,
"While promoting ["What It Means"] Hood has been desperately—
almost pathologically—signaling his negrophilia to salivating left-wing
rock journos. Certainly, his recent political awakening will elicit hearty
high fives and fist bumps from the band's five black fans." It's true that
the Truckers' audience is largely white and politically left, but that language echoes the taunts of racists who target Black homes and bombed
Black churches.

To hell with 'em is the Truckers' usual response. "You take it with a
grain of salt," says Patterson. "It's brought out the worst in a lot of people, but I feel like far more people have been wholeheartedly accepting."
Aside from a few editorials in the *New York Times* or the *Bitter Southerner*,
they typically engage with their detractors only through music, particularly in songs like "Watching the Orange Clouds" (which contains a
pointed line about "boys too dumb to be proud"). But grievance culture
has become a favorite topic for Cooley, and he writes about it with an elo-
quence at odds with its ugliness. "What I've noticed with people is that
when you try to avoid certain topics or saying something that might set
them off, inevitably you do anyway, because once they consume enough
of this stuff"—meaning Fox News, alt-right forums, and other outlets
that prickle a sense of grievance in some white men—"everything sets
them off. Everything is evidence of something that's out to get them. It's
a mess out there."

Outside Gillsburg, Mississippi

▼

When Lynyrd Skynyrd's Convair turbo prop crashed in Amite County, Mississippi, on October 20, 1977, they were one of the biggest bands in the country and on their way to getting even bigger. Since their first rehearsal more than a decade earlier, they had crammed a lifetime into a short career full of ups and downs, triumphs and failures. In four years, they'd released five albums, all but one of them selling platinum. "Sweet Home Alabama" had been a number-eight hit in 1974 and was still in heavy rotation at radio stations. The band had stumbled with their 1976 release *Gimme Back My Bullets*, on which they ruminated on hit singles the way some rock stars sang about broken hearts and blowjobs, but then they hired a kid named Steve Gaines and rebounded with *Street Survivors*. It hit stores just three days before the plane crash.

There's so much about the crash that seems far-fetched, and you might not believe some of the details if you read them in a novel or saw them in a movie or heard them from your uncle over Thanksgiving dinner. But there they are. The title of their latest album took on a grim irony that was amplified by the cover art depicting the band standing amid flaming wreckage, and it included a song called "That Smell," written by front man Ronnie Van Zant about two bandmates who nearly got themselves killed pursuing their hedonistic rock-star dreams: "Whiskey bottles, brand new cars," goes the opening line. "Oak tree, you're in my way."

Even before they took off from Greenville, South Carolina, to fly to Baton Rouge, where they were scheduled to perform at Louisiana State University, most of the band members and their entourage were wary of the Convair's airworthiness, in particular the faulty fuel delivery system to the second engine. They had been renting the plane for less than a month, and after a bad scare flying into Greenville, they had decided this would be their final flight aboard the jalopy. Cassie Gaines, one of Skynyrd's Honkettes, went so far as to purchase a one-way ticket on a commercial airline, although she ultimately chose to fly with the rest of the band. They had to get down to a show and couldn't wait another day for repairs or replacements. Reportedly, Ronnie Van Zant just shrugged his shoulders. Or, as Mike Cooley puts it on *Southern Rock Opera*, he said, "Shut your mouth and get your ass on the plane."

These details have fed the kind of urban legends that typically stem from tragedies and elevate the dead to the realm of American myth, like Elvis Presley or Buddy Holly. The Truckers heard all the stories growing up. "These guys became southern martyrs after their plane crashed," says Cooley. "There was this legend that there was a Betamax machine on Lynyrd Skynyrd's plane. The legend goes that it went flying across the cabin while the plane was crashing and decapitated Ronnie Van Zant. But there's another legend that except for one small wound on his head, his body was perfectly intact. Which one is true, I don't know." The Drive-By Truckers' mission with *Southern Rock Opera* wasn't to parse fact from fabrication but to explore the nature of those legends, to figure out why Skynyrd became Southern martyrs and what that meant.

The site of that crash occupies an unusual place in this book. Neither Patterson nor Cooley nor any other member of the Truckers past or present has ever lived anywhere near the crash site, and the research they conducted for *Southern Rock Opera* didn't actually include a pilgrimage to Amite County. Similarly, Skynyrd had no real connection to the place either. It was on the way to where they were going; it was simply as far as they got. In fact, they crashed into a place with no real name. It was Mississippi, so far south there was debris in Louisiana. It was twenty miles southwest of McComb, a town of about ten thousand souls and the site of civil rights protests and KKK violence in the '60s. It was Amite County, but just a small corner of it. The closest road is some distance away, referred to even before the crash as Slaughterhouse Road.

It was about five miles outside a tiny unincorporated community called Gillsburg, but it wasn't *in* Gillsburg. The plane touched ground even farther out in the country, deep into bottomland clotted with underbrush, its soil so soft that chunks of wreckage were buried on impact, to be excavated years later as souvenirs for fans. This was a fine spot of nowhere, as good as any other place to go down. For years it was unmarked, hard to find. As of October 2019, however, a monument stands out on Highway 568: three columns of black granite with the names of the dead, about one thousand feet from the actual crash site. The spot looms large in Skynyrd lore—and therefore in Trucker lore—but not for any reason native to the place. It has no music scene aside from hymns sung in church and boasts no celebrities whatsoever (although nearby Kentwood, just over the border in Louisiana, is the hometown of Britney Spears). But that anonymity, along with the unfathomable pointlessness of the tragedy, creates a blank space in the saga of Lynyrd Skynyrd. It leaves room for rumor and hearsay to pool around the actual details and flood them out. The story always feels slightly unsettled, unfinished even, so that anybody can retell it to fit their own needs or even write themselves into it. The Truckers did both.

Southern Rock Opera begins with a very different kind of crash. It opens with a brief bit of noise and distortion, a voice barely audible and not quite intelligible, interrupted by a stab of heavy guitar that heralds the arrival of the full band. In a spoken-word delivery that highlights his North Alabama twang and his narrator's eye for grisly detail, Patterson relates the night his best friend and his best girl went out driving together. Bobby's got his lights off, reckless as ever, and, sure enough, the car goes off the road, colliding with a telephone pole and splitting in two. The next day—the day of his high school graduation—there are already rumors passing among their classmates: "Everyone said that when the ambulance came, the paramedics could hear 'Free Bird' still playing on the stereo. You know it's a very long song."

I heard variations of this story in high school, just an hour or so northwest of the Shoals. Whenever a local kid died in a car crash—which was strikingly often, come to think of it—there were rumors about the condition of the body, particularly the head. The cranium of a car crash fatality was always described as looking like a busted cantaloupe. When I heard these rural legends, however, it was always Led Zeppelin's "Stairway to Heaven" playing into the night. It's not quite as long as "Free Bird" but perhaps more thematically fitting to the final moments of a teenager's life in the '70s and '80s. Especially in a Christian community, that particular song made a certain kind of gruesome sense. If "Free Bird" is about leaving and being remembered, then "Stairway" is about learning where you'll be spending eternity.

Right at the start of *Southern Rock Opera*, "Free Bird" and Skynyrd are part of something fantastical, and the first half of the album toggles between the real South and a collectively imagined South. The Truckers are more than happy to blur the lines between those worlds, to treat the graduation day legend as gospel and reality as a rumor. As teenagers, they had perpetuated some of those very myths themselves. Patterson was only thirteen when that plane went down, and he associated Skynyrd and their music with the kids who bullied him in junior high but also with his dad's friends and colleagues, who had worked with the band when they came through the Shoals. He heard the stories they passed down, but he wouldn't come around to their sound until much later. In the meantime, he listened to R.E.M., a very different but no less southern group.

Cooley was only eleven and had no such associations. He'd just heard them on the radio and liked their faster songs, the ones grounded in blues and boogie. A few years later he bought their first live record, *One More from the Road* (1976), and "wore it out." It took him a while to get into "Free Bird," though, despite it being Skynyrd's signature song—the one that closed nearly every show, the one that showed off both the specificity of Van Zant's songwriting and the intensity of the band's jamming, the one whose title has been shouted at nearly every band that has taken a stage. "I didn't listen to it because it was slow. I didn't want to hear any slow shit. I had no idea about the ins and outs of the band. I was never a fan boy. I'm still not . . . of anything, actually. I resist it. But I kept hearing people talk about 'Free Bird.' It was such a big deal. So I finally listened to it."

That intro, with its flourishes of piano and its bed of organ that morphs as if by magic into Rossington's elegant guitar riff, still sounded like "slow shit" to the boy, but he endured. "I finally waited long enough for *that* to happen"—that being the moment at four minutes and forty seconds into the song when the music takes flight. The tempo jumps, the mood quickens, and the entire band gracefully glides into a propulsive jam, acting as a single organism to create one of the most galvanizing moments in rock music, albeit one that has lost some of its luster over the years thanks to its overfamiliarity. Young Cooley was finally hearing why the song is still played to death on classic rock radio and why its title is still shouted at Skynyrd, and more often non-Skynyrd, concerts. "I was jumping up and down on the bed, shouting, 'Fuck Yeah!' I finally saw what the big deal was. *Oh, that happens!*"

Those experiences fueled *Southern Rock Opera*. Skynyrd provided an easy daydream of stardom for a generation of young men growing up in the South, largely because there is nothing innately special about the band beyond its work ethic. They weren't David Bowie, disappearing into the role of an alien messiah. They weren't the Stones either, playing Satanists to the squares. Nor were they Bob Dylan, with his fancy words. Skynyrd weren't even like that *other* massive southern rock band, either; none of them were instrumental virtuosos like Duane Allman. They were amazing players for sure, and they could shred and wail and jam hard enough to blow the Stones and the Who off their own stages. But they could do all that because they buckled down and worked hard at it.

As teenagers in Jacksonville, Florida, they spent hours playing their songs over and over and over again, perfecting the tempo changes, mapping out the solos, and polishing every riff and rhythm, all inside the blazing-hot Hell House, their tin-roof practice shed located in a literal swamp. Skynyrd took their modest gifts and made something bigger from them, which meant that even at the height of their fame, back when "Sweet Home Alabama" was wedging itself into rock radio for a half-century run, the band was never quite larger than life. They were life size. It was the plane crash that lent the band their weird mystique.

The first half of *Southern Rock Opera* explores the pathology of a certain breed of southern man, one who finds himself anchored in a small town, unable to flee down those highways leading who knows where but away. We follow him as he listens to Skynyrd, practices his guitar loud enough to annoy the neighbors on "Guitar Man Upstairs," bids farewell to his teenage girlfriend on "Zip City," then imbibes and recovers on "Dead Drunk and Naked" like the rock star he longs to become. The Truckers are drawing from their own dreams and experiences; in fact,

Southern Rock Opera couldn't have been made—or, at least made as well—without Adam's House Cat, without the band's enduring failure and disappointment, without that nagging doubt in their minds that everything could go south at any moment.

In between those semiautobiographical songs, Patterson introduces larger themes and settings, in particular the three great Alabama icons: Van Zant, of course, but also the Alabama governor and failed presidential candidate George Wallace and the head football coach at the University of Alabama, Paul "Bear" Bryant. Bryant doesn't get much screen time, despite his name being spoken by southerners with the same reverence and awe they reserve for Jesus himself (well, maybe not by Auburn fans). Wallace, though, gets his comeuppance in a song written by Patterson, sung by Rob Malone, and told from the devil's point of view as he "brews up some sweet tea and whoops up some southern hospitality for the arrival of the new guest."

Van Zant, however, gets nearly a full LP, although he shares it with his Skynyrd bandmates. The second half of *Southern Rock Opera* is more streamlined in its narrative, shifting from that fictional band to the real Lynyrd Skynyrd with "Cassie's Brother." They're jumping right in at the end of the story, with Steve Gaines joining the band in 1976. Then "Life in the Factory" looks back to how they got to that moment, calculating the stakes in their story by locating the either/or choice to take a safe but deadening factory job or risk everything for a chance at something bigger. "They hit the road doing ninety. Leave them steel mills far behind," Patterson sings. "Ain't no good life at the Ford plant. Three guitars or a life of crime?"

Those were the choices facing Van Zant and the boys playing behind him, and so many other kids, not just in the South but everywhere. We hear about them in the boardwalk anthems of Bruce Springsteen and in the midwestern story-songs of John Mellencamp. Ronnie was a juvenile delinquent, a teenage father and husband, and in his Gainesville neighborhood a notoriously tough scrapper who took on guys twice his size. He was a good fighter but a better singer, and the band's long hours at the Hell House were driven by a certain desperation as they realized their lives depended on mastering their music. Those impossibly high stakes, even more than their blues- and boogie-based southern rock, are perhaps what the Truckers identify with most of all in this story.

But success always comes with a price, especially in the land where Robert Johnson and George Wallace sold their souls to the devil. Life on the road was just as ragged as life in the factory, but Skynyrd's determination barely waned. They toured heavily, kept writing, kept working, and then made the horrible decision to board that final flight. The Truckers created something like a roadside memorial for the band with "Angels and Fuselage," which closes the double album. After the streamlined boogie rock of "Shut Up and Get on the Plane" and the almost manic urgency of "Greenville to Baton Rouge," the Truckers slow the tempo way down. "Angels and Fuselage" opens with a slow, tenuous guitar riff that leaves lots of space between the notes and evokes that feeling of time standing still. It's immediately a powerful moment, almost unbearable, and I've seen fans in tears when the Truckers play it live. The band is trying to create a quiet moment of clarity in which Steve and Cassie and Ronnie can meet their fate with dignity and humanity rather than carry on as legends.

"Angels and Fuselage" brings *Southern Rock Opera* to a climax with a series of violent guitar shifts that sound like metal being torn apart, and Cooley's guitar solo—jumbles of bent, strewn notes—conveys what Patterson's lyrics cannot. The song fades out: a cinematic touch, like rolling the credits on a film. It's a supremely moving finale, and during subsequent tours they ended more than one show with the song, each Trucker setting his instrument down and leaving the stage, one by one, until only Brad Morgan remained, keeping that beat stoically—a beat that could go on forever.

Patterson doesn't describe himself as an especially religious person, yet he often writes songs about heaven and hell, morality and faith. "Angels and Fuselage" hinges on a startlingly spiritual chorus: "I'm scared shitless of what's coming next." As he drawls out the word "scared" and turns the next word into a soft exclamation, Patterson is boiling down the worries of life to their most primal and irreducible: What happens when we die? Where do we go? What is it like to stop living? The vulgarity of his phrasing somehow makes the question all the more immediate and relatable, never letting you forget that that there are actual humans, with all their dreams and flaws, inhabiting this song and that plane. Do they make their way to heaven, or do they join Wallace in hell? Perhaps Patterson was still weighing their sins against their graces. He leaves them with a question mark, their mortal bodies strewn among the wreckage outside of Gillsburg but their souls gone off to only God knows where.

Among Skynyrd's many graces was Van Zant's willingness to examine and undermine certain ideas about southern masculinity, which is all the more impressive considering he was doing so at a time when the rest of pop culture was lauding southern rednecks as paragons of manliness: think Burt Reynolds in *White Lightning*, Joe Don Baker in *Walking Tall*, or Bo and Luke in *The Dukes of Hazzard*. Gently puncturing those ideas seems to have been Van Zant's goal from the very beginning: for Skynyrd's 1973 debut, *(Pronounced 'Lĕh-'nérd 'Skin-'nérd)*, he wrote a scrappy single called "Gimme Three Steps" about avoiding a bar fight. Rather than portray himself as the scrapper that he was, Van Zant plays the coward "shaking like a leaf on a tree" and maybe even pissing himself (or at least that's how I've always heard the line "the water fell on the floor"). Humiliating though it may be, running away and screaming was the smart strategy, given that the other guy was not only bigger but also had a gun pointed at him. "I'm telling you, son," Van Zant sings, and you can imagine him delivering the lines with a rakish grin on his face. "Well, it ain't no fun staring straight down a .44."

If his mama told him to "be a simple kind of man," as the song "Simple Man" goes, Van Zant took no heed. Lynyrd Skynyrd songs are complicated and contradictory to what we imagine as the '70s stereotypical redneck, and they've only grown trickier over the years. It's easy to see why the Truckers might be fascinated with him as both a songwriting influence and a songwriting subject. "That's what we were drawn to when we were writing those songs and exploring that story," says Cooley. "Skynyrd weren't ashamed of what they were. They were comfortable in their skin as ordinary people, as southern people, as rural people. And they weren't dumb, not by a long shot. They weren't educated. None of them finished high school. They didn't speak the King's English. But Ronnie Van Zant was not a dumb guy. If you listen to those songs, that's a thinking man writing those songs."

Among Skynyrd's sins, however, was their association with the Confederate flag—a symbol of primarily racial hatred in America and beyond. Skynyrd used it as a backdrop on several tours, as though audiences needed to be reminded that these hard-tourin', hard-jammin', hard-livin' Florida rednecks were indeed southerners. Over the years that banner became so closely associated with the band that when Mark Ribowsky published his excellent biography, *Whiskey Bottles and Brand-New Cars: The Fast Life and Sudden Death of Lynyrd Skynyrd*, in 2015, the musicians were pictured on the cover with the Confederate flag behind them.

The rebel flag has become a contentious subject among fans as well as band members, and it may explain why Skynyrd have not received the same critical reappraisal granted their contemporaries. It's the cement block around their feet. That relationship between band and flag has obscured the music and spawned as much fantasy and debate as the incorruptibility of Van Zant's corpse. There are some who view that association favorably, who might carve a rebel flag on a tree near Gillsburg. But there are many others who claim that MCA Records foisted the flag on Skynyrd at a time when the band felt that it had worked too hard to push back. There are likewise theories that they stopped using the flag later in the 1970s, although there is footage of Steve Gaines jamming furiously in front of the banner. Because he joined Skynyrd in late 1976, that means they were flying it within a year of the plane crash.

There is some evidence to suggest they were consciously distancing themselves from the rebel flag around the time they were recording *Street Survivors*. As Cooley points out, "There's not a single Confederate flag anywhere on their last album. They never made any public statement about it, but allegedly it was a conscious decision, mainly on Ronnie's part, because he could see the writing on the wall. He could tell they needed to distance themselves from that imagery, because he was already seeing where they needed to go in the future, and maybe that wasn't the best image to put forward."

"I firmly believe those guys weren't a bunch of racists," says Malone, who since leaving the Truckers has played in a Skynyrd tribute band and even opened for Skynyrd themselves. He brings up "The Ballad of Curtis Loew," a song from their 1974 album *Second Helping*. It's a bit of Southern mythmaking from Van Zant, who sings about watching a fictional Black bluesman playing his "old dobro" all day and chastises the white community for viewing the elderly musician as useless. When he sings about Curtis's funeral—"Ol' preacher said some words, and they chunked him in the clay"—there's outrage in his voice for an artist denied his due. "All those rock and rollers were into the old blues guys," Malone says. "But to me that rebel flag is like a swastika. What it represents, when you get right down to it, is slavery. I don't feel like liking their music is aligning me with some kind of racism, but fundamentally, I don't think there's a way to defend it."

Whatever their motivations, it's clear Skynyrd knew on some level that this symbol could be controversial even in the '70s. They knew it might read as offensive even as it might endear some southerners to their cause. That there is any controversy at all suggests some level of shame attached to the rebel flag, which like so many things associated with the South has some fantasy around it. For one thing, this is not *the* Confederate flag. Designed by William Miles in the early years of the Civil War but roundly rejected by the fledgling Confederate government—it was too dissimilar to the American flag, which apparently still inspired some reverence among the treasonous—it never flew over the Confederate capitol, not at its original location in Montgomery, Alabama, nor in its later headquarters in Richmond, Virginia. That dubious honor went to a very different flag, with a blue field on the left containing eleven or thirteen stars (one for each Confederate state) and red and white horizontal bars on the right.

The banner that became synonymous with Southern rebellion and all that entailed (i.e., slavery as well as the insistence that slavery had nothing to do with it whatsoever) was actually a battle flag, first adopted by the Army of Virginia under General Pierre Gustave Toutant-Beauregard in 1861. Originally square rather than rectangular, it lessened the confusion on the battlefield regarding which regiments were enemies and which were allies. It was only one of many battle flags flown by Confederate forces, and it rose to prominence only after the war had been lost, when southerners were looking for ways to cast their loss in a romantic light.

For many years the display of this or any other Confederate insignia was strictly forbidden throughout the South, at risk of punishment by occupying Union forces. Flying the flag or even decorating the graves of Confederate soldiers was viewed as a continuation of treason, which only reinforced its power as a symbol of Lost Cause sentiments: that romantic idea that the South was righteous in its fight but overwhelmed by aggressive Union forces that had access to more powerful weapons and greater technology. Such prohibitions were eventually dropped when the Union found it advantageous to reconcile with the South, a craven compromise that came at the expense of freed Black slaves and led to decades of Jim Crow laws that segregated the races.

The flag's popularity has alternately surged and abated with advances made by Black Americans. When the Ku Klux Klan grew in power and popularity during the 1920s, the rebel flag spoke a visual language similar to white sheets and burning crosses, only less violent. You could fly it at one of the Klan picnics held throughout the South and, increasingly, in the Midwest, and everyone would understand exactly what it meant. From there the flag infiltrated state institutions and imagery: Georgia added Miles's design to its state flag nearly eighty years after the Civil War, around the time the civil rights movement was growing in the 1940s. It was flying high over the state capitol in Atlanta when the Truckers played their first notes, and it was still flying when they recorded *Southern Rock Opera*. Georgia's flag was finally redesigned in early 2001, shrinking but not jettisoning the rebel insignia. That was finally excised in 2003.

Georgia looks positively progressive compared to Mississippi, where until 2020 a version of the Confederate flag was still incorporated into the official state flag design. Several pieces of legislation had been introduced and several lawsuits filed to force a redesign, but none had progressed very far in the courts, even after a young white supremacist in 2015 posted photos of himself with the Confederate flag on social media and the next day walked through the door of the Emmanuel African Methodist Episcopal Church in Charleston, South Carolina, and killed nine Christians, including state senator and senior pastor Clementa Pinckney. This was supposed to be the young white man's attack on Fort Sumter: the opening volley in a race war he was certain his side would win. In summer 2020, during the countrywide protests over the death of George Floyd, the Mississippi legislature agreed to change the flag, putting the final design to a popular vote in November.

The Confederate flag remains very much a battle flag, and its supporters still associate it with military valor and sacrifice. Whether it's posted in internet forums, brandished at right-wing demonstrations, plastered on pickup truck bumpers, flown on flagpoles in front yards, or carried into the US Capitol by pro-Trump seditionists, it marks public spaces as battlefields in a larger culture war. It signifies not only certain beliefs about the Confederacy, about whiteness and Blackness, but also a hostility toward anyone who disagrees with those beliefs. It transforms its supporters into soldiers fighting for a Lost Cause and potentially willing to launch a second civil war. And just as in war, when teenage flag-bearers were usually targeted first and when toppling a flag could destroy the enemy's morale, those who still fly the Confederate flag understand that it is under heavy and constant fire.

For a generation of southern men and women, myself and my brothers included, our first exposure to the Confederate flag was through popular culture. Just as our grandparents grew up with *Gone with the Wind*, we came of age with *Smokey and the Bandit* and *The Dukes of Hazzard*. Every kid I knew growing up wanted a Trans Am with a flaming chicken on the hood or an orange Dodge Charger with the doors welded shut, and most of us thought sliding across the hood and climbing through the window was a legitimate means of entering any automobile. The Bandit's car is an iconic gas guzzler running interference for Jerry Reed's semi full of illegal beer. The Duke boys' hot rod had the flag emblazoned on the hood, and it was nicknamed the General Lee, a reference to the Confederate general whose reputation as an upstanding Christian gentleman was burnished by the Lost Cause. Before I even knew what the Civil War was, I was playing *Dukes of Hazzard* with my brothers in the woods behind our house, building rickety ramps to jump our bikes across the creek.

Patterson and Cooley initially loved the show but very quickly outgrew it. *Smokey and the Bandit* was another story. Released the same year Skynyrd's plane went down outside Gillsburg, *Smokey and the Bandit* was a big film for them and their friends. "It's Burt fucking Reynolds," explains Cooley. "He drives a cool car and he bangs Sally Field. For a generation of guys coming of age and looking for some kind of identity, he was our icon in every way. But when that black Trans Am makes its debut, it comes flying out of that semi-trailer in such a way that the license plate is right at eye level, and it's got Georgia plates with the stars and bars up in the corner."

Kids—especially boys—growing up in the South at this time were surrounded by rebel flags and rebel culture on television sets, movie screens, and even the radio. "It didn't even occur to me until fairly recently that all that imagery wasn't coming from our ancestors," says Cooley. "It wasn't being passed from one generation to the next. It was all from Hollywood. And it was put to us as romance, as nostalgia, as identity, so no wonder so many people have trouble separating that out." This is an important reason why some southerners still cling to the Confederate flag: even more than a historical artifact, it is a symbol of youth and innocence, tangled up in formative experiences and comforting ideas of home. When heritage is mentioned in defense of the symbol, it may be a very personal heritage: a pride that permits no shame.

As Patterson and Cooley grew up, they grew out of it. On *Southern Rock Opera* they wrote what they intended to be a rejection of the flag and the ugliness surrounding it. Full of knotty guitar riffs and blustery power chords, "The Southern Thing" examines that popular phrase that appeared in the '70s on bumper stickers and T-shirts, usually illustrated by the rebel flag: "It's a southern thing…you wouldn't understand." What is that southern thing? In his lyrics Patterson defines it by what it isn't. "Ain't about my pistol, ain't about my boots," he declares. "Ain't about no cotton fields or cotton picking lies." And it certainly "ain't about no flag." In the song's final verse—and in his onstage introductions to the song—he recounts the story of his great-great-grandfather, who he believes enlisted in the Confederate Army not out of belief in slavery and definitely not because he had strong opinions about states' rights, but because Union soldiers had ransacked his farm. He was shot clean through at Shiloh, not thirty miles from home, but lived to regale his children and grandchildren and great-grandchildren with his old war stories.

Patterson never really settles on what the southern thing really *is* about or what it should be about. Such is the duality of the southern thing. This is a song of *ain't*s, which leaves something murky behind, something that is open to misinterpretation by fans who might not listen too hard beyond the cautioning refrain: "Stay out the way of the southern thing." Honestly, I wish the song were more explicit. I wish it didn't hide behind family lore and loyalty to exonerate the everyday southerners who, sure, might not have had the wealth to buy and sell actual human beings but nevertheless fought to preserve that culture.

And maybe the band wished that, too. While the flag doesn't appear in the packaging for *Southern Rock Opera*, or on any of their albums for that matter, on tour they had to work to distance themselves from the Confederate imagery that so many southern rock bands, including the one they were singing about, had embraced. If fans raised the flag at a show, the Truckers would stop a song and demand they put it away. Cooley has dog-cussed audience members. And the band researched it, understanding that they had to be on the right side of facts to be on the right side of history.

"The people in the South who still cling to it, honestly they're not hateful people," says Cooley. "It's more just out of ignorance. A lot of them are very decent people, but there's no talking to them. 'This is not what it means to you? Okay, I get that, but it's what it means to the entire rest of the world.' Whenever there was a lynching or a beating, that flag was nearby. And now when young men latch onto this hateful ideology, that symbol is one of the first things they latch onto."

The flag doesn't appear in many of their subsequent songs, but you can hear them taking aim at it on "What It Means" and "The Perilous Night," the latter inspired by the violence in Charlottesville. (The song was first released in 2017 as a B-side to a live version of "What It Means." When they re-recorded it for their 2020 release *The New OK*, they didn't even need to update the lyrics. The details and sentiments were, sadly, still relevant.) Their most explicit condemnation of the flag came not in song but on the editorial page of the *New York Times*. Patterson, whose prose has appeared in various outlets, including *The Bitter Southerner* and *Oxford American*, was asked to write about the place of the Confederate flag in the South, and he responded with a passionate defense of his home and an explanation of why the flag doesn't figure more prominently on *Southern Rock Opera*. "We made a conscious decision not to discuss the so-called rebel flag," he writes before acknowledging the fact that the flag has risen in prominence since they recorded that album, and he has adjusted his thinking: "It's high time that a symbol so divisive be removed. . . . Why would we want to fly a symbol that has been used by the K.K.K. and terrorists like Dylann Roof? Why would a people steeped in the teachings of Jesus Christ and the Bible want to rally around a flag that so many associate with hatred and violence? Why fly a flag that stands for the very things we as Southerners have worked so hard to move beyond?"

Decades deep into his long career in rock music, Cooley revisits Skynyrd from time to time, but he isn't exactly jumping around the room anymore. "I feel the same way about Skynyrd these days as I do about Jesus. I admire most of the work, but the fans suck. I want nothing to do with their biggest fans." In their reincarnated form, Skynyrd has become so closely identified with right-wing politics that the subtleties, political as well as musical, of their earliest songs have been lost.

Who could have imagined an afterlife so wild and so completely mundane for such a band? On the tenth anniversary of the plane crash, right at the tail end of Reagan's second term as president, the surviving members of Lynyrd Skynyrd launched a reunion tour, with Ronnie's brother Johnny Van Zant taking over vocals. They intended it as a one-off event, but it proved so popular that they kept going. This iteration of the band embraced the rebel flag with even less hesitation, using it once again as a backdrop and printing it on T-shirts, trucker caps, shot glasses, and belt buckles. The complicated and often contradictory band that died in that plane crash died in that plane crash. What rose from the dead was a zombie version of Lynyrd Skynyrd: they played the same songs, sang the same lyrics, but somehow it all sounded less complicated, less subversive.

Decades later, when they tried to distance themselves from that flag, it was too late. In 2012 Gary Rossington, the last surviving member of the original lineup, told CNN, "Through the years, people like the KKK and skinheads kidnapped the Dixie or southern flag from its tradition and the heritage of the soldier. That's what it was about. We didn't want that to go to our fans or show the image like we agreed with any of the race stuff or any of the bad things."

There is a lot of hedging in that statement, especially the suggestion that the rebel flag has more to do with the soldiers than the cause they were fighting for, but still it seemed like a long overdue announcement. But outcry from fans was so swift and vehement that the guitarist had to clarify that the band would still be using the Confederate flag, but only alongside the American flag, as though that made it okay, as though that simplified everything rather than introducing a whole new set of much less revealing complications. "We know what the Dixie flag represents and its heritage," he wrote on the band's website. "The Civil War was fought over States rights.... I only stated my opinion that the confederate [sic] flag, at times, was unfairly being used as a symbol by various hate groups, which is something that we don't support the flag being used for. The Confederate flag means something more to us, Heritage not Hate."

In the woods at the crash site in Mississippi, there can be found all sorts of homemade memorials, poignant and heartfelt, mostly carvings on the same trees that scraped the bottom of the band's plane, tore off the wings, split flesh, and caught the contents of exploding suitcases, leaving socks and pants and T-shirts hanging in the branches like tinsel on a Christmas tree. Skynyrd fans—and even Truckers fans, so intertwined are the two bands—still make pilgrimages to the site more than forty years later, parking on the side of the road and wandering into the underbrush. Some leave tokens of appreciation or search for those buried hunks of metal, or carve those messages into those trees: their names and the date of their visit, song lyrics, the names of band members who died.

The more ambitious fans, who have either more time on their hands or more coordination with a knife, carve out on a stout trunk what we commonly identify as the Confederate flag, notching the St. Andrew's cross and the decorative stars as deeply into the bark as they can. Even in death Skynyrd cannot escape this tarnished symbol of southern defiance and treason.

This isn't the only area in which the revivified Skynyrd differs from the original version or reveals how tricky these waters are to navigate. Gun control—or at least the virulent opposition to any legislation concerning who can buy guns and under what conditions—is an important issue to many Skynyrd fans. The band has made a slogan of the phrase "Gimme back my bullets," the title of their 1976 album, although it's perhaps not quite the way Ronnie Van Zant intended. According to a 1992 interview with the magazine *Goldmine*, Rossington explained that the bullets weren't literal bullets but those attached to the singles that made their way quickly up the charts. "I've been on top, and then it seems I lost my dream," Van Zant sings. "Tell all those pencil pushers, better get out of my way."

And then there's "Saturday Night Special," which is somehow among Skynyrd's most popular songs. Originally penned for the 1974 film *The Longest Yard* starring "Burt fucking Reynolds," it opens Skynyrd's third album, *Nuthin' Fancy*, and the first verse follows a guy shooting his cheating wife and her lover. The second verse is about Big Jim, who drinks a little more than he gambles and ends up shooting a bar full of holes. (He could be the man threatening Ronnie on "Gimme

Three Steps.") "Mr. Saturday Night Special, got a barrel that's blue and cold," goes the chorus. "Ain't good for nothin' but put a man six feet in a hole." In case you don't get the point, Ronnie Van Zant lays it all out for you: "Handguns are made for killin'. They ain't no good for nothin' else," he preaches. "So why don't we dump 'em, people, to the bottom of the sea, before some ol' fool come around here wanna shoot either you or me." It sure sounds like Ronnie's coming to take your guns.

Guns are perhaps an even bigger and more pervasive part of southern culture than the rebel flag itself. The biggest demographic of gun owners in the United States is southern white men, according to a 2013 Gallup poll, and more than twice as many conservatives own guns than liberals. What is now a divisive issue once had much more gray area, especially when it came to who could buy which types of guns. Van Zant was criticizing the popularity of the so-called Saturday night special, which refers to a range of small, inexpensive handguns that could be purchased quickly and with little hassle. They weren't accurate, and there's very little uniformity within brands and lines. The term may have dog-whistle origins, as it possibly derives from the "Niggertown Saturday night special," slang for the guns African American men were supposedly buying to use against whites. It was an insidious rumor to stoke fears of violence and uprising and ultimately to sell more guns. By the mid '70s the term had shed some, if not all, of its racist connotations and was viewed as referring to a weapon for hotheads rather than the pistols and rifles used by law enforcement and the military, not to mention hunters and marksmen.

In the late 1960s the National Rifle Association actually supported a ban on Saturday night specials, but it wasn't until after Watergate that Congress banned the import of these cheap handguns. Foreign manufacturers then simply shipped them to the States unassembled, and vendors sold the parts instead of the whole gun—an ingenious workaround that allowed John Hinckley Jr. to shoot Reagan in 1982. By then, a coup by a man named Harlon Carter had redirected the NRA toward increasingly extreme positions. "That's when the NRA transformed and they became who they are today," says Cooley, "which is primarily a right-wing organization. Guns are just a fundraiser."

Ronnie Van Zant owned a .22 pistol and more than one .38 when he wrote "Saturday Night Special," but he understood that gun ownership brought with it a certain responsibility: having your finger on a trigger ought to make you less violent, not more. Strangely, the song became something of a rallying cry for the resurrected Skynyrd, as the band not only kept it in set lists but often opened with it. Says Cooley, "It's a pro-gun-control song. Blatantly. Their fans are still willing to overlook the song's subject matter or just not get it."

Harlon Carter, no relation to the US president who was working to push even tougher gun legislation through Congress, became the patron saint of the modern-day NRA, not to mention the subject of Cooley's song "Ramon Casiano," which opens *American Band*. Ramón Casiano is the name of the kid Harlon Carter shot and killed back in 1931, when they were both just teenagers. The instigating factor was a stolen automobile, and the teenage Carter appointed himself detective and judge before aggressively questioning suspicious characters in his small Texas town. When sixteen-year-old Casiano refused to answer his questions, Carter shot him with a shotgun. He was initially convicted of murder, but the sentence was overturned on appeal, based on a loophole regarding the judge's comments to the jury about the definition of *self-defense*. So Carter, a white man, was never punished for murdering an American of color.

In the Truckers song, Cooley depicts Carter, nicknamed the Bullet, as an ideologue, a huckster "never forced to make amends." He's a grievance merchant deploying paranoia and bigotry to rally his troops. "He had the makings of a leader, of a certain kind of men who need to feel the world's against him, out to get him if it can," the song goes. The Truckers trace the NRA's current stances regarding legislation and research (hostile opposition to both) to this one man who bent the organization to his will, whose pride and grievance defines a potent strain of twenty-first-century politics. "Killing's been the Bullet's business since back in 1931," Cooley sings. "Someone killed Ramon Casiano, and Ramon still ain't dead enough."

Skynyrd's crash was the end of something more than just Skynyrd. Bands like the Allman Brothers Band and 38 Special (fronted by Ronnie's brother Donnie Van Zant) survived and even thrived well into the 1980s, although few if any found a place on MTV, and the harder edges of rock and roll were ceded to metal bands from the Mid-Atlantic and the West

Coast. *The Dukes of Hazzard* ran until 1985 and has been in syndication ever since, but it never pretended to offer any kind of realistic or probing depiction of the South. Jimmy Carter lost his bid for reelection in 1980 to Ronald Reagan, who finally brought Nixon's Southern Strategy to fruition and introduced twelve years of Republican rule. Would that have changed had Skynyrd not crashed? Or were they like their peers destined for nostalgia tours and an increasingly niche market? Could they have survived that onslaught of synths and drum machines?

But that plane did go down. And it went down where a Black woman named Mae Miller had been free for just over a decade. In 1977 she was working as a glass cutter and raising four adopted children, and had no idea she would become her community's most notable citizen. Her childhood in Amite County was anything but happy. Miller's parents, Cain and Lela Wall, along with her six siblings, were held in what was called peonage until 1961. Akin to indentured servitude, peonage is an old and—by the middle of the twentieth century—illegal practice that essentially allowed slavery to persist under a different name, as Black men, women, and children were forced into unpaid labor to pay off debts that were often fabricated or exaggerated. "We been though pure-D hell," she told *People* magazine in 2007. "I mean hell right here on earth."

The Walls lived in a small, dirt-floor shack with no electricity or running water, reminiscent of nineteenth-century slave quarters, and they did housework and farm work for several families around Amite County and Tangipahoa Parish, just over the Louisiana line. They faced the constant threat of violence; Miller recalls her father being beaten with chains so badly that his children jumped on top of him to shield him from the blows, and she remembers being raped repeatedly as a child. With no connection to the outside world—they were not allowed to travel or see family—the Walls had no inkling of the Jim Crow laws that defined life in the South during the early twentieth century, nor were they aware of the strides that Black Americans were making toward civil rights. Most of all they didn't understand that the oppression they faced was not just immoral but illegal. They were free, but not freed.

It wasn't until 1961, nearly one hundred years after the signing of the Emancipation Proclamation, that Mae Miller escaped that life. She simply fled, figuring that what she might run into was better than what she was running from, and her disappearance led to her family being kicked out of their shack and left homeless. It wasn't until the very early 2000s that Miller began to tell their story. As she told ABC News in 2006, "We thought everybody was in the same predicament. We didn't know everybody wasn't living the same life that we were living. We thought this was just for the black folks."

Slavery seems like something buried deep in the past, abandoned with the South's great loss, so much so that many southern whites scoff at the very idea of reparations. But it persisted in a dark corner of America long after the Civil War and coexisted with the Great Depression, with World War II, with rock and roll, with the civil rights movement. The Wall family's story is impossible to ignore when discussing this corner of Mississippi. It is, of course, merely a coincidence that one of the most consequential white bands from the South died in a place that held the last remnants of such a brutal and defining institution. But this is the heart of the South. Slavery is its original sin and its persistent lie: that it did not exist, or that Black Americans were better off slaves than free, or that it was not the underlying reason America went to war with itself, or that its symbols have nothing to do with white supremacy.

And so the South that was presented in so many songs and on so many television shows was itself a "cotton-picking lie," as Patterson put it. After Van Zant's death, most depictions of the South as more than hate and ignorance began to ignore the hate and ignorance in order to focus on the *more than*, as though we had moved so far beyond the ugliness of history that it could no longer haunt us, as though it had to be pride or shame, but never both. But Skynyrd, in their finest, most graceful moments, stared that down and focused on the contradictions, the shame and pride, the duality of the southern thing, just as Van Zant had stared down the barrels of those guns in "Gimme Three Steps" and "Saturday Night Special." This is the animating force behind both Skynyrd and the Truckers, and therefore it is the heart of *Southern Rock Opera*: an overwhelming desire to capture the South as it is and the South as it might be, if we could ever move past the lie.

Back to the Shoals

▼

It was not the homecoming they were hoping for.

By fall 2001 the Drive-By Truckers had hand-sold enough copies of *Southern Rock Opera* that they were finally getting serious label consideration, including interest from Lost Highway Records, a subsidiary of Universal Music Group and home to Lucinda Williams, Lyle Lovett, and the best-selling *O Brother, Where Art Thou?* soundtrack. Journalists and critics were starting to pay attention, and *Spin* magazine wanted to do a feature on the band, which looked to be their first bit of mainstream press. The magazine was sending down to the Shoals a photographer named Mark Heithoff and a writer named Eric Weisbard (a prominent rock critic and later founder of the annual Pop Conference in Seattle), but its staff wanted to center the article on a concert. Could the band book a show someplace in their old stomping grounds?

Well, no. Many of the same old blue laws were in place, still prohibiting local alcohol sales. Florence had gone wet, but Lauderdale County and most of the Shoals were still dry and still a no-man's-land for bars and clubs. That meant pickin's were as slim as ever for the Truckers, who were determined to play *here*, determined to be portrayed as a Shoals band, determined to showcase North Alabama in this first bit of major press. Maybe it was only because the place figured so prominently on their new album, or maybe Patterson Hood still wanted to put his hometown on the map. They had played a local karaoke club once or twice, but the owner refused to book them again, despite the free press and the crowds they were beginning to attract. So the band scheduled another local club, but it closed down for good just a few days before the show. With too little time to rebook anywhere else—and, really, with no other places to rebook—they turned to their friend Dick Cooper, who had served as a resource for *Southern Rock Opera*: a jack of all trades, "a sort of technical adviser, historian, guru, sounding board, mediator, mood elevator, assistant engineer, and coproducer," as Patterson puts it. Could they hold the gig out at his house on the lake?

Cooper lived in a big A-frame house out by Wilson Lake, which was a hangout for local musicians and those just passing through. He had two housemates. One was Scott Boyer, who in the early '70s had fronted a band called Cowboy and scored a modest hit with the song "Please Be with Me" (which Eric Clapton famously covered on his 1974 album *461 Ocean Boulevard*). The other was a young bass player named Shonna Tucker, barely drinking age, from Killen, a small town east of Florence. She had a close friend named Jason Isbell who was over there more often than not; everybody thought they were dating, but they were then only close friends. That would come later. "Jason was always over there," says Tucker. "We would all sit around, drink whiskey, and swap songs."

Other musicians would crash at Cooper and Boyer's house, too, including Patterson, who would stay there whenever he was in town. And he was in town often, cooling his jets between Truckers tours. Most of all, he was trying to get out of Jenn Bryant's hair. After his second marriage had ended and after his ill-advised relationship with the band's manager had soured, he'd found himself homeless, couch-surfing and occasionally even sleeping in his car. So Bryant, his old friend and the Truckers' webmaster and number-one fan, had cleaned out a storage closet just big enough for a sleeping bag and let Patterson crash there for a few weeks, much to the chagrin of her boyfriend. The Trucker bunked in her closet, booked gigs on her computer while Bryant was at work, and left town whenever he could so as not to overstay his welcome.

So he was in the Shoals a lot, which allowed him to book solo shows at the Nick down in Birmingham or at the Tip Top up in Huntsville. Sometimes Shonna's friend Jason called shotgun and rode with Patterson, even sitting in with him a time or two. Fresh out of college at the University of Memphis, he could play some sharp guitar licks, sang with a burr that sounded much older than his years, and was already working on his own songs. The kid was a sponge who soaked up lessons from Patterson and was always looking for opportunities to play or just talk music. "I was a fan of the Truckers," says Isbell. "I had gone to see them at the Hi-Tone when I was at school in Memphis. When Patterson asked if I wanted to ride down with him and play on a few songs, I said, 'Fuck yeah.'"

So Isbell was there the night the Truckers set up a small stage and some chairs in Dick Cooper's yard. With the lake in the background, the setting resembled a small wedding or a church potluck more than a rock show, but they seeded the crowd with friends and family members, fewer than a hundred altogether, including Weisbard and Heithoff. Then the Truckers played *Southern Rock Opera* in its entirety, completely acoustic—surely a subdued way to hear the album, but with such short notice, it would have to suffice. Patterson talked his way through "Days of Graduation" and "The Three Great Alabama Icons," and Mike Cooley strummed out the riffs on "Ronnie and Neil" and "72 (This Highway's Mean)." The band broke more strings than they could repair along the way. It was, in its own way, a thoroughly Truckers show.

When the article finally ran almost a year later—in the December 2002 issue, with Eminem on the cover—Weisbard called the music "poetry among the wreckage"—an evocative phrase that tipped its hat to the failure of Reconstruction, to civil rights, to the mess that was the Truckers' Dirty South, even if the band hadn't yet settled on that phrase for this thing they were just beginning to get in their sights. But "wreckage" might also apply to the band itself, which had weathered all manner of tribulation to get to this pivotal point in its life. They were suffering an unexpected indignity in that very moment at the lake, because Rob Malone was not there. Nobody knew where he had gotten off to. The night before, up in Nashville, they had played a showcase for the Americana Music Festival, then in its inaugural year, after which they'd all driven down to the Shoals, a trip of about two or three hours depending on how hot your foot is. Malone had left with his girlfriend rather than ride in the van. He never made it to the show.

"We get there and no Rob," says Patterson. "We set up and still no Rob. Eric and the photographer arrive. No Rob. People are starting to show up for the concert, and Rob's still not there. So we had to play without him."

The Truckers were fuming over the empty folding chair up on the stage with them, which they saw as a sure sign that they weren't ready to make this next step. It made them look like amateurs, like yokels rather than the road-tested, hardworking band they had become. The Truckers had spent years boasting a come-as-you-are mentality, taking no attendance at shows and refusing to rehearse the spontaneity out of their songs. Now it looked like those rules were biting them on the ass. Where the hell was Rob?

"About seven or eight songs in," says Patterson, "I'm sitting there watching Jason Isbell in the crowd, knowing full well that he knew how to play every song we were playing. And I'm sitting next to an empty chair. So I'm like, 'Hey, man, why don't you grab a guitar and join in?'" He meant join in for the set, but Isbell stuck around for more than five years. The next day, when Heithoff shot the band for the *Spin* article, Jason was there in the frame, albeit slightly apart from the band: in the main image, the band members are perched on a rusted bridge over a remote creek, but the newest and youngest Trucker is standing down in the corner, in the water up to his knees. He was in, but only so far.

Rob finally got in touch. He wasn't dead in a ditch somewhere. There was no wreck on the highway, no oak tree in his way, no rock star self-obliteration to launch a thousand what-ifs. The Devil Himself, as he was known in the band, had simply gotten waylaid. "I'd met this chick in New York who was from Florida, and I was kinda seeing her off and on," he says. "She called me up and said, 'Hey, let's go to New Orleans. This guy's got some really good mushrooms, and we'll trip for a couple of days.'" So he did that instead of playing the Truckers' most important show to date.

Even with this new kid in the band, Malone was a tough loss. He had been a key part of the Truckers' first solid lineup, a guy who tore up roads and stages for *Alabama Ass Whuppin'* and who had holed up in a warehouse in downtown Birmingham to record a double album, with ambitions to change the way listeners thought about the South. He had switched from guitar and bass and back to guitar as needed, and he'd been present when they played the first Heathen Songs, a group of tunes that depicted their home in unsentimental terms and would set the band on its course for the next ten years. Now he was gone. "I never want to be overly negative about Rob," says Patterson. "When we were playing all those crazy shows in '99, riding in that crappy van and sleeping on floors, he was rock solid. A drunken derelict and a wild man, but rock solid. We ended up having to kick him out of the band, but we viewed it as him leaving. Did he jump or was he pushed?" Years later, nobody's entirely sure.

"Honestly," says Malone, "I think I just wanted to do something different, 'cause I was riding a different style of music that didn't seem to fit in well with what those cats were doing. I definitely felt like they wanted a change too. The way it came about, that probably wasn't the wisest way to do it. But there was so much dysfunction going on at the time, and we were all a little out of our minds from touring and lots of substances." Malone doesn't regret leaving the Truckers, but he still thinks he could have chosen a more diplomatic way to depart. "Everything worked out beautifully, and I feel like they're happy with where they are, their state in life, and I'm happy where I am." Malone still lives in the Shoals, where he gives music lessons and plays in a variety of outfits, including Fiddle Worms and a Skynyrd cover band called the Curtis Loew Project.

Malone's exit and Isbell's entrance meant the Truckers were no longer what you might call an Athens band, but something else. Critics were calling them "southern rock" and placing them in a lineage with the Allman Brothers Band, Lynyrd Skynyrd, Wet Willie, and others. Over the next decade they would gradually migrate back to the Shoals, back to the sweet soul music that seemed to seep out of the river, which is why this place warrants a second chapter: Patterson and Cooley were different people in the 2000s than they had been in the 1980s, and the Shoals was a different place than it had been in the past. They would pick up other band members from this region, some just for a tour but others for an impressive run of albums that found them building on their influences in unexpected ways. They would soon be recording songs in the Shoals, delving deep into the region's musical history, and expanding their riff-heavy rock and roll to encompass swampier grooves and gritty R&B. And when they went on tour, it was a different kind of leaving: they represented the Shoals to thousands of fans and on hundreds of stages across the country. Home went with them on the road.

The version of the Truckers that left the Shoals that November weekend for the next gig in Norman, Oklahoma, was very different than the one that had played the Americana Music Festival just a few days before. Patterson remembers Isbell's mother dropping him off to start his first tour as a professional rock and roller. "It was like that scene in *Almost Famous* where Cameron Crowe's mother tells that guy in Stillwater, 'Don't kill my son.' Jason's mother was in high school the same time I was. She's about a year older than me, and she's watching me throw his shit in our beat-up, crappy van, and she must have been wondering, *Is he going to come back alive?* I promised her, 'Yes, I'll take care of him.'"

Born and raised in Green Hill, Alabama, a rural suburb of Florence, Isbell came of age in a place that had grown slightly more comfortable with its musical past and therefore more accepting of those citizens who wanted to build on that. Clubs and venues were still few and far between, but, paradoxically, that meant live music was more accessible to aspiring young players. Though the Shoals had ignored and disdained Adam's House Cat, the place nurtured Isbell. It gave him greater access to mentors and provided more opportunities to play in front of live and usually enthusiastic audiences, even if it was at the back of a Mexican restaurant rather than at a real rock club.

Isbell started playing guitar when he was a kid, teaching himself to strum and finger chords along with songs on the radio, mostly classic rock but also mainstream pop and country. He loved Prince and R.E.M. and the wave of alt-rock bands infiltrating the mainstream. "I got lucky because in the mid '90s there was some real serious guitar music going down. To be fifteen when the Braves won the World Series and Nirvana was putting out albums was pretty fortunate for a kid from Alabama who liked to rock."

His family encouraged his creative pursuits, he recalls. "My uncle was in a cover band, and they played a bunch of southern rock songs. He was teaching me to play when I was seven or eight years old." His grandfather was a Pentecostal preacher who recruited Isbell to play guitar in church. "I spent a lot of formative time with him playing music. We would go through hours of gospel songs, him playing lead instrument and I would play rhythm guitar. And he would reward me by tuning the guitar to an open tuning and playing blues guitar using his pocketknife as a slide."

As a teenager Isbell was usually at La Fonda Mexicana, a locally owned restaurant in Florence that hosted shows in its back room and gave local musicians, including members of the Swampers, a regular venue. In particular, a group called Iguana Party—led by a guitarist named Barry Billings, who had played in the country-rock outfit the Shooters and in Marie Osmond's touring band—would play for four or five hours a night at least once a week, running through a set list heavy on songs that had been recorded or published in the Shoals. Before he could even legally drive, Isbell's parents would drop him off there and return to pick him up hours later, during which time he'd just watch the old-timers jam.

Sometimes they would invite him or one of his friends to sit in, and between sets Isbell would pick their brains for tricks or lessons. Billings taught the kid how to make room in a song for other players, to back up the singers and soloists rather than play over them. Similarly, David Hood provided some guidance for how to behave during a session. "I remember asking David for advice," says Isbell, "and his advice was always 'Show up on time. Make sure your gear works. Be nice.' *What the fuck? I want you to tell me how to be a rock star.* But it's true! Taking me under their wing was not part of their job. They weren't getting paid to do that. But they did it. Those guys really took care of us. It's not lost on me how lucky I was to grow up around that."

Isbell's generation had a very different relationship to music from the heyday of the Shoals. They didn't make it, like David Hood's generation had. And they were much further removed from it than Patterson's generation had been. They didn't hear "Mustang Sally" or "When a Man Loves a Woman" or "I Never Loved a Man (The Way I Love You)" on the radio or on MTV (which by then was barely even playing music videos). When they heard these songs, they heard them straight from the musicians themselves, which made them sound less like oldies and more like current songs. There was no dust on them, no distance from them. "We all knew early on" about the region's history, says Isbell,

but the weight of it didn't hit me until I got older and could understand the music better. The real beauty of the place is in these very adult concepts and very adult struggles that I, as a rural white kid in Alabama, did not in any way understand. I enjoyed the way it sounded, but when I got in my twenties and started traveling and seeing what other people's lives were like, it hit me: *Oh my god, this is what Aretha was talking about. This is why Otis's voice sounds the way it does.* It wasn't just a gift from God. It was a response to something.

When that sunk in, I started to understand the magic of what they made down there.

And maybe because he was a generation removed from that music, that realization allowed Isbell to grapple with the legacy of the South and how it affected Black Americans on a personal and creative level. About growing to understand and appreciate the music that had made the Shoals famous, Isbell says, "I realized that I'm not going to be able to make blues music or my precious R&B. That's what I listened to more than anything else. Luckily I gave up trying to sound like Otis Redding or Etta James and just tried to follow what I was good at. I realized I'm not qualified to make that kind of music." Why?

Because I'm a white person. Bottom line. I have such a respect for that music, so I try really hard to understand the emotions that went into it. They didn't sound that way because they were trying to sound that way. They sounded that way because that was something that had to come out of them because of the life they had led or because of the way they had been treated and in a lot of cases marginalized. There's a huge combination of things that added up to Otis Redding, and most of those things I will never be able to understand. But the beauty of that music is that when I listen to it, I can feel it, even though the details are lost on me. And I'm somebody who's gone looking for the details and tried to understand. So I can imitate those sounds but to actually make the art that they're making, you would have to live a life similar to theirs.

Isbell took that lesson and applied it to the songs he was only just beginning to write. After high school, he enrolled in the writing program at the University of Memphis, studying fiction rather than songwriting. He worked at a restaurant near campus, and one night another waiter asked Isbell to open for him at a local coffee shop. The only condition: Isbell couldn't play covers. He had to write his own songs. It was the goose he needed, and he quickly came up with a half hour of material. Even then he was trying to emulate his Shoals idols without imitating them, writing in country-rock mode rather than straight R&B. That opening slot was the first of several small shows he played in Memphis, mostly at coffee shops and open-mic nights, and it gave him an opportunity to sharpen this initial batch of songs and figure out what listeners liked and what they didn't.

When he moved back to the Shoals in early 2001, he and some friends made demos of his songs and took them to FAME, hoping the studio might bankroll an album—or at least give them a discount on studio time. That didn't happen, but based on the quality of his songs, Isbell was offered a publishing deal: a couple hundred dollars a week to be on the FAME writing staff. He felt like he had won the lottery. The Shoals was doing for Isbell what it hadn't done for Patterson. It was giving him opportunities. It was encouraging him to refine his craft as a songwriter and performer. It was amplifying his voice rather than dampening it. "So I was prepared when lucky things happened," he says.

And the luckiest thing was the Truckers needing a new member.

Almost as soon as Isbell joined the band, they all left the Shoals and hit the road. The kid spent that first tour sitting in the back of the van, headphones on, Truckers CDs in his Discman, taking scrupulous notes. He was learning the material, figuring out his place in every song. Most of them were familiar from the acoustic shows he had already played with Patterson, but now he would be playing with several other guys, the third guitar in a three-guitar attack. Any jitters he might have had weren't evident onstage, and after one or two shows, it was like he'd been in the band for years.

Hitting the road, Isbell left behind his new girlfriend. After years of close friendship, he and Tucker had finally acknowledged their attraction to each other, although the timing wasn't great. As she recalls, "We professed our love for each other right before he was asked to jump in the van and join the Truckers. We had been best friends for a long time, and I think it was inevitable that we'd get together. People always thought we were dating even when we weren't. He always had a girlfriend and I had a boyfriend. Finally it happened and then he left."

Riding in the same van with the Truckers was an education, even just in terms of exposing him to music he'd never heard before. While they were being touted as a southern rock band and associated with Lynyrd Skynyrd, the Truckers were listening to a much wider range of records. Earl Hicks, having taken over bass when Rob Malone switched to guitar, played Captain Beefheart and Sonic Youth, and Patterson dashboard-DJed the Pixies, Pylon, PJ Harvey, Neutral Milk Hotel, and the Glands. "I'd never heard any of them before," says Isbell. "There just wasn't access to that kind of stuff where I was. The first two or three times I heard some of those albums, it sounded too weird and I thought I had to try to find something to like about it. But then I became obsessed. I think that has served me well. It's given me influences that a lot of people in my world probably don't have."

But mostly he was listening to Truckers songs, studying up on them, not only finding his place in them but figuring out how they worked. He went back through the three studio albums and one live album they had released, a small catalog but a mountain of material. "When I first heard the songs, I thought they had a way of discussing southern tropes and rural tropes that I hadn't heard before. I couldn't tell when they were kidding and when they weren't, and that meant *I fucking love this!* It's a caricature, but it's also very moving." He found in these songs lessons that he would apply to his own compositions: about how to write sympathetic characters, how to invest a song with particularity and peculiarity, how to make sure the language matched the narrator, how to avoid overwriting, and most of all how to turn his own experiences in the South into compelling rock and roll.

Within days of joining the Truckers, Isbell began writing his own songs in this mode. He wrote "TVA," about three generations of his family living in the shadow of Wilson Dam. He wrote "Outfit," about his father's advice to him as he embarked on his first tour with a professional rock band. And he wrote "Decoration Day," about a feud between southern families. The latter was written when the Truckers were staying with their friend Joe Swank, a radio DJ and Bloodshot Records rep who lived in Carbondale, Illinois. Isbell says, "I woke up before everybody else did and started thinking, *What kind of song could I write that these guys would like?* I knew there was this kind of southern gothic strain going through their music, and I thought of this crazy story I'd heard about my great uncle killing somebody. So, *I'll just write a song about that.*"

In the quiet morning hours, his bandmates snoring in the next room, Isbell reflected on his family's past, especially his Great Uncle Holland, who was purported to be something of a kingpin in the Shoals. "I didn't have all the details, and I know that a lot of the things I said in that song aren't true. There's a lot of artistic license, to the point where I wish I had tried to learn more about what had actually gone down. It's a little insensitive in hindsight. But it's still a good song, I think."

There are, of course, two sides to this story, but they both rip open the polite veneer of small-town life to reveal something much darker. According to local reports, in May 1982, Deward "Dude" Lawson was visiting his son Calvin and Calvin's girlfriend, Mary Ann, at their trailer home in Florence one day. The three of them were outside planting tomatoes when Holland Hill pulled up with his sons, Dennis and John Barton Hill. They had shotguns with them, and they shot Dude multiple times—bloody retribution for some crime or other; nobody remembers what it might have been. Before they left, they threatened more bloodshed to come. Calvin rushed his father to the hospital, meeting the ambulance halfway, but Dude died from his wounds.

In the Hill family's telling, Holland and his boys weren't anywhere near Calvin Lawson's trailer. Thanks to testimony that painted Calvin as a drunk and Mary Ann as a woman of loose morals—therefore rendering them both untrustworthy witnesses—Holland's lawyers convinced a jury that the defendant was a good man, an upstanding citizen, and something of a local celebrity, thanks to his fiddle playing in a popular bluegrass band. After only an hour of deliberation, the jury acquitted him of all charges.

What Isbell wrote constitutes something like a Dirty South version of the Hatfields and McCoys: two families engaged in a bloody feud for so long that nobody remembers how it all started. It has just always been that way; each family exists to defy the other. And maybe it's fitting that he wrote the song from the point of view not of his own family but of a Lawson—Calvin Lawson, specifically, who is so shaken by his father's murder that he denounces the whole business. He understands that this feud, which started before he was born, leads nowhere and creates nothing but misery for all involved. Rather than promise vengeance against the Hills, he refuses to even mourn his father: "I've got a mind to go spit on his grave," Isbell sings, noting that it's not even marked.

Isbell called this new song "Decoration Day." The title is a reference to what is now known as Memorial Day, which originated in the tradition of commemorating the Civil War dead, Union and Confederate alike. Public displays of Confederate loyalty were forbidden during Reconstruction. In the Reconstruction South, men flying the rebel flag or wearing their old gray uniforms were likely to be stopped by occupying Union forces, arrested and jailed, or worse. Only southern women—wives and daughters and mothers and sisters—could openly mourn fallen Confederate soldiers, so they were the ones who lay wreaths on graves or draped Confederate flags over headstones. The tradition was practiced in the North and the South throughout the twentieth century, finally recognized as a national holiday in 1971. It has shed any Confederate trappings, such that it is now more about honoring the dead from all wars rather than just the Civil War.

"When I grew up, we decorated all the graves, and it didn't have any kind of antebellum or Civil War connotations whatsoever." That's how Isbell remembers it; it was never about southern tradition, more about family. Still, you don't have to work hard to hear "Decoration Day" as a refutation of certain poisonous ideas about the region, in particular Confederate imagery as "heritage." When Lawson spits on his father's grave, he might be spitting on the notion of the Lost Cause and the family loyalties that perpetuate the conflict.

All that came from one early morning writing session when Isbell was lonely and far from home and most likely hung way over. First, Isbell played the song for bass player Earl Hicks, and Isbell remembers that he was dismissive. Patterson was just the opposite. "He goes, 'Holy shit! Holy shit! You wrote that today? Goddamn!'" And let me pause just a moment here to remark on Isbell's dead-on impersonation of Patterson. I've spent hours talking to them both for this book, and when Isbell mimics Patterson's North Alabama twang and his supremely enthusiastic southern cadence, I feel like I might be talking to the man himself.

Isbell's impersonation of his former bandmate is, of course, completely affectionate and perhaps reveals just how close the two became during the 2000s. Patterson rejects the notion, but Isbell embraces it: the elder songwriter became a mentor for the young musician, just like David Hood and Barry Billings had been. "Patterson and I were really close," says Isbell. "We hit it off immediately. But he's good at making friends. I'm not. And Cooley's not. Patterson's an adult with friends, which is weird. He's like, *Until you let me down, we're buddies.* And that's a brave way to go through the world. I come from the other direction: *Prove to me that you can be my friend.*"

Patterson was impressed enough that the band started including "Decoration Day" in its live sets and eventually recorded it for their follow-up to *Southern Rock Opera*. The song turned out so well that the Truckers named the album after it. "That was a big deal because I'd never even had a song on a record before," Isbell says, "and I remember Patterson giving me a copy of the album at me and Shonna's wedding party. We just had a party out in a field, a friend's backyard, and he gave me a copy of *Decoration Day*. I was very, very happy to have that."

Isbell arrived in the band as a talented songwriter still developing a distinctive voice, one who could hold his own against his more experienced bandmates, but he was also a sharp guitar player who, like Malone before him, bolstered the Truckers' three-guitar attack. He's a polished and precise player, especially compared to Patterson and Cooley. Together, they established a dynamic that blended the loud, reckless spirit of punk with the more practiced riffing of Skynyrd and other southern rock bands. Isbell made it sound like he'd played these songs hundreds of times already, while Cooley, who actually had played them hundreds of times already, made it sound like he was playing them for the first time. And in between them was Patterson, who toggled between lead and rhythm, between wailing on a solo and pushing the songs along at a chugging pace. Together they turned "Decoration Day" into something epic and almost violent, a barrage of guitars that's more Crazy Horse than Skynyrd, or maybe like Sonic Youth if they weren't city folk. The song's loud, dramatic coda sounds like a bag of snakes, as each guitarist tries to outdo the others. That meant "Decoration Day" had to come a little later in their sets, so they could build up to it and wring every ounce of bitterness and angst out of it.

It had been nearly a decade since Patterson had left the Shoals, yet he remained tethered to the place, connected to its legacy and finally in a position where he could put his hometown back on the map. He was not the only one. The fashion designer Billy Reid moved from New York City to Florence in 2001, setting up a studio to launch a new label out of Alabama. He came to know and love the place through his wife, who was born there, and rather than a liability, this new headquarters, though far from the catwalks of New York and Paris, became a selling point. In 2005 he opened a Billy Reid store—his third—on Court Street. It sparked something like a local renaissance, attracting high-end restaurants like Odette to the thoroughfare.

In fact, the Shoals had grown tremendously in the ten years since

Adam's House Cat died its inglorious death, blurring some of the distinctions between the sticks and the city as the suburbs sprawled into the countryside. FAME had been built out in the middle of nowhere, essentially in a big cornfield, but the town of Muscle Shoals had grown right up to its doorstep. By the time Isbell signed a contract with the studio, it was surrounded by a CVS and a McDonald's and several other chain stores that Patterson laments in songs like "After It's Gone" and "21st Century USA." While FAME remains a fully operating recording studio, it has become a popular tourist spot for the people who understand its significance—which has grown since the release of "that movie." The time capsule aspect of the place has only intensified over the years, with its worn shag carpeting, ancient wood paneling, and faded black-and-white photos of the stars who had come through town. But the Truckers were determined to record there at the height of their success, and since then the studio has hosted sessions by Dylan LeBlanc, Gregg Allman, Phish, and the Blind Boys of Alabama, among others.

By contrast Muscle Shoals Sound Studio was flailing. The Swampers had moved their facility from its original location at 3614 Jackson Highway to a larger building on the banks of the Tennessee River, but after struggling through the early 1980s, they sold the building and their archives to Malaco, a label consortium based in Jackson, Mississippi. The new owners saw enough potential in the Muscle Shoals brand to keep the name in place for another twenty years, but by the time the Drive-By Truckers released *Southern Rock Opera*, the future of the studio looked bleak. It closed in 2005 and is now a film studio, but the original facility out on Jackson Highway has been restored to its '70s glory, with original wood paneling, some of the original equipment, and ancient graffiti marking David Hood's spot near the back of the room.

Song publishing was still a crucial part of the Shoals music industry, but new studios were popping up around the region, including the NuttHouse in Sheffield, which hosted sessions by the Nashville bluegrass band Steeldrivers and the Birmingham indie-gospel outfit St. Paul and the Broken Bones. There were also new labels like Single Lock Records, run by John Paul White, a Shoals native who had been one-half of the country duo the Civil Wars. The local music industry was booming once again, but few of the Truckers were around much to enjoy the city's renaissance. Patterson and drummer Brad Morgan still lived in Athens and Cooley was in Birmingham, and besides, they were spending more time on the road than they did at home. And when they weren't touring, they were recording. Or writing.

The whole enterprise still had a DIY spirit to it. They were still touring in a van, and they had one cell phone between them, which is to say that Patterson had a cell phone that the others used from time to time. He'd be riding shotgun, a notebook on the dashboard, calling up promoters and booking shows six months out. "The whole Truckers thing was just a circus," says Isbell. "At times I felt like I was in a gang, and at other times I felt like I was in a cult. And sometimes I felt like I was riding around with my uncles and they were all hung over and grumpy. And sometimes I felt like a rock star."

They still depended on the largesse of fans and fellow musicians for lodging. Before they graduated from van to bus, they slept on sofas or in spare bedrooms or even on bare floors. "Once Cooley went to sleep, he was out," Isbell says. "He would never wake up. I remember being so cold that we had to roll him up against the door to keep the wind from coming in." Someone—usually Earl Hicks—would sleep in the van to protect their equipment. In Baltimore one night, he woke to the sound of someone jimmying the door, although Hicks might have scared the would-be thieves more than they scared him.

Whoever they stayed with, they had one strict rule: leave the place neater than you found it. That's just good southern manners. They understood that many of their fans and hosts had to go to work the morning after a show, so the Truckers made sure to fold sheets, wash dishes, and pick up after themselves, no matter how tired or hung over they might be. Their mess should not be their host's mess. One night they stayed with their old friend Kelly Hogan and her roommate, Neko Case, in Chicago, and Hogan had warned them that she had to work the next day and wouldn't be able to see them off in the morning. She says, "I woke up and made my coffee, and it was like that scene in *Gone with the Wind* when Scarlett is walking through the railyard with all the Confederate wounded laid across the ground. I felt like I was lifting my big hoop skirt to step over the bodies."

After she left, the Truckers painstakingly cleaned the apartment. "I opened the door that night and it was the cleanest it had ever been. They'd done all the dishes; the floor was shiny; the towels were all washed and folded. But there was a streetlight shining through the window on the floor, and right there in the light was Cooley's toothpick. That was the only sign the little shoemaker's elves had been there. Those boys' mamas raised them right. They knew how to behave."

Perhaps because they were finally realizing their rock dreams at a time in life when most people are settling down, or perhaps because their biggest record was released so close to 9/11, there was a shift in the Truckers' songwriting, although not in their sound. Isbell noticed it right away: on the band's first albums, Patterson in particular had embraced southern clichés and punchlines, and wrote lyrics full of humor and humanity, but his songs were growing much more straightforward. "I'm not saying there's causation here," says Isbell, "but around that time the music got a little more genuine and a little more direct. They left behind that sense of *I don't know if they're fucking with me or not.* There was something very ridiculous and absurd about what they had been doing. There had been this weird route to poignancy."

One song that took that weird route was "The Deeper In," Patterson's opening salvo on *Decoration Day*. What's the ultimate insult you can hurl at a southerner? What's the most clichéd joke about rural folks? Incest: anybody who lives out in the country is busy making time with their cousins and sisters and anyone else they're related to. That's the setup for "The Deeper In," about a romance between siblings. But it's not a joke of a song. It starts quietly, with Patterson singing a cappella about a young woman with few opportunities and an older brother who's been away most of her life. "You only met him when you were nineteen years old," Patterson sings. "Old enough to know better, but you took to his jawline and his long sandy hair." They run off together, a Bonnie and Clyde of forbidden love. They have children. They make a family. They get arrested and sent to prison. Their children are taken away and placed in foster homes.

The song's arrangement is spare: first Patterson alone, then the band enters, playing a gentle and deeply sympathetic country waltz, and the song ends tragically and tenderly. One night the young woman dreams of the Lord bestowing grace and forgiveness on one of his less fortunate souls, but she awakens "in a jail cell, alone and so lonely," with seven long years in a Michigan prison stretching out in front of her. "The Deeper In" cuts off abruptly with a fading chord from John Neff's pedal steel, which sounds like a tear rolling down a cheek. It's a small miracle

of a song, despite the unseemliness at its center: a redneck joke decon-
structed, with life breathed into it, and transformed into a genuinely affecting love song. As Isbell puts it, "it's Patterson saying, *This is what
you say about us, so we're going to tell you what it's really like.* To me that's
as good an example as you can get of trying to extend humanity with
music, and there's nothing to me that's more of a higher calling for music
than that."

Decoration Day marks a subtle shift in the band's lyrical priorities.
"The Deeper In" is one of only a handful of character-driven songs on
the album; most of the others draw from Patterson's and Cooley's own
lives and struggles. They both sing angry, grieving songs about the suicide of Adam's House Cat bassist John Cahoon as well as sober, devastating songs about the state of their marriages, which they had been
collecting for a few years by then. It's a far cry from many of the early
songs that Isbell had been learning in the back of the van, and the contrast between grizzled veteran and green newcomer is pronounced. Isbell
contributes the album's title track, but "Outfit" recounts the advice his
father gave him when he embarked on this career in rock and roll. "Don't
sing with a fake British accent. . . . Have fun, and stay clear of the needle."
He was starting his journey, but his bandmates were already far along in
theirs. As if to highlight the differences between them, Patterson would
introduce him onstage as Jason "Nearly Famous" Isbell.

The age difference between Isbell and his bandmates was nowhere
more apparent than in Europe, where the band toured in May 2002. It
was Isbell's first time out of the country, not to mention his first time on
an airplane. He was nervous and terrified: "I got shit-hammered at the
hotel bar, and Earl had to help me get to the airport and get on the plane,"
he says. Once they landed, the kid was in no better shape. The pair immediately found a shop selling psilocybin mushrooms. "I ate half of my
carton, but nothing was happening. So I ate the other half and some of
Earl's, too. I didn't know to give it some time. I'd just had cowshit mushrooms. I went to a place that I never want to return to in my life. I was
literally running up and down the hallways screaming. We'd only been
there twenty-four hours. My brain was probably reprogrammed in some
crazy ways."

More than Isbell, though, Hicks was getting out of hand. The bass
player was a "Beefheart hippie," to use Isbell's term, and he seemed

intent on rebelling against anything that smacked of tradition, which in some cases meant the other Truckers. He was becoming increasingly difficult on the road, and it came to a head while the band was traveling in Europe. Hicks wasn't coming to sound checks, and when he was around, he could be volatile, unpredictable, antagonistic. "One night he ordered his dinner to be delivered to the stage," says Isbell. "He was eating steak while he was playing bass. Then he jumped into the drum kit and shit went everywhere. He was yelling at people, and then one night he yelled at Cooley, and that was it. They let him go." Lesson: don't piss off Cooley.

"We weren't equipped to handle each other's mental health issues," says Isbell. "We were doing our best and we cared a lot about each other, but we were not the kind of people who would say, *Let me help you get some therapy* or *Let me help you figure out how to handle this*. Letting Earl go, I know that was really hard on Patterson, because Patterson wears his heart on his sleeve." Hicks has since become something of a shadowy figure in Trucker lore. Today, he's one of very few former bandmates out of contact with the band, which means he's a ghost haunting this book. (Hicks politely declined a request for an interview.)

"It's something that's still real sad to me, because we were really close friends," says Patterson. "And we owed him this debt. He made *Pizza Deliverance*, *Alabama Ass Whuppin'*, and *Southern Rock Opera*. All three of those records would not have happened if it weren't for Earl. We didn't have money to go into a studio or hire anybody, so he got the gear specifically to make those records and to produce us. He produced *Southern Rock Opera*, but he refused a credit. He could be a really surly, contrary guy, but he was fun and he was sweet." In tribute, Patterson wrote a song called simply "Goodbye," which would eventually appear on the 2006 album *A Blessing and a Curse*. The song opens with a bit of studio chatter, perhaps as a nod to Hicks's role as the band's expert recording engineer. Then the band enters playing a slow crawl of a melody, a rickety groove that at times seems to barely hold together, much like the band itself. Patterson is measured in his remembrance as he struggles to decide how much of the blame to shoulder for this severed friendship. "I feel so damned nostalgic every time I think about those times," he sings in a soulful but searching performance, as though he's figuring it all out in real time. "I start to feel so guilty but goddamnit I swear to you I tried."

Even as they were venturing farther away from home than they had ever been, their idea of home was changing. The addition of Isbell to the lineup was a big part of their transition from being an Athens band to a Shoals band again, and the Truckers were recording more often in their old stomping grounds. Half of *Decoration Day* and most of *The Dirty South* was recorded at FAME. For the latter Patterson even resurrected "Lookout Mountain," his suicide note inspired by the hard times he'd faced with Adam's House Cat. Now the song took on a different tone: it felt less like a first-person account of depression and more like a character study, as though the narrator of one of Patterson's other songs was singing it.

For Patterson that meant coming to terms with his experiences in Adam's House Cat and, to some extent, forgiving his hometown for rejecting him so long ago. But he and his band were returning as something like conquering heroes, or at the very least as hometown boys done good. He'd achieved enough with the Truckers that he didn't have to listen when folks said that he wasn't doing it right or that he wouldn't amount to anything.

When it came time to replace Hicks, the Truckers didn't look in Athens for a new member, although there would have been more than a few worthy candidates back where Patterson still got his mail. In fact, the band didn't have to look very far at all: Isbell's new wife, Shonna, played bass. The decision was easy. Also, there wasn't really a decision. "We didn't have a second choice other than Shonna," says Patterson, who had actually known her before he met Isbell. "I felt like she was the right person for the band. Everybody else thought she was the right person too. But the narrative that people just assumed out there in public was, *Oh, okay, now they've got Jason's wife on bass.*"

She and Isbell were living in a small house in Center Star, Alabama, just east of Killen, and she remembers being awakened by an early morning call from her husband. "I was dead asleep when the phone rang. I think it was 4:00 a.m., and Jason was calling from somewhere in Europe. So there was a time difference. He didn't explain what happened, but he said they'd all talked about it and wanted to know if I wanted to play bass with them. I was silent for a minute. 'Are you *sure* you've talked about this? They know we're married, right?' It seemed like such a crazy idea."

But she didn't hesitate. "I was a passionate musician, and that's what I wanted to do with my life. So I said yes."

The implication was that she was hired to placate this new singer-songwriter who had already emerged as a star on his first album with the band—a kneejerk assumption with a whiff of misogyny to it. But it was far from the case. "The fact that they were married would have played against it," says Patterson, "but there were enough reasons for why we wanted her in that band that we refused to acknowledge their marriage as a negative. We just bulldozed through that part of it." They made Tucker a full partner in the band—not just a salaried player, but a full member with creative input. It seemed unfair to them to make her a subordinate of her husband, and besides, they wouldn't even know Isbell if not for her. "When it went south, though, it sucked on so many levels."

Tucker earned her Truckers spot on merit alone. By the time she joined the band, she'd been playing bass more than half her life. Her father had given her guitar lessons when she was eight years old. "We had this shitty little acoustic guitar that Daddy said he paid ten dollars for in Mexico when he was in the Navy. He showed me a few chords and I kept picking at it. He would hear me in my bedroom playing along with songs on the radio. I was playing the bass lines. I had no idea what I was doing, but I guess I had a natural inclination to play the bass lines. Luckily, he recognized that and got me a bass for my tenth birthday."

In high school she joined a bluegrass band playing upright and was so devoted that she skipped her senior prom to play a gig at the Indian Camp Creek Bluegrass Festival in nearby St. Florian, Alabama. And like so many local teenagers, she received endless encouragement from veteran musicians associated with FAME and Muscle Shoals Sound. "When I met Spooner [Oldham], that's when the roof came off. Not only did I get to learn about the musical history of my home on a very intimate and personal level, but Spooner showed me that this is really something you can do for a living. I got to see that it was a real thing, a real job."

Schooled in what might seem like disparate styles—white bluegrass and Black R&B—Tucker was and remains a badass bassist, playing with agility and authority whether on Patterson's classic rock anthems or Cooley's boogie-rock songs or Isbell's country-rock waltzes; even more crucially, she clicked immediately with drummer Brad Morgan, which gave the band an even more formidable and versatile rhythm section. Tucker allowed the Truckers to expand their repertoire throughout the 2000s and gave them a solid grounding as they explored new facets of their hometown's music history, especially on the deep soul cut "Purgatory Line" (from the 2008 release *Brighter Than Creation's Dark*), the swamp-noir groove of "The Wig He Made Her Wear" (from the 2010 release *The Big To-Do*), and my personal favorite Shonna moment, the discofied "Used to Be a Cop," which sounds like Chic gone country rock.

"I was a young female musician, and I think people enjoyed seeing that," she says. "The Truckers weren't a dainty band. They were a big, loud, dirty, belligerent rock and roll band. I think fans were fascinated at first by this woman in a dude's band. I'd already had to get used to that just being a female musician. I'd always had to prove myself. But I don't remember getting a negative vibe from anybody. The fans seemed to be very accepting."

Even with his wife in the band and onstage with him every night, Isbell's adventures with drugs and alcohol soured into dependency. What had once been an occasional rock star indulgence ramped up into a continuous nightmare, which is partly the result of what he admits is an addictive personality but also due to his lack of experience: almost overnight he had gone from an aspiring nobody to a celebrated songwriter hailed by fans as a talent equal to his elder bandmates. He experienced something like the bends from rising too quickly, without the blood and sweat that Patterson and Cooley had put into it. "The audience was already there," he says, "and they were already intense—loud, noisy hell-raisers, a thousand people in a room drunk off their asses, and I'm in the middle of it thinking, *AAAAAAhhhhhh, this is awesome!*"

The more Isbell drank, the more he and Tucker fought. Even after the Truckers sold their old clunker of a van and graduated to a touring bus, there was still no privacy—nowhere they could go to hash things out. "We were having trouble in front of every-*fucking*-body," Isbell says. "I wouldn't wish that on anybody, having to get a divorce in front of your closest friends. *Let's scream at each other on the bus with everybody around.*" And when they got off the road and headed home to Center Star, they could barely stand to be around each other in their small house. "I was not fit to be in a relationship, and things got real bad. My drinking went from recreational to escapist, and then it all caught up with me."

"He was a mess and getting more and more difficult to live with and be around," says Tucker. "Those were hard years. I was basically his caretaker when he was in some of the worst places he's ever been in his life. But I never took the time to deal with any of it. It was always like, *Let's just fix this and play the show. Let's get through this and play the show.* I was just putting Band-Aids on things. But he wasn't in control of himself in any way."

Isbell hinted at his unhappiness in some of the songs he was writing at the time. "Danko/Manuel" compared his situation to that of members of The Band, who had shortsightedly sold their publishing rights to guitarist Robbie Robertson and were left to tour endlessly for the rest of their lives. Even as he ponders the mistakes of his heroes, Isbell expresses the weariness of a man twice his age: "I ain't livin' like I should. A little rest might do me good." That song comes midway through *The Dirty South*, and the album ends with what may be his best and most devastating Truckers song, "Goddamn Lonely Love." His guitar riff spirals downward like his emotions, and he lays everything out pretty bluntly: "I could take Greyhound home, but when I got there, it'd be gone, along with everything a home is made up of," he sings. "So I'll take two of what you're having and I'll take all of what you've got, to kill this goddamn lonely, goddamn lonely love." Did these songs ease his troubles, or did playing them every night with his increasingly estranged wife make his troubles worse?

In his songs Isbell could be his best self—or at least a better self—and his lyrics display a remarkable generosity as well as a startling degree of self-awareness. Outside of his songs, he was blunt to the point of cruelty. During one show he drunkenly announced that he was getting a divorce, which prompted Shonna to take a swing at him. She missed and hit the microphone, jamming her fingers. "They had vodka and it got ugly," says Traci Thomas, their manager at the time. "That was the night we coined the phrase 'Rednecks don't drink white liquor.'"

That tension made their summer 2006 tour opening for the Black

Crowes even more of a nightmare and poisoned sessions for their 2007 album, *A Blessing and a Curse*, whose title may or may not refer to Isbell's status in the band. "It was a miserable experience," Patterson says. "I know it's wrong not to separate that out when you're judging a record, but maybe if the experience had been a little *more* miserable, it would have been a better record." It was the first album they worked up primarily in the studio instead of onstage, an interesting experiment that nevertheless produced songs that sound uprooted, too slick compared to what had come before and lacking many of the details that typically add up to rich characters and specific settings. But there are highlights, including Patterson's "World of Hurt" and Cooley's "Gravity's Gone." And "Space City," a eulogy for Cooley's grandmother, is one of his finest and most emotionally complex compositions, turning Huntsville's history with space travel into a metaphor for grief and longing. Especially from the stoic songwriter, it's a weeper.

Isbell's two songs, however, are among his weakest with the Truckers, and his relationship with the band was fraying beyond repair, especially his friendship with Patterson. That came to a head over a new song he had written called "Dress Blues," inspired by the death of an old high school classmate. Marine Corporal Matthew D. Conly had been killed when his Humvee triggered an IED while on patrol in the Iraqi province of Al-Anbar. He was a week from his twenty-second birthday and a month from returning home.

Even at such a low point, Isbell could still write songs like finely observed short stories, deftly depicting the small-town setting through careful details: "The high school gymnasium's ready, full of flowers and old Legionnaires," he sings. The bleachers are festooned with red, white, and blue bunting—an oddly celebratory touch. "Nobody showed up to protest, just sniffle and stare." In its understatement the song is a vivid and sympathetic portrayal of communal grieving, of the ways in which an international war can reverberate on a local level. And who says nobody shows up to protest? Isbell himself calls out the mourners for not saying anything when Conly was sent "to fight somebody's Hollywood war."

Like most of their freshly penned songs, the Truckers added "Dress Blues" to their setlist, first playing the song live in April 2006. It stayed there for a year as the band worked on an arrangement, but nothing seemed to click. "I got really mad about the way they performed that song live," Isbell admits. "It seemed like we couldn't get the tempo right." One night his anger got the better of him, and he made some disparaging remarks to the crowd concerning both the band and the song. "I was so mad. Of course, I was also drunk, and there was no way I should have said that. It upset Patterson really badly. That might have been the worst fight we ever had while we were all on tour together, but I was just so fucking mad that it didn't sound right to me. Out of all the personal issues that we had, it was actually a creative difference that was the worst fight."

But they did keep playing that song, at least until March 30, 2007, when Isbell sang it at the Music Farm in Charleston, South Carolina. The next night—their second show at the same venue—was his final performance as a full-fledged Trucker. Onstage they made no mention of his departure, but a week later Patterson posted an announcement on the band's Myspace page wishing Isbell the best of luck and noting some upcoming dates. Accompanying that notice was news that John Neff, a pedal steel player from Athens who had toured and recorded with the band off and on, was joining the Truckers full time. Isbell responded with his own terse message on his Myspace page: "I am not in the Drive By Truckers anymore. Go figure. I wish them luck. I will not answer questions about it."

"It became obvious that he was nowhere near ready to help himself," says Shonna Tucker. "I couldn't be married to this person anymore, which is an awful thing to realize. But we kept playing in the band together a little while after we split up, which made things even worse. It all blew up and we finally decided, *Okay, he's got to go.* It was a long, rough journey to get to that point, but we finally got there."

Just like that, this very productive and very tumultuous period in the Truckers' history was over, and nobody knew exactly what to do next. Isbell already had a solo album lined up, *Sirens of the Ditch,* which he'd been recording piecemeal at FAME over the past four years, with Patterson coproducing and most of the Truckers and Spooner Oldham backing him. It was released in July 2007—just three months after he left the band. Almost immediately, he went back out on the road with his backing band, the 400 Unit, featuring old friends from the Shoals area. It took him a while to find his feet as a solo artist. As a Trucker, he had only two or three songs on an album, which meant he could pick his best and most memorable compositions. Sustaining a full-length album by himself proved much trickier. There are moments of grace and brilliance on his first three albums, but they sound like an artist trying to figure himself out. Tellingly, once he got sober in 2012, Isbell's albums grew much more confident, much more consistent, much more compelling in his depictions of small-town characters and real-life marriage. He has become one of the most celebrated singer-songwriters in Nashville, his sales and celebrity far outstripping that of his former band.

"The positives I take away from that experience [with the Truckers]," he says, "were so great that I don't look back on it with any kind of bitterness. I was not in good emotional health, but it was so good for things that I would need later. I don't know what I would have done, what avenue I would have taken, and there's a very good chance that had I not been in the band at that time in my life, I might be making music that I don't love right now. And to me that trumps everything else."

With Isbell gone, Tucker was the Truckers' strongest connection to the Shoals as well as to a generation that grew up revering rather than rebelling against their Shoals forebears. The differences between all of those generations came to bear in 2007, when the Truckers were hired to back Bettye LaVette on her album *The Scene of the Crime*. Back in the early 1970s, LaVette had been a promising young R&B artist with a few minor hits to her name but without a chart smash commensurate with her talent and promise. After signing with Atlantic Records—the same label as Aretha Franklin and Wilson Pickett—she headed down to the Shoals and recorded with the Swampers, cutting a record that was gritty and groovy as she blurred the lines between country, R&B, and rock. She cut Ron Davies's "It Ain't Easy" a year after David Bowie covered it as Ziggy Stardust, along with Neil Young's "Heart of Gold" and John Prine's "Souvenirs." Her cover of Joe Simon's "Your Time to Cry" could have made her a star or at least given her a smaller hit on which to build a fan base, but Atlantic Records declined to promote the single or even release what was to be her debut full-length album. Her label never gave LaVette a reason.

"I can think of that album and my dog Mickey that I had when I was eleven and just burst into tears at any time," says LaVette nearly fifty years later. "When they told me they weren't going to release the album, I crawled under the dining room table and stayed there three or four days. I had people bring me food and wine and joints." For decades, no one—not even LaVette herself—understood why the album was shelved. Whenever someone asked her about it, she was embarrassed that she had no answer. It wasn't until much later that she learned that she had unknowingly gotten caught up in a split between Atlantic cofounders Ahmet Ertegun and Jerry Wexler. "Jerry was on my side," she explains, "but Ahmet was on Aretha's side. It wasn't going to work with me and Aretha. What you wanted to have at a label was one of everything, so it wouldn't have worked to have the both of us."

LaVette might have been just one of so many artists who recorded in the Shoals and then disappeared, to be resurrected occasionally on deep-cut anthologies or niche-market reissues. But she spent years scrambling to assemble something like a musical career, which often meant taking gigs in hotel lounges and recording catch as catch can. She released a comeback record in 2003 called *A Woman Like Me* on the tiny label Blues Express. When Andy Kaulkin, cofounder of the punk label Epitaph and its offshoot Anti, heard her sing, he immediately signed her to a roster that already included R&B legend Solomon Burke and would eventually add Mavis Staples. On her 2005 release, *I've Got My Own Hell to Raise*, she emerged as a survivor, something like a legend at a time when her peers had either lost their voices or were too stymied by old-school sales and chart expectations to release anything of substance. In fact, LaVette had refined her instrument over the years, becoming a superbly imaginative and exacting interpreter of a wide range of songs.

Because of their similar histories with the Shoals—histories that involved neglect and rejection—LaVette and the Truckers seemed a good match; the Truckers turned themselves into a backing band for their sessions together at FAME. (Isbell was asked not to attend the sessions but showed up anyway.) They titled their record *The Scene of the Crime*, in reference to the murder of her '72 album. But the sessions were anything but pleasant, as three very different generations of musicians had three very different approaches to making music in the studio. When LaVette had recorded some thirty-five years before, the session players had everything worked out by the time she went in to sing. They had chosen the songs, had arranged and rehearsed them, and could knock them out quickly and efficiently. Most of the Truckers, on the other hand, viewed sessions as looser and more exploratory. They might know their parts, but they were to some extent winging it.

Most of the sessions with LaVette involved hollering and yelling and more than a few heated disagreements, such that Patterson even mentions them in his liner notes for the album. Only Tucker seemed to endear herself to the R&B legend. LaVette, however, blames herself for the outbursts, not the band. After so much heartbreak, she was bound and determined to make things go her way. "It had to be my way, period," she says. "Every time they wouldn't do something I wanted them to do, I would get mad and start cussing and crying. But they knew I knew what I was doing, even if I couldn't always figure out how to say what I wanted. But it was worse for them."

The Scene of the Crime further established LaVette's reputation as a song interpreter and remains one of the standouts in the busy 2000s soul revival, a movement that made late-in-life stars of similar should-have-beens like Sharon Jones and Charles Bradley. The record harks back to the original country-soul sound LaVette and the Swampers had hammered out years before, but without being too precious about it, without sounding like actors in a historical reenactment. Today, it remains one of her favorite albums, now that she has recorded so many. She says, "I still probably do more tunes from that album in my show than any of the other ones."

The Scene of the Crime ends with a Stonesesque vamp called "Before the Money Came (The Battle of Bettye LaVette)," which is the only writing credit she has earned in her career. LaVette styles herself a song interpreter rather than a songwriter, and Patterson had to coax her into a collaboration. When she hits the chorus and puts every professional disappointment, every setback, every heartbreak into the lines, "I got so much to say, so damn proud I was built this way," it's clear they've found some common ground in their experiences of this place.

While certainly not laid-back and relaxing, the LaVette sessions were nevertheless something like a balm during what might be the darkest time in the Truckers' history. Even with Isbell gone, there was still tension within the band, a crisis of identity as the members struggled to figure out what kind of band they were without him. Frequently this indirection played out in the rock show, which was often more ragged than glorious, uncomfortably tense.

It didn't take the Truckers very long to right themselves, and they emerged stronger from that dark period, immediately producing one of their longest and finest albums, *Brighter Than Creation's Dark*, released in 2008. Recorded largely at FAME and featuring contributions from Spooner Oldham (who had been touring with the band), it's a record full of war songs—actual war, not just combat between bandmates. It's about class and struggle in the South, with songs about dying music scenes, songs about family, songs about the Weird Harolds that populate the corners of small towns, songs about chicken-wing puke eating the shine off candy-apple red Corvettes. "It was a total strip-down," says multi-instrumentalist John Neff, "a great opportunity for more pedal steel."

Out of the shadow of her ex, Tucker emerged as a compelling third singer-songwriter, further rooting the band in Shoals R&B with songs like "Home Field Advantage" and "Purgatory Line." Her compositions took different shapes; she wrote in different forms, with humor, warmth, and a penchant for eccentric turns of phrase. Isbell had avoided R&B because he didn't feel qualified to sing it, but Tucker eased into it with no fuss or second-guessing. She wrote comfortably in that vein, and she sang with a powerful and expressive twang. That total strip-down allowed the band to come back with a broader palette, mixing their southern riff rock with swampier grooves.

Tucker had been writing songs for a few years, inspired by country artists like Tom T. Hall and Dolly Parton as well as locals like Dan Penn and Donnie Fritts. "They knew I wrote and always encouraged me, but it took a lot of courage for me to bring my songs to these two people I thought were two of the greatest songwriters ever. I played 'I'm Sorry, Huston' and 'Purgatory Line' for Patterson, and he's like, 'Holy shit! I love both of those songs!' *Okay, I guess I'm going to be a singer now. I'll have to figure that out.*"

Her growing confidence culminated on the 2011 release *Go-Go Boots*, the Truckers album most grounded in the Shoals. Steeped in North Alabama R&B, it was recorded in tandem with the previous year's *The Big To-Do*, during long and very productive sessions at David Barbe's Chase Park Transduction studio in Athens. Songs like "Go-Go Boots" and "The Fireplace Poker," both about murderous preachers, use those swampy rhythms toward cinematic ends, with the band scoring Patterson's lyrics of lust and conspiracy like they would a movie. In fact, in a letter to fans, Patterson described it as a "noir film" about the murder of Elizabeth Dorlene Sennett, reportedly by her husband, Rev. Charles Sennett. And they cover not one but two songs written by a guy named Eddie Hinton: Tucker sings "Where's Eddie," which had been a minor hit for the Scottish singer Lulu in 1970, and Patterson tackles "Everybody Needs Love," which became something like the band's theme song for the tours that followed.

Hinton remains a minor, slightly elusive character in Shoals lore, never as celebrated as he ought to be for his session playing and songwriting, and that may be due to the fact that he played not one defining role but many. He was a superb guitar player with an ear for mimicry; that's him soloing on the Staple Singers' "I'll Take You There" and nailing Pops's distinctive tone and style so dead on that everybody thought it was Pops playing. He was a curious songwriter: whether working with Fritts in the late 1960s or by himself in the 1970s, Hinton trafficked in oddball imagery (as in Tony Joe White's "300 Pounds of Hongry"), unwieldy but still compelling concepts (the Box Tops' "Choo Choo Train"), and overly earnest social critique (Cher's "Save the Children"). But he also had a way of taking a scenario and locating its kernel of melancholy and longing, as he did on his most famous composition, a co-write with Fritts: "Breakfast in Bed," which kicks off Dusty Springfield's 1969 breakout album, *Dusty in Memphis*, is about a woman comforting the man she loves as he cries over another woman.

After he heard Hinton sing, none other than Atlantic Records president Jerry Wexler declared he would be the next big thing, that he was a superstar in the making. But any chance at a solo career was wrecked when Hinton was busted for possession in the early 1970s. He left the Shoals and wandered in the wilderness, finally releasing his solo debut, *Very Extremely Dangerous* (one of Patterson's favorite albums), in 1978. As solid a chunk of white soul as it is, the album had the misfortune of being released just weeks before his label, Capricorn Records, went bankrupt. For the rest of his life, Hinton battled mental illness, drug addiction, and homelessness.

Perhaps the Truckers saw something familiar in Hinton and his thwarted career, shades of the woman in Nashville who appeared like a vision to Patterson and Cooley just as Adam's House Cat were breaking up. He seems like a local cautionary tale, but Patterson knew Hinton first and foremost as a family friend and colleague of his father, David Hood. He knew him as one of the few adults from that scene who would really interact with him as a kid. And as an adult Patterson saw Hinton perform a small show in Sheffield and was floored by the way the performer drove his backing band and engaged his audience. Long before Discogs made it easy, he sought out the hard-to-find and out-of-print albums that Hinton had recorded in the 1980s, when he was living in a city park in Decatur, Alabama.

When Hinton died of a heart attack in 1995, at only fifty-one years old, Patterson was inspired to write "Sandwiches for the Road," a sympathetic eulogy that neither ignores nor romanticizes the musician's mental illness. "The voice in my brain can be a little unkind sometimes," he sings. "Go ahead, point at me, I ain't scared. . . . Nothing can hurt you but yourself." The song closes out the band's debut, *Gangstabilly*, presenting Hinton as something like a spiritual guide for the Truckers.

Thirteen years and countless rock shows later, Hinton was on their minds again. Shake-It Records in Cincinnati, Ohio, had started a series of seven-inch singles called *Dangerous Highways* featuring different artists covering Hinton's songs. He had no real connection to the Magic City or the Buckeye State, but the first installments were by Ohio artists: Greg Dulli of the Afghan Whigs and the Twilight Singers, followed by a split between the Heartless Bastards and Wussy. The Truckers' song choices on their single show a deep familiarity with Hinton's work and a keen understanding of how his songs might accrue new implications nearly fifteen years after his sad death. "Where's Eddie" is on its surface about a woman who breaks Eddie's heart and then tries frantically to make it up to him, but Tucker finds new depths in the song that weren't available to Lulu forty years earlier. She sings it to the real Eddie Hinton, wondering what became of him and wishing he could know the extent of her appreciation for his music. Making it a song about more than heartbreak, Tucker gestures to every demon that haunted him.

That sensibility extends to the Truckers' cover of "Everybody Needs Love," a song they had played years before at Cooley's wedding. "It was one we could do pretty easily, simple to work up," the groom recalls.

It's the Truckers' "Johnny B. Goode" or "Mustang Sally"—a song so ingrained in them as fans and as players that they really didn't have to labor over an arrangement. They debuted it (or, as the case may be, re-debuted it) at a homecoming show at the historic Shoals Theatre in Florence, with David Hood and Spooner Oldham sitting in. "We got some special shit about to go down," Patterson told the crowd by way of introduction to their "tribute to one of the greatest, greatest artists that ever came out of this area." The studio version that ended up on the Shake-It seven-inch and later on *Go-Go Boots* features one of Patterson's most ecstatic vocal performances, totally open and unguarded in its commitment to that simple and sublime statement. Against the band's exquisite country-soul arrangement, which foregrounds Neff's pedal steel and Morgan's excited drumbeat, it sounds like Patterson could be singing those words to his hometown, or to his bandmates, or to his new wife, or to Eddie himself. If the mark of a good cover is that the artist sings it like he wrote it, with no distance between the material and the performance, then Patterson might have stolen the song from Hinton.

"Everybody Needs Love" became something like a mission statement for the band—not just a single but a spiritually generous and musically exuberant anthem. They played the song on *The David Letterman Show* in June 2011, and they made sure to include it on their set list when they recorded a show straight to acetate at Jack White's Third Man Records in Nashville (which was released on vinyl later that year). In 2015, when the Supreme Court ruled in favor of marriage equality, Wes Freed, the Richmond-based artist who has worked closely with the Truckers for most of their career, created a poster featuring the song title and a Cooley bird with a rainbow banner in its beak. Cooley had the print framed and hung it prominently in his kitchen.

What might have been a triumphant year instead turned into another moment when the band might have swerved into the ditch. In December 2011 the Truckers announced that Tucker was leaving the band, along with John Neff. The two had started dating, which she now acknowledges was a mistake, and while their relationship wasn't as dark as her marriage to Isbell, it was similarly toxic and did introduce new tensions within the band. By all outward appearances the split seemed much more amicable than Tucker and Isbell's, with Tucker making the announcement on the band's website and Patterson adding his own tribute to her: "Her charm and spark will be irreplaceable and her part in our last decade of this band's history is indisputable. We will share in our fans missing of her."

"I had had so many wonderful experiences in the band," she says, "but it was also incredibly exhausting. It was a lot of trauma that I experienced. I made some bad choices. A lot of what I went through was not my fault, but some of it was. I decided it was best to take a break, which ended up being the best thing for me." She released a record, *A Tell All*, with her band Eye Candy but eventually moved back to Center Star and started farming. She didn't pick up an instrument for nearly two years but then gradually returned to the music scene, recording an EP with Spooner Oldham and touring with Pegi Young, John Paul White, and a new Shoals act called the Secret Sisters.

David Barbe filled in for her until the Truckers could find a replacement, which turned out to be a player from Mississippi named Matt Patton, formerly of a Tuscaloosa band called the Dexateens. The Dexateens and the Truckers had a long affiliation, the former having opened for the latter on numerous tours and at a handful of HeAthens Homecoming shows, and Patterson having produced their gritty and imaginative *Hardwire Healing* in 2008. Growing up as part of a Pentecostal church, Patton was raised on punk and gospel and saw no difference between the two, and he immediately cut a striking figure onstage: tall and lanky, he sported a bowl cut and muttonchops and wore a constant beatific grin whenever he played, as though he was in the midst of spiritual rapture. "If my eyes are closed and my head is back, I'm not really thinking," he says. "My fingers are just moving. That's the old Pentecostal thing coming back. I feel a similar way playing rock and roll shows as I felt playing churches. You're connecting with people around you, grabbing on to an energy that's outside of you and possibly bigger than us."

Tucker had been the Truckers' last connection to the Shoals, the last band member who lived there, and her departure signaled a sea change even more than Isbell's did. To survive in the new decade, they would have to become something new, something other than a Shoals band. That transition defined their next album, the 2014 release *English Oceans*, which they were just getting ready to record when Patton came aboard. "I wouldn't say I was disappointed in how that record came out," says the new bass player, "but it was made right when we were regrouping and trying to figure out what kind of band we were then." It's a fine album, with some songs that hew perhaps a bit too closely to what they had done in the past and others—in particular Cooley's title track, an evisceration of white supremacy conspiracy theories—that point the way forward, but generally it sounds tentative: a group of players in search of a purpose, working it out and gelling as a band almost in real time.

Given that album's muted reception among critics and fans, the Truckers faced a new crisis: Had they simply run their course? "I got the sense with the last couple of records," Patterson told me at the time, "that people were considering us this old band that didn't know when to break up. We hadn't embarrassed ourselves, I don't think, but each record seemed to get a little less attention than the one before it." They had kept up a remarkable pace, releasing ten studio albums, touring almost constantly, and weathering one debacle after another during their nearly twenty years together, but was a hiatus in order for them? Should they take some time off? Did they need to go away so that people could miss and appreciate them?

Those were the questions they were asking themselves in the months leading up to the sessions of *American Band*, and they make that album all the more miraculous. It wasn't just a comeback, and it wasn't just a band capturing the horrors of the times in smart, angry, passionate rock songs that were somehow both hopeful and pessimistic. It showed a band willing itself into a new form, painfully realigning itself, fighting to make itself heard. The lineup was the same one that had made *English Oceans*, but it's a totally different band. Partly that's due to the songs themselves, which express outrage and dissent without self-congratulation. Only a handful of rock bands have managed to strike that balance in the twenty-first century, and fewer still have done so while so visibly rooted in red state America.

Richmond, Virginia

▼

Let's start with pink flamingos. Designed in 1957 by a Massachusetts man with the improbable name of Don Featherstone and marketed exclusively by Union Products, the cheap plastic fowl lived many lives throughout the second half of the twentieth century. The flamingo was a sign of the exotic and the modern in the 1960s, with its bold new color and space-age material accentuating its S-shaped neck and compensating for its simple wire legs, but its ubiquity eased its transformation into a signal of bad taste even before John Waters made his deliciously distasteful midnight movie *Pink Flamingos* in 1972. For a generation of Boomers in that decade, as Jennifer Price writes in her book, *Flight Maps: Adventures with Nature in Modern America,* "the bird became a useful thing to have around if you were doing anything outrageous, rebellious, oxymoronic, inappropriate or transgressive. It became an effective way to post a sign: Something Subversive Happening Here."

Somehow the 1980s proved to be the pink flamingo's heyday, as live versions of the bird lent the opening credits of *Miami Vice* a sense of the exotic—never mind that the species had been hunted to extinction in Florida. There were services you could hire to plastic-flamingo-bomb your friend's yard and mail-order stores that branded the bird onto welcome mats, playing cards, pool toys, bowling shirts—you name it. Thirty years after their creation, the plastic birds were selling better than ever, with enough copycats (or mockingbirds?) that Featherstone adjusted his design for the first time to include his authenticating signature. Out in the sticks, however, it played as rural kitsch, never quite shedding its associations with the less fortunate, the low class, any poor soul with poor taste.

Wes Freed remembers when the pink flamingo craze hit Richmond in the late 1980s. He was studying art at Virginia Commonwealth University, and "all the girls were really into pink flamingos," says the unofficial Trucker in his slow, careful drawl. "I thought a black flamingo would look cool. So I started drawing those and painted them on the backs of some of the girls' jackets." Those black flamingos joined a menagerie of fantastical animals on his canvases, staggering over his sloping hills alongside an anthropomorphic possum by the name of Hexter and a gang of voluptuous women in various states of undress and a shared state of don't-give-a-damn. They appear on some of the concert posters Freed designed in the 1990s, in the weird comic strip called "Willard's Garage" he drew for the *Richmond City Paper*, and on the large canvases he painted, sometimes on reclaimed lumber or cardboard or whatever flat surface might be on hand.

An early fan of the Truckers who hosted local shows for them and even invited them to crash at his house, Freed painted the image that appears on the cover of *Southern Rock Opera*, which depicts a gigantic owl hovering ominously over Highway 72. The band loved his blend of the real and the fantastical, so they asked him to work on their follow-up, the 2003 release *Decoration Day*. The owl had been Patterson Hood's idea, based on a giant neon sign he remembered back in Florence, Alabama, but for this new album Freed received no guidelines. *"Oh shit, what am I going to do? Maybe I'll use that black flamingo thing.* So I did the drawing for the cover, and it was a pair of black flamingos in a sinkhole," Freed says. Two short, squat, squawking birds totter about the cover on stubby, gnarled legs, flapping wings that don't look capable of lifting anything into the sky. Utterly fantastical yet strangely familiar in this rural landscape, they have long, snakelike necks supporting heads with fevered red-yellow eyes and sharp beaks. It's impossible to tell if they're sprouting from or repelled by the homemade wooden cross memorializing... *something.*

Built from spare parts of dumb chicken, violent flamingo, and sinister crow, these odd birds creep into the booklet art for the Truckers' CDs and LPs as well, as though haunting these songs. The painting that accompanies Jason Isbell's "Outfit" in the *Decoration Day* booklet shows a young, skeletal man, almost like a redneck Día de los Muertos figure with overalls and a buzz cut, sitting on the gate of a battered pickup smoking a cigarette and working on a six-pack. Behind him is a rusted-out mobile home, and the black flamingos infest the picture like termites or black mold. One of them appears to be asking him for a smoke, while the other eyeballs a pink flamingo with suspicion or maybe even lust. Still carrying traces of their low-rent lawn-decoration associations, they're like gremlins in the works, sabotaging the expected symbolism of the South. Like the Truckers did with their early songs, Freed takes a rural southern cliché and gives it new life and gravity and menace.

Truckers fans took to these birds immediately, some labeling them death birds and others categorizing them as crowmingos. It was Wes's wife, Jyl Freed, a talented artist and musician who passed in 2017, who came up with the name Cooley bird. "It just stuck," he says. "Cooley's got black hair, and he's got kind of a beak." Ever since they appeared on *Decoration Day*, these twisted black birds have become synonymous with the band, serving as a mascot similar to Iron Maiden's Eddie or the Descendants' Milo or Dio's Murray. They appear on stage backdrops, T-shirts, shot glasses, tour posters, turntable slip mats, fan tattoos, and of course every single album since *Decoration Day*. One of them chats up a young woman at a bar on *The Dirty South*, spouting Isbell's lyrics like pickup lines, and another one peeks out from what looks like a garden hedge on the cover of *A Blessing and a Curse* in 2006. There are two Cooley birds hidden on the cover of *English Oceans* and one perching on the finger of a child in the booklet for the 2020 release *The Unraveling*, either hounding or possibly protecting these two kids as they watch the sun set on their uncertain future.

Like the band it has come to represent, the bird evolved over time. It has learned to fly, its wings growing longer and its frame more graceful, all of which only makes it more visually striking but also more symbolically elusive. At one point it even jumped out of the frame and into the real world, when Freed created a gigantic Cooley bird hat out of couch foam. The man himself dutifully wore it for a few shows until the damned thing, all four feet of it painted black, became too unwieldy. "It's turned into a more fearsome sort of creature, with bigger wings and flies a lot more," says Freed. "But it's emblematic and looks good on a sticker or a T-shirt. The Cooley bird's got a face for merch."

Connecting every image he does for the Truckers—as well as for Patterson's and Cooley's solo tours, their joint shows as the Dimmer Twins, and assorted related and unrelated projects—is Freed's unique visual style, which might be described as redneck folk art. In addition to the Cooley bird, there are characters that show up from one album to the next, including the latest addition to the zoo: a swirling, distorted cat silhouette that is spot-glossed on the booklet for *The Unraveling*. "Patterson did coin the phrase Cattersons for all those black and red cats," says Freed. "He decided that they should be called Cattersons, although he said that in a fucking Facebook comment. It might have been just an offhand joke, but I'm going to start calling them that."

The relationship is unique among contemporary bands, but rock and roll—especially as embodied by the Truckers' heroes—has always emphasized the visual. In the 1960s, groups like the Who and the Rolling Stones came out of art school and used theories and practices they learned in the classroom, whether it was the pop-art cover of *Who's Next* or the big lips-and-tongue logo that the Stones adopted. Even the Velvet Underground was sort of a prefab art-rock outfit assembled by Andy Warhol, who designed the banana cover of their 1967 self-titled debut. The Swedish design firm Hipgnosis created almost all of Pink Floyd's album covers, and Roger Dean crafted the fantastical landscapes for Yes and so many other prog bands. But few artists of that or any era have worked as closely with an artist as the Truckers have with Freed.

His artwork has become so prominent over the years, so closely associated with the Truckers and their music, that he's become something like an auxiliary member of the band, like David Barbe or Jenn Bryant: someone who has had a hand in their success, who has helped mold the band's identity from the outside. Freed's art connects the songs, ties everything together, and sets everything within the same half-real world of their Dirty South. "You know how Marvel has its own universe?" says Patterson. "That's us. We have our own universe. The way Wes paints is literally the way he sees the world. He sees those birds flying around when he looks up at the sky. They're very real to him. That marriage between his artistic vision and our artistic vision is very special and unique."

Even after so many years as the Truckers' bizarre avatar, the Cooley bird remains an inscrutable damn thing. Born in the former capital of the Confederacy—a city always atoning for its history, not to mention the first market to embrace the Truckers—it doesn't represent hate or racism necessarily, but it does appear like a dark embodiment of some essential southern impulse, some rebellious urge: *Something Subversive Happening Here.* Freed can't get much more specific than that, and he's content to let the Truckers' mascot remain elusive. "I'd probably be stupid enough to babble it off if I knew the answer," says Freed. "I think it just has to do with the music I like."

"I've never separated the two, the music and the art," says Freed. "To me it's all art. It's visual art and art that you hear. Songs put images in my mind, and images put songs in my mind. It all seems to be drawn together. It's a weird way I have of seeing things." He grew into both early in life, showing a talent for drawing around the time he developed an obsession with rock and roll. Growing up on a farm out in Waynesboro, Virginia, about an hour and a half northwest of Richmond, he had plenty of subjects both domesticated and wild. In fact, the kid wanted to be a veterinarian. That is, he says, "until I learned that I had to do a lot of math and I had to put animals to sleep. I grew up on a farm, so I was no stranger to death. But just having to do it on a daily basis. On the farm, until you send them off to slaughter, you're concentrating on keeping them alive. So I decided that music or art was probably better suited to me."

But that experience was formative. Freed took what he saw on the farm and put it on his canvases. "We were fostering kittens all the time. We had possums living in the house that we had rescued. I've always liked possums. I can't stand rats, but for some reason possums fascinate me."

As a teenager he couldn't decide which he wanted to pursue, music or visual art. So he chose both. He got his first commission at thirteen, when a classmate paid him a nickel to draw a portrait of Gene Simmons. Album art fascinated him, especially the Kiss covers; something about those painted faces piqued his imagination. A misfit kid, he could play a little guitar, just enough for everybody else in his high school band to realize he should probably sing. He loved hard rock, the Stones and the Who and Skynyrd, but his tastes changed when he went away to art school. He moved to Richmond in 1983, the year R.E.M. released their full-length debut, *Murmur*, which still exerts a strong pull on Freed. "The music of your college years is so important, and nothing will ever equal *Chronic Town* and *Reckoning* and *Murmur* for me."

Like many artists, especially those misfit kids from small towns, he dreamed of moving to the city. But his mission of going to New York and maybe squatting in an abandoned building until his art career surely took off did not go as planned. "I got to Richmond and thought, *This place is pretty fucking big*. Then I went to New York—not to live there, but for a recording session or something—and I loved it. It's fucking *New York City*. But I didn't think I could live there. Too much going on. I can get anything in Richmond that I can get in New York, just not as much of it."

So he stayed put. Freed worked odd jobs to pay rent and buy art supplies. He and some friends started a band called Dirtball, whose membership, like that of the Truckers, was based on whim and opportunity, on the demands of those day jobs. Some nights it might sprawl into the double digits; other nights it might be just Wes and his wife, Jyl, up on stage. Musically, it was anything goes: cosmic country, psych-bluegrass, redneck folk, or reckless garage rock, usually with an upright bass player, several guitarists, and a makeshift drumkit. As ramshackle as they were, Dirtball fit well in a bustling music scene that had no single defining sound or aesthetic but did have a strong DIY philosophy. A hub on the East Coast touring circuit and a true rock and roll town—as praised by none other than Bruce Springsteen—Richmond had birthed metal acts like Lamb of God and the almighty Gwar, punks like Avail and Honor Role, rootsy pop acts like the Pat McGee Band, and folk groups like Pelt, along with more alternative-friendly outfits like the two-man House of Freaks and the one-man Sparklehorse.

Like the Truckers, Dirtball were part of a scene that was reappraising country as one element in a much larger musical palette, combining it with punk or metal or whatever might be on hand. Freed played lead guitar and sang songs in a reedy twang while his band churned up a rickety noise behind him. Their 1994 release, *Hillbilly Soul*, sounds just like its title, and Freed did the artwork, which depicts an angry, moon-faced figure traversing a dark landscape with a pitchfork and a jug of moonshine. The music and art were both primitive but developing in unusual ways.

Four years later, when Dirtball released their second album, *The Well*, the cover revealed a much more refined artist able to relate a bizarre and elaborate narrative in a single frame—a trait that would serve him well with the Truckers. A gigantic skeleton looms over an Appalachian landscape, carrying a mandolin the size of a log cabin and a slide like a telephone booth. It has disturbed a group of revelers around a campfire, who run in all directions. It's as if they have summoned an ancient god from some mystical holler—which may be the best explanation of making art.

Freed's brushwork was heavy and rough-hewn, like he'd carved each painting out of old bubblegum. But it was refining itself, growing more graceful and elaborate in its primitiveness. "I try to *let* it evolve, not *make* it evolve. A person changes, so their art is going to change. And their music is going to change." Part of that change was in priority; instead of an artist and musician, he gradually became an artist who played music, although the two would always be intermingled, inseparable. In addition to his comic strip, he did DIY shows around town, exhibiting paintings anywhere that would give him a wall to hang them on. Gradually, as Dirtball ran their course and he started a new band called Shiners, new characters began to appear and populate his world, connecting each canvas to every other one. Some were animals like Hexter the possum or the then-unnamed black flamingo. Others were his interpretations of real figures, like Keith Richards and Ronnie Wood speeding through Fordyce, Arkansas, in their rented Impala or Hank Williams playing cards and drinkin' shine with Lemmy Kilmister from Motörhead. He also did one album cover: Cracker, having relocated to Richmond and just a few years after their massive hit "Low," commissioned art for their 1998 album, *Gentleman's Blues*, and Freed flew out to Los Angeles to meet with Virgin Records' graphic designer. He was appalled by the results: the image is still recognizably his, but it's been shrunk, pulled out of proportion, and rendered in an ugly black and brown color scheme. He vowed to maintain more control over his contributions in the future.

When the Truckers first played Richmond in September 1997—a decisive show that I'll get into later in this chapter—they bunked with the Freeds at their house up in the working-class suburb Mechanicsville, just north of the city. On an otherwise unremarkable street, the couple had decorated their house like every day was Halloween: tombstones standing in the yard, skeletons clawing out of shallow graves. Inside was essentially a gallery devoted to Freed's art. Rooms were lined with paintings on canvas and lumber, some with homemade frames adorned with moonshine jugs and S-shaped mandolin sound holes. Some depicted weird-ass skeletons; others showed dead and decaying rock stars. There were portraits of bipedal possums, pinups of naked or nearly naked women with names like the Desert Witch and the Dixie Butcher. There were black flamingos alongside bright, white owls and full moons with women's faces in the center.

"I wish I had photos of that house," recalls Rob Malone. "It was the type of house where if you decided you wanted to take a shower, you'd probably end up dirtier for having gone into the bathroom. But that was all part of the fun of touring."

The Truckers would stay there every time they were in town, even as the band grew more popular, even as the lineup changed, sometimes even when they could afford a hotel. "Whenever we stayed there," says Isbell, "I slept on the couch with their dog, this gigantic old dog that would not move. The cushions had long since been removed from this couch, which was very small—more like a settee. So I was just wadded up with this dog that weighed seventy-five pounds and had fingernails out to here because they'd never had his nails clipped."

In addition to free lodging and two fans who would introduce them to a rabid local audience, the Truckers got something much more unexpected: a visual artist as distinctive with his paints as Patterson and Cooley are with their lyrics, for whom each slash of the brush across wood was something like a guitar riff or a swampy bassline. It gave them a visual signature to complement their music, to enlarge the universe of their lyrics, to grace their album covers and T-shirts and tour posters. "The first time we walked in that door," says Patterson, "was like walking into Wes's head. So immersive. Cooley and I looked around, then looked at each other, and said, 'He's got to illustrate *Betamax Guillotine*,' which is what we were calling the *Southern Rock Opera* at the time."

They hadn't even released their debut when they first bunked with the Freeds, but they were already thinking ahead to their ambitious third studio album. They had some visuals they knew they wanted on the cover and in the booklet, specifically a giant owl based on the sign advertising the radio station WOWL back in the Shoals. Perched on a hilltop near O'Neal Bridge, which crosses the Tennessee River to connect Florence and Muscle Shoals, that neon bird kept drivers appraised of highway conditions, much like Vulcan down in Birmingham: If its eye was burning green, there had been no traffic fatalities that day. If it burned red, it meant someone had died on the road. Death is such a crucial aspect of the record: spectacular car crashes that everyone talks about at the next day's graduation ceremony, that inspire legends among friends of the dead, that haunt the mean, old highways all over the South. When Freed painted the image, he made sure the owl's eyes were red.

For the booklet he painted a car careening in front of a giant moon, headed for an oak tree. Lilla Hood, who had grown up to become a graphic designer (thanks in part to her childhood experience helping to create concert posters for Adam's House Cat), created an owl die-cut outline to hold the booklet in place, and as a happy accident it looks like the owl is holding that full moon in its horns. Grounding the music in the mythical, Freed's image plays off of the real-world elements of the songs, as though such figures as George Wallace and Ronnie Van Zant and even the band members themselves inhabit the space in between the fantastical and the factual. It's a striking package, and it helped the band sell thousands of copies without any help from a label.

Since then, the band and the artist (and Lilla) have worked together less by commission and more by collaboration. Typically Freed finds inspiration in the band's songs, as he did on the 2004 release *The Dirty South*. Listening to Cooley's opening track, "Where the Devil Don't Stay," about a moonshiner in the Prohibition South, Freed created a spooky, midnight-toned forest full of bare trees wrapped in withering kudzu, lit by a full moon with a hint of a face in its sphere. A dapper devil in hat and vest sits at a stump with a poker hand dealt atop the inner rings. The painting wraps around to the back cover, where a funnel cloud emerges from the smokestack of a locomotive, a reference to Patterson's song "Tornadoes": "And as the thing came through, it sounded like a train." Freed's image is somehow both literal and figurative at once.

Inspiration travels both ways. *English Oceans* from 2014 features two heads half-submerged in a river—not baptized, but emerging almost like the ghouls in the 1962 horror film *Carnival of Souls*. They might be witches or banshees or wives of the Confederate dead. It's based on a painting Freed did for the DC filmmaker Barr Weissman, who directed the 2009 Truckers documentary *The Secret to a Happy Ending*. But when

Patterson saw the finished work, he loved it and felt it summed up some of the ideas they were playing with on these new songs. It could be the made-up English ocean Cooley sings about on the title track.

What Freed doesn't draw—at least not often—are rebel flags. They pop up occasionally but usually as insignias embedded in a particular character and not in a way that glorifies the thing. Partly he leaves it out because he knows the Truckers don't cotton to it. But mostly, despite his previous interest in alternative Confederate imagery—his second album with Shiners was titled *Bonnie Blue* in reference to the South Carolina flag and palmetto tree, which were briefly symbols of southern secession—he's not interested in the rebel flag as a symbol of the South. His relationship to it is fraught, as it should be for southerners of a certain generation. "I grew up in the Valley," he says, referring to the Shenandoah Valley in Virginia.

> My grandfather had uncles who fought with Jeb Stuart, so Confederate flags meant something different to us back then than they do now. My grandfather was not at all a racist person, but he grew up listening to stories from his uncles, who came home from the war, busted the tips off their sabers, and used them as corn cutters. Up until Obama was elected, my philosophy was, *If we let the terrorists have the flag, then the terrorists win.* But it soured. I defended the stupid thing for a long time, and then I realized it's not defensible. I don't want to see them anymore.

Even before Patterson convened the Drive-By Truckers in June 1996, they were already on their way to Richmond. In May of that year, the annual Atlanta rock festival Bubbapalooza booked a Virginia band called Used Carlotta, fronted by a singer-songwriter named Louis Ledford. They drove all day in order to play all night, and they missed the opening slot by Patterson's band the Lot Lizards. But they were awed by the event itself, impressed by the turnout and by the rowdy response their unknown band received. Bubbapalooza seemed to bring together a community that went beyond the city limits, defining the Redneck Underground for the outside world.

When Used Carlotta returned home, tired but triumphant, Ledford hatched a plan with his bandmate George Reuther and Wes and

Jyl Freed from Dirtball: they would host a similar event, except theirs would be monthly instead of yearly. In retrospect, it was the definition of biting off more tobacco than they could chew, but the whole point was to be ambitious. "Back in the mid-1990s the music scene had gotten kind of insulated," recalls Ledford. "In the '80s there were all kinds of bands coming through Richmond, but that had petered out. So we had this idea to put on a show, a monthly version of Bubbapalooza. Or down in Chapel Hill they had Sleazefest. They had a lot of these big to-dos back then."

Originally they called it the New Dominion Barn Dance based on a local country music radio program called the Old Dominion Barn Dance, but someone else owned the rights to that name. It was Freed who came up with an alternative: the Capital City Barn Dance, which he promptly put on concert posters, using sideways horseshoes for the capital Cs. This was no half-assed showcase: they transformed the warehouse-turned-venue Flood Zone into a barnyard, complete with a red-frame backdrop and hay bales on the stage. They hung homemade stars from the ceiling, which Freed admits was a pain in the ass. Usually either Dirtball or Used Carlotta would serve as the house band, or they would have a fast-talkin' emcee introducing the acts. Card girls dressed in Daisy Dukes or cutoff overalls gave the proceedings the feel of a DIY *Hee Haw* production. They were known to host square dances between acts. "We made a real show of it," says Freed.

On a given night, there might be up to three, maybe four bands on the bill, who would play abbreviated sets before the stage manager—who worked part-time as a dominatrix—ran them off so the next band could set up. "You know how slow things go when a band is trying to leave the stage?" says Freed. "We got people on and off the stage on time with her cracking the whip."

Payment was paltry—just $200 per act. "Sometimes we had to pay them out of our own pocket," says Freed, "because we didn't make enough money that night. We fuckin' lost money. We paid out of pocket on a regular basis. We had a bank account, but it was always in the red." Cracker played the Barn Dance twice, once in June 1997 and again in April 1998. The latter was a secret show featuring special guest Joan Osborne, which meant they could post no ads or flyers. But they let the word get out through other channels, resulting in a line around the block.

"Then we actually had some money to work with," says Freed, "which was cool."

At a moment when alt-country was coalescing online, the Barn Dance was one of many real-world endeavors to build a national, potentially international community of like-minded players and fans, all coming together to play idiosyncratic iterations of related styles of music. That included Split Lip Rayfield, a rambunctious acoustic act from Wichita, Kansas; the Damnations TX, an Austin band with high-lonesome harmonies; Two Dollar Pistols from North Carolina; and even the Holy Modal Rounders featuring legendary freak-folkie Michael Hurley. Says Freed, "The whole idea was to make it a showcase for bands playing the same kind of music that we were playing. They would come play this thing that we did once a month, and then when we were looking for shows in their town, they'd hook us up with whatever they could."

Dirtball and Used Carlotta tours became A&R trips, with Ledford and the Freeds scouting acts for the Barn Dance. One tour took Dirtball down South, where in March 1997 they represented Richmond at Bubbapalooza. After speeding to Atlanta just hours before their show, the Freeds were exhausted by the time a strange band of burly guys from nearby Athens took the stage. It was the first Bubbapalooza after the death of its founder, Gregory Dean Smalley, and the first one the Truckers played. "It was special," Patterson recalls, "because we were playing in front of a sold-out house, and we'd never played in front of a packed-out house before."

For the Freeds it wasn't life changing; they were far too exhausted for that. But they were impressed: the Truckers still had that new-car smell about them, but they already had a strong set of sturdy songs, a charismatic front man, and a noisy, boisterous take on alt-country that fit the Barn Dance ethos perfectly. Jyl approached them after the show, and *Hell yeah*, they wanted to drive up and play Richmond. Four months later the Truckers were booked at the Flood Zone. They became fast friends with the Freeds, who saw them as kindred spirits. None of them were cut out for regular workaday jobs with cubicles and paychecks and health insurance. Like Patterson and Cooley, Freed took odd jobs wherever he could, anything that would allow him the flexibility to paint and play. And like the Truckers, he realized that he had to invest everything in these pursuits. "I learned a long time ago, if we're going to do this, if music is how we're going to make a living, then we really gotta do more. I was painting houses, and I was ready to fucking give that up."

Freed did the poster for the Truckers' first Barn Dance and thought enough of the result to include it in his 2019 book, *The Art of Wes Freed: Paintings, Posters, Pin-Ups and Possums*. It's another midnight landscape, with fat, twisted trees sprouting from black-dirt hills. In the starry sky the words *Capital City* are neatly printed with those sideways horseshoes for Cs. And the big, bright moon holds not the face of a man but the quizzical countenance of a woman side-eyeing a jug of moonshine stashed in one of the tree trunks. The Drive-By Truckers headline the bill, right above Dirtball and Used Carlotta plus Celebrity Corn-Shuckin' and Big "Scotty" Price and the Barn Dance Gals. Admission is seven dollars until 9:30 p.m., when it goes up to ten. Students get a two-dollar discount.

That show in September 1997 was a rousing success for the Truckers—and reassuring proof that their music could travel. "They just seemed to click, and everybody seemed to love them here," says Freed. "It was a really good time for that kind of alternative-country-whatever punk-roots-rock thing. A lot of people were into that. And rockabilly has always been big in Richmond, although that doesn't really have anything to do with the Truckers. But their music appeals to people who like rockabilly because it's rockin' and they're kinda hillbilly."

The Truckers played three more Barn Dances: in March 1998 after the event had moved across the street to a bar called Alley Katz, and twice in 1999 at its final location at the Dogtown Lounge. "That gave us an instant crowd," says Patterson. "The next time we came to Richmond, we packed out a small club. We had a big following there." They continued playing Richmond even after the Freeds closed the barn door for good, each show receiving a better response than the last: more tickets punched, more merch sold, more noise from the audiences, more shouted requests for songs that had become something like live staples by then. "Our first shows there were really encouraging for a bunch of Alabama boys that had failed so miserably with our previous bands," says Cooley. "*Oh shit, we're gonna make this work!* To us it felt immediate. We felt like we were finally getting somewhere."

Playing Richmond also put Patterson back with an old friend from the Shoals named Jay Leavitt, who managed a record store called Plan 9

Music (after the gloriously bad 1959 alien invasion flick directed by Ed Wood). They had been out of touch for years, until Leavitt caught one of their Barn Dance shows. He was not completely impressed. "I remember thinking, *These are good songs, but maybe Patterson needs to get him a front man who can sing.* Back in those days his voice was *rough.* He hadn't quite come into his own yet. But he stuck to his guns and turned himself into one of the great front men in the business today."

Even as the Truckers worked things out, Richmond remained one of their top markets for a good decade, but that popularity was pretty much annihilated with the release of *A Blessing and a Curse* in 2006. That album was made under some duress, at another low point in the Truckers' existence, right around the time when Isbell was on his way out. Critics were less than kind, but Richmond took it especially hard, although no one's sure exactly why. Perhaps it had something to do with a beloved band seeming to shed its redneck image on an album that sounded too polished, or maybe it's because they had been working at such a high level that even a slight dip looked like ruination. "That record absolutely repelled our audience in Richmond," says Patterson. "It seemed like a betrayal to them. There were longtime Richmond fans who never came back after that record." He doesn't necessarily disagree—he's called it the Truckers' worst record—but it's not *that* bad.

When they played those Barn Dances, the Truckers were already touring heavily, almost nonstop, straying very far from home to find audiences sometimes hostile to their music and sometimes enthusiastic. But crowds were still generally small, especially in the South. "The South was the last to know," says Cooley. "Being from the South, you get big everywhere else first. Folks like stuff from other places, I guess. We started out doing really good in Atlanta, but that was pretty much the Star Bar—the one environment that embraced us. Then we started doing good in Richmond and New York City. We were doing great in all those markets before we could even sell out the Nick in Birmingham. If you're from the South, that's the last market you're going to break."

The Barn Dance was crucial to that success. It gave them a ready-made audience, larger than average for a band with no name recognition outside its home state and barely any inside. It also became a useful stepping stone to bigger cities even farther into Union territory, primarily New York, Boston, and Philadelphia, but they also trekked out to State

College, Pennsylvania, and parts farther west. Most crucially of all, their Barn Dance success gave the Truckers encouragement to keep going, reassured them that there would be an audience *somewhere* for what they were doing. It wouldn't be in vain. It told Patterson and Cooley that the Truckers would not suffer the same fate as Adam's House Cat.

"The things that would have discouraged other bands, we didn't even see any of that," says Patterson. "We didn't see it that way. Are you kidding? We're finally getting somewhere. And we're ten years older than other bands on the circuit, which I think gave us an advantage. We were meaner. It meant something to us. Every goddamn night. If there's 12 people or 50 people or 250 people, every night we're up there trying to save souls."

Looking back on this period in the band's life, he's shocked at the conditions they cheerily endured. "It amazes me how bad the bad times were. If I had been able to honestly see how bad it was, I don't know what we would have done. But at the time it was a sense of mission, the Blues Brothers thing: we're on a mission from God. That allowed me to keep my blinders on and not see how fucked up everything was."

It's impossible to ignore the fact that the first market to embrace the Truckers—a band already rethinking and subverting many southern conventions—was also the capital of the Confederacy, the locus of the Lost Cause, a city forever mired in its history. It's tempting to speculate about some lofty reasons, and perhaps there really is in the local psyche some need to distance Richmond's present from its past. Perhaps that made the Drive-By Truckers sound even meaner when they played on local stages—rebellious in the right way. That impulse seems to drive a lot of economic and especially cultural development in the city, which is littered with old Confederate monuments as well as newer ones meant to present a very different view of history. The city has faced something like a historical reckoning in recent years, as the worthiness and therefore the fate of some of its most popular monuments has been called into question.

Nestled near the mouth of the James River—named by English settlers after King James I, famous for the translation of the Bible he sponsored—Richmond was a major hub for human trafficking in the early nineteenth century, with some three hundred thousand Africans imported, imprisoned, auctioned, and shipped along the river to plantations throughout the South. The slave trade grew in parallel with early industrialization, in particular metal foundries. Soon after Jefferson Davis ordered shots fired on Fort Sumter in South Carolina, which ignited the Civil War and demonstrated that the South would not secede peacefully, he moved the Confederate capital from Montgomery, Alabama, to Richmond in order to make more strategic use of the Tredegar Iron Works, which manufactured armor for war machines like the CSS *Virginia*. That made the city a strategic target for Union forces, which launched several campaigns to conquer Richmond. The earliest of them, in 1862, was thwarted by a quartet of Confederate generals: John B. Magruder, Stonewall Jackson, James Ewell Brown "Jeb" Stuart, and Robert E. Lee. In April 1865, with the momentum finally shifting decisively against the South, Confederate forces abandoned the city, looting and burning armories, warehouses, and farms on their retreat. Locals more or less welcomed Union forces—a moment The Band commemorated nearly a century later on their 1969 song "The Night They Drove Old Dixie Down." (Following the breakup of Adam's House Cat, Patterson and Cooley formed a very short-lived acoustic duo called Virgil Kane, named for the Confederate protagonist of that song.)

The city recovered quickly, and its population quadrupled between 1860 and 1920, during which time Richmond bolstered its agricultural economy with railroads, factories, and more foundries. Many of the vestiges of that era remain, although most of them have been repurposed for more useful, less treasonous purposes. The Confederate White House, built in 1818 as a private residence for a local doctor, now houses the American Civil War Museum, as does the old Tredegar Iron Works. Buildings in the Shockoe Bottom neighborhood that were associated with the slave trade, however, have been torn down and in some cases the locations paved over, with few markers to acknowledge their importance to American history.

Through the middle of the city runs a 1.5-mile stretch of grand boulevard, lined with towering trees and expensive houses built during the first decades of the twentieth century, leading all the way to the Governor's Mansion. At points along this tony thoroughfare have long stood large monuments to a crew of Confederate figures, most of them military. In addition to Matthew Fontaine Maury, here commemorated for his achievements in oceanography rather than his feats as a naval commander, Monument Avenue had three of the officers who staved off Union forces in 1862. Lee, Jackson, and Stuart are all on horseback, as though leading troops into glorious battle, perched atop massive pedestals that elevate them above the level of everyday Richmonders.

Controversy accompanied these monuments from the moment they were erected in the 1890s as part of the celebration of the twenty-fifth anniversary of the Civil War. Richmond was pulling itself into the industrialized twentieth century and undergoing an economic transformation, and many locals believed these monuments to a lost war ran counter to those aspirations. But these efforts to commemorate the war and more specifically the Confederacy were part of a national wave of public memorials that subtly—or sometimes with no subtlety whatsoever—buttressed the Lost Cause mythology. This strategic reinterpretation of history recast the war as a skirmish regarding states' rights in which both sides maintained valor in battle and righteousness in intent. It allowed the South to argue that slavery was not the primary motivation for going to war, despite the fact that slavery is mentioned in every state's articles of secession.

One consequence of this fallacy is the whitewashing of these generals who watched over Monument Avenue, whose wartime heroism is commended and whose transgressions are ignored. Lee was the worst of them, a man who not only owned slaves on a plantation outside Arlington, Virginia, but notoriously abused them. He ordered frequent whippings and other punishments that amounted to torture, and he separated families by selling parents and children to different plantations. On the battlefield he was no gentleman, but a tyrant who stood by as Confederate soldiers massacred Black Union troops even after they had surrendered Fort Pillow, in Tennessee. Yet, the Lost Cause mythology has erased many of those sins, and he has been remembered as a shrewd strategist and righteous Christian leader. Slowly, that is now changing.

But no monument on Monument Avenue, not even Lee's, drew as much ire as the very large and elaborate memorial to Jefferson Davis, president of the Confederacy and architect of the South's treason. At his monument, located near North Allen Avenue—formerly the site of the Star Fort, a Confederate defense post—Davis was depicted mid-oration, standing awkward and stiff even for bronze, his left arm outstretched in what might have been intended as a dramatic flourish but more resembles a gesture of reconciliation. He looked like he was checking for rain. Behind him was a massive granite column rising sixty feet into the air, atop which perched a sculpture of Vindicatrix, the vengeful spirit of the South (perhaps a distant ancestor of Freed's Desert Witch). She and Davis were flanked by a colonnade of thirteen columns, one for each state in the Confederacy.

Once upon a time, the issue was what to do with these monuments. Should they be torn down? Placed in museums alongside other Confederate artifacts? Should they be melted down to make new statues to heroes who better reflect the American values of equality, fairness, and democracy? Or should we leave them in place, perhaps with new inscriptions offering more accurate historical context? The answer, which becomes clearer every day, is to remove them from public spaces, although that may not be feasible in every case. Some are protected by state laws and—ironically, considering the whole states' rights smokescreen—by federal laws, others by public sentiment. A few actually have some artistic value. The Lee statue in Richmond, for example, was designed by French sculptor Antonin Mercié, creator of the Francis Scott Key Monument in Baltimore, among other pieces of public art. But many others across the country are mass-produced, with little to argue in favor of their existence.

One of Richmond's strategies had been to add to its collection of monuments, in the hope of diluting the message conveyed by the Confederate ones. In 1996 the city unveiled a statue honoring the tennis star Arthur Ashe, who became the first Black presence on Monument Avenue. It was followed twelve years later by the Virginia Civil Rights Memorial on the grounds of the State Capitol. Rather than a military hero, it depicts teenage education activist Barbara Johns leading a demonstration at her segregated high school in 1951. Instead of a lone vaunted white man, it depicts a community of Black Americans. Both newer monuments exist in pointed debate with older monuments in this uniquely conflicted city.

Perhaps the most notable addition is *Rumors of War*, a massive equestrian statue by the artist Kehinde Wiley, best known by many for painting the presidential portrait of Barack Obama. Unveiled in Times Square before moving to the Virginia Museum of Fine Arts in December 2019, it is based on Richmond's Jeb Stuart monument, but the nineteenth-century

Confederate general has been replaced with a twenty-first-century Black man sporting dreads, sneakers, and ripped jeans. The statue uses the visual language of military heroism to depict a subject with no sword in his hand, no battalion at his back, no Lost Cause to defend. He looks triumphant, simultaneously mocking the Confederate generals while also transcending the local reference. Freed watched from the balcony of his downtown condo as the statue was erected and unveiled. When he declares, "I fucking love it!" he does so with a devious laugh.

A farm boy who wanted to be a veterinarian, a painter whose canvases host a bizarre menagerie of animals real and imagined, Freed long thought the solution to the monument problem was to strip the riders from their mounts, leaving their loyal steeds atop their pedestals to bear empty saddles and acknowledge the pointed absence of the men themselves. "People love horses. They should just take Lee off his horse and leave Traveler there. Nobody's got a complaint against Traveler. Traveler wasn't a racist. Traveler never owned a slave. Traveler didn't know a white man from a Black man."

It shouldn't be terribly difficult to see why many Richmonders, both Black and white, still object to lionizing the leaders of a failed government dedicated to preserving slavery and white supremacy. In June 2015, the back of the Davis monument was tagged with the words *Black Lives Matter* scrawled in black spray paint, a photo of which appeared the next day in the Richmond paper (around the same time the Truckers were displaying a Black Lives Matter banner onstage at their shows). Calls for its destruction, or at the very least its removal, intensified following the deadly 2017 Unite the Right rally in nearby Charlottesville, and in 2018 the Monument Avenue Commission, created by Mayor Levar Stoney, recommended that Davis be removed and the others be appended with new interpretive signage. "Of all the statues," read their official report, "[Davis] is the most unabashedly Lost Cause in its design and sentiment."

That local debate came to a head during the summer of 2020, when hundreds of thousands of Americans—despite a global pandemic—took to the streets of their communities to protest the murder of Black men and women by white police officers. In Richmond the Confederate monuments became popular gathering places, hubs for protest and dissent, targets for graffiti and vandalism. After being paint-bombed repeatedly, the Davis statue was finally toppled on the evening of June 10 and was eventually hauled away. Mayor Stoney ordered that the Stuart statue and three others be removed and placed in storage until their fates could be determined.

But Lee was on state property, which made his removal much trickier. Governor Ralph Northam ordered the removal of the Lee statue from its pedestal: "It was wrong then, and it's wrong now," he stated. "So we're taking it down." Toppling this monument wasn't easy. In August 2020 a local circuit court judge issued a temporary injunction based on Virginia's promise more than one hundred years earlier to "affectionately protect" the statue, although two months later another judge reversed that ruling and effectively dissolved the injunction. By then, Lee was already covered in bright spray paint: ACAB, BLM, the names of the dead. Demonstrators knelt around the pedestal in a sign of peaceful protest popularized by outcast quarterback Colin Kaepernick. When Rep. John Lewis, a civil rights hero who had marched across the Pettis Bridge in Selma, Alabama, nearly sixty years earlier, died in July, his visage was projected onto the monument, obscuring horse and rider. Those images became viral because they were so powerful, and they were so powerful because they so decisively answered the question of what to do with these statues. Outraged Virginians had created a new work of art, new ideas overwriting old ideologies: not a metaphor for but an enactment of how we might engage with history, how we can dig deeper into our shared past, how we can unearth the truths of prejudice and slavery, how we can write boldly over the historical revisions that perpetuate white supremacy. Freed commemorated the demonstrations on the cover of the Truckers' late-2020 album, *The New OK*, which depicts the base of a monument with no statue. Instead, it has been painted with Pride colors and tagged with "BLM." It is crawling with Cooley birds and Cattersons.

Statues like these have become lodged into everyday life, not only in Richmond but all over the country, even in states that weren't yet states when the Civil War ended. Every place in this book has a monument: Florence has one dedicated to Confederate soldiers in front of the Lauderdale County Courthouse, and until recently Athens had a soldiers' monument on Broad Street, near the UGA campus. In 2017 Memphis removed memorials to Robert E. Lee and Nathan Bedford Forrest, skirting the Tennessee Heritage Protection Act by selling those two local parks to a private organization. There are active efforts in all of those places to remove similar statues.

Confederate monuments are so common in the South that many people don't even see them anymore. They've been absorbed into the landscape, taken for granted. Until recently I couldn't have told you anything about the soldiers' memorial in Selmer, my hometown, despite the fact that it stands on the courthouse grounds across the street from my father's law office. I have driven or walked past it thousands of times but never bothered to look at it, much less study it or reflect on the virtues it might promote. I imagine that experience is the rule rather than the exception for people who enjoy the privilege of merely looking through these monuments, at least until the controversy surrounding them flares up again. Instead of reflecting some deficiency in the monument designs—or, more generally, in the concept of monuments as daily reminders of sacrifice and heroism—I think that southern duality of seeing and not seeing allows racist notions of white supremacy to linger without examination. We let ourselves off the hook.

"Everybody takes for granted growing up and seeing that stuff and walking by it," says Cooley. "There's this notion that's far too easy for most people to fall into—that something has just always been that way. More things are more recent than you think. Many of these monuments and statues were placed there pretty recently, usually in response to greater advancements by Black people. Most of those things are not there to honor these brave men who fought, blah blah blah. They were put there to remind Black people what their place was. You gotta think of the intent behind it. It's not at all what these people need to believe it is."

In 2019, the Southern Poverty Law Center published a report titled *Whose Heritage? Public Symbols of the Confederacy*, which found that "two distinct periods saw a significant rise in the dedication of monuments and other symbols. The first began around 1900, amid the period in which states were enacting Jim Crow laws to disenfranchise newly freed African Americans and re-segregate society. This spike lasted well into the 1920s, a period that saw a dramatic resurgence of the Ku Klux Klan." The Stuart and Davis monuments in Richmond belong to this era. According to the report, "the second spike began in the early 1950s and lasted through the 1960s, as the civil rights movement led to a backlash against desegregationists." The Jefferson Davis monument in Memphis and the Robert E. Lee monument in Roanoke, Virginia, both belong to this era.

Cooley wrote about this historical short-sightedness on "Surrender under Protest," the first single released for *American Band*. Although it became known as an anthem of defiance after the 2016 presidential election, it's actually a song about the Lost Cause and why that romantic narrative of Confederate loss appeals to "the lonely, fragile minds of angry youths." That idea has thrived for so long because it offers a good out: "If it's all you can remember, then it's been that way forever," he sings, calling out the people who cling to tradition but don't care to look beyond their own lives.

How is this for a statue? A woman stands in front of her flat-screen TV, crying toddler in her arms, hair mussed and clothes wrinkled, a shock drawing across her face as she watches the news. The talking head on Fox News reports there are no weapons of mass destruction to be found in Iraq. This is the moment when she realizes that there was nothing to justify the invasion of that country in 2003 or the loss of life that resulted. This is the moment when she realizes that her husband and her baby's father died for no reason. This is the moment when she braces herself for a hard future. This is a moment as worthy of a public commemoration as any act of battlefield bravery.

Patterson describes this scene in "The Home Front," one of two wartime songs he wrote for the 2008 release *Brighter Than Creation's Dark*, although he makes no mention of any statue. The song itself is the monument, and despite being one of his shortest compositions—not even one hundred words—and not among his most popular, "The Home Front" was important enough at the time that the band named its early 2008 tour after it. Brad Morgan kicks things off with a big drumbeat, to which Cooley adds some hand-on-shoulder guitar riffs. Hints of organ, courtesy of Shoals legend Spooner Oldham, fill the spaces in between the notes before giving way to smears of John Neff's pedal steel. Patterson sounds beaten down, his voice tired and sympathetic even when the lyrics convey anger and outrage, and Shonna Tucker joins him on the last line—"She's left standing there on the home front, the two of them alone"—before the song shifts into an instrumental coda that sounds like the closing credits to an incredibly sad movie. It ends with Morgan alone again, his snare drum suggesting a military funeral.

If most of the statues on Monument Avenue extol battlefield heroism, then "The Man I Shot," the other war song on *Brighter*, offers a very different military experience: the aftermath of combat, when a soldier questions his decisions and confronts his actions. It's a scorched, scoured blues, played at a slightly frantic pace, the guitars frayed at the edges, Morgan's drumbeat trying to buck the groove, keep the listener off balance, as an Iraq veteran wrestles with his guilt over killing a man. Patterson repeats the line "He was trying to kill me," as though trying to convince himself. Was he justified in taking another life? Did he rob children of their father? "I was trying to do good," he concludes. "I just don't understand."

Both of these songs were inspired by backstage visits, one from a veteran still dogged by the horrors he witnessed and the other by the family of a soldier killed just days before he was supposed to return home. As songs about the Iraq War go, they are a bit late. The middle of the 2000s had seen a spike in protest music, such as Bright Eyes' "When the President Talks with God" and Steve Earle's 2004 album *The Revolution Starts...Now*, but much of that spirit had died down by the time the Truckers released *Brighter Than Creation's Dark* and the economic crisis was overshadowing Bush's military blunders. These two songs aren't necessarily protest songs, at least not like the kind we associate with Dylan and Ochs and others. By the later years of the decade, artists across various media—such as Kathryn Bigelow, director of *The Hurt Locker* and *Zero Dark Thirty*—were exploring the aftermath of the war, especially as it played out away from the battlefield. And in 2009, the US military dropped a decades-old ban and allowed the publication of photographs of the flag-draped caskets of the war dead being shipped back to the States, which brought home the personal costs of the war.

Patterson didn't write "The Home Front" or "The Man I Shot" with war monuments in mind, but the songs work as something like anti-monuments. "To commemorate is to seek historical closure," the art historian Kirk Savage wrote in his groundbreaking 1997 study *Standing Soldiers, Kneeling Slaves*. By contrast, the Truckers want to leave history open-ended, to put it in the hands of those who experienced that despair and that grief and that loss and that guilt, rather than leave it to politicians or businessmen who might skew history to their own ends. This is a fine line to walk, to commemorate the fallen by saying their sacrifices added up to very little, but it's an important way of holding accountable the leaders who created that war. It's as though Patterson is attempting to forestall efforts to assign some Lost Cause rationalization to this war. And yet, as recently as 2019, Bush's former press secretary Ari Fleischer was attempting to dismiss the idea that Bush lied to the American people. That claim, he asserted on Twitter, was itself a lie, one perpetuated by liberals and the media. (Same thing, right?) It's an excuse for a failed war, an attempt to rejigger history: a different kind of Lost Cause.

Brighter Than Creation's Dark ends with "Monument Valley," a song that was inspired by the Westerns of John Ford and that inspired Freed's inner-sleeve painting of a haunted desert landscape. A huge film buff and a fan of the director, Patterson wrote the song as an epic show closer, and the Truckers ended many of their Home Front Tour appearances with it. It subtly comments on his approach to writing about war—or really about anything. "And when the dust settles and the story is told, history is made by the side of the road," Patterson sings, as the band churns up a righteous intensity that demands raised lighters and raised voices, "by the men and women that can persevere and rage through the storm, no matter how severe."

They had pushed the record bins up against the wall to clear a space for the 200, maybe 250 fans who bought tickets to see the Drive-By Truckers play an in-store at Plan 9 Music, in Richmond. At the back end of the store, they had built a small stage that barely held the six musicians, but they all seemed to love being all up in each other's business like this. It had been ten years since the band formed, and they had played this city several times and even this particular record store before. But this was a special night in July 2006, both for the band and for the city that had cheered them on for nearly a decade. (The poster in the store window promised, "This live performance . . . will be recorded for future release," although it would be fourteen years before the Truckers released it as a *triple* live album.)

The Truckers—which sported what many fans consider the classic lineup, with Jason Isbell, Shonna Tucker, and pedal steel player John

Neff—had been itching to play a real rock show, and they were as close as they were going to get that summer. Out of something like financial desperation, they had accepted a relatively lucrative gig opening for the Black Crowes on a summer amphitheater tour, which paid well but didn't exactly play to the Truckers' strengths. They were doing short sets to a lot of empty seats, and anybody who had bothered to show up so early wasn't there for the first band and wasn't very deep into a long night of drinking. But the Truckers kept their heads down, hoped they would win a few fans out of the deal or maybe some good press, and played their best in the hot summer sun.

When they just happened to have a free night on the East Coast, Jay Leavitt—Patterson's friend from back in the Shoals and the manager at Plan 9—invited them to play a fundraiser for a new charity called the Harvey Foundation, which benefitted local arts organizations. They eagerly accepted the in-store appearance, said they would play for about ninety minutes, then went for nearly three hours. Isbell covered the Stones' "Moonlight Mile" and dedicated it to Leavitt, and they played a handful of new songs that they had just set to tape for a record they were calling *A Blessing and a Curse*. "They were obviously having such a good time, and they got really loose," recalls Leavitt. "The Jack was flowing that night. And the crowd was just wasted."

About forty-five minutes into their set—by which time Patterson's green shirt was more sweat than fabric—Leavitt walked onto the small stage and stepped up to the microphone. First, he applauded the band for playing this fundraiser for "a case of beer and a bottle of Jack Daniels." ("Two cases of beer and four bottles of Jack," Cooley corrects him.) Then he described an evening just a few months before when he had heard the worst news possible, and everybody in the audience knew exactly what he was talking about: his friends Bryan and Kathy Harvey had been killed, along with their young daughters, Stella and Ruby. He didn't go into detail about what had happened to them, mostly out of respect but also because there wasn't anybody in Richmond who didn't know what had happened to the Harveys.

"Grief is a process in life," Leavitt said when introducing a new Truckers song called "World of Hurt." He had been in the studio with the Truckers when they recorded it, and Patterson had given him his handwritten lyrics about the nature of love and life. "That song helped me a lot. . . . Through the month of January, I probably listened to 'World of Hurt' a hundred times. I cried a bunch while listening to it. As the month progressed, the hole started getting better. This song is a song of hope to me." He ended his speech by shouting the song's climactic chorus, "It's fucking great to be alive!"

A midtempo number that's both melancholy and majestic, "World of Hurt" opens with a chiming guitar and Patterson speaking directly to the audience the way a preacher might address a revival tent or a commencement speaker might encourage a graduating class. "Once upon a time my advice to you would've been to go out and find yourself a whore," he says (not sings, but says) by way of introduction, splitting that last word in two—*ho-were*—but somehow not making it sound like a joke. "But I guess I've grown up 'cause I don't give that kind of advice anymore." As the song continues, he ponders the nature of love and the risks we all take just getting out of bed each morning, but underlying the song is this idea of what makes a man: at one point he believed the answer was sexual experience and social domination, a kind of muscled toughness that brooked no fear or sadness. The chorus of the song even twists that threat so common to bar brawls and parking-lot ass whuppin's: *You're about to enter a world of hurt*. But the Truckers know we're all already inhabiting that world.

"World of Hurt" is a song they usually play late in the rock show, often as an encore or closer, because it's a song that gains so much power and perspective from all of their other songs about messing up your life, destroying your band, contemplating death, and trying to stay focused on the righteous path. It's a song that puts their catalog into a slightly different perspective, even if it's just saying that none of the travails they describe, however horrible or insurmountable, negate the worth of life. They just make it sweeter. So you don't necessarily need to know that Patterson contemplated ending his own life to get goosebumps when he shouts, "It's great to be alive!" as the guitars crash around him.

In 2006 "World of Hurt" was prophecy. Over the next several months, the Truckers would drive through hell. The new album would land with a thud, alienating many in Richmond who had been following them for so long. Isbell would slide further into addiction, his relationship with Tucker would fray beyond repair, and he would leave the group. The band would briefly lose its way and nearly break up for good.

When they played it back then, the song was a way to brace for impact. When they play "World of Hurt" now, all of those horrible experiences are bound up in the guitars and drums and bass and organ.

At Plan 9, the song takes on a different meaning altogether with the recent tragedy weighing on everybody's mind. This performance becomes a wake for the Harveys, a way of remembering the family but also a way to find some meaning in their deaths. The Truckers play "World of Hurt" as though living your best and truest life is the kindest way you can memorialize the dear departed. "Remember, it ain't too late to take a deep breath and throw yourself into it with everything you got," the forty-two-year-old rock star exclaims, his hands stretching out at his sides like he's trying to welcome the entire audience into the song. It's a big moment, bigger than the stage and the record store, and the Truckers follow it up by immediately slurring into "Why Henry Drinks"—a tonal shift that few other bands could pull off. But it's all part of the rock show.

Patterson didn't know Bryan Harvey very well, but he knew the guy well enough. The Richmond native had gained some notoriety among the college rock circuit of the late 1980s and early 1990s as one half of the Richmond band House of Freaks, the other half being percussionist Johnny Hott. Known for penning sharp, supremely catchy songs and performing them in a way that made two men sound like six or seven, the duo signed with Rhino Records, moved from the East Coast out to Los Angeles, and released their debut album, *Monkey on a Chain*, in 1988. Two years later their follow-up, *Tantilla*, took its title from a demolished Richmond dance hall and meditated somberly and soberly on local history. They toured with Midnight Oil, formed a supergroup with members of the Dream Syndicate and the Long Ryders, and backed Mark Linkous on his debut as Sparklehorse. After two more albums, they disbanded in the mid-1990s, with Hott joining Cracker and Harvey focusing on family. He and his wife, Kathy—the inspiration for the House of Freaks song "I Got Happy"—bought a house in the Woodland Heights neighborhood, where they lived with Ruby and Stella.

On January 1, 2006, Bryan Harvey walked out of his home to get the morning paper. He and Kathy had been up later than usual the night before, and one of their daughters had stayed the night at a friend's house. She was due home any moment. Bryan was still sleepy when he left the front door open, although that was something he and his neighbors often did without thinking. It's one of those all-American tropes that people cite as supposed proof that they live in a safe neighborhood or a small town. Two men saw that open door and went through it. When they left hours later, carrying only a stolen laptop and a pittance in cash, the Harvey family were dead, their final moments filled with almost incomprehensible horror.

Moments later, Hott arrived at his friend's home, ready to wish them all a happy new year. He noticed the front door still open and, more alarming, smoke billowing from the windows. The house was on fire. He called 911.

Because they did not bother to switch out the stolen car they drove through Richmond, the two murderers were captured a few days later in Philadelphia, putting an end to what news outlets described as a crime spree. The story horrified Richmond, as it would any city anywhere. Locals grew suspicious of strangers. They lay wreaths and stuffed animals in the yard of the Harveys' house and in front of the toy store Kathy owned, World of Mirth. And they read all about the crime in local and national newspapers. They debated every detail, argued about the fates of the killers, and tried to figure out what it said about their city.

It became the biggest local news story of the year, so much so that a year later the city's alternative newspaper *Style Weekly* named the Harvey Family its 2006 Richmonders of the Year, noting how their deaths had opened old wounds in the city: "The Harvey family has become a symbol of sorts, a painful reminder that no matter how far we think we've come, we haven't come far enough," news editor Scott Bass wrote in the cover story. "Richmonders have responded with good works in many ways, through memorials and foundations, a children's run and a scholarship fund. Yet this awful tragedy also forced us to rethink what we thought we knew about crime and violence, and whether we could, in reality, protect ourselves and our loved ones from them. And then we all proceeded to lock our doors just a little bit tighter."

The Harveys were white, and their murderers were not just Black but portrayed as Black in a way that seemed to confirm so many thug stereotypes and even more unspoken prejudices. They were uneducated, unemployed, in and out of prison, addicted to drugs, prone to violence, disregarding so many social barriers. They seemed to bear out the Jim

Crow warnings that Black men presented a danger to white women and children, to white families and white society. While nobody defended the murders, some locals tried to muster sympathy for the perpetrators, explaining that both had been born into abject poverty. Both had been sexually abused as children. Both had been arrested multiple times and released back on the streets. Both, it appeared, had been failed by the system. This, in a city where, at the time, a quarter of all Black residents lived below the poverty line and nearly 90 percent of all prison inmates were Black.

In death, the Harveys took on the burden of an uncomfortable symbolism that did not reflect who they were in life, and it's ironic—grimly, perhaps—that their murders and the aftermath would have made for a good House of Freaks song. The South was one of Harvey's favorite subjects as a songwriter, specifically how the South he saw around him still bore the weight of its past atrocities, still clung to its old prejudices, still used the Bible to assert its righteousness. The past is "a festered wound that never heals," Harvey proclaims on "White Folk's Blood," a procession of fever-dream images that paints a dismal picture of southern life. "Dusting off their guns, words like worms crawl through their brains," he sings, and there is something unflinching in his delivery, as though he must bear witness when he might rather turn away. "Sermons fly from the preacher's mouth, but the auction block still remains."

Patterson had seen House of Freaks back in their heyday, when they played the Don't Care Danceteria in Huntsville, Alabama, and Bryan Harvey would show up whenever the Truckers played Richmond. Sometimes he would bring Kathy and the girls. "They were cute kids," Patterson says. "The family stood out. They were definitely part of that scene. They were so beloved in the city, and they were in all these different communities—the arts community, the music community, the small business community. It was like dropping a bomb in Richmond."

Patterson doesn't write about any of this on "Two Daughters and a Beautiful Wife," which is a very different kind of song than "World of Hurt" and a very different kind of memorial than the ones that once stood along Monument Row. He's not distracted by race or class or southern history or anything larger than the Harveys as people. Instead, he gives them a gentle, sad song, opening with a strummed guitar and an odd thump of percussion—perhaps a subtle and affectionate nod to the two-man drums-and-guitar lineup of House of Freaks. He imagines Bryan Harvey reaching the Pearly Gates to find his beautiful family waiting there for him, while back on Earth "everybody cried and cried." The song pares away every aspect of the story until only the man remains, with Shonna Tucker harmonizing sweetly on some of the tougher questions: "Is there vengeance up in heaven? Or are these things left behind?"

Patterson will tell you himself that he's not an especially spiritual person, and that makes "Two Daughters and a Beautiful Wife" all the more poignant and generous: it imagines an afterlife that he knows probably doesn't exist. It used to bother me, though, that the two daughters and the beautiful wife weren't imagined as characters in the song, that they were just precious things that a white man had lost. But I think the song speaks to Patterson's life at the time, and it may be as much about him as it is about Bryan Harvey. When he learned of his friend's death, Patterson was a husband for the third time, but he had the maturity and perspective to make this one stick. And he was a father for the first time. His daughter, Ava Ruth, was just over a year old. Patterson was growing into a life similar to the Harveys'.

After chasing his rock dreams for most of his life, he had finally caught them. Yet he was at the same time leaving behind the partying, the carousing, the hard drinking, the drugs. Most of it, anyway. Right when everything was firming up, right when the Truckers appeared to be settling into a career as something more than just a one-shot band, right when he was reaping the rewards of all their touring and playing, he was growing up. Patterson was feeling like an adult in his early forties, working to balance his family life with the rock shows. He would take "Two Daughters and a Beautiful Wife" out on the road with him even when his own daughter and beautiful wife stayed home, and the song became a message from his past self to his future self, from his home self to his road self: a reminder of what he was leaving behind and how utterly precious and precarious it all was.

McNairy County, Tennessee

▼

If you want to pinpoint the moment when something changes in the fabric of southern life, mark this date on your calendar: August 12, 1967. That's the day one of the South's defining legends was born and the day Pauline Pusser was murdered.

That morning, Pauline's husband, Sheriff Buford Hayse Pusser, received a call reporting a disturbance on New Hope Road, roughly fifteen miles south of the county seat of Selmer. Two drunks were fighting, the caller said, and there would be a murder to investigate if he didn't get down there and break it up. This was not convenient timing, as the Pusser family was planning to leave for a trip later that morning. But he dutifully confirmed that he'd check on it, and Pauline offered to join him for the thirty-minute drive down to the southern end of the county. They thought it probably wouldn't take more than a few minutes; then they could get on with their vacation.

New Hope Road was down in a remote part of McNairy County, which itself lies about ninety miles due east of Memphis, one in a line of counties along the Mississippi state line. The Pussers had to make the drive from their home outside Adamsville, then turn left toward Corinth, Mississippi, way out into the country, past the line of motels that were known fronts for liquor, gambling, and prostitution, and then down a backroad toward the New Hope Methodist Church. They were in no particular hurry; those two drunks had probably passed out by now. A car pulled up alongside them, and Pusser noticed a gun barrel protruding from the back window. He had no chance to react before it fired. Pauline was struck in the back of the head, and she was likely dead before she even understood what was happening. Her husband was struck multiple times as he struggled to maintain control of the car. His jaw was blown off its hinge, leaving the bottom half of his face hanging down. Somehow he managed to bring the car to a halt as their assassins sped away, but Pusser had no way to radio for help.

He survived the attack, a feat that seems inhuman. He spent nearly three weeks in the hospital and underwent several rounds of reconstructive surgery to reattach his jaw. As he recuperated in a full facial cast, however, the sheriff became a national celebrity. The incident was reported in newspapers around the country, including notices in the *New York Times* and the *Washington Post*, bringing national attention to the war Pusser had been waging against the State Line Mob. He inspired the 1971 best-selling book *The Twelfth of August*, by W. R. Morris, as well as a country song, "The Legend of Buford Pusser," by Eddie Bond, a rockabilly performer who was less famous for his music than for telling Elvis to stick to driving trucks.

In her 2013 memoir, *Walking On*, Pusser's daughter, Dwana, credits Bond's song with establishing some of the popular elements of his notoriety: "The first hint of the shaping of Daddy's legend and turning it into a commodity was being spun on turntables around the Mid-South. I think Daddy enjoyed and encouraged the attention." The song was enough of a regional hit for Bond that he soon followed it up with a full album. Released in 1973 on the Enterprise imprint of Stax Records, *Eddie Bond Sings the Legend of Buford Pusser* is a fawning hagiography with banjos and Bakersfield guitars, but it's also really, really weird. "The Prettiest Dress," by far the album's longest song, is presented as Pusser's soliloquy to his wife's casket, despite the fact that the sheriff was unable to attend his wife's funeral and the facial cast made it impossible for him to even speak. But Bond's song imagines him in the funeral home, promising his wife they'll meet again: "You wait for me when you reach the edge of time, and if there's such a thing as shopping in heaven, I'll get you the prettiest dress we can find."

Pusser identified the shooters who killed his wife as members of the State Line Mob, who operated a vice racket in the county. He suspected

the attack was ordered by a guy named Carl "Towhead" White in re-
taliation for an incident the previous year: Pusser had received a report
about a break-in at the Shamrock Hotel, run by a woman named Louise
Hathcock, who was White's lover. When he entered the property, she
fired at him with a Smith & Wesson .38, which in the close quarters only
grazed him. He returned fire and killed her with a shot to the head. No
charges were ever filed against White or his alleged accomplices, but
within a few years each of the suspects turned up dead under suspicious
circumstances. One of them, a hitman from Massachusetts, was dredged
out of the Boston Harbor, his body riddled with bullets. Two more were
found in Texas. White was shot outside a hotel in Corinth, Mississippi.
There was nothing to tie Pusser directly to the killings, of course, except
for gossip and legend.

Because state law prohibits anyone from serving more than two con-
secutive terms, Pusser was forced to sit out the 1970 election. In an un-
coordinated campaign, the residents of Adamsville elected him local
constable, which allowed him to continue chasing crooks and busting
stills and generally representing law and order. Meanwhile he was becoming not simply a regional figure but a national celebrity, making public appearances at car dealerships and even briefly dating Miss Tennessee
Anne Galloway.

By that time, however, McNairy County was tiring of its notoriety
and soured at the depiction of their home as a locus of crime and corruption. When producers associated with Bing Crosby Productions began
developing a biopic called *Walking Tall*, local leaders declined their requests to shoot there in the county, on the roads and backwoods where it
all happened. Instead, production moved north to Chester County, but
the battle for who defined the place—McNairy County and, more generally, the South—raged on.

By then, Pusser had transformed into a tall tale: a celebrity lawman as
redneck Rasputin, the living embodiment of law and order, an exemplar
of southern manhood. As his celebrity grew, so did the legends around
him: Did his enemies shoot his dog, bomb his house, threaten his kids,
beat and stab him on an almost daily basis? Did he really break protocol
and wear street clothes instead of a uniform, as though he was always un-
dercover? Was there really a bulletproof room in the back of his house in
Adamsville? Many people claimed that he refused to carry a gun. Word

spread that he cleaned up the county armed only with a big stick. Was it an ax handle? Or, as many swore, a fence post? Maybe it was a 2 × 4 tempered with the blood of so many heads smashed in. How much was true and how much legend? It all depends on who's telling the story.

Using the murder of Pauline Pusser as its climax—rendering her a casualty in the transformation of her husband from small-town lawman to American hero—*Walking Tall* embraced the legend and cemented it in place for a national audience. It's a brutal, bloody film, with Joe Don Baker projecting a physical intensity that curdles into plain old meanness as his body registers every punch, stab, and bullet. Not especially well reviewed, *Walking Tall* wasn't initially a hit in theaters, where it was sold as a highbrow film. It didn't catch on until it hit drive-ins and small-town theaters, where it played for months on end.

Along with *Deliverance* in 1972 and *White Lightning* in 1973, *Walking Tall* established a national market for hicksploitation flicks that lasted well into the 1980s. Low-budget B movies like *Dixie Dynamite* in 1976 and *Moonshine County Express* in 1977 depicted the adventures of bootleggers in the rural South, presenting these criminals as American daredevils and rebels. Released in 1975, *Moonrunners*, starring Robert Mitchum's brother James, spawned the hit television show *The Dukes of Hazzard*, which ran from 1979 to 1985. Its premise was simple and endlessly repeatable: Bo and Luke Duke were two good ol' boys "never meanin' no harm," as Waylon Jennings's theme song vouched. They drove around in a souped-up Dodge Charger, painted bright orange and emblazoned with a Confederate flag on the roof. With the help of their cousin Daisy and their uncle Jesse, they would help strangers passing through town or run moonshine around the county while avoiding police officers and outwitting a harmless crime lord named Boss Hogg. That show informed how entire generations of viewers defined the South and themselves as southern. Few people had quite as much of an impact on southern pop culture in the 1970s or did so much to define southern masculinity as Pusser.

Patterson Hood and Mike Cooley grew up barely an hour's drive from McNairy County. After *Walking Tall* opened in their hometown, it continued to play at one theater for nearly a year and inspired a deep fascination with the sheriff in the two future songwriters. As kids, they played Buford and Bootleggers the way some kids played Cops and Robbers.

Even at such a young age, however, they understood they were seeing something of themselves up on the screen. "We all grew up knowing that some of the 'bad guys' in that movie were from our home region," says Patterson. "Everybody knew some of those people. It would get whispered about, and they were, to some extent...I wouldn't say they were pillars of the community, but they weren't necessarily *not* liked. They might be somebody's uncle, but they might also be somebody else's drug dealer. You knew not to cross them. That's the whole small-town thing of what you tolerate and turn a blind eye to, because, well, that's just ol' Uncle Bill." Folks rooted for Pusser, even if many of them understood he was fighting Uncle Bill.

Years later, those memories would inform their songs with the Drive-By Truckers—in particular what they called the Heathen Songs, which "were largely based on tall tales, local legends, myths, and imagination," says Hood. "We were telling stories, but not presenting anything as fact." Pusser was the perfect subject for this songwriting project: a real person whose life, while well documented, was equally constituted by rumor and hearsay, exaggeration and legend. He remains both real and mythological, actual and imaginary. He was also, they realized, a compromised figure: both hero and villain. Their fellow southerners "made him out to be this almost supernatural superhero," says Cooley. "He was a big, tough, scary motherfucker, but he was also allegedly a dirty cop. That's a very common theme in American entertainment— the tough lawman who's willing to bend the rules to put the bad guy away. Well, he might be willing to bend the rules to fuck you over, too. You gotta be careful who you hero-worship."

A songwriting project perhaps even more ambitious than the rock opera but much less defined, the Heathen Songs form the foundation of the Truckers' early catalog, in particular the run of albums up to their 2004 release, *The Dirty South*. The songs skew wildly from third person to first, from the barely fictional to the all too real, from songs about redneck sheriffs to laments for their own crumbling marriages. What connects them all is their embrace of the lowly, the poor, the socially disreputable. But they refuse to paint these people in broad strokes, instead filling these songs with fine details: shotguns loaded with black-eyed peas, car salesmen gunned down on their showroom floors, guys just trying to get by in a bad economy.

That word *heathen* has a long and complicated history in America, where it was applied to any group viewed as unenlightened: the Indigenous people encountered by European explorers as well as the Asians and Africans imported as cheap labor for railways and on plantations. The word contained a subtle argument for their enslavement: those heathen races needed to be educated, fostered, civilized, and redeemed by the benevolent hand of the white race. I didn't know any of that history growing up in McNairy County, but I heard that word frequently. It was applied to anybody, regardless of race, who didn't go to church. Heathens were the poor souls who slept in on Sunday morning, who had never heard the good news. Or else they were poor people who didn't have the sense or the smarts to lift themselves out of their dire situation. Or else it was a name for misbehaving children: when I threw a fit at the Big Star when my mother wouldn't buy me that comic book, I was acting like a *heathen*. Over time I heard folks exaggerate the southernness of the word, twisting it into *heathern* and using it interchangeably with *redneck* or *white trash*. In that regard it retained some of its old-world implications, in that it allowed the speaker to feel socially or morally superior.

It's crucial to note that Patterson and Cooley and eventually Isbell weren't using the word that way. The Heathen Songs are written and sung from the point of view of the heathens themselves: people who might have a car up on cinder blocks in their front yard or a mobile home with pink flamingos out front, people who've been cast off from polite society. Patterson was identifying himself as a heathen, in particular on an early song called "Heathens." It took him years to write, but that long process helped shape the entire project. It started with a guitar part, a short theme that bounces between two notes, sounding both miserable and a little conniving, and Patterson understood right away that it was too special to waste on a joke song. It needed to be good, needed to make a statement, needed to be something he could spend a lifetime playing night after night after night.

So he just lived with it for a while, until the first verse came to him while bouncing on a trampoline outside his second wife's hairdresser's house in Athens. The marriage had frayed, not quite beyond repair but getting there, which explains that first line: "Something about the wrinkle in your forehead tells me there's a fit 'bout to get thrown." There was a van in the ditch, a cul-de-sac of sleeping neighbors, and an unrepentant narrator: a whole world in a song. "We were heathens in their eyes. I guess I'm just a heathen still," Patterson sings. "I never have repented for the wrongs that they say I've done. I done what I feel." Featuring a delicate melody at odds with its messy milieu, it's one of several songs about doomed relationships on the 2003 album *Decoration Day*.

The Heathen Songs, which sprawl across the Truckers' early albums, took root in an intensely creative and prolific time for the band, starting in the late 1990s when they were touring constantly behind their first two records, *Gangstabilly* in 1998 and *Pizza Deliverance* in 1999. Although Patterson and Cooley had been playing together for fifteen years by then, they were still staking their claim on the South as their subject. The songs came almost faster than they could write them down and work them out, infused with humor and pathos. "We were prolific as shit back then," recalls Patterson. "I had a pretty massive notebook of songs for each album." He was too broke to afford an actual computer, so he kept multiple notepads full of lyrics, notes, and song ideas, all scribbled in chicken scratch and stashed in a backpack.

The Truckers would tour one album while recording the next one and writing the one after that, which means the Heathen Songs are scattered across multiple studio albums, as well as Patterson's first solo record and the band's odds-and-sods comp *The Fine Print* in 2009. "When Jason Isbell joined [in 2001], we were touring behind *Southern Rock Opera*, about to record *Decoration Day*, and were deep into writing *The Dirty South*," says Patterson. "He loved the concepts and embraced what we were doing. He wrote 'Never Gonna Change' from a similar point of view and 'The Day John Henry Died' to capture that blue-collar aspect of the area we grew up in." It was a heavy workload, but the result is a string of albums that feel thoroughly interconnected as they conjure a world that's large yet specific, familiar yet exotic, dangerous yet inviting. "Home was more violent than the big cities, in a lot of cases," says Patterson. "Rednecks will whip your ass."

Pusser was too large a figure to fit into just one Heathen Song and too complex to approach directly. On the band's 2004 album, *The Dirty South*, they tackle him with a full trilogy: two songs by Patterson and one by Cooley, composing what is sometimes referred to as the Buford Suite. Patterson opens the set with "The Boys from Alabama," drawing the listener in with a sinister invitation. "We're gonna take you up to McNairy County, Tennessee," he narrates over the seediest organ lick you could imagine and a heavy industrial drumbeat credited as "auto parts" in the liner notes. "Sheriff Buford Pusser was trying to clean up McNairy County, Tennessee, from all them bootleggers who were bringing crime and corruption into his little dry county. And for his troubles he got ambushed and his wife was murdered and his house got blown up and they made a movie about it called *Walking Tall*."

So far so legendary, but the Truckers' version is no mere retelling of the tale. Patterson's introduction concludes with an important announcement: "This is the other side of that story." To get to that other side, the band pushes Pusser out of the frame, and he becomes a character only briefly glimpsed, a mighty force impacting a full cast of bootleggers, pimps, gamblers, racketeers, murderers, and worse. The Truckers are much more interested in "the other side of that story"—the Uncle Bills of the Dirty South. "The Boys from Alabama" takes the form of a monologue by a veteran crook recruiting—or cajoling, or blackmailing, or aggressively threatening—a first-time offender into joining a much larger network of criminals. Neither character is named, not the speaker nor whoever he's addressing, and they are likely only loosely modeled on real people. But the song makes clear the ruthlessness of these rural criminals and the extensive underworld they represent.

As the guitars gnarl and crunch, Patterson drawls his syllables to evoke the bluster of a man caught up in his own power. He makes the word "opportunism" sound melodic and sing-songy. He insinuates some things ("Ain't nobody gonna stick anything up your ass if you remember who your friends are") and states others outright ("They might find your body in the Tennessee River or they might not find it at all"). And as the song shifts into a major key and the guitars explode, he howls the chorus, "I wouldn't piss off the boys from Alabama if I were you."

Who were the boys from Alabama? They were the higher-ups in the Dixie Mafia chain of command, to whom the State Line Mob in McNairy County reported. In the years after World War II, the crew was based in Phenix City, Alabama, a small town right on the Georgia border known for decades as Sin City. Thanks to nearby Fort Benning, bootleggers and brothel owners had a large customer base of soldiers, who were easy marks for grifters, dealers, pimps, and hucksters. As crime became the dominant industry, Phenix City grew increasingly corrupt and violent. In 1954, following the assassination of a leading anti-vice advocate, Governor Gordon Persons sent in the Alabama National Guard and imposed martial law. Many of the criminals moved north, expanding the syndicate to Alcorn County in Mississippi and McNairy County in Tennessee.

They congregated in the southern end of McNairy County, running motels, lounges, and the occasional restaurant. Most of them were fronts for illegal liquor sales in this dry county, much of it manufactured locally in an extensive underground economy of homemade stills and hooch runners. Other businesses concealed backroom casinos, money laundering operations, or trailer-park brothels. Tourists and travelers passing through town offered a profitable side hustle; they might stop in at the White Iris Restaurant or the Shamrock Motel and find themselves a wallet or a purse lighter when they left—and that's if they were lucky. As Dwana Pusser notes in her memoir, that stretch of highway was referred to locally as "Little Chicago" and "Murder City USA."

It should be noted that all of these activities were against the law, but one in particular was *especially* against the law. In dry McNairy County, the manufacture, importation, sale, and possession of liquor was forbidden. Dry counties were the planned outcome of what are called local option laws; a product of the nineteenth-century Temperance Movement, local option laws grant jurisdiction to county and city governments to determine how liquor is bought and sold. There are varying degrees of dryness: almost all prohibit liquor, while others might include wine and/or beer. McNairy County allowed beer sales but not wine. Hardin County to the east allowed wine but not beer. McNairy County went dry in the late 1890s, long before Prohibition made every county in America dry. But the Eighteenth Amendment was no great success, serving not to curtail the consumption of alcohol but rather to send it underground. Speakeasies opened in basements and attics, selling bathtub gin to high and low society alike.

In rural areas juke joints sprang up in remote shacks, entrepreneurs devised ingenious ways of hiding their merchandise, and rural buccaneers outfitted early hot rods with secret tanks for smuggling hooch across state lines (a trend that would eventually grow into NASCAR). Stills popped up throughout the dense backwoods of the county, each one an independent business venture in a community where the raw materials—sugar, wheat chaff, copper tubing—could all be purchased with little suspicion at the local farmer's co-op. The West Tennessee terrain is full of remote hollers and valleys, which made it difficult for law enforcement to find, let alone reach, these stills. Moonshiners would haul barrels out to the site, one of which they would bury in the ground. They'd fill this one with water, sugar, and wheat chaff; left alone for up to two weeks, the mixture would ferment and produce the base for the whiskey—known as the mash. Some shiners would throw a dead possum or squirrel in the barrel to discourage their men from sampling the product.

Over a nearby firepit the mash would be boiled and distilled, and the stringent white whiskey transferred to jugs or barrels for transport. The distillation process produced a great deal of smoke, which usually tipped off law enforcement. Police would organize surprise raids and bust up the stills with pickaxes, leaving telltale square puncture marks. The whiskey would drain out into the soil, and the shiners would be taken to jail. However, if they eluded the cops—if they were wily enough, or if they had gone deep enough into the woods, or if they had paid someone off—the whiskey would be shipped around the county and beyond, usually sold under the counter at straight businesses like those along Highway 45. For most law enforcement officials, this bootleg economy was simply a fact of life, and officers might let it slide if the money or the threat was sufficient. Even today, locals occasionally uncover the ruins of old stills, rusted-out barrels and neat piles of rocks still bearing the scorches of the fire.

The Truckers grew up in dry counties like these. Both Patterson and Cooley knew that dry counties were never really dry and that local option laws only forced drinkers to be sneakier, craftier, less conspicuous in their consumption. They sang about those experiences in numerous Heathen Songs, most famously on "Let There Be Rock" from *Southern Rock Opera*, which recounts a particularly perilous parking job Patterson performed after downing a fifth of vodka. And it's the unspoken setting of "The Boys from Alabama," the only place where such a criminal syndicate could flourish. "I knew it was all bullshit," Patterson says of his own dry county. "The church was full of hypocrisy and the cops were enforcing a prohibition. Fuck that."

In the 1960s and 1970s, the people making money off these operations in McNairy County were all part of a larger system, predominantly white and based along the southern coast in Alabama and Mississippi, where tourism supported the bootlegging industry. The syndicate had tendrils stretching far north, with soldiers throughout the South, including a notorious gangster in northern Alabama named DeWitt Dawson, who is the subject and narrator of "Cottonseed," the second song in the Truckers' Buford Suite. Cooley wrote it based on a run-in he had with Dawson at a church in his hometown of Tuscumbia. As the din of "The Boys from Alabama" fades, Cooley strums a jump cut into a starkly acoustic monologue that claims, "I put more lawmen in the ground than Alabama put cottonseed." It's a wild boast, the outlaw inflating his legend, cultivating his own myth.

DeWitt Dawson was as violent as he was charismatic. He was the leader of the notorious Dawson Gang, which also included his brothers Pride and Homer Gene and a few conscripted cousins. They had been busted for robbery, grand theft auto, and—much less entertainingly— tax evasion over the years, and DeWitt had developed the cockiness and self-regard of a '30s gangster. According to a *Washington Post* article from 1977, when the IRS raided his home, they found a note that read, "I gave at the office." He pled guilty, but he had the audacity to buy an ad in the local newspaper proclaiming his innocence.

As part of his sentence, Dawson had to do community service, which in this case involved speaking at churches and telling his story as a cautionary tale. Cooley was at one of those appearances:

> I was at this church youth retreat and they had booked him to speak, this local gangster celebrity. I don't know if he was doing it for points toward his parole or what the nature of it was, but he made it very clear that he wasn't coming as a minister. He kept stressing that it wasn't a come-to-Jesus moment. He comes in thinking he's going to be talking to about thirty or forty teenagers, but he was such a big deal that all of these people showed up, all these kids' parents. I couldn't get that part into the song—what did they want from him? Did they want him to beg for their forgiveness? Did they think he was going to reveal some big secret to them? Tell them where the bodies are buried? Maybe I can write about that at some point.

Dawson was, of course, defiantly unrepentant. Even as a kid, Cooley could sense as much. The local celebrity might have played the part of the reformed criminal, but there are rumors that he carried a gun to the pulpit. Rather than confessing his sins, in "Cottonseed" he treats those sins like gospel, as though bombing a judge was akin to healing the sick. Through Cooley's song Dawson explains to the congregants and to us how the world works: "The meanest of the mean I see you lock away and toss the key, but they're all just loud-mouth punks to me. I've scraped meaner off my shoes."

He has no redemptive mission, no higher calling; in fact, he seems to have no motivation at all, but rather exists as the embodiment of some violent impulse in the Truckers' Dirty South, as dark as it is self-justifying.

By the time Cooley met Dawson, Pusser was already dead. On August 21, 1974, the former sheriff had signed a contract with Bing Crosby Productions to star in a sequel to *Walking Tall* and had spent the rest of the day at the county fair just outside Selmer. On his way home to Adamsville, his souped-up Corvette crashed into an embankment and flipped. The T-top was open, and Pusser was thrown from the car, his neck broken and his body pulverized. His daughter and her friends were following him, and while they didn't see the crash—Pusser had a notoriously heavy foot and was said to have been going 120 miles per hour when his car left the road—they were first on the scene. Pusser was pronounced dead where he lay. Today the charred and twisted remains of his Corvette serve as a grim exhibition in the Buford Pusser Home and Museum, right next to a display of collectible Buford sticks for sale.

Like nearly everything else about Pusser, the crash still serves as a source of rumor and debate. Eyewitnesses at the county fair said he appeared intoxicated before he headed home. Was he driving drunk? Or did he simply lose control of his vehicle? Everyone knew he loved driving as fast as he could down McNairy County's back roads. Or maybe he was murdered? In *Walking On*, Dwana Pusser suggests that her father was the victim of a political conspiracy. Although a Republican, Pusser was campaigning for fellow Adamsville resident Roy Blanton, a Democrat running for governor. The rumor was that Blanton would return the favor by appointing Pusser as the commissioner of safety for Tennessee, a position that would allow him to open any criminal files in the state and possibly reveal a criminal network that extended far beyond McNairy County. There was no way they could let that happen.

The Truckers' theory is much more local. In "The Buford Stick," the final installment in the suite, the sheriff is portrayed as someone perhaps corrupted by celebrity, or, at the very least, distracted by the glint of light off the news cameras. The song opens with a minor-key riff, gnarly and heavy and just plain mean, recalling the musical setting of "The Boys from Alabama," and Patterson sets about dissecting the bluster of Pusser's celebrity: "With his book reviews and movie deals . . . he gets a hot new car to keep us on our toes, and that ridiculous stick where the press corps goes." Patterson is, of course, singing in character, in this case adopting the voice of a small-time hood caught in the crossfire of Pusser's war with the State Line Mob, ostensibly a bootlegger bristling at the way fame has erased the lawman's transgressions and exaggerated his triumphs. Besides, all those flashbulbs around McNairy County make it hard for an honest criminal to do his job.

This may be the ultimate point of the Buford Suite: the rural South had long been economically depressed, with more and more people leaving small towns for big cities. Agriculture was still a lucrative business, but changing technology called for a smaller labor force. Gradually timber overtook farming as the dominant use of the land, as lumber companies rented fields that had once grown cotton and soybeans. In such a landscape, honest yet desperate men might turn to something like bootlegging purely as a means of survival, out of not desire but necessity. This is an idea that illuminates so many of the Heathen Songs, including "Goode's Field Road," from the 2008 release *Brighter Than Creation's Dark*, about a tow-truck driver caught up in a criminal conspiracy. (Patterson calls that song "one of the best things I've ever written.") Or "Putting People on the Moon," where a laid-off auto worker takes to selling coke just to scrape by. Or Isbell's "Never Gonna Change," about a family of bootleggers in Alabama who protect their business as their birthright. The Truckers aren't necessarily defending these men and women who operate on the outermost fringes of capitalism. But they are trying to understand them, to appreciate their plight and give them some kind of a voice in pop culture. "We want to be fair to whatever story we're telling," says Patterson. "I would hate to condescend or be overly romantic, but I do want it to be an entertaining story."

And so "The Buford Stick" becomes almost Shakespearean, presenting Pusser as a tragic hero felled by his own fame—someone whose success has obscured his mission. The song's narrator daydreams about sabotaging that flashy sports car: "It wouldn't take my man long to do the job, just a partially sawed-through steering rod, and I wouldn't have to worry about the good sheriff anymore." But he stops just shy of self-incrimination, even as he describes that fatal crash: "Hit an embankment going 120 miles per hour on a straightaway. The Lord works in mysterious ways." It's not necessarily an admission of guilt, maybe just a sinister daydream; even in this Heathen song, Pusser's death remains unsolved.

"After we got those songs out there," says Cooley, "these folks who grew up in McNairy County would come to shows and talk to us about Pusser. He was no white knight by any stretch of the imagination. People would tell us about growing up and hearing their parents and grandparents talk about Pusser like he was some piece of shit. They told us about the bootlegging gang he was going after in the movie. That's all true but it wasn't because he wouldn't take their money. It was because someone else had made him a better offer. He was on the take."

Hearsay, of course, isn't evidence, and shortly after the album was released, Patterson received what he calls a "really nasty note" from Dwana Pusser, who took exception to this portrayal of her father. "I was writing about the mythology and didn't take the real people into account," he says. "I hate that I offended his family. That was never my intent. Same time, the things my song said were very plainly stated as being from a specific person's point of view and not mine. The song was narrated by a guy who wanted Pusser dead, and I'm not sure she got that."

It's not hard to see Dwana's side of the story or to understand why she might object to a song calling for the murder of her father. But it is valuable to get "the other side to that story," to complicate a southern legend whose moral equivalencies are perhaps too settled, too perfect: good guys against bad guys, the agents of law and order against the perpetrators of crime and chaos. In some ways, the story of Pusser as the Truckers tell it is about the South fighting to portray itself to the rest of the world. Whose story becomes the established narrative? And whose is omitted altogether?

In that regard, the Buford Suite reveals something essential about the Drive-By Truckers, something that defined the band early in their career and continues to define them even now that their scope has widened on their recent albums, when the South is no longer their primary subject. It has to do with the direction of southern rebellion. Historically, the South has pushed against the intrusion of outside forces, whether it's Union troops, General Sherman, northern abolitionists, carpetbaggers, revenuers, interlopers, civil rights activists, or movie stars with bad accents. And in the aftermath of the 2016 election, there's been a loud outcry against allowing the South to tell its side of the story through what amounts to a renewal and shoring up of its self-aggrandizing Lost Cause rebel narratives. By taking on the legend of Pusser—one not imposed on the South but regionally generated to present the South as it wished to see itself—the Truckers direct that rebellion inward instead of outward or northward. They're pushing back against the South itself and its pieties, its self-defining myths. It's a truly heathen move.

This idea echoes throughout their catalog, including *American Band*, *The Unraveling*, and *The New OK*. In fact, like so many of their albums, the Buford Suite is a call not only to adopt new and more constructive symbols of the South but also to interrogate our attitudes toward old symbols through which our identities, collective and individual, are built and defended. By telling "the other side of that story" and by complicating the legend of Buford Pusser, the Drive-By Truckers attempt to rescue the man from the myth and the South from his shadow.

I grew up in McNairy County in the 1980s, but the place the Truckers describe is not the place I knew. By the time Pusser died, the State Line Mob had largely scattered. The Dixie Mafia remained intact, but if they continued doing business in McNairy County, they did it with much less audacity and much more discretion than they previously had. I heard people talk about Pusser reverently, although some criticized his embrace of celebrity along with the county's refusal to let *Walking Tall* film there. The motels and restaurants along Highway 45 were shuttered and abandoned, although they stood hollowed out and haunted for years to come: ghosts from the past, cautionary tales to the local populace, question marks for travelers who perhaps clutched their purses closer until they were safely in Mississippi. I knew them only as boarded-up buildings, left to weed and rust. We passed them on our way to my brother's

T-ball games in Eastview or to soccer practice in Corinth. They seemed like the ruins of some ancient civilization; I had no idea what went on between those crumbling walls.

The place where I grew up was quiet, enclosed. My whole world was home, school, church, friends' houses, and the woods just beyond our backyard. Pusser died the year I was born, so I never met him, never knew him as anything more than a tall tale: a name spoken with a shake of the head, a grainy photo in the *Independent Appeal* to mark this or that anniversary, a giant mural at Pusser's Restaurant in Adamsville. Aside from the new sheriff, Robert K. Lee, who taught my Sunday school class, my main connection to that part of McNairy County was my father, an attorney who had moved to Selmer in 1970. He had some dealings with Pusser, as any local lawyer would, but he was understandably unforthcoming around his three sons. But that was his way: occasionally he might joke about financing someone's "double-long" trailer, but generally he did not talk about the details of his work or tell us about those late-night phone calls that distressed him so much. It was only later that I learned that those calls were from a worried parent whose ex had taken the kid.

As I grew up and moved away from Selmer—first to Memphis for college, then out of the South completely—I came to think of McNairy County as a place tinged with tragedy. Everyone waxes poetic about their origins, however far away they get from them, but the local tragedies continued to pile up long after I left, and I followed them from afar: The 2000 fire that destroyed the First Baptist Church up on the north side of town, caused by a stray spark during the installation of a new steeple, burning so hot it melted the handbells I'd played as a kid in the youth choir. The accident during the annual Cars for Kids charity parade in 2007, when a funny car revved its engines and spun out of control into the crowd, killing seven teenagers and injuring many more. The old man who drove his car into a crowd at the 2016 Rockabilly Festival, killing two.

And the death of my father. In 2001 doctors discovered a glioblastoma the size of a golf ball wedged ominously in his brain, a diagnosis that explained the last few months of forgetfulness, clumsiness, and headaches. Because this was a ridiculously malignant and relentlessly aggressive cancer, he was given just six months.

That was June.

I moved away from the South in July.

He died the next May at the McNairy General Hospital, the same hospital where I was born. Because he was an Army veteran, he was buried at Shiloh National Cemetery, just a thirty-minute drive from our home, interring his—and my—personal history within an equally painful national one, the Civil War burial ground and mourning site for Confederate defeat.

That is the prologue to my discovery of the Drive-By Truckers. In a way, the world they created in their songs reminded me of my father, who admittedly wouldn't have understood my fascination with the band. Like him, they provided an alternative example of southern masculinity, one that didn't always jibe with the guys who flew the Confederate flag and claimed to be southern *by the grace of God*. My father seemed out of place in Selmer, although he loved his community. He was a southern liberal Democrat with a framed poster of President Kennedy in his law office and an oval cutout of turf from the football field where Paul "Bear" Bryant won his 315th game as coach at the University of Alabama. My father was fit, but not physically strong. He couldn't fix a car or unclog a sink to save his life, yet he traded legal services for fruits and vegetables his clients had grown in their own garden: watermelons bigger than your head, bushels of green beans and snap peas, ears of corn by the armful. "Different people have different ways of paying you," he told his sons.

Similarly, the Truckers measure a man not by his ability to wrassle a bear (which Pusser famously did) or by how he handles a gun or a 2 × 4, but by how he treats the people around him, friend or stranger, rich or poor, criminal or Christian (or both).

The Truckers returned to McNairy County in 2010, this time to document a very different kind of crime. In March 2006, Matthew Winkler, the young pastor at the Fourth Street Church of Christ in Selmer, was found dead on his bedroom floor, shot in the back at close range. His wife, Mary, and their three young daughters were missing. The murder startled the town and especially his small congregation, who knew Matthew as a faithful family man. An Amber Alert was issued for Mary and her kids, who were eventually found in Orange Beach, Alabama, down on the Gulf Coast. Mary was questioned and claimed that Matthew had abused her physically, emotionally, and sexually. They had fought constantly, about finances among other things; she had lost money to a scam involving someone pretending to be a Nigerian prince. Mary claimed that she did not remember getting the gun, but she did remember firing it by accident. When Matthew rolled off the bed, dying, he whispered a word to his wife: "Why?"

I heard about the incident the way most people did—through CNN—but it wasn't long before old friends were emailing me with grisly details about the murder. News reports quoted congregants and citizens, parents of my high school friends or pastors who had shaken my hand and prayed for my family. I remember the shock of seeing a photograph of the Winklers' house on Mollie Drive, because there next to it was the red-brick ranch house with blue trim and wooden shingles where I grew up. There was my old bedroom window on the front of the house, the one that had once shattered when lightning struck a tree in our yard, scaring me senseless. Reading about my hometown in the news made me feel impossibly far away.

I never knew the Winklers. I had gone to college, graduated, and married before the family took up residence in the Church of Christ parsonage. In fact, no one was living in our house at the time of the murder, as my recently widowed mother had moved down to Birmingham to be closer to her family. She recalled meeting both Matthew and Mary Winkler but never formed much of an impression of the family. In fact, few on Mollie Drive seemed to have interacted with the couple at all, save one neighbor who recalls Matthew threatening to shoot his barking dog.

Patterson was all the way over in Norway when he heard about the murder, and he immediately associated it with the Buford Suite. He wouldn't write about it for another year or two, after the case had gone to trial. "I was in Hernando, Mississippi, working on a project with Jim Dickinson and his sons Luther and Cody, and the trial was playing out on some reality channel in our ratty motel room. I wasn't meaning to watch, but I remembered the story. I felt I knew some of those people from childhood, the people in that courtroom." He was watching with much more than distracted interest when the defense attorney entered into evidence the go-go boots and blonde wig Matthew forced his wife to wear in the bedroom. "I literally heard the crowd gasp. I knew at that moment she would walk. I knew those people weren't going to convict her after that."

The jury deliberated for eight hours before finding her guilty. Instead of first-degree murder, however, the charge was reduced to voluntary manslaughter, which defined the murder as a crime of passion. She was sentenced to 210 days in prison but got credit for the five months she had already served. She also spent two months at a mental health facility for treatment of depression and post-traumatic stress disorder, and was eventually awarded custody of her children. The lightness of the sentence infuriated Matthew Winkler's family and many who believed she got away with only a light smack on the wrist.

Patterson was not surprised in the least. He knew he wanted to tell the story in song—not the story of the murder, which sadly is not different from so many similar domestic abuse cases, but the story of Mary Winkler's sentencing. He started with a title, "The Audible Gasp," but soon changed it to "The Wig He Made Her Wear." The band recorded it for the 2010 release *The Big To-Do*, and musically, the song is all rhythm section, with drummer Brad Morgan and bassist Shonna Tucker creating a taut noir groove that's as tangled and clotted as a ravine full of kudzu. Patterson doesn't sing the lyrics, and he foregoes any hint of a chorus or bridge. His lyrics are surprisingly literal, as if he's sharing lunchtime gossip over slugburgers at Pat's Café.

"It was as open and shut as I have seen," he tells the listener by way of introduction; then he lays out the gist of the story. More than just a convincing summation of the facts of the case, "The Wig He Made Her Wear" offers a moment of true southern storytelling: as it proceeds, it becomes wilder, darker, and more outrageous, just like the Winkler trial itself. "Nobody at church would ever suspect, he made her dress up slutty before they had sex," he says before describing, in a careful deadpan, the moment when the defense attorney plunked down the wig and hooker heels on the witness box for the whole town to see. "In the courtroom that day there was an audible gasp. What they put up on display the locals couldn't quite grasp." Savoring your shock and maybe stealing a fry off your plate, Patterson seems to ask his listener, *Can you believe it?*

"I took some criticism for my writing of that song," says Patterson, "but I feel like it was misunderstood. People say I just reported the facts and there's no emotional depth to it, but I always I felt like the song was about that audible gasp and the mores of small towns in the Bible Belt. Everything else was just to set that up. It's all about that gasp in the courtroom."

Even more than the murder itself, there is something violent and irreparable about the airing of small-town secrets, the excavation and exposure of personal predilections that we pretend don't exist except in gossip and rumor. It's a theme that drives so much American fiction, from *Winesburg, Ohio* to *Gone Girl*, but especially southern gothic literature, the tradition in which Patterson is operating. It thrives on the contrast between extremes: the heavenly and the earthly, the spiritual and the carnal, the righteousness of a beloved preacher and his fetish for fishnets. It's unfathomable that murder becomes justifiable, although Patterson tells the tale in such a way that morals remain murkier than motives. Did the sexual and emotional ordeals of the Winkler marriage excuse such violence, or did the jury recognize something deep in themselves? Did reducing Mary's charge tamp down those secrets and give them the illusion of security? Did the townspeople identify more with Mary or with Matthew? Everybody has their wigs and go-go boots.

There are no real heroes or villains in this story; the characters can't be distinguished as lawmen or outlaws, murderers or victims. But what makes all these McNairy County stories so similar, aside from their shared setting, is that nobody really wins. Everybody loses something essential: their lives, their livelihoods, their freedom, and their secrets, but most of all their faith. McNairy County is a place where faith is repeatedly bolstered and shattered, and perhaps that is why it has captivated the Truckers so thoroughly: both mundane and strange, it's a place no different from any other except in how it sits in our imagination. And how it sits in my memory.

Out West

▼

It's November 21, 2014, and the Drive-By Truckers are closing out the second show of their three-night stand at the Fillmore Auditorium in San Francisco with a thirteen-minute version of a song called "Grand Canyon." It was inspired by the death of their longtime merch guy Craig Lieske, a tragedy made all the more unfathomable by its happening right in the middle of a HeAthens Homecoming weekend.

They take their time with the song, leaving some spaces in the music, little bits of thoughtful silence between the clicks of Brad Morgan's drums and the etch of Mike Cooley's guitar. Jay Gonzalez plays his organ like he's painting the first morning rays of sunlight on a lonely highway. There is a sense of steady westward motion in this performance: the click of highway lines, the regular rhythm of exits and rest stops and gas stations. If it's a road song, tonight it's a road song of nostalgia, as Patterson Hood describes long tours and late nights with his beloved friend, including an afternoon watching the sun set over the largest ditch in America. "I'll think about Grand Canyon, and I'll lift my glass and smile," he sings.

It's a moment he has written into the song as a way of remembering it, maybe a way of keeping Lieske alive even just for a few moments every night. But "Grand Canyon" has become something of an all-purpose eulogy, with Patterson raising a glass to all his dead heroes: Vic Chesnutt, Chris Quillen, Jimmy Johnson, John Cahoon, Bryan Harvey, Sissy

Patterson, George A., Gladys Sizemore. Sometimes he'll call them out by name, a running list of People Who've Died, but some nights he knows that his audience knows, even allows them a moment to toast their own fallen friends. I think of my father in those last minutes of the song, and I lift a glass and try to smile.

Tonight at the Fillmore, as on many evenings, the song doesn't end with its climax but starts anew, first with Morgan's stoic beat, accentuated by Matt Patton's bass notes. Then there are great waves of distortion from Cooley's guitar, carving canyons into earth. They deconstruct the song, finding weird grooves and themes, taking the scenic route to get back to that climax. Patterson is largely quiet tonight, willing to let the guitars do the talking and the toasting and the weeping: a bit of Crazy Horse, a bit of Skynyrd, a lot of just themselves. Out of the din come a few lines from "Sleepwalking," the old Santo & Johnny hit, like a song they can't remember the name of. Finally, only a squall of concentrated distortion remains, as the band members one by one walk off the stage, Morgan pounding out the final measures like he doesn't want the song to end just yet. It's a beautiful moment in the rock show, bitingly loud but bittersweet in its understatement.

That run of shows felt like something of a culmination, as the Truckers took their place among the great rock bands that had played the Fillmore Auditorium before them. In 2015 they released excerpts from those three shows in a triple-live box set called *It's Great to Be Alive!* and sequenced this performance of "Grand Canyon" at the very end. Because they dig deep into their catalog for every show, the set serves as an unofficial career retrospective: a survey of every corner of their remarkable catalog, some of their newest songs (from that year's *English Oceans*) mixed in with rarities like "Girls Who Smoke" and early cuts like "Box of Spiders." The Truckers even revive an old Adam's House Cat song called "Runaway Train," which at that point had never been officially released in any form. As a greatest hits package, it sounds more convincing than their actual greatest hits, the 2011 single-disc *Ugly Buildings, Whores & Politicians*.

As such, it might have felt like the culmination of something important: the end of an era. *English Oceans* earned modest praise and notched modest sales. Tickets to the Fillmore shows went fast, but even Patterson, ever the optimist, sensed a shift in the winds around them and feared the Truckers might be running out of gas. If the secret to a happy ending was knowing when to roll the credits, as "World of Hurt" asserts, had they just blown past the right moment long ago? The band had spent decades trying to keep it between the ditches, hiring and firing members, recording on frayed-shoestring budgets, touring by the seat of their pants, and nearly coming to blows repeatedly, but they had emerged in this new decade with their steadiest lineup yet, a streamlined quintet that could do more than justice to any song in their catalog. Hitting a wall at this point would have been ironic after so many years of toil and frustration.

That, of course, didn't happen. They followed *It's Great to Be Alive!* with *American Band*, which reinvigorated them and helped rebrand them as the Dance Band of the Resistance, putting our gnawing fears and outrage to music. But that performance of "Grand Canyon" in San Francisco nevertheless sounds like an important mile marker in their long journey, yet another stretch of road where they might have ended up in the ditch.

Halfway through "Grand Canyon," Patterson takes an existential flight of fancy and wonders aloud "if the recently departed make the sunsets to say farewell to the ones they leave behind." It's a lovely thought, especially from someone who doesn't regard himself as especially religious. But Patterson has a thing for sunsets. "Monument Valley," which closes their 2008 release, *Brighter Than Creation's Dark*, opens with a quote from John Ford, the director of poetic Westerns, about where to put the horizon, and from there the song crescendos into a show-closing anthem about how every one of us one day rides off into our own sunset.

When Patterson moved to Portland, Oregon, just months before the release of *It's Great to Be Alive!* in 2015, those sunsets took on a slightly more menacing quality. The cover of *The Unraveling*, their first album from 2020 and one that Patterson describes as "really fucking dark," shows two kids standing on the beach watching the sun sink into the water, casting pinks and reds across the sky. *Was this sunset created by the death of the American dream?* the album seemed to ask. On *The New OK*, their second album of 2020 and one somehow more optimistic than its predecessor, what appears to be a sunset is actually a city on fire. He wrote the song in response to the protests that rocked Portland, Oregon, the weekend after George Floyd was murdered, and the band members recorded their parts in isolation. There's an eerie, precarious beauty to the music, the way these distanced band members play, even as Patterson wonders how to talk to his children about what's going on in their city. This isn't a song about what it means; it's a song about what a person can do. "I'm trying really hard to find a way to make it all better," he sings with a barely contained urgency in his voice, "as I struggle with how or if I should share stories that are so upsetting."

The Truckers might be bound to the South, but Patterson always seems to be facing west, always driving into the sun. The West has held enormous imaginative power over him, first as a place seen in the films of Ford and John Huston and Dennis Hopper (in particular *Easy Rider*, which he says inspired the *Unraveling* cover), but also as a place to visit on tour or on vacation. The Truckers have played frequently in states between them and the sunset, markets many other bands avoid. They have made off-season jaunts into cities hungry for live music and willing to shell out to see any band, even these weirdos from Georgia. "Seen the mountains of Montana at seven AM," Patterson sings on "Hell No, I Ain't Happy," a sober account of those long drives between gigs and those long months away from home—which get a little longer once your tour van crosses the Mississippi.

When he left Athens and moved to Portland, Patterson felt right at home as soon as he saw the Columbia River cutting through downtown; it reminded him of home, of growing up in the Shoals, of falling in love with the Tennessee River. He quickly found a foothold in the local music scene, even if he didn't immerse himself as deeply in it as he had in the Athens scene two decades earlier. He haunted the clubs and watched younger bands cut their teeth and hung out with locals like Chris Funk, the Decemberists guitarist and producer of his one-off solo track "Airplane Screams" (featured on a 2017 benefit EP for the Southern Poverty Law Center).

That move westward gave Patterson a new perspective on his own southernness. His North Alabama twang was exotic in Portland, making him something of an odd man out and allowing him to see the South from the outside. While *American Band*—the Truckers' first album after his move—signaled an expansion of their sound and their subject matter, it also included meditations on his origins, in particular the song "Ever

South," a family tree set to music. Tracing his roots back to Alabama and from there back to Ellis Island and across the Atlantic to Ireland and Scotland, the song is epic in its depictions of generations of Hoods across the centuries, yet personal in its reckoning of himself and his children as both culmination and continuation of those family lines. It sounds like it could come only from someone who has moved far away from home and can look back on the South from afar, turning the defining southern yearning—the nostalgia for a home and a time you can't reclaim—into something wiser, more measured, more humane. Even in Portland, Oregon, about as far from Athens, Georgia, as you can get without leaving the continental United States, he's defined as southern: "Everyone takes notice of the drawl that leaves our mouths," Patterson sings, "so that no matter where we are we're ever South."

By enlarging their scope to take in not just this one region of the country but all of America, the Truckers are implicitly denying the idea of southern exceptionalism—the notion that the South remains a place removed from the rest of the United States. Regional differences are disappearing with the big box stores and digital retailers he sings about in songs like "21st Century USA." The South is becoming more like the rest of America, and the rest of America is becoming more like the South: infected with similar prejudices and racked by similar violence.

It's not the most romantic depiction of home, but the point of a song like "Ever South" is that we take the South with us wherever we go. That's exactly the kind of realization you can read about but really comprehend only by leaving home. In fact, the one thing all the places in this book have in common, aside from geography, is that they were all places for the band to leave. It's never as important how these musicians got to these cities. What's more compelling and what truly pushes their story along is how they left, and why: Adam's House Cat left the Shoals in defeat. Patterson and Cooley left Memphis separately and in disgust. Several different iterations of the band left Athens with great promise and excitement. That determines how they write about those points on the map and how they set about constructing this idea of a South. It's the leaving, not the arriving, that shapes their story.

Actually, it's not just leaving, but *leaving behind*. Their songs sift through the "poetry among the wreckage," to resurrect Eric Weisbard's phrase, to find what they can carry forward and what they can resign to history. Leave the Confederate flag and the Lee monuments and the Lost Cause and the heritage arguments and the racism. As Patterson put it in his *New York Times* editorial, "if we want to truly honor our Southern forefathers, we should do it by moving on from the symbols and prejudices of their time and building on the diversity, the art and the literary traditions we've inherited from them. It's time to study and learn about who we are and where we came from while finding a way forward without the baggage of our ancestors' fears and superstitions."

That is not easy, but the miracle of the Truckers' music is that their songs make it sound possible. The South is always changing, always shedding some traditions and starting new ones, always reinventing itself; and who's to say a rock and roll band can't show the way forward? Who's to say salvation can't be found at a rock show? The Truckers describe just one iteration of this place so many of us still call home, but they have a notion that something better is coming next, just after the next sunset.

Acknowledgments

▼

Much of the information in this book was gathered through lengthy and enlightening interviews with the band, and I am grateful to Patterson Hood, Mike Cooley, Brad Morgan, Matt Patton, and Jay Gonzalez for giving me so much of their time and trusting me with their stories. I would also like to thank past members, as well, in particular Shonna Tucker, Jason Isbell, Rob Malone, John Neff, Matt Lane, and the great Chuck Tremblay. I've benefitted from the insights and input from the sprawling Truckers family: Wes Freed, David Barbe, Jenn Bryant, Lilla Hood, Brandon Haynie, Bettye LaVette, Dave Schools, Jay Leavitt, Pudd Sharp, Mark Lynn, Traci Thomas, Kelly Hogan, David Hood, John Hornyak, Luther Dickinson, Cody Dickinson, Kevin Sweeney, Nick Bielli, Slim Chance, Kandia Crazy Horse, Robby Grant, and many, many others. A special shout-out to Christine Stauder at Red Light Management, who put up with my endless requests for info and interviews. Every band should have such a badass manager.

This book could not have been written without the patience, perseverance, and encouragement of Casey Kittrell at the University of Texas Press, who had faith in me even on those days when I felt his faith might be misplaced. David Menconi believed in this project from the very beginning; I've been reading his writing for half my life and consider myself lucky for the chance to work with him. Thanks as well go to Sarah Hudgens and the American Music Series editors Jessica Hopper and Charles Hughes.

Brady Brock and Alyssa Jones took the time to show me around Athens and make me feel right at home, and I'm grateful as well to New West Records and ATO Records. Ken Weinstein, Jakub Blackman, and Kim Grant helped put me in touch with many of these fine musicians. Adam Rudolphi proved invaluable as a transcriber, assistant, sounding board, and friend. The amazing Faye Gleisser read portions of the manuscript and provided invaluable feedback. Jason and Shannon Speth and Darren Hawkins showed me the stills in McNairy County.

Chris Avino sold me my first Drive-By Truckers CD back in Newark, Delaware, which set me on this journey. A few years later, Candice Jones and Rohan Mahadevan took me to my first Truckers rock show in Baltimore. My conversations with Brady Potts and Mary McCoy (aka the Star-Crossed Truckers) about the Truckers, about rock and roll, about the South, and about everything over the years have been invaluable.

I've had the opportunity to work with some wise editors over the years, who have made me a better writer: Fredric Koeppel, Lynn Conlee, Chris Herrington, Leonard Gill, Caine O'Rear, Scott Plagenhoef, Mark Richardson, Rob Harvilla, Craig Shelburne, Scott Lapatine, David Daley, Jeremy Larson, Brent Baldwin, John Mulvey, Tom Pinnock, John Robinson, Sam Richards, and especially Michael Bonner at *Uncut*.

I couldn't ask for better, smarter, more generous, or more creative neighbors and friends than Ryan Powell and Tim Bell. I'm fortunate to have such an amazing group of friends and colleagues here in Bloomington, where the conversation is always lively: Sammy Joe Osborne, David Brent Johnson, Kate Crum, Jeffrey Saletnik, Jooyoung Shin, Dr. Amanda Quinby, Dorothy M. Burford, Scot Ausborn and Joanna Woronkowicz, Mike Adams, Athena Kirke and Andrew Moisey, Jason Nickey, Heath Byers, Peter Ermey and Joanna Davis, Sam Stephenson, Andy Hollinden, Margaret Graves and Ally Batten, Kate Althizer, Mike McAfee, Phil Ford, Ben Wittkugel, Jon Lawrence and Jan Sorby, and David and Janet James. I'm indebted (perhaps literally at this point) to the fine people at Landlocked Music in Bloomington, the finest record store in the land, and the equally fine people at Hopscotch Coffee, also in Bloomington, the finest coffee shop in the land.

Beyond Bloomington: Toby Manning, Catherine Lewis, Joe Sankey, Mike Long, Nina Gray, Josh Klein, Althea Legaspi, Gerritt Lagemann, Genie Deusner, Todd and Leigh Richardson, James Spears, Christina

Huntington, Henry Murphy, Teresa Vivolo, Daniel Cooper, Travis Morgan, David McCarthy, and Marina Pacini, and the amazing people at Burke's Book Store, the finest book store in the world. Owners Corey and Cheryl Mesler have had an immeasurable impact on my life as a reader and writer.

Writing can be a lonely pursuit, but there are other writers whose words and wisdom I find endlessly rejuvenating. I am fortunate to know Laura Snapes, Tom Carson, Nate Patrin, Joe Tangari, Eric Harvey, Amanda Petrusich, Aaron Cohen, Ann Powers, Eric Weisbard, Grayson Haver Currin, Jewly Hight, Bob Mehr, David Cantwell, Andria Lisle, Alex Greene, Robert Ham, and Erin Osmon, among many others.

I'm blessed to have family everywhere I go. In Nashville: Rose and Bill Carver, Deidre Carver, Nancy Carver, Matt and Carrie Malone, Sadie, and Sam. In Birmingham: Maloy Love, Anita and Jerry O'Neal, Suzanne Hart, Renee and Chris Schmidt, Alison and David Skinner. In Texas: Owen and Judy Barnett, the most incredible in-laws anybody could wish for, and Owen Finley Barnett, my other brother and a huge Truckers fan.

My brothers, Edwin and David, grew up in the same South that I grew up in and know it as well as I do. I hope their kids, Wil and Shelby and Shiloh and Truett, will make that South a better place. I've learned so much from Ron Montgomery about how to tell a good story. And I am blessed to have parents who raised me right: Ann Deusner Montgomery, who instilled in me a great sense of adventure and love of life, and Earl Deusner, whom I miss every day.

And finally, like everything I do in this life, I wrote this book for my wife, Melody. She talked through every idea in these pages, proofread chapters, cranked *Decoration Day* even louder, talked me down from every ledge, and continually fills my life with so much joy and beauty and wonder.

Selected Discography

▼

As of this writing, the Drive-By Truckers have released thirteen studio albums, several live releases, one odds-and-ends collection, one Adam's House Cat do-over, one career retrospective, and three albums as a backing band, not to mention a bundle of EPs, mini-albums, promotional releases, and seven-inch singles. Patterson Hood has released several solo albums, Mike Cooley has a live one under his belt, and Jason Isbell has his own busy career. There are some live shows on their Bandcamp web page and literally thousands of bootlegs available elsewhere on the internet. *Massive* seems like an understatement to describe their catalog. What follows necessarily collects only a fraction of their output, concentrating on official physical releases.

Drive-By Truckers: *Gangstabilly*
(Soul Dump, 1998)

Their debut, a self-financed and self-released collection of songs, splits the difference between alt-country and rock and roll. But this new band sounds ragged and rowdy whether they're strumming electric guitars or pummeling acoustic instruments. "The Living Bubba" signals Patterson's deeply empathetic, character-driven songwriting, while "Panties in Your Purse" hints that Cooley might actually be his equal.

Drive-By Truckers: *Pizza Deliverance* (Soul Dump, 1999)

Their follow-up, mostly recorded at Patterson's haunted house in Athens, is full of songs that they had originally planned to include on their debut. Less twangy and much louder, it's perhaps closer to their late-'90s rock show, and almost every one of these songs remains in their setlist decades later—except the Clinton-era "The President's Penis Is Missing," about a scandal that now seems so quaint.

Drive-By Truckers: *Alabama Ass Whuppin'*
(Second Heaven, 1999)

Recorded largely at the Nick in Birmingham, the band's first concert album was the product of relentless white-knuckle touring and established the Truckers as a premier live act even before they had a record contract. "The Avon Lady" may be four-and-a-half minutes of Patterson shooting the shit with the audience, but it presents him as a consummate southern storyteller.

Drive-By Truckers: *Southern Rock Opera*
(Soul Dump, 2001; Lost Highway, 2002)

The idea had been around long before the Drive-By Truckers formed in 1996, but it took them years to become the band that could actually pull it off. The result is one of the best and most consequential rock-and-roll albums of the twenty-first century, launching countless scholarly papers about "the duality of the southern thing." But the most affecting songs recount their Alabama adolescences, catalog their rock-star dreams, and use the tragedy of Lynyrd Skynyrd to show how those dreams might ultimately doom them.

Drive-By Truckers: *Decoration Day* (New West, 2003)

Jason Isbell joined the band pretty much the day they released *Southern Rock Opera* and immediately proved himself an equal to his new bandmates, as though the Truckers were greedily hoarding ace songwriters. His "Outfit" recollects advice from his dad, while Cooley's "Sounds Better in the Song" and Patterson's "(Something's Got To) Give Pretty

Soon" show what the newcomer can look forward to in his new job. Apologies to Skynyrd, but this is the best point of entry for Trucker newcomers.

Drive-By Truckers: *The Dirty South* (New West, 2004)

Almost as long as they had been working on the rock opera, the Truckers had been writing what they called Heathen Songs, which chronicle a class of loose-ends southerners who rarely appeared in pop culture except as caricatures and villains. "Putting People on the Moon," "Daddy's Cup," and the three songs about Buford Pusser and the Dixie Mafia bypass Southern clichés and sensationalist details in favor of portraits of people pushed to the fringes.

Patterson Hood: *Killers and Stars* (New West, 2004)

Patterson's solo debut—well, his first to get a wide release on a format other than homemade cassette—is his version of Springsteen's *Nebraska*: a lo-fi field recording with only his voice and guitar. He made it in the wake of his second divorce, left the songs deliberately unfinished, and sold copies at shows before New West Records gave it a proper release. It's quiet, often intense, and even more often just plain weird.

Drive-By Truckers: *A Blessing and a Curse* (New West, 2006)

Considered by many—including Patterson himself—to be their worst album, it was recorded at Drive-In Studios in Kernersville, North Carolina, where R.E.M. and Pylon both made epochal Athens records. But the Truckers' fifth LP was marred by their decision to write songs in the studio and even more by the tensions arising from Isbell's worsening alcoholism. There are, however, some standouts, including Cooley's devastating "Space City," a eulogy for his beloved grandmother.

Bettye LaVette: *The Scene of the Crime* (Anti, 2007)

LaVette recorded an album down in Muscle Shoals in the early 1970s, but Atlantic Records shelved it and effectively thwarted her promising career. Thirty-five years later, she returned to the scene of the crime with the Truckers as her backing band. The sessions were notoriously tense, as LaVette clashed with the younger musicians, but none of that comes through on their lively covers of songs by Eddie Hinton, Willie Nelson, and Elton John.

Drive-By Truckers: *Brighter Than Creation's Dark* (New West, 2008)

With Isbell out of the band, the Truckers regrouped, promoted bassist Shonna Tucker to full singer-songwriter, and returned with their longest album: four sides full of Gulf War veterans, dying music scenes, Weird Harolds, and brutally murdered musicians. Given the tone of the material and the dark years they had barely survived, the hope and humor on these nineteen songs are unexpected and disarming.

Drive-By Truckers: *Live from Austin, TX* (New West, 2009)

This one is subdued compared to a typical rock show but positively chaotic by the standards of *Austin City Limits*. The highlight is a twelve-minute version of "18 Wheels of Love," which provides a bittersweet update on the ongoing love story between Patterson's mama and her second husband, a trucker named Chester.

Drive-By Truckers: *The Fine Print (A Collection of Oddities and Rarities 2003–2008)* (New West, 2009)

A contractual obligation odds-and-ends collection that nevertheless sheds more light on their previous albums than does the "greatest hits" comp released two years later. The song about George Jones is a little too mean, the one about Mrs. Claus a little too vicious, but "Goode's Field Road" is one of Patterson's best Heathen Songs, and their cover of Warren Zevon's "Play It All Night Long" is a sly rock-geek commentary on the Ronnie Van Zant–Neil Young contretemps from *Southern Rock Opera*.

Booker T.: *Potato Hole* (Anti, 2009)

This was their second support gig, this time for the legendary Stax organist and Booker T. and the MGs namesake. His playing conveys as much as a singer's voice or a songwriter's lyrics, and the chemistry between them on covers of OutKast, Tom Waits, and Cooley songs was so strong that they launched a lengthy tour together.

Patterson Hood: *Murdering Oscar (And Other Love Songs)* (Ruth Street, 2009)

Like his debut, Patterson's follow-up gathers songs dating back years (including one written in the wake of Kurt Cobain's suicide in 1994) and originally recorded to cassette. Not all of these ideas have aged well, especially the one about Courtney Love, but his band the Screwtopians—which features his father, legendary Shoals bassist David Hood—rip through them vigorously.

Drive-By Truckers: *The Big To-Do* (ATO, 2010)

Proving just how crucial a bass player can be to a rock band, Shonna Tucker allowed the Truckers to expand their sound beyond southern rock to encompass the Shoals R&B they had all grown up with. This underrated gem in their catalog is among their most character-driven albums and therefore one of their most empathetic, following strippers, alcoholics, homicidal wives, unemployed husbands, and doomed trapeze artists as they navigate rock bottom.

Drive-By Truckers: *Go-Go Boots* (ATO, 2011)

Recorded during the same sessions as *The Big To-Do*, this is a much more violent album, with not one but two songs about the same murder of a preacher's wife, another about a haunted assault rifle, another about a bitter breakup with their longtime label, and one about an ex-cop anchored by Tucker's Chic-gone-country bass line. They balance it all out with an exuberant cover of Eddie Hinton's big-hearted "Everybody Needs Love."

Drive-By Truckers: *Ugly Buildings, Whores & Politicians: Greatest Hits 1998–2009* (New West, 2011)

Summing up a band like the Truckers with only sixteen tracks is folly, and there's no way this single-disc retrospective could satisfy every fan or do the band justice. Where's "Goddamn Lonely Love"? "The Southern Thing"? "One of These Days"? You're better off springing for every single album.

Drive-By Truckers: *Live from Third Man Records* (Third Man, 2011)

This muted set recorded for Jack White's label in Nashville is notable for David Hood playing bass on two tracks, including an affectionate cover of Percy Sledge's 1968 Shoals classic "Take Time to Know Her."

Patterson Hood: *Heat Lightning Rumbles in the Distance* (ATO, 2012)

This is Patterson's third solo album but his first solo album not composed of new recordings of old songs (or old recordings of old songs, for that matter). It presents a more stripped-down and thoughtful folk-rock sound that gives a cinematic shine to his intimate story-songs. Best of all is "Come Back Little Star," a touching eulogy to Vic Chesnutt cowritten and sung with Kelly Hogan.

Mike Cooley: *The Fool on Every Corner* (Cooley Records, 2012)

Cooley's only solo album to date is a live recording from a three-night run at the Earl in Atlanta. He strips down his Trucker songs to their acoustic bones and adds a few new tunes, including a cover of Charlie Rich's "Behind Closed Doors" and an original called "Drinking Coke and Eating Ice" that sounds like it could have been a hit for Merle Haggard.

Drive-By Truckers: *English Oceans* (ATO, 2014)

Following the departure of Tucker and the hiring of the Dexateens' gospel-loving bass player Matt Patton, the Truckers settled into the quintet that remains their most durable lineup to date. Their debut is a little shaky, but Cooley's "Made-Up English Oceans" gestures to the more explicitly political songs on their next albums and Patterson's

"Grand Canyon," about the death of their merch guy Craig Lieske, is a show-closer for the ages.

Drive-By Truckers: *Black Ice Vérité* (ATO, 2014)

In February 2014—the night of a freak Georgia ice storm—the Truckers invited a few friends and fans to the 40 Watt to preview songs from *English Oceans*. This live document, which accompanies a DVD of the full performances, collects a handful of tracks and rounds them out with a few songs recorded at Bonnaroo that year.

Drive-By Truckers: *Dragon Pants* EP (ATO, 2014)

A Record Store Day lark, this is also one of their strangest and funniest releases, thanks to their well-observed and self-deprecating songs about growing old in rock and roll. They're the butts of their own jokes, whether it's Patterson fantasizing about strutting around the house in Jimmy Page's *Song Remains the Same* wardrobe or Cooley sweet-talkin' the missus on the sultry slow jam "Trying to Be the Boss on a Beaver Brown Budget."

Drive-By Truckers: *It's Great to Be Alive!* (ATO, 2015)

They recorded their fourth live album during a three-night stand at the Fillmore Auditorium in San Francisco, and it's maybe their best career retrospective yet—and not just because it's three and a half hours and thirty-five tracks long. Rising to the occasion that the venue demands, they dig deep into their sprawling catalog, mixing fan favorites and rarities like they're all the band's signature tunes.

Drive-By Truckers: *American Band* (ATO, 2016)

The Truckers have always written about politics, but they never did so as explicitly or as angrily as they did on this career-revitalizing album, released just two months before the 2016 election. Since then, songs like

"What It Means" and even "Kinky Hypocrite" have remained tragically relevant in America.

Drive-By Truckers: *Live In Studio * New York, NY * 07/12/16* (ATO, 2017)

Recording at legendary Electric Lady Studios (where Patti Smith made *Horses* and Stevie Wonder made *Talking Book*) must have been a blast for these rock geeks, but their performances of *American Band* songs add little to the originals.

Adam's House Cat: *Town Burned Down* (ATO, 2018)

Patterson and Cooley's first band recorded this album at Muscle Shoals Sound Studio in November 1990, shopped it around to labels, got roundly rejected, and eventually split up. After discovering the masters twenty-five years later and reuniting with original drummer Chuck Tremblay, they finally released this artifact from another era, which puts a southern twist on the underground rock of the Replacements and early Soul Asylum.

Drive-By Truckers: *The Unraveling* (ATO, 2020)

The Truckers traveled down to Memphis to make their long-awaited follow-up to *American Band*, recording at Sam Phillips Recording Company with engineer Matt Ross-Spang. "It's a dark fucking record," says Patterson, and he's not wrong. "Awaiting Resurrection," their bleakest closer to date, barely lets any light in or entertains any optimism, but there's something cathartic about them sneering at shirking politicians: "Stick it up your ass with your useless thoughts and prayers." Nobody cusses like Patterson Hood.

Jerry Joseph: *The Beautiful Madness* (Cosmo Sex School, 2020)

The Truckers toured with Jerry Joseph back in the 1990s, so this was a reunion in more ways than one. Patterson produced the album, and all the

Truckers—including Isbell—backed him up. It's somewhere between Beat poetry and southern rock, "Howl" if Ginsburg had been a grouchy southern punk. "Sugar Smacks" is Joseph's apocalyptic account of just barely surviving a morning spent watching the news over breakfast.

Drive-By Truckers: *The New OK* (ATO, 2020)

The Truckers' second album of 2020 was their first under quarantine. Several of the songs, including the soulful "Tough to Let Go" and the funky "Perilous Night," were recorded in Memphis during the *Unraveling* sessions, but the title track and "Watching the Orange Clouds" were written and assembled by the band during lockdown. And Patton gets not one but two lead vocals, including the closing cover of the Ramones' sadly timely "The KKK Took My Baby Away."

Drive-By Truckers: *Plan 9 Records July 13, 2006* (New West, 2020)

In July 2006 the Truckers took a break from their arduous tour with the Black Crowes to play an in-store at Plan 9 Music in Richmond. You can hear how relieved and excited they are to play a real rock show again, which makes it arguably their finest live album. It's also the only one so far featuring Jason Isbell, who covers the Rolling Stones' "Moonlight Mile" and rampages through "Decoration Day." Within a year, he would be out of the band.

Mike Cooley, Patterson Hood, Jason Isbell: *Live at the Shoals Theatre* (Southeastern, 2021)

In June 2014 the three core singer-songwriters from the early to mid 2000s lineup reunited for a one-off acoustic show to raise medical funds for the local reporter and professor Terry Pace. They treated the occasion like a casual guitar pull, trading off songs and stories from throughout their careers together and apart. It's a master class in songwriting, but what really makes this quadruple live album distinctive is the way it showcases their singing voices blending together in rough-hewn, extemporaneous harmonies.

Selected Bibliography

▼

All the quotations in this book, unless otherwise noted, are from interviews I conducted with the band over several years. Where applicable, I've checked their stories and memories against contemporaneous newspaper reports, album reviews, and concert reviews. Below is a selected bibliography of sources that shaped my thinking about the band and their music.

Abad-Santos, Alexander. "Racists Ruined the Confederate Flag for Lynyrd Skynyrd." *The Atlantic*, September 21, 2012. https://www.theatlantic .com/culture/archive/2012/09/racists-ruined-confederate-flag-lynyrd -skynyrd/323381/.

Barbee, Matthew Mace. *Race and Masculinity in Southern Memory: History of Richmond, Virginia's Monument Avenue, 1948–1996*. Lanham, MD: Lexington Books, 2014.

Beetham, Sarah. "From Spray Cans to Minivans: Contesting the Legacy of Confederate Soldier Monuments in the Age of Black Lives Matter." *Public Art Dialogue* 6, no. 1 (Spring 2016): 9–33.

Bingham, Shawn Chandler, and Lindsey A. Freeman, eds. *The Bohemian South: Creating Countercultures, from Poe to Punk*. Chapel Hill: University of North Carolina Press, 2017.

Blair, William A. *Cities of the Dead: Contesting the Memory of the Civil War in the South, 1865–1914*. Chapel Hill: University of North Carolina Press, 2004.

Blight, David W. "Decoration Days: The Origins of Memorial Day in North and South." In *The Memory of the Civil War in American Culture*, edited by Alice Fahs and Joan Waugh, 94–129. Chapel Hill: University of North Carolina Press, 2004.

Blistein, Jon. "This Is Normal: The Enduring, Knotty Relevance of Randy Newman and Drive-By Truckers." *Rolling Stone*, September 6, 2019. https://www.rollingstone.com/music/music-news/randy-newman-good -old-boys-drive-by-truckers-dirty-south-873957/.

Boles, John B., ed. *Masters and Slaves in the House of the Lord: Race and Religion in the American South, 1740–1870*. Lexington: University Press of Kentucky, 1988.

Bragg, Rick. "In Birmingham, a Big Iron Man Gets No Respect." *New York Times*, March 22, 1997. https://www.nytimes.com/1997/03/22/us/in -birmingham-a-big-iron-man-gets-no-respect.html.

Broughton, Robert D., and Revonda Foster Kirby. *Ghost Tales of the State Line Mob: Stories Based on Actual Events, 1900–1974*. Rev. ed. CreateSpace Independent Publishing Platform, 2016.

Brown, Rodger Lyle. *Party Out of Bounds: The B-52's, R.E.M., and the Kids Who Rocked Athens, Georgia*. Athens: University of Georgia Press, 2016.

Buckner, D. B. "Decoration Day: The True Story behind Jason Isbell's Drive-By Truckers Song." AXS Entertainment, June 27, 2014. Accessed via the Internet Archive Wayback Machine. http://www.examiner.com /article/decoration-day-the-true-story-behind-jason-isbell-s-drive-by -truckers-song.

Buma, Michael. "'Stand Tall, Turn Your Three Guitars Up Real Loud, and Do What You Do': The Redneck Liberation Theology of the Drive-By Truckers." *Journal of Religion and Popular Culture* 13 (Summer 2006). https:// doi.org/10.3138/jrpc.13.1.002.

Byrd, Jodi A. "A Return to the South." Special issue, *Southern Quarterly: Las Americas Quarterly* 66, no. 3 (September 2014): 609–620.

Cantwell, Robert. *If Beale Street Could Talk: Music, Community, Culture*. Urbana: University of Illinois Press, 2009.

Castle, Emery N., ed. *The Changing American Countryside: Rural People and Places*. Lawrence: University Press of Kansas, 1995.

Ching, Barbara. "Where Has the Free Bird Flown? Lynyrd Skynyrd and White Southern Manhood." In *White Masculinity in the Recent South*, edited by Trent Watts, 251–265. Baton Rouge: Louisiana State University Press, 2008.

Cobb, James C. *Away Down South: A History of Southern Identity*. Oxford, UK: Oxford University Press, 2005.

Cobb, James C. *Georgia Odyssey: A Short History of the State.* 2nd ed. Athens: University of Georgia Press, 2008.

The Company We Keep: Drive-By Truckers' Homecoming and the Fan Community. Athens, GA: Nuçi Phillips Memorial Foundation, 2019.

Coski, John M. *The Confederate Battle Flag: America's Most Embattled Emblem.* Cambridge, MA: Belknap, 2005.

Courrier, Kevin. *Randy Newman's American Dreams.* Toronto: ECW Press, 2005.

Covington, Abigail. "When the Fire Broke Out." *Oxford American,* January 25, 2016. https://www.oxfordamerican.org/magazine/item/755-when-the-fire-broke-out.

Crazy Horse, Kandia. "Drive-By Truckers." PopMatters, December 14, 2001. https://www.popmatters.com/drive-by-truckers1-2496085416.html.

Dechert, S. Renee, and George H. Lewis. "The Drive-By Truckers and the Redneck Underground: A Subcultural Analysis." *Country Music Annual* (2002): 130–150.

Doig, Will, "Walmart Threatens the Town R.E.M. Made Famous." Salon, February 25, 2012. https://www.salon.com/2012/02/25/walmart_threatens_the_town_r_e_m_made_famous/.

Duncan, Cynthia M. *Worlds Apart: Poverty and Politics in Rural America.* 2nd ed. New Haven, CT: Yale University Press, 2014.

Elkington, John. *Beale Street: Resurrecting the Home of the Blues.* Charleston, SC: History Press, 2008.

Ells, Blake. *The Muscle Shoals Legacy of FAME.* Charleston, SC: History Press, 2015.

Ezzell, Patricia B. *TVA Photography: Thirty Years of Life in the Tennessee Valley.* Jackson: University Press of Mississippi, 2003.

Fertel, Rien. *Southern Rock Opera.* 33 1/3 Series. New York: Bloomsbury Academic, 2019.

Fishman, Charles. *The Wal-Mart Effect: How the World's Most Powerful Company Really Works—and How It's Transforming the American Economy.* New York: Penguin Press, 2006.

Fredrickson, George M. *White Supremacy: A Comparative Study in American and South African History.* New York: Oxford University Press, 1981.

Freed, Wes. *The Art of Wes Freed: Paintings, Posters, Pin-Ups, and Possums.* Winter Park, FL: Story Farm, 2019.

Genovese, Eugene D. *A Consuming Fire: The Fall of the Confederacy in the White Christian South.* Athens: University of Georgia Press, 1998.

Goodman, David. *Modern Twang: An Alternative Country Music Guide and Directory.* Nashville, TN: Dowling, 1999.

Gordon, Linda. *The Second Coming of the KKK: The Ku Klux Klan of the 1920s and the American Political Tradition*. New York: Liveright, 2017.

Gose, Joe. "A Return to Downtown Birmingham." *New York Times*, August 6, 2013. https://www.nytimes.com/2013/08/07/realestate/commercial/a-return-to-downtown-birmingham.html.

Greer, Jim. "Underground: G. G. Allin." *Spin*, January 1991, 80–81.

Grooms, Anthony. *Bombingham: A Novel*. New York: Free Press, 2001.

Guralnick, Peter. *Sam Phillips: The Man Who Invented Rock 'n' Roll*. New York: Little, Brown, 2015.

Guralnick, Peter. *Sweet Soul Music: Rhythm and Blues and the Southern Dream of Freedom*. Boston: Little, Brown, 1999.

Hale, Grace Elizabeth. *Cool Town: How Athens, Georgia, Launched Alternative Music and Changed American Culture*. Chapel Hill: University of North Carolina Press, 2020.

Hamilton, Jack. *Just Around Midnight: Rock and Roll and the Racial Imagination*. Cambridge, MA: Harvard University Press, 2016.

Hood, Patterson. "Ballad of the Leaning Man." *Bitter Southerner*, September 4, 2019. https://bittersoutherner.com/from-the-southern-perspective/ballad-of-the-leaning-man-funky-donnie-fritts-patterson-hood.

Hood, Patterson. "The Cos-Mo-Pol-I-Tan Sound." *Oxford American*, December 24, 2015. https://www.oxfordamerican.org/magazine/item/728-the-cos-mo-pol-i-tan-sound.

Hood, Patterson. "The Houses Aretha Built." *Bitter Southerner*, August 17, 2018. https://bittersoutherner.com/the-houses-aretha-built-patterson-hood.

Hood, Patterson. "I Know a Place: Growing Up Muscle Shoals." *Oxford American*, November 10, 2020. https://www.oxfordamerican.org/magazine/item/1987-i-know-a-place.

Hood, Patterson. "Into the Perilous Night." *Bitter Southerner*, November 15, 2014. https://bittersoutherner.com/into-the-perilous-night-patterson-hood.

Hood, Patterson. "'Like Sonny Liston': An Appreciation of Tom Petty." *Bitter Southerner*, October 6, 2017. https://bittersoutherner.com/from-the-southern-perspective/music/like-sonny-liston-tom-petty-patterson-hood.

Hood, Patterson. "Now, about the Bad Name I Gave My Band." NPR, June 17, 2020. https://www.npr.org/2020/06/17/879393187/now-about-the-bad-name-i-gave-my-band.

Hood, Patterson. "Ronnie & Neil (and Jimmy Johnson)." *Bitter Southerner*, September 11, 2019. https://bittersoutherner.com/from-the-southern-perspective/ronnie-and-neil-and-jimmy-johnson-patterson-hood.

Hood, Patterson. "The South's Heritage Is So Much More Than a Flag." *New York Times*, July 9, 2015.

Hughes, Charles L. *Country Soul: Making Music and Making Race in the American South*. Chapel Hill: University of North Carolina Press, 2015.

Jeter, Sena. *Four Spirits: A Novel*. New York: Morrow, 2003.

Johnson, Kenneth M. *Demographic Trends in Rural and Small Town America*. Reports on Rural America. Durham, NH: Carsey Institute, 2006. https://dx.doi.org/10.34051/p/2020.6.

Johnson, Kenneth M., and Calvin L. Beale. "The Rural Rebound." *Wilson Quarterly* 22, no. 2 (Spring 1998): 16–27.

Jones, Booker T. *Time Is Tight: My Life, Note by Note*. New York: Little Brown, 2019.

Kemp, Mark. *Dixie Lullaby: A Story of Music, Race, and New Beginnings in a New South*. New York: Simon & Schuster, 2004.

Kronenburg, Robert. *Live Architecture: Venues, Stages and Arenas for Popular Music*. London: Routledge, 2012.

Lassiter, Matthew D., and Joseph Crespino, eds. *The Myth of Southern Exceptionalism*. New York: Oxford University Press, 2010.

Lassiter, Matthew D., and Kevin M. Kruse. "The Bulldozer Revolution: Suburbs and Southern History since World War II." *Journal of Southern History* 75, no. 3 (August 2009): 691–706.

Lauterbach, Preston. *Beale Street Dynasty: Sex, Song, and the Struggle for the Soul of Memphis*. New York: W. W. Norton & Company, 2015.

Lechner, Zachary J. *The South of the Mind: American Imaginings of White Southernness, 1960–1980*. Athens: University of Georgia Press, 2018.

Leib, Jonathan. "The Witting Autobiography of Richmond, Virginia: Arthur Ashe, the Civil War, and Monument Avenue's Racialized Landscape." In *Landscape and Race in the United States*, edited by Richard H. Shein, 187–212. New York: Routledge, 2006.

Luckerson, Victor. "Dismantling Dixie: The Summer the Confederate Monuments Came Crashing Down." *The Ringer*, August 17, 2017. https://www.theringer.com/2017/8/17/16160286/charlottesville-richmond-montgomery-confederate-monuments.

Maxwell, Angie. "'The Duality of the Southern Thing': A Snapshot of Southern Politics in the Twenty-First Century." *Southern Cultures* 20, no. 4 (Winter 2014): 89–105.

McWhorter, Diane. *Carry Me Home: Birmingham, Alabama: The Climactic Battle of the Civil Rights Revolution*. New York: Simon & Schuster, 2002.

Meadows, Bob. "The Last Slaves of Mississippi?" *People*, March 26, 2007, 132.

Meister, Hillary, and David Barbe. "Localzine: Athens, Georgia." *CMJ New Music Monthly* 30 (February 1996): 61–62.

Millikin, Patrick, ed. *The Highway Kind: Tales of Fast Cars, Desperate Drivers, and Dark Roads.* New York: Mulholland Books, 2016.

Mills, Cynthia, and Pamela H. Simpson, eds. *Monuments to the Lost Cause: Women, Art, and the Landscapes of Southern Memory.* Knoxville: University of Tennessee Press, 2003.

Odom, Gene, and Frank Dorman. *Lynyrd Skynyrd: Remembering the Free Birds of Southern Rock.* New York: Broadway Books, 2003.

Paddison, Joshua. *American Heathens: Religion, Race, and Reconstruction in California.* Berkeley: University of California Press, 2012.

Pohlmann, Marcus D., and Michael P. Kirby. *Racial Politics at the Crossroads: Memphis Elects Dr. W. W. Herenton.* Knoxville: University of Tennessee Press, 1996.

Price, Jennifer. *Flight Maps: Adventures with Nature in Modern America.* New York: Basic Books, 1999.

Pusser, Dwana, with Ken Beck and Jim Clark. *Walking On: A Daughter's Journey with Legendary Sheriff Buford Pusser.* Gretna, LA: Pelican, 2009.

Reece, Chuck. "Patterson Hood: The Bitter Southerner Interview." *Bitter Southerner*, September 27, 2016. https://bittersoutherner.com/patterson-hood-bitter-southerner-interview-drive-by-truckers.

Ribowsky, Mark. *Whiskey Bottles and Brand-New Cars: The Fast Life and Sudden Death of Lynyrd Skynyrd.* Chicago: Chicago Review Press, 2015.

Runtagh, Jordan. "Remembering Lynyrd Skynyrd's Deadly 1977 Plane Crash." *Rolling Stone*, October 20, 2017. https://www.rollingstone.com/feature/remembering-lynyrd-skynyrds-deadly-1977-plane-crash-2-195371/.

Savage, Kirk. *Standing Soldiers, Kneeling Slaves: Race, War, and Monument in Nineteenth Century America.* Princeton, NJ: Princeton University Press, 1997.

Shafer, Byron E., and Richard Johnston. *The End of Southern Exceptionalism: Class, Race, and Partisan Change in the Postwar South.* Cambridge, MA: Harvard University Press, 2006.

Shaw, Chris, and Chris McCoy. "Worst Gig Ever! Memphis Musicians Share the Worst Night of Their Career." *Memphis Flyer*, September 22, 2016, 12–14.

Terrell, Steve. "Song of a Preacher Man." *Pasatiempo*, March 18, 2011, 24.

Tracy, Janice Branch. *Mississippi Moonshine Politics: How Bootleggers and the Law Kept a Dry State Soaked.* Charleston, SC: History Press, 2015.

Upton, Dell. *What Can and Can't Be Said: Race, Uplift, and Monument Building in the Contemporary South.* New Haven, CT: Yale University Press, 2015.

Wake, Matt. "The Nick: A Dangerous History of Alabama's Coolest Bar." Alabama Life and Culture, December 17, 2018. https://www.al.com /life/2018/12/the-nick-a-dangerous-history-of-alabamas-coolest-bar .html.

Weisbard, Eric. "The Mouth of the South." *Spin*, December 2002, 106–108.

Whitley, Carla Jean. *Muscle Shoals Sound Studio: How the Swampers Changed American Music*. Charleston, SC: History Press, 2014.

"Whose Heritage? Public Symbols of the Confederacy." Southern Poverty Law Center, February 1, 2019. https://www.splcenter.org/20190201 /whose-heritage-public-symbols-confederacy.

Willman, Chris. *Rednecks and Bluenecks: The Politics of Country Music*. New York: New Press, 2005.

Wilson, Charles Reagan, et al., eds. *New Encyclopedia of Southern Culture*. Chapel Hill: University of North Carolina Press, 2006–2013.

Wilson, David. *Inventing Black-on-Black Violence: Discourse, Space, and Representation*. Syracuse, NY: Syracuse University Press, 2005.

Wood, Roy, Jr. "For Roy Wood Jr., Alabama Is Painful History, New Hope and Home." *New York Times*, September 19, 2018. https://www.nytimes .com/2018/09/19/travel/for-roy-wood-jr-alabama-is-painful-history -new-hope-and-home.html.

Index

▼

Dinosaur Jr. (band), 66
Dio (band), 195
Dirtball (band), 198–199, 202–205
"Dirty South" (concept), 1, 7–9, 11, 16–19, 161, 169, 196, 230, 234
Dirty South, The (Drive-By Truckers, 2004), 8–9, 21, 38, 42, 73, 177, 180, 195, 201, 227, 229, 255
Dirty South music scene, 94
Dixie Dynamite (film), 226
Dixie flag. *See* flag: Confederate
Dixie Mafia, 230, 237, 255
Doig, Will, 106
"Do It Yourself" (Hood), 47–48
Downtown 13. *See* "After It's Gone"
Dragon Pants (Drive-By Truckers, 2014), 259
Dread Zeppelin (band), 56
Dreams So Real (band), 85
"Dress Blues" (Isbell), 181
Dressy Bessy (band), 86
drinking: and Adam's House Cat, 67; in art, 199; at bars and clubs, 77–78, 80, 82, 109, 217; and Drive-By Truckers, 19, 94, 100, 104, 126, 160, 163, 179–180, 182, 222, 232; and Buford Pusser, 223–224; as subject of songs, 35, 49, 72, 80, 90, 139, 143, 154, 169, 219, 232. *See also* moonshine; Prohibition; whiskey
"Drinking Coke and Eating Ice" (Cooley), 258
drive-by shootings, 93–94
Drive-In Studios, 255
Drive-By Truckers: and Adam's House Cat, 50, 58–59, 92, 100, 103, 144, 207; and Athens, GA, 11, 12, 18, 74, 92, 163, 177; and Atlanta, GA, 92, 206; and Auburn, AL, 18, 123–124; audience behavior, 12, 63, 92, 102–103, 108–110, 136–137, 152, 179, 205–206, 244; band name, 13, 93–95, 136; and David Barbe, 11, 98, 111, 132, 186, 190, 196; and Birmingham, AL, 118–121, 124–137, 206; and Confederate flag, 12, 14, 151–152, 202, 248; and country music, 198; and Dexateens, 190; early financial struggles, 98–100; expanding focus to America writ large, 2, 136, 191, 237, 246–247; fans, 108–110, 133–134, 136–137, 145, 151, 154, 173, 179, 189–190, 194–195, 200, 206–207, 216; first live shows, 91–92, 98, 149, 205; first recording session, 90–92; and HeAthens Homecoming, 12, 100, 108, 110–111; and Eddie Hinton, 187–188; and

Lilla Hood, 201; idea of place, 17, 95–96, 101–103, 159, 177, 247–248; interrogating southern stereotypes, 95–96, 136, 151, 168, 175, 207, 235; and Jay Leavitt, 205–206, 217–218; as liberal reformulation of southern rock, 36; and Lot Lizards, 90; and Lynyrd Skynyrd, 7, 9, 28, 37, 119–120, 122, 123, 126, 128, 131, 142–148, 153, 158, 167, 171, 244, 254; managers, 105, 132, 160; and McNairy County, TN, 18, 237, 239; merch, 92, 103, 109, 110, 195–196, 200, 205, 243; musical influences, 167; and Randy Newman, 128; and New York City, 206; and North Mississippi Allstars, 55; and opening acts, 100, 108; origins, 9–10, 202; and Tom Petty, 110; on politics, 136–137; possible break-up, 10, 105, 125, 132, 161, 191, 218, 244–245; and the Quadrajets, 123; and race, 62, 131, 136, 158; recording, 229, 245–246; rehearsals, 162; relationships, 103–105, 124, 126, 131–133, 160, 175–180, 189, 196, 206, 227, 245; and Richmond, VA, 197, 199, 204–206, 218; and Dave Schools, 98–100, 122, 132; self-releasing albums, 133–134; and John "Pudd" Sharp, 123–124; and the Shoals, 159, 162–163, 172, 177, 184, 186, 189–190; songwriting, 2, 7, 9, 17, 96, 104, 123, 136, 140–141, 146, 174, 227, 229, 235–236; structure of live shows, 11–13, 100, 109, 162, 171, 205, 216, 218–219, 243–244; touring, 100–105, 110, 160, 162–164, 167, 173, 175–176, 179–180, 187, 191, 199–200, 204, 206–207, 214, 217, 222, 229, 243, 245–246; visual style, 200; website, 102–103, 133
Drivin' N Cryin' (band), 87
drugs, 10, 19, 22, 71, 73, 82, 93, 131, 175, 179–180, 187, 220, 222, 227
dry counties, 30, 41–42, 159, 231–232
"duality of the southern thing" (concept), 6, 8, 62, 96, 126–128, 135, 151, 158, 213. *See also* "The Southern Thing"
Dukes of Hazzard, The (TV show), 8, 16, 84, 146, 150, 157, 226
Dulli, Greg, 188
Durham, NC, 68, 92–93
Dylan, Bob, 26, 69, 143, 215

Earl, the (club), 258
Earle, Steve, 215
economic crises, 41, 215, 228

complex relationship to southern identity, 9, 146, 153, 158; and Confederate flag, 146–148, 153–154; cover bands, 163; and Drive-By Truckers, 7, 9, 28, 37, 119–120, 122, 123, 126, 128, 131, 142–148, 153, 158, 167, 171, 244, 254–255; fans, 141–142, 153–154, 156; and guns, 154–156, 158; and Hell House, 143–144; influence, 67, 146; and LeBlanc and Carr, 125; and MCA Records, 147; merch, 153; as musicians, 142–145, 171; performances, 146; rumors and legends, 122, 140–141, 143, 145, 147; and the Shoals, 27–28, 142; songwriting, 139, 146, 154; as southern rock, 7, 16, 119, 163; touring, 145–146, 153, 157. See also *Southern Rock Opera; and individual members and songs*

Macon, Georgia, 84
"Made-Up English Oceans" (Cooley), 191, 258
Magruder, John B., 208
Malaco, 49, 172
Malone, Rob: and Athens, GA, 85; on Confederate flag, 148; and Drive-By Truckers, 103, 105, 122, 126, 144, 147, 167, 171, 200; growing up in the Shoals, 22, 48, 101; leaving Drive-By Truckers, 10, 161–163
Mangum, Jeff, 87
"Man I Shot, The" (Hood), 215
"Margo and Harold" (Hood), 90
marriage equality, 189
"Marry Me" (Cooley), 11
Martin, Trayvon, 3, 136
masculinity, southern ideas of, 84, 128–129, 143, 146, 218, 225–226, 239
Maury, Matthew Fontaine, 208–209
MCA Records, 147
McCain, John, 129–130
McComb, Mississippi, 140
McCullers, Carson, 15
McDowell, Ronald, 130
McNairy County, TN: crime, 223–227, 230–237, 239; deaths and tragedies, 238–239, 242; as the Dirty South, 9, 18; economic decline, 237–238; geography, 223, 231–232, 234, 237–239; monumental landscape, 213; as place to grow up in the 1970s and 1980s, 13–15, 237–239; racism, 15. See also *Dirty South, The*; bootlegging; moonshine; Pusser, Buford Hayse
McWhorter, Diane, 114

Mellencamp, John, 144
Memorial Day. See Decoration Day
memorials. See monuments and memorials
Memphis, TN: and Confederate flag, 60–61; crime in, 57–58, 62, 74–75; as the Dirty South, 18; and Drive-By Truckers, 18; garbage worker's strike of 1968, 60; geography, 51–52, 223; mayoral election of 1991, 59–62; memorial landscape, 212–214; musical and cultural legacy, 15, 26, 60, 75; music scene, 41, 53, 58; and Nashville, TN, 65; race relations and racism in, 58–62; tourism, 60, 75; violence in, 60–61. See also Adam's House Cat; Beale Street
Mercié, Antonin, 210
Method Actors, the (band), 85
Miles, William, 148–149
Miller, Mae, 157–158
Mills, Mike, 80, 107
Milsap, Ronnie, 65
Mississippi, 55, 149, 158. See also Amite County, MS; Gillsburg, MS; Jackson, MS; McComb, MS; Oxford, MS; Shoals, the, AL
Mitchell, Margaret. See *Gone with the Wind*
Molly Hatchet (band), 121
Montgomery, AL, 148, 208
monuments and memorials: and the Civil War, 8–9, 19, 169–170, 207–216, 221, 248; and the Harvey family, 220–221; and Lynyrd Skynyrd, 141, 145, 147, 154
"Monument Valley" (Hood), 10, 216, 245
Moonrunners (film), 226
moonshine, 19, 80, 115, 198–201, 205, 225–226, 232. See also bootlegging; whiskey
Moonshine County Express (film), 226
Moretti, Giuseppe, 113
Morgan, Brad: in Athens, GA, 85, 109, 172; and Drive-By Truckers, 10, 103–104, 133, 145, 189, 243–244; on "The Home Front," 214–215; and Shonna Tucker, 179, 241
Morris, W. R., 224
MTV, 56, 66, 156, 165
Mueller, Karl, 67–68
Murdering Oscar (And Other Love Songs) (Patterson Hood, 2009), 54, 79, 257
Murder Junkies, the (band). See G. G. Allin
Murphy Howze (band), 40
Muscle Shoals (film), 32, 172
Muscle Shoals, AL. See Shoals, the, AL

political manipulation, 2; as Drive-By Truckers subject matter, 39, 62, 63–64, 169, 219–221; and guns, 63–64; history of, in the South, 6, 19, 127, 129, 247; killing of James Byrd Jr., 62; in McNairy County, TN, 15, 223–225, 239–242; in Memphis, TN, 60–62; murder of Harvey family, 219–221; in music, 8, 93–94; in the Shoals, 38–40, 169

Virgil Kane (band), 67, 208

Virgin Records, 199

Virginia Civil Rights Memorial, 210

Virginia Museum of Fine Arts, 210

Vulcan, 113–117, 119, 128–130, 201

Waits, Tom, 257

Walking Tall (film), 13, 16, 146, 225–226, 230, 234, 237. *See also* Pusser, Buford Hayse

Wall, Cain, 157

Wall, Lela, 157

"Wallace" (Hood), 121–122, 125, 144

Wallace, George, 9, 27, 121, 125, 144–145, 201

Walmart, 105–106

Warhol, Andy, 196

Warner Brothers Records, 44

"Watching the Orange Clouds" (Hood), 137, 261

Watergate, 27, 155

Waters, John, 193

W. C. Handy Festival, 45

websites. *See* internet, impact of

Weisbard, Eric, 159, 161, 247

Weissman, Barr, 201

Well, The (Dirtball, 1998), 199

Welty, Eudora, 15

West, Kanye, 101

West Coast, 115, 156–157

Westerns, 216, 245

Wet Willie, 7, 163

Wexler, Jerry, 29, 184, 187

"What It Means" (Hood), 3–6, 12, 62, 137, 152, 260

"When the Pin Hits the Shell" (Cooley), 47–48

"Where's Eddie" (Hinton, Fritts), 187–188

"Where the Devil Don't Stay" (Cooley), 115, 201

whiskey, 23, 82, 109, 124, 139, 160, 217, 232. *See also* bootlegging; drinking; moonshine

White, Jack, 189, 258

White, John Paul, 172, 190

White, Tony Joe, 187

White Lightning (film), 146, 226

whiteness: in Birmingham, AL, 114–115, 129; and Confederate imagery, 149–150, 158, 211–213; Drive-By Truckers' awareness of, 3, 19, 136–137; and Joel Chandler Harris, 134–135; and the Harvey family, 220–221; in Memphis, TN, 58–62; in Nashville, TN, 65; and Elvis Presley, 59; in Shoals music scene, 26–27, 30–31, 124, 165–166; and the term "heathens," 228; and violence, 8, 9; and white culpability, 2

white privilege, 213

white supremacy, 135, 158, 191, 211–213

Who, the (band), 143, 196, 198

"Why Henry Drinks" (Hood), 219

Widespread Panic (band), 77, 84, 98–100, 107

"Wife Beater" (Hood), 95

"Wig He Made Her Wear, The" (Hood), 179, 241

Wiley, Kehende, 210–211

Williams, Hank, 15, 199

Williams, Lucinda, 159

Wilson, David, 94

Wilson Lake. *See* Wilson Reservoir and Dam

Wilson Reservoir and Dam, 21–25, 46, 160, 168

Winesburg, Ohio (Sherwood Anderson, 1919), 243

Winkler, Mary, 239–242

Winkler, Matthew, 239–242

"Women Without Whiskey" (Cooley), 109

Wonder, Stevie, 260

Wood, Ronnie, 199

Wood, Roy, Jr., 130–131

Wooden Nickel. *See* Nick, the

"World of Hurt" (Hood), 181, 217–219, 245

WPA, 114

WREC, 52

Wussy (band), 188

Wuxtry (store), 92, 108

Yahoo. *See* internet, impact of

"You Better Move On" (Alexander), 25

Young, Neil, 27–28, 64, 97, 123, 126, 183

Young, Pegi, 190

Zebra Ranch, 55

Zevon, Warren, 256

Ziggy Stardust. *See* David Bowie: as Ziggy Stardust

"Zip City" (Cooley), 143

"Zoloft" (Hood), 90